Like ghosts through the night they came, the faint noise of their horses' hooves being my first indication of their approach. As the quiet noise became louder, I first sat up in my bed, then rose and went for my Winchester that sat against the wall beside the door. Sam came up behind me, his face fearful and his Sharps in his hands. Neither of us spoke.

Directly in front of the cabin they rode, then there was the sudden blasting of rifles in tandem with the crashing of a glass pane. Sam gave a low cry in his throat and moved to the front door, throwing it open and sending a quick and useless shot out into the darkness. Then they were gone, riding into the thick, black night. Above us the moon swam in a pool of murky clouds.

Still neither my brother nor I spoke. Sam stood in the doorway, staring after the riders, his face invisible to me but his rage and tension filling the air like electricity. I moved over to where a stone, wrapped in paper, lay on the dirt floor. I picked it up, noting with irritation the trembling of my fingers, and removed the wadded paper.

Another threat, another warning of "death for fence-stringers" if the fences weren't removed. . . .

DEVIL
WIRE

CAMERON
JUDD

St. Martin's Paperbacks

This is a work of fiction. All of the characters, organizations and events portrayed in this novel are either products of the author's imagination or are used fictitiously.

DEVIL WIRE / BRAZOS

Devil Wire copyright © 1981 by Cameron Judd.
Brazos copyright © 1994 by Cameron Judd.
Excerpt from *Dead Man's Gold* copyright © 1999 by Cameron Judd.

For information address St. Martin's Press, 175 Fifth Avenue, New York, NY 10010.

ISBN: 0-312-94436-5
EAN: 978-0-312-94436-0

Printed in the United States of America

Devil Wire Zebra edition published 1981
Bantam Domain edition / February 1995
St. Martin's Paperbacks edition / June 1999

Brazos Bantam Domain edition / March 1994
St. Martin's Paperbacks edition / January 2000

St. Martin's Paperbacks are published by St. Martin's Press, 175 Fifth Avenue, New York, NY 10010.

10 9 8 7 6 5 4 3 2 1

CHAPTER 1

IT'S never an easy thing for a man to admit that he's been a failure, but such was the assessment I had to make of myself as I rode through the Montana night aboard the unreserved coach section of this train on the Northern Pacific rail line. I was tired to my very soul, the thrill of my first ride long left behind me somewhere around Bismarck, the endless rumblings of the rail now a torment rather than a pleasure.

There was little I could do as I stared out through the dark windows except relive the past. And that was an unpleasant pastime, for I had few things I could recollect with pride.

I had failed. I had failed myself, my family, the memory of my father and mother. Everything I had dreamed of had crumbled away bit by bit, leaving me with the realization that it was time to give up. So here I was, a Tennessee farmer without a single success to call my own, Miles City bound and watching the Montana plains slip swiftly past my window, the land lit with the dim glow of the night sky, and my mind in such a turmoil I couldn't even appreciate the rugged beauty of it all.

Gloomily my mind moved back over the years, as steady and relentless as the rumbling, smoke-belching train on which I rode. The memories were sometimes pleasant, causing me to smile at my reflection in the dark window, but largely they were painful.

I was born a farmer and a Baptist in 1849 in the same tall oak bed in which I had been conceived the year before, and the same bed in which my brother had come into the world some five years prior to me. There was no doctor to assist my mother with either birth; the other women from further up the valley served as midwives while my father paced about in the yard, nervously puffing his pipe. In both cases his apprehensions were quickly relieved, for both my brother and I were strong, fat, healthy babies that grew to be strong young men. In those days, weakness and sickness in the family were things no hard-working Tennessee farmer could afford.

I grew up on the family homestead in Powell's Valley, a long valley that runs southwest to northeast in eastern Tennessee and western Virginia. It is a green, fertile valley that is bordered on the south by Wallen's Ridge and the Powell Mountains and on the north by the Cumberlands, and through it ran a portion of the great road that first led settlers from the hills and valleys of Virginia and the Carolinas on through Cumberland Gap and into Kentucky. Our farm lay southwest of Cumberland Gap, our home built right up against the base of the steep Cumberlands that stood in a tall, proud line, projecting gray faces of rock through the trees on their crests.

My father was typical of the breed that populated the valley in those days—few smiles and little mirth, but lots of back-breaking work. He worked from the first light of dawn, sometimes even before that, until that same light faded at dusk. And my brother and I were always with him, and together we made the farm into something of which we all were proud.

I received just enough schooling to teach me to read and write, though my mother taught me many other things as well. I developed a passion to learn, one that could not be squelched, and I read every book I could get my hands on. My mother was proud of that, as was my father to a lesser degree, for they both sensed that learning would take the place of brawn as the country grew and developed. I think that somehow they always looked on me as the one who would carry on the farm's life after they were gone. My older brother had too much of the wanderlust in him to stay in the place of his birth until the end of his days; I was a more stable fellow, not as prone to wander.

My brother went by the name of Sam, his full name being Samuel Adams Hartford. My name is James Monroe Hartford, and my callen name is Jim. My father chose the names not out of any interest in history, but simply because he had heard them and liked the ring of them. My mother would have preferred biblical names, I think, for she always called me James and my brother Samuel, rather than the Jim and Sam the rest of the world knew us by. But seemed fitting, somehow, for she had a dignity about her that didn't lend itself to slang or nicknames. It was a quiet dignity, a humble one, a very real one.

When the war came I was just a sprout of a boy, twelve years old, but fired up by the controversy of the times and the endless debates between the southern and northern sympathizers in the valley. Both factions were there, and the very air was tense in those days with dissension. When the fighting began, many local men and boys swarmed up through Cumberland Gap to join the northern forces while my father and brother decided to join with the south. It wasn't political reasons that motivated my father's decision, for he was a highly unpolitical man and could not, I think, have said just what the fighting was all about. And while his localized, almost isolated existence made it difficult for him to visualize something as big as a nation, he did have a clear concept of statehood, and he knew that his home state had joined the secession. So as a loyal Tennessean, he went with it, fighting for a cause he did not understand.

He fought with Zollicoffer in that general's last fight. My father was shot just before the near-sighted Zolli-coffer was blown from his saddle while barking orders to Union troops that he took to be his own men. And the rag-tag army of farmers broke ranks after that and scurried back to their farms and families, leaving their out-dated 1812 army issue flintlocks in the mud beside the bodies of their comrades. My father's corpse was among those left behind, but my brother Sam did not leave his side, and as a result was taken prisoner by the northern troops and hauled away to a prison camp in Bryant's Fork, Illinois. The stories he told me of the atrocities heaped upon the prisoners in that camp, the cruelties engineered by the heartless, sadistic overseer of that hellish place . . . many times those stories have made me shudder.

It was after the war that my failures truly began. My mother died the year after the war ended, my brother reaching home scarcely in time to see her alive for one last time. We buried her on the grounds of the farm, near the creek and beneath an oak. Sam stayed on with me long enough to get the farm back on its feet again, then he was gone, the wanderlust claiming him, driving him west to make his fortune in the gold fields of Con-federate Gulch, Montana Territory. And though he never gained the riches he hoped for, he did get enough to set himself up as a small-time rancher on the eastern Montana plains, making his living amid a growing cattle industry. And I was left alone in Tennessee, a boy not yet twenty years old, trying with all that was in me to make a success of the old Powell's Valley farm, doing my best to continue what my father had begun, working as hard as I would have if he had been looking over my shoulder. I wanted to make the farm back into a thing he would have been proud of.

And I was failing. Miserably failing. It seemed that God himself was against me, for whenever blight struck the valley, it was my crops that died first. Whenever disease ravaged the cattle, mine were the first to die. I watched my profits decrease year by year, and soon I had to begin selling portions of my farm to make up for the losses. I sold more and more, eating away at the borders of the farm, each year becoming poorer than the year before, until at last, in this year of 1884, I had sold the rest of it, even the house itself, and boarded the train with Montana as my destination.

It hurt me to have to give up on the task left to me by my father, but I tried to comfort myself with the realization that I had done my best. Yet it seemed a vague comfort, and I dreaded the prospect of having to face Sam and tell him of my failure. And the fact that I would have to ask him for work until I could somehow set myself up to make a living on my own was a cause of constant anxiety for me.

My spirits had revived somewhat as the journey progressed and my mind was overwhelmed by the new, and to me, amazing things that I was seeing. I had never in my life seen a city of any real size—I hadn't even traveled the distance south to Knoxville—and when first I set eyes on Chicago it took my breath away. I had the same reaction when I saw St. Paul, and if anyone had talked to me right then they would have found me the most enthusiastic traveler in the country, I think.

Those optimistic thoughts had come several days ago when the journey was young. But now, here in the late Montana night in the darkness just before dawn I felt quite differently. I was growing close to my destination now, my anticipated and dreaded meeting with Sam only a short time away, and my entire worldly fortune in a carpetbag at my feet. I was beginning to realize just how ignorant I was of life on the plains. I was going to cattle country, and the only experience I had with cattle was on the farm in a world utterly apart from the rolling, seemingly endless plains around me. Would Sam be able to use me, to provide me work? I felt certain he would give me a place to stay and feed me, even if there was nothing I could do to help him, but the idea of taking something without giving in return was repulsive to me, a violation of the pride of my raising.

"Good evening, sir. May I sit down?"

The speaker's voice jarred me from my thoughts, and I looked up at him sharply—and rather stupidly, I'm afraid. As soon as my mind came around to reality again, I remembered my manners and offered him the seat across from me. The unreserved coach was set up in a series of stalls, with two benches in each one set facing each other. I had been seated alone in my stall, and this fellow had been up further ahead in the car, also alone. I had noticed him earlier.

He was sharply dressed, a gold watch chain draped across his stomach, accenting the neat gray suit which he wore. On his head sat a gray derby, matching the suit, and his mustache also was gray. He was slim, tall, and distinguished, obviously a businessman, and as he sat down before me the shabbiness of my own clothing became embarrassingly apparent. But I smiled pleasantly, glad to have someone to talk to.

"Aaron P. McCuen," he said, extending his hand. "I hope I'm not intruding, but this trip is getting rather tedious, and I thought you might find a little companionship as pleasant as I would."

"I certainly would," I replied. "The name's Jim Hartford. I noticed you got on in Bismarck. You from around there?"

"No sir, though I have been there in connection with my business. Stayed about two months—meetings and all that garbage. I'm heading into Miles City now. More business."

He had a pleasant voice, smooth and clean. I wanted to get him to talk some more just to hear it. "What's your line of work, Mr. McCuen?"

"Call me Aaron—or just McCuen, if you prefer. I'm affiliated with the Washburn and Moen Manufacturing Company in Worcester. More of a salesman than anything else, and a spokesman on occasion for the company. I deal in barbed wire."

Barbed wire. Now there was something I had heard about, though indirectly. I had never actually seen the stuff, though I knew it was available in Tennessee. Most folks in the valley still used rails or stones for fencing.

But I had heard reports, second or third hand, of those who talked of the trouble the wire was causing west of the Mississippi in the cattle country, where many still wanted the ranges open. But beyond that I knew little of the matter. I wondered if Sam used the wire.

"Barbed wire, you say? I assume you're going into Miles City to make some sales. I hear the stuff has caused a little trouble at spots."

He nodded dolefully. "There's been some trouble, I'll admit, some areas worse than others. Texas has been pure hell over the matter, with wire cutting organizations and anti–wire cutting organizations, with secret signals and passwords and such things as that. There's been a good deal of violence at some spots. The wire is getting all over the country now. My company is producing not far from twenty million pounds of the wire every year. Business is booming."

"What brings you out this way? Isn't there any wire being sold here yet?"

"Oh, yes," he said, pulling out an expensive-looking cigar and offering it to me. I refused, and he paused to slowly light up. "But rail service had been in Montana only a short time—transcontinental rail service, I mean. Before last year we had to ship the wire in by freight wagon for the most part. Now we haul it by rail and most of the time just dump and sell it right beside the tracks. We sell to homesteaders and quite a few ranchers. Cattlemen are buying more and more of the wire. I guess they're starting to realize they can't really fight the stuff—it's here to stay. And it can be a real advantage to them if they use it correctly. I'm heading into Miles City to try to set up a better distribution system, maybe to try to get a few more cattlemen converted over to our side. There's been a real flurry of trouble between ranchers who use it and those who don't in the last few months. Maybe you haven't heard. The railroad tries to keep it quiet and all."

My heart sank within me. I had heard of no major trouble in the area I was going. I was suddenly fearful for Sam's safety, though I had no idea if he was involved at all in the barbed wire controversy. And I feared for myself too, for in the back of my mind was a plan to obtain some land for myself and get into the cattle business myself once I learned what I needed to know from my brother. My face must have reflected my thoughts, for McCuen frowned slightly, as if he sensed I was bothered by something.

"Well, enough talk about me and my barbed wire," he said. "What brings you out this way? And where do you call home?"

"I'm a Tennessee boy—a farmer up until now," I said. "I came out here . . . to see what my luck might be like in the cattle business." I found myself hesitant to tell the entire truth, for I was not at all proud of the way I was running for refuge to my brother.

McCuen smiled. "That's good to hear. I wish you the best of luck. Perhaps when the time comes we can talk about doing a little business about fencing."

"Maybe so. I'll admit I'm a little bothered about that trouble you mentioned. I hope I don't run into any of it."

"Oh, I doubt that you will," he said. "I intend to see what I can do to still any unrest that seems to have arisen over the situation."

I forced a grin at him. "I'll certainly keep you in mind if I ever need any wire," I said.

"Thanks. By the way . . . if you plan to stay in a hotel there, then perhaps we could share the cost of a room. I certainly don't want to seem presumptuous, but . . ."

"Thanks but no thanks," I said. "I have a brother out here, and I figure to spend some time with him before I get myself set up."

"That's good. And I hope you find some good land. A few years back you could have walked out anywhere and made a claim, just about. But since the government granted most of the land to the railroad it's pretty much a matter of buying whatever half-decent places you can find. The old-timers have all the land near town. New settlers have to range further out."

I felt a growing depression. It seemed every piece of news I was hearing made me wonder more and more if I had done the right thing in selling the Powell's Valley farm. I turned toward the dark window, brooding.

Outside the plains were bathed in a soft light, and the distant horizon was a lightening shade of purple and lavender. The newly rising sun was invisible to me as I stared southward, but I could follow its course as the shadows stretched black and long toward the west, then shortened rapidly as the sun rose higher. I heard the noise of the train's brakes, and we pulled to a halt in front of a station platform marked "Glendive."

Passengers rose and moved off while others got on.
McCuen had been dozing, and a man brushed roughly
past him, his jacket knocking McCuen's hat off and
waking him up. My companion stirred, frowned at the
man's back, and picked up his hat.

"I didn't realize I had gone to sleep," he said. "I
couldn't even think of sleeping all night, and now that
daylight is here I'm getting drowsy." He looked at his
cigar and frowned to see it had gone out. He began to
dig in his pocket for a match, then murmured something
and cast the smoke to the floor. He leaned back, pulled
his hat low over his eyes, and dozed off again as the
train began pulling forward again. He lay with his sup-
ple fingers folded across his stomach, snoring faintly. I
had to smile. This elegant man could even snore elegantly.

I turned and looked out again over the Montana
plains, my stomach tying itself in knots inside me.
Could I do it? Could I really make a success of myself
here in this unknown land, or would I be simply a burden to Sam?

I looked around me at the other passengers. Some sat
sleeping; others were staring out the windows. How
many of these were other men bringing their families to
the Montana Territory to try to make up for past failures? Children roamed the aisle. Many larger families
were traveling together, probably hoping to buy or
claim enough land to make some sort of living. From
what I had heard, many were predicting a great influx
of settlers to Montana within the next twenty years. The
railroad literature promoting the land showed pictures
of neat cottages surrounded by flowers in a land that
looked like a depiction of paradise. As I looked out the
window I saw a land that was unlike that in the pictures,
and felt certain many other men in the train were just

beginning to realize that the land was not the promised country they had dreamed about. The train stopped again, and again. More passengers.

Like me, many new settlers were southerners, I guessed, probably trying to remake fortunes lost during the war. It was a standing joke that the Confederacy was not dead—it had just moved to Montana. Broken men, shattered families that had lost a lifetime's worth of homebuilding and hard labor when the war swept through the south . . . many were surely desperate, with only a few dollars and a bagful of dreams between themselves and starvation.

At least I had some money from the sale of my land—enough to take care of me for a time, and hope-fully enough to buy a good piece of railroad property. I reached down to pat the side of my carpetbag.

It was gone.

The shock spread over me like the touch of death, chilling me, filling me with an overwhelming panic. Gone! Suddenly I stood, a violent gasp breaking from my lips. McCuen stirred but did not wake. I looked about the car in desperation.

There . . . there it was, in the hands of a tousle-headed boy, a lad that could not be more than ten years old, lugging it as fast as he could toward the rear of the car. Apparently he had only just now slipped the bag from beneath my feet while I was lost in contemplation.

But now I had him. He couldn't get away. I ran from the stall where I had been seated and headed after him just as he made it out the car's rear door. The other passengers looked at me with dull eyes, not concerned about what I was doing.

I caught the little devil on the platform at the rear of the car. My hand grasped his shoulder and the other reached for the bag.

"Give it back, you little beggar! Give it back, or I'll box your ears until your jaws ring!"

I've heard plenty of cussing in my day, but none to match in vigor and vileness the language that burst from that young throat. And as his words damned me, his hands pushed me with unexpected force, upsetting me, sending me back against the platform railing as the bag slipped from my grasp.

And then I was over, falling, striking the embankment beside the tracks and rolling down it, landing at last almost twenty feet from the fast-moving train, the morning dew soaking my pants and a dazed expression shaping my features as the train moved past me, the young devil waving my bag at me with a taunting look on his face.

For several long minutes I sat there, my dulled brain unable to take it all in. I was stranded, without a horse or weapon, here on the Montana plains, every cent I had in the world being carried away from me by a young thief who was probably anticipating an orgy of candy and licorice water. I was stuck, alone and isolated. Miles City was on down the track, a long walk. Maybe I could find that young robber there and recover my cash, but I wasn't sure Miles City was where he would get off. I was broke, unarmed, and alone in a place where I knew no one. Sam's spread was out there somewhere, but I had no idea of its exact location.

So I got up, brushed myself off, and started walking.

CHAPTER 2

I followed the tracks closely, taking the opportunity to view the country to which I had come. For the most part it was grasslands, generally flat but with low hills that stretched far in all directions. There were larger hills, too, and cottonwoods that grew tall and lonesome out on the grasslands. More cottonwoods grew along the course of a meandering brook. I debated whether or not to take a drink from the brook, but the brown tint of the water killed the idea.

Occasionally I saw cattle roaming lazily in the distance, and I could see why Montana had perhaps the biggest cattle industry in the west. I could also understand the hesitancy of some ranchers to have the land fenced in. Many of them had come to the Montana Territory many years before, riding a weary gelding and leading a handful of scrawny cattle. Many with just such a humble beginning were rich today, for on the open range many calves were born who were the fair and legal property of whoever first managed to get a rope around their necks. A good active rope could make a cattleman successful back in those old days even if he had little money to invest in stock. Those days were ending now, being killed by fences and railroads. No wonder many were sad to see the coming of the new settlers. The whistle of the railroad engines marked the beginning of the end of the west that was. Civilization was reaching across the plains on a track of steel.

I noted the irony of having to walk slowly beneath the sun along the railroad, the modern miracle that could move a man from one end of the nation to the other in a fraction of the time it took to travel by river or horseback. The passenger car in which I had been riding had hardly qualified as luxurious, but now I wished fervently that I was back on it. Into my mind flashed a report I had read some months back of how the people of Bozeman, a town west of Miles City, had greeted the arrival of the first passenger train last March with a huge banquet. When I arrived in Miles City there would be no such welcome for me. I didn't even know how I could get in touch with my brother.

I spotted a small dwelling nearby a creek that was hardly more than a trickle. Though I wasn't certain, I thought myself about fifteen miles from Miles City, also called Milestown by some of the older residents of the area. It was still early, and I knew I could easily reach my destination on foot, but I hoped I could hitch a ride on a passing wagon. I walked toward the isolated little dwelling, noting a narrow wagon road leading from it and roughly paralleling the railroad.

As I drew near I looked for some sign of life about the place, but there was none save for a lone horse in a split-rail corral near the house.

The place was small, one of the sort of houses I later learned was almost standard in the territory. It was a log house, obviously well constructed, with evenly sized, tight-fitting logs. I looked the place over very carefully. I had gained some limited experience with log buildings in Tennessee, and always I found them fascinating. Whoever had built this one was a craftsman. This was no loosely chinked dirt-roofed structure; the roof was made of hand-split shingles, and the chinking was tight. The builder had put real glass into the windows, as well as store-bought shutters. It was an appealing spot, with a restful and calm atmosphere about it. I noticed an extensive garden behind the house, beside which the small stream widened into a large pond of the sort that was good for watering animals. I found myself envious of whoever owned this little spread, for although it didn't appear to be a ranch as such, it was obviously a well-kept and productive little spot. I assumed whoever lived here was a self-sufficient individual who lived on what he raised and hunted, for I could figure no other way he could survive out here unless he was a rancher. Large-scale farms were a rarity in these parts, and I saw no signs of extensive cultivation.

"That's far enough, buddy. You just reach good and high and turn around real slow."

The voice was gentle, its tone belying the threatening content of the words. But I wasn't about to call the bluff, if bluff it was, and very quickly I obeyed. I thrust my hands straight up and turned completely around.

It was a gray-bearded fellow that I saw step from behind a cottonwood, a Spencer rifle aimed at my gut. His voice may have sounded calm, but the look in his eye sent a chill through me, and I had the unnerving sensation that this fellow would not hesitate to put a bullet through my gut. I wondered just what I had walked into.

"Easy, mister . . . I meant no harm. I got thrown off the train a ways back, and thought maybe you might have a cup of water. I was just about to holler for you."

"Good thing you didn't," he said. "I might have blowed your head off. I been right skittish lately. I reckon you must be new to these parts. A man don't just walk up on somebody else with no warnin', especially the way things is right now."

I wasn't sure what he meant by that last comment,

but I was in no mood to quiz him. The gun was still aimed at my abdomen, and my hands still reached for the clouds. And as long as that big Spencer's muzzle was giving me its one-eyed stare, I wasn't about to lower them. My father had carried a Spencer, and I knew of the tendency of that sort of weapon to go off with only a slight bump to the stock, and I prayed that he wouldn't bump the butt end of that cannon against one of those cottonwoods.

He was looking me over, obviously in no hurry to make any changes in the present situation. I felt I was being sized up. And with my sweat-soaked condition, along with the dirt that had smeared on my trousers when I fell from the train, I wasn't sure I would pass whatever mental test he was putting me through. But apparently I looked more pitiful than threatening, for slowly he let the muzzle of his weapon drop and he looked at me with almost a disdainful expression.

"Well, you don't look any too dangerous. But with the trouble we've been havin' the last few months I ain't about to be careless 'bout no one that comes up unexpected. But you're on foot, so I reckon you ain't one of them riders."

I let out a sigh as the gun's barrel dropped, and slowly I lowered my hands. "Thanks for dropping that gun, mister. I had no intention of disturbing you. I'll be on my way."

"No—not until you've had that water you wanted," he said, now just as amiable as he had been hostile moments before. "I ain't gonna have it said that Jasper Maddux sent anybody away thirsty."

He supplied me with a dipper of ice-cold water fresh from the well. It was a luxury, cool and refreshing, filling me with vigor and clearing my mind even as I drank it. When I had finished I had another, then another. The old fellow grinned at me all the while.

"I reckon you were right thirsty, feller," he laughed. "What can I call you?"

"Jim Hartford," I said. "I'm from Tennessee. I just got into the territory this morning."

"You say you fell off the train?"

I flushed, ashamed to tell him what had happened, but I managed to get my story out, and actually felt grateful when the old fellow didn't laugh. I omitted any reference to my brother, for still it filled me with shame to have to come crawling to him, and I had no desire to talk about it.

"What is it you aim on doin', now that your cash is gone?" he asked. "I wish I could help you out, but I'm about as busted as you are."

I found I couldn't answer him. I had no desire to face Sam until I had at least tried to regain my cash. I shook my head.

"I don't really know, Mr. Maddux. I reckon I'll go into Miles City and try to get a little work somewhere and maybe find that little jackass that took my money. Right now I just need to get on into town."

"You came by at a good time, then. I'm headin' in that direction, though I ain't goin' but within about five miles of town. You can probably hitch a ride with somebody from there who'll take you the rest of the way."

Within ten minutes we were bumping along in an old flatbed, following a wagon trail with the deepest ruts I had ever seen. It was ten times rougher than any wagon ride I had ever taken, but Maddux didn't seem to notice. The vague references to trouble that I had heard both from him and McCuen came to my mind, and I inquired about the matter.

"It's been a real problem lately," he said. "Worse than any I've ever seen. Riders are what are causin' it all, night riders that cut wires and threaten folks that fence in their land. They gave me a bit of trouble the

other night, tryin' to cut the fence I got around my wa-
terin' hole. I ran 'em off, though. That Spencer roars
good and loud.'' He grinned and displayed red gums
with two yellow teeth in the front worn down to nubs.

I hadn't noticed the fence around the water hole. And
though I was grateful to Maddux for the help he was
giving me, I couldn't help but feel he had done the
wrong thing to fence in his watering hole. No wonder
ranchers were angry at fence-stringers! Water holes
were precious in cattle country.

''Does anybody know who these riders are?'' I
asked. ''Whose men are they?''

''Nobody knows. They're all strangers to these parts,
best anybody can tell. I figger somebody has hired 'em,
moved 'em in from somewheres to cause trouble. Cattlemen, probably . . . maybe several of 'em together. So
far there ain't no proof that they're tied in with anybody
in particular, and all the ranchers say they don't know
a thing about it. But I figure somebody has hired 'em.
We'll find out sooner or later.''

We rode the remainder of the distance with few
words. When we reached an area where an even rougher
road led southward off the one we were on, Maddux
stopped the wagon and I climbed down.

I gave him my thanks and he headed down the side
road. I waved at him until he disappeared from view,
then I started walking again, moving west toward Miles
City.

The sun was high in the east, beaming down much
hotter than before. But the air was pleasant, and though
I was hungry I felt quite vigorous, and walked with a
fast and firm stride. I felt fortunate in one way to have
no burden to carry, but I also missed the feeling of my
carpetbag in my hand. I refused to let myself worry
excessively about my loss, for I knew that worry would

do nothing to help me replace my lost money or get started as a rancher.

I had it in mind to find work somewhere around Miles City. I had no idea what sort of jobs were available, but I was confident enough of my abilities to give me the assurance that I would find something. And in the time I was not working I could scout around and see if there was any sign of that young thief who stole my bag.

I turned when I heard the noise of a buggy on the road behind me. A one-horse buckboard approached me at a good clip, raising a sizeable cloud of dust on the road. It was a fine vehicle, a very expensive model, I could tell, but the driver was of far more interest than the buckboard itself.

It was a young lady, pretty and auburn-haired. She was steering the buckboard like an expert, and her bearing and confidence in her task caused me to sense immediately that this was a lady of strength and pride. And if the expensive buggy was any indication, she was also a lady of some wealth.

I smiled at her and nodded as she approached. She slowed the buggy down and pulled up beside me, looking down at me from her perch like a queen from her coach. My lands, she was pretty!

"Hello, ma'am. How are you today?"

"Fine, sir. And yourself?"

"Very well, thank you. I couldn't be better." It was a lie, of course, but I had learned long ago that people making polite conversation weren't interested in hearing honest answers.

"What puts you on foot, sir? Has your horse had some trouble?" Her voice was clear and bell-like, perfectly suiting her appearance. I felt warmth steal over me.

"No, ma'am. You might say I had the misfortune to

fall off the Northern Pacific back some ways up the track. I hitched a ride with an old fellow just this far. I'm heading for Miles City.''

She looked at me carefully, curling her lip in a way that made my heart beat faster. She sighed loudly.

''My father would thrash me if he knew I picked up a stranger on the road,'' she said. ''But I'm going into Miles City and would be glad to have some company. Hop in. My name's Jennifer Guthrie.''

''Jim Hartford, ma'am. I appreciate the ride.''

The buggy rode a lot smoother than Maddux's wagon. I settled back on the soft upholstery and enjoyed the scent of her perfume as it wafted over to me.

''Miss Guthrie, I can't tell you how grateful I am for the ride. I was getting a bit weary out there.''

''I imagine so. How did you manage to fall off the train?''

There it was . . . the same embarrassing question Maddux had asked. I gave her an abbreviated version of the story, again omitting any mention of my brother. It crossed my mind that she might be from a ranching family, and should she and Sam be on opposite sides of the barbed wire struggle it might be the end of my free ride. She didn't react with the same reserve Maddux had shown toward my story; she laughed, and I blushed crimson. It was very difficult to admit to a pretty young lady like this that a child had outwitted me.

She apologized profusely for her laughter. ''I'm sorry . . . I guess it isn't funny to you at all. Please forgive me.'' She smiled silently to herself for a time, and I could almost see the pictures flashing through her mind—pictures of me falling off the platform of that passenger car while a five-foot devil laughed at me. I had to admit there was a certain comical element in it.

She asked me about myself, my background, my

plans. I told her a little, though very little, and in the process learned much about her.

Her father was Luther Guthrie, she said—a man whose name was known even in Tennessee as the owner of the fantastically successful Muster Creek Cattle Company, one of the biggest dealers in beef in the territory. I had heard of him and his company through talk back home and in my reading in preparation for the trip. From what I gathered, Luther Guthrie owned millions of dollars and had almost complete control over huge tracts of the best grazing land to be found in hundreds of miles. It astounded me to realize that I was sitting beside his daughter, smiling and talking with her almost as if we were old friends.

"You're needing a job," she said. "Have you ever done any cooking? I mean for large groups of people."

It was an unexpected query, but I managed to bluff my way through it. "Yes," I lied. "I was a cook in the army a few years after the war. I cooked for dozens at a time." There wasn't a trace of truth in it, but I sensed a job offer coming on, and I intended to take advantage of it. Working for Luther Guthrie could be a very lucrative job, just what I needed right now.

"I'm glad to hear that. You see, our cook died just two weeks ago, and we've been just scraping by since then. You'll need to work to make up for that money you lost. Would you consider coming to work for us?"

I had assented to the offer scarcely after the words had left her lips. She smiled, apparently sincerely pleased that I would be working for them, and I sat back with a sense of gratification. I had managed to bluff my way into a job . . . now if only I could bluff my way through a few meals, maybe I would have some money.

We talked casually until we reached Miles City. Miles City! The very place I had dreamed of, the place where I hoped to rebuild my life. Miles City of the

Montana Territory—several hundred people, over twenty saloons, and several businesses of the type a man doesn't mention in polite society. I felt a thrill of excitement as the buckboard entered the wide dirt street.

There were a goodly number of people walking about in the street, and many of the men paused to politely tip their hats to Jennifer, and she smiled and nodded back. I could feel them looking me over, wondering who I was and what I was doing in the company of Miss Jennifer Guthrie. I felt a little like a plucked chicken hung for display in a butcher's window.

Miles City was not an exceptionally large town, though the coming of the railroad had started a spurt of growth. Many of the town's retail establishments were lined up in two facing rows on either side of the wide street. I looked over some of the signs. Ringer and Johnson Livery . . . Lodging-Rooms . . . Chinese Laundry . . . The owner of the laundry smiled and gave a curt bow as we passed his business. Leaning up against the wall of the building beside him was a slender young man with a neatly-trimmed mustache and sideburns. He too waved at the lady and stepped back inside the building sporting the sign that read Huffman's Portraits.

"It seems that you're pretty well-known in this town," I said as she pulled the buggy to a stop. I leaped down to circle the buggy and give her a hand as she stepped out.

"Oh, I guess my family has been around these parts for quite some time," she said. "My father has done well with cattle, and the family name has spread pretty far."

"Ma'am, I think I'll walk over to the livery and enjoy the shade while you take care of your business. Maybe I'll explore the town a bit. If you would like I would be happy to take over the driving when it's time to head back to your ranch."

"Why, thank you, Mr. Hartford. I would appreciate that."

She turned and moved on down the boardwalk, entering a textile and general merchandise store. I looked after her, unable to take my eyes from her until she was gone. Sitting in the buggy with her had made me forget my troubles very quickly. I think if that little railroad thief had popped up before me right then I would have patted him on the head.

I loitered about for awhile, finally heading across to the nearest saloon for a glass of water, the only drink that didn't cost any money. I was halfway across the street when I heard a voice calling my name.

I turned to see Aaron McCuen approaching me. In his hand was my bag.

"Thank heaven!" I exclaimed, opening the bag to find all my money intact where I had stowed it in a side pocket. "How did you come by this?"

"Oh, I took it from that little fellow that had it. I knew it was yours, but I couldn't figure out where you had gone."

And so again I had the humiliating experience of telling my story, and again it was greeted with laughter. I didn't really mind this time—I was growing used to it.

"Come in and join me for a bite," he said, gesturing toward a cafe. I accepted the invitation.

We sat in a cool, dark corner of the cafe with our meals before us, and into my mind came the tale of the wire-cutting night riders Maddux had told me about. I related it to McCuen, and he seemed upset by the news.

"This is bad . . . bad," he said, shaking his head. "I don't know what kind of effect this will have on my business. It isn't good at all for people to associate barbed wire with violence and threats. Something is going to have to be done."

He sat brooding for awhile, and I stayed with him

until I saw Jennifer Guthrie emerge from the store across the street, a full basket in her arms. She headed back toward the buggy, and I took my leave of McCuen, again thanking him for the safe return of my bag.

She was pleased to see my bag had been returned. I told her about McCuen, not mentioning his business for fear she would not be pleased if the subject of barbed wire came up.

"Was your money in the bag?" she asked.

I started to answer, then caught my breath. If I said yes, she might assume that I would not be interested anymore in her offer of work at the Guthrie ranch. And I suddenly realized that money or no money, I wanted that job. I wanted to be near her.

"No . . . the money was gone," I said. She shook her head sympathetically.

"I'm sorry. I guess you'll be coming to work for us then. Will you watch my things for me? I have a bit more to do before I'm ready to leave."

The "bit more" took the rest of the day. By the time we at last climbed aboard and headed for the Guthrie ranch on Muster Creek it was late afternoon.

CHAPTER 3

IT was getting dark when we made the turn north off the main road toward the Guthrie ranch near Muster Creek. The horse was slow—hungry, I suspected, for it had not grazed for quite some time—but Miss Guthrie assured me the ranch was not far.

I noticed as we drew nearer the ranch that Jennifer Guthrie was growing nervous. Her face appeared slightly pale, and she clenched her fists in her lap, responding to my attempts at conversation with a minimum of words, staring ahead into the growing darkness.

At last I asked her what was bothering her, and she began to deny that anything was on her mind. But she paused, smiled sadly, and said, ''I'm a bit worried about how my father will react when I get back. You see, I stayed much longer in town than I thought I would, and he always likes to know where I am at every minute. He's very protective, you know—still thinks of me as a child.''

I sighed. That didn't sound good. If Luther Guthrie was the type to grow angry just because his daughter came in late from town, then he probably would be even more upset to meet a fellow she picked up on the road. I grew apprehensive. I suspected that my greeting at the Guthrie ranch might be something less than cordial.

We came upon the ranch quickly, and in the moonlight it was an impressive sight. The house was one story tall, built of logs, and spread out long and narrow. I could tell that the place had been expanded several times, and as we rounded a turn in the road I could see that there was another large extension on the rear of the house, making the structure into something like a large L.

Light streamed from the windows, making a soft glow about the front of the house. It looked friendly, somehow, like a place where a traveler would be welcome. My fears eased a little. After all, I had been assured a job at the place, so what was there to worry about?

There were several outbuildings, also log structures, and a few smaller sod buildings set further off. A hill covered with scraggly brush rose up behind the ranch, and in a pen built on the hillside I saw the faint white forms of chickens. There was a corral built alongside one of the larger outbuildings, and several horses were inside. The moon was growing brighter as it climbed through the sky, and the whole scene was bathed in dim light, giving it all a sort of dream-like quality.

We pulled the buggy up right before the house, and the dream became a nightmare.

The front door burst open suddenly, and a big figure stalked out, approaching us with obvious anger. My self-confidence vanished like a drop of water on a hot rock. I had no doubt that this was Luther Guthrie.

"Jennifer, where have you been? Do you think that I haven't been worried about you?" Then he looked at me. "And who is this melon head?"

I glanced over at the young lady. Even in the darkness I could see that she was pale. It was a long moment before she could speak, and I suddenly realized that she was afraid, terrified of her own father.

"I . . . I'm sorry, Pa . . . I just stayed longer than I meant . . . I'm sorry . . ."

Her voice was quaking, making her sound like a small child. Yet she was at least twenty-five years old, I estimated. It seemed incongruous. What kind of man was this Luther Guthrie, to raise a daughter in such a manner that even as a grown woman she was terrified of him?

"Stayed longer than you meant, did you? Well, that's a blamed fine reason!" He snorted, then looked again at me. "I asked you who this joker was. What do you mean riding home after dark with a stranger, like some brothel girl? Mister, you better have an awful convincin' explanation as to why you're here, or else . . ."

Hot anger flashed through me, and my voice spoke before my mind did. "My name is Jim Hartford, sir," I said with mock respect. "Your daughter was kind enough to let me ride with her into Miles City. I wanted to return the favor by driving her back. I planned to discuss the possibility of working as a cook for you, but I think that would be pointless now." I turned to Miss Guthrie. "Thank you for the job offer, but I don't think it's going to work out." Then I immediately regretted my words, for they were new fuel to the fire of wrath which the rancher heaped upon his daughter.

"Jennifer, do you mean to tell me you offered this man a job?" he exclaimed. "Without even checking with me? If you were a few years younger, I'd turn you over and . . ." He glowered at her with an expression that looked very much like one of hate. It disturbed me, and I felt an instinctive urge to protect the young lady. "Get out of that buggy, Jennifer! And you too, whoever you are."

Jennifer Guthrie obeyed, her cheeks now wet with tears. I too climbed down, but my face was calm, for this loud man had stirred up my pride. I stood to my full height, better than six feet, and looked down on his face. I would not cower before him.

His eyes looked up into mine, and he spoke through gritted teeth. "Get out of here, mister . . . get out before I turn the dogs loose on you! And if I ever see you near my daughter again I'll kill you. Is that clear? Now hit the trail!"

Jennifer Guthrie was sobbing, pleading. "But Pa, he did nothing! He helped me! Please . . . he doesn't even have a horse."

"He's got his legs. Get inside, girl. I'll deal with you in a moment. And as for you, mister, you'd best be movin' on right now!"

I was bitter angry, deadly angry. But I kept my temper and looked at him without losing one bit of my calm. And then I smiled, deliberately and slowly, purposely showing that he could not make me run. When I walked away, it would be under my own power and by my own will.

"Good evening to you, sir," I said. "Perhaps we will meet again."

And then I picked up my bag from the floor of the buggy and started walking away. I didn't look back once, but I could feel his gaze like a prickle in the back of my neck. I walked proud and firm, like a king.

I was almost back to the main road before my anger had cooled to the point that I could think clearly again. I was still mad over the way I had been treated, but in that small portion of the mind where cold objectivity is often at odds with self-pride, I sensed that the rancher's reaction to my presence was understandable. This was not a country where strangers were to be trusted, and Jennifer Guthrie's willingness to pick me up without question on the road this morning told me that she was a bit naive about her own safety. No wonder her father was protective. If I had a daughter like that I would be protective too.

But still, he had treated her quite rudely, and for some reason I could not understand I felt that his rudeness to her was also a personal affront to me. And I knew that I had to see her again. Not only in contempt for her father's demand that I not do so, but for another reason as well, though I couldn't put it into words. But I had to see her, somehow. And I knew that I would.

I reached Miles City again at about midnight. I slipped into the livery and spent the night on a scratchy mound of hay, my bag as my pillow. All night my nostrils were choked with the smell of hay, dust, and manure.

I woke up with the sun, more refreshed than I would have expected. I stretched, straightened my rumpled clothes, and pulled loose hay from my collar. Today I would buy a horse, and a gun. Out on the plains, a man had to have a gun.

But first he had to have breakfast, so I headed across to the cafe to wait for it to open.

On the boardwalk I found the little varmint who had taken my bag on the train. He had his back to me, and he was puffing a huge cigar. I grabbed him by the collar and yanked the cigar from his mouth and crushed it beneath my boot.

"You're too young to smoke," I said, giving him three or four smacks on the rump that sent him wailing down the street. It was all very satisfying.

I bought a good breakfast of steak and fried eggs, along with several large hunks of good wheat bread and three big mugs of strong black coffee. It was by far the best meal I had enjoyed since I left Tennessee, and I exulted in the satisfaction of having a full belly. I praised the meal as I paid my bill, and the lady who took the money smiled proudly. I left feeling very good.

The gun shop was just opening across the street, and I walked over and looked over the stock. There were many good weapons for sale here, most at good prices. I had owned a rifle back in Tennessee, as well as a pistol, but both were now outdated weapons and I had sold them before I began my westward trip. I had it in mind to buy a '73 Winchester, along with a Colt Peacemaker. I had read of these guns, and seen a Peacemaker in action once, and I admired them as fine weapons. The fact that they fired the same ammunition was a real advantage, too, for it eliminated the possibility of confusion in a pinch and generally simplified things all around. It was a mark of distinction to carry a '73.

There were cheaper guns for sale, and the temptation to save some money was strong, but my desire for the Colt and Winchester was stronger. I yielded, and walked out of the store the proud owner of two fine firearms. I felt like a true westerner.

I set out in search of a horse dealer, and found one bending his elbow in a saloon at the end of the street. Horses and horse dealers were as numerous as bedbugs around Miles City, and many local ranchers ran almost as many horses as cattle out on the range. I knew I would have to deal carefully, though, for many of these dealers were very adept at passing off a bad deal to a greenhorn. And unflattering though the thought was, I had to admit that I was a greenhorn. But it didn't necessarily follow that I was gullible, for I knew horses.

The horse dealer smelled of his trade, mixed with the odor of earthy sweat and not a little alcohol. He led me to the area where he ran his stock. It didn't take me long to spot a bay that looked like a good mount, but I took my time in bringing it up, discussing with him the merits and disadvantages of many of the other animals before at last getting around to it. I had already haggled down to a more reasonable price than he had first named by the time I brought up the horse I wanted, and after further argument I got him down to a figure that I could afford. I bought the horse, making him throw a halter and bridle in the deal, and headed for the livery.

There was an old saddle for sale there; I had seen it the night before. It was in pretty poor shape, but the price was low, and I was confident that with a little work I could turn it into a saddle worth owning. I also purchased a blanket and a scabbard for my rifle. I was pleased with the fit of the saddle on the horse, and when I mounted a new sense of confidence swept through me. Now I had transportation, a means of getting around to look over available land. And still I had spent only a small portion of my cash. I felt that all around I had made a good deal.

All my dealings had worn away the morning very quickly, and my big breakfast was feeling ever smaller in my stomach. I rode back over to the same cafe once more, proudly tethering my horse outside at the hitching post. A burly fellow dressed in skin clothing sat outside in the shade, looking with an expert eye at my horse.

"That's a good hoss," he commented as I came up beside him on the shaded porch. "It ain't no puddin' foot."

"I think I got a good deal," I said. "You know horses pretty well?"

"I know 'em right well," he said. "A man can get cheated pretty quick if he don't. I got me a good hoss, a sorrel, but it's got a pretty bad turn of the ankle right now. There's a hoss doctor here in town—he ain't no official doctor or nothin', just an old boozer who has a good way with an animal—and he's takin' a look right now. That's why I'm here instead of out on the plains shootin' buffalo."

He talked in a fast flurry, and I was rather surprised, for men of the plains rarely tell much about themselves

to a stranger. But as I looked at him closely I could see
why he was so verbose. His eyes refused to turn to
mine, and in them was a faint mist of tears. This man
was grieving, worrying over his hurt horse. It was
strangely touching, and told me much about the feeling
of a plainsman for his horse. Over the years a man's
mount became more than a means of transportation; it
was a companion, a partner. To lose it was like losing
a part of one's self. If this buffalo hunter's horse was
injured to any great extent, he would be forced to shoot
it. And from looking into the sad eyes of this man I
could tell that he would sooner shoot himself.

I felt a strong compassion for this fellow, and I invited him to share a meal with me. He seemed glad to
accept, and we moved quickly into the coolness of the
cafe.

I ate less than I had earlier in the morning, and while
my companion, whose name was Jack Tatum, ordered
a huge meal, he ate little of it. I tried to turn the conversation to pleasant topics, hoping to relieve my partner's melancholy.

He told me of buffalo hunting, of how the animals
were almost gone now, wiped out with such speed that
at times the ground north of town had been littered with
dead carcasses like leaves under a tree in late fall. The
railroad had brought an increase in the hunting of the
buffalo, he said, and Miles City was becoming a center
for the trade of hides of the disappearing animals.

"There's a lot of new things springin' up all over
these days," he said. "And I figure it's only the start.
The railroad is the biggest change—some call it im-
provement, but I ain't sure—and in the next few years
folks will start pourin' in thick as sorghum. That ain't
the only changes, neither. The sheep herders are movin'
their woolies in from the west more and more lately.
The cattlemen don't like it for the most part, but there

ain't been too much trouble. The main trouble is between the cattlemen themselves. I reckon you've heard
about the riders that have been cuttin' fences. Well, they
hit again last night, at several places, or so I heard. They
really hate that 'devil wire,' as the ranchers have took
to callin' it.''

"Where did they hit?'' I asked absently.

"I don't know all the places, but I seen 'em myself
headin' over toward Sam Hartford's spread near South
Sunday Creek . . .''

My glass dropped from my hand, and Tatum's words
were suddenly interrupted. He looked at me strangely,
and I was embarrassed.

"Did you say Sam Hartford?''

"Yes . . . you know him? He's a good one—a good
feller.''

I looked straight into Tatum's eyes. "He's my
brother, Mr. Tatum. I'm Jim Hartford.''

I don't know just why I revealed myself to him, for
I didn't want Sam to hear of my presence here until I
had seen him myself. But the mention of the night riders
sent a chill through me. I had the sudden gripping fear
that perhaps Sam had been hurt, or was in some sort of
danger.

"You . . . you're Sam's brother? Why, he's spoken
of you, lots of times!'' He leaned back and looked at
me as if I had suddenly become a new person. "Land
o' Goshen, I never would have figured! Does Sam know
you're about these parts? Last he said you was in Tennessee.''

"No, Mr. Tatum, he doesn't know, and to tell you
the truth, I hadn't aimed on telling him 'til a little later.
But these riders . . . you say they were heading for
Sam's place? Do you think . . .''

Tatum shook his head. "Don't you worry. Sam's alright. I heard from a friend that nobody was hurt no-

wheres last night. Sam's been usin' fencin' the last year or so, keepin' his stock confined instead of runnin' over the range. Probably those riders cut that fence in a lot of places. It'll cost Sam to replace it. But he'll do it, I reckon. He's done it before.''

I frowned. The idea of Sam being harassed by those riders bothered me, for my family had always been a close and protective one, every member standing up to fight if any one of us was threatened. And Sam had a temper, which was another thing that worried me. He wouldn't long stand for anyone damaging his property, if he was the same Sam that I knew from years back. I felt a sudden strong impulse to see him. If he needed help I intended to give it to him.

"Mr. Tatum, where is this South Sunday Creek? I think I'll ride out to see my brother.''

He gave me quick directions. I could reach Sam's spread by riding up the Fort Buford road for a short distance, then cutting northwest until I reached a creek. If I followed that creek northwest I would come to Sam's spread.

I didn't tarry long after that. The desire to see my brother was overwhelming. I gave Tatum best wishes for the recovery of his horse, thanked him for the directions, and walked out into the sunlight. I mounted my newly purchased horse, and headed off to find my brother. It felt good to be in the saddle, but I was nervous about the task before me.

As I rode I thought of the years that had passed since we had last seen each other. How would he be? Would he seem much older? He had married many years before. Whether he had children I didn't know. We had been boys when last we saw each other, and now we were both far into manhood. It seemed like only days since I had watched him leave for Montana, yet in a paradoxical way it seemed an eternity ago at the same time.

The passing of time had brought changes not only to the west but also to our own lives. I would soon be faced with the torment of telling Sam of my failure to sustain the old Tennessee homestead. How would he react? Would he be pleased to see me? I didn't know, and the realization of the momentous nature of this occasion sank further into my mind as I plodded along.

I reached the South Sunday and began riding northwest. It was then that I saw my first barbed-wire fence.

CHAPTER 4

IT was a fearsome-looking stuff, this barbed wire. I stopped long enough to examine it.

This wire could be pretty rough on a fellow's leg should he allow his horse to brush him up against it. The barbs looked more like miniature daggers than anything else, at least a half inch long. It wasn't what I had expected, somehow. No wonder this stuff kept such good control over cattle.

This wire was rusted, reminding me that the prickly wire had been available for about ten years now. The railroads were of course carrying it across in greater quantities than before, but there was nothing really new about barbed wire. Just why there was so much trouble right now over the stuff I couldn't really say; apparently something had set off hard feelings about it—the coming of a larger number of settlers with more fences, maybe.

I continued on, following the course of the creek. I found myself repeatedly swallowing an unrelenting lump in my throat, and my mouth was dry. I could feel my chest throbbing with the continual beating of my heart. Soon I would see my brother for the first time in many years. It was a frightening thought, making me anxious and full of a sort of dread.

I don't know with what instinct I realized that the

spread I next encountered was Sam's, but somehow I knew it at first glance. There was certainly nothing glorious about the place. I recalled the literature of the railroad and its promise of neat, white cottages. No neat cottage this dwelling! Just a low, dirt-roofed cabin with a couple of outbuildings and a sprouting garden behind it. Grass grew on the roof, which seemed to be so low that I wondered how Sam managed to stand upright without bumping his head. I felt a kind of sadness steal over me. Back in Tennessee I had talked proudly of my pioneering brother and the beautiful spread he worked in the Montana Territory. Somehow actually seeing the place let me know just how rough this sort of life could be. This was the life my brother had chosen. And now, it was also to be mine.

My horse plodded steadily toward the little dwelling, and I found my hands trembling as they held the reins. My eyes darted about the place, looking for Sam, scanning the entire area. I couldn't see him.

The door was standing open, though I could not see into the dark interior of the cabin. But then a figure filled that door, and a Sharps aimed its fearsome muzzle at me.

"Who are you and what do you want?" It was Sam all right. The gravelly voice was just the same as it had always been.

"Sam, don't you know me?"

There was only long silence. I couldn't see his face because of the shadows in the doorway, but I could guess at his expression as the realization of who I was stole over him. The muzzle of the gun dropped slowly, then the weapon was leaned against the doorpost. Sam's voice came, scarcely audible, its query tentative in tone.

"Jim?" Then again, more loudly and with assurance, "Jim!"

I was down off my horse and moving toward him as

he came out of the doorway. I recognized his face immediately, those same blue eyes, the sandy hair, thinner now. I threw my arms around him, and he did the same to me, and he gave me a bone-crushing hug of the sort that only a brother can inflict. Then he backed away, his hands on my shoulders pushing me back so he could study my face.

"My Lord, boy, I never thought I would lay eyes on you for a long, long time—maybe never. But you ain't a boy no more, are you? My gosh, you're a man, a full grown man!" He beamed at me, shaking his head at the wonder of it all, thrilled to his soul to see me and making no effort to hide the fact.

"Jim . . . Jim!" He sounded my name with satisfaction. Then a sudden look of trouble came over his face, and he said, "I'm sorry about the gun . . . I didn't know who you were. There's been some trouble here just last night, and I thought maybe . . ."

"I know, Sam. That's part of the reason I came out here. I didn't plan on seeing you until . . . well, I have a long story to tell, and I'd rather not start it here."

"Then come inside, brother, and meet my wife. Becky! We've got a guest . . . my brother! It's Jim, Becky, come from Tennessee!"

He hustled me inside, and I saw Becky. It was a strange feeling, looking at a woman I knew was my sister-in-law, and had been for years, but who I was just now seeing for the first time.

I shook her hand and noted the calluses. Her face was like that of many ranchers' wives I was later to meet. It was neither young nor old, unattractive nor pretty. Her eyes were brown and limpid, and her features told of a beauty that had long ago faded from toil and hot sun. She smiled, but her smile was weary, and her mouth had something which I can only describe as a hardness, a firmness molded forever into her face from years of wind, sweat, labor, and more labor. But she was a pleasant enough woman, and it was with real happiness that I greeted her.

Minutes later I was seated at a rough, hand-made table, my hands around a mug of coffee, telling my story. It was, as I had promised, a long story, one which spanned all the time since Sam and I had separated sixteen years before. And it was not a pleasant story, and when at last I had to tell Sam the thing I dreaded most—the fact that I had been forced to sell the family homestead—it was all I could do to force out the words. But he looked at me with no trace of condemnation in his gaze and with no tone of accusation in his voice.

"You tried, Jim. That's what counts. Some of us try to farm in Tennessee and don't quite make it, and some of us head to Montana to strike it rich and don't quite do that either. There ain't no hard feelings, in case you were worried about that. You did your best."

I can't describe the relief that swept over me with those words. Like Bunyan's Christian before the cross I felt a burden fall from my shoulders to never return. I looked down at my coffee mug, hoping not to blubber like some woman.

Sam told then of all that had happened to him, and I found myself fascinated by the tale. It had been a far rougher life than the one he had anticipated when he left Tennessee, and things had not worked out quite as he had planned. But he had lived, managing to get a good piece of land not far from town, a real asset in these days, for he could easily afford to make several trips to town each year, while most dwellers of the plains were more limited in the extent to which they could travel.

For two hours we sat at that table, squeezing in the events of sixteen years, feeling the same sense of family unity which we had known back in Powell's Valley growing between us again. Sam was older, much older, and his face showed it, but still he was Sam, my brother and companion. It was good to be close to him again.

Becky refilled my cup and I looked down at the table. "Sam," I said, "I've heard talk in town of trouble with fence cutters, and I heard they hit here last night. Is that right?"

Sam's face clouded. "You'd better believe it's right. They cut my fence last night, five places. And it ain't the first time, and I ain't the only victim. This situation is getting bad, Jim, real bad. There's gonna be blood before this is over."

To hear my own brother saying those words chilled me. He had an air of morbid certainty about what he was saying, and Sam had never been one for idle or unfounded talk. Something was brewing around here; I had felt it from the first time McCuen had mentioned the subject on the train. And apparently my own brother was going to be involved in whatever trouble erupted.

"How can you be so sure things will get that bad, Sam?" I asked. He was silent. Becky looked at him inquisitively.

"Sam, should I show him . . ."

He nodded. She moved over to the opposite side of the cabin and delved into a trunk. She returned with a crumpled paper in her hand. Without a word Sam took it and handed it to me.

The words on it were scribbled in large, crude letters, and to read them sent a spasm of fear through me.

"We have given our warning—the devil wire must go, else there will be blood on the land—no home, no wife, no child will escape—the land shall run red with fence-stringer blood."

I looked up into Sam's cold blue eyes. "Where . . ."

"Tied on a rock, tossed through my window last night," he said. He gestured over toward the front window. A pane of glass was broken, the hole temporarily covered with a piece of muslin. My numb hands let the paper fall from my fingers back onto the table.

"Do you have any idea who is behind all of this, Sam?" I asked. "Any clue at all?"

Sam stood and paced toward the center of the cabin. "I have no proof, only the rumors that I've heard," he said. "And because of that I've been slow to put the blame on anyone. But there's been those who say they've seen the riders mostly around one place, a ranch not too far from here. Have you heard of Luther Guthrie?"

I felt a sudden redness come to my face, and my breath quickened. Sam noted my sudden start, and eyed me curiously.

"Yes, I've heard of him," I said. "Do you think that he's the one behind this?"

"The riders have been spotted several times. Always they move back toward the Guthrie spread. I have friends around here, other ranchers, shepherds, buffalo hunters. Many of them feel there's no doubt that Guthrie has hired the riders. I know from meeting him on a couple of occasions that he is a totally unreasonable man. It goes beyond what you might think. A lot of cattlemen have a dislike for 'devil wire,' as they call it, but most of 'em manage to tolerate it, or so it appears. But this Guthrie . . . I can't figure him out. He literally gets red with rage and anytime anybody even thinks of fencing in the range, and on occasion he's even threatened lives. If anybody around here would hire those riders, it would be him."

Although I knew nothing of Guthrie's hate for fences, I knew quite well of his personality. He was obviously a man easily angered, especially concerning anything that was his—his daughter, for example, I thought ruefully. I could easily imagine him being much the same way toward his land, his cattle, his profession. There was a logic in what Sam was saying. It was quite possible that Guthrie was the culprit.

But why did that bother me so? Why did I feel the sudden panic that was overwhelming me? I didn't want to admit the answer, but I knew it full well.

It was because of her—because of Jennifer Guthrie. If her father was involved in this, and if in fact it did come down to open conflict and bloodshed, then she could be hurt. If not physically, at least mentally through seeing her father fighting, maybe even injured or killed, if things went that far. I had no love for Luther Guthrie, but I did not want to see him hurt, for that would in turn hurt Jennifer. Jennifer . . . in my mind she was no longer "Miss Guthrie" . . . she was Jennifer. I frowned. What was coming over me?

If there was a conflict between the angry cattlemen, then I would have no choice but to support Sam's side. And then in a sense, Jennifer would become my enemy. And that was a surprisingly painful thought.

I stood. "Sam, you have no plans to make some sort of move against Guthrie, do you? Do I sense that kind of notion rolling around in your mind?"

Sam said nothing. The silence was a ringing affirmative.

I moved toward him. "Sam! What could you do? Guthrie has men, cowboys. And if he is the guilty one, which he well might not be, he would have the riders, too. What chance would you have against him? What would you do?"

"I wouldn't have to go alone. There're others like me."

"But they're spread all over the plains."

"We could unify. It's been done in other places."

"But . . . violence, Sam? Violence? Would it be worth it?"

He looked at me coldly. "I'll not see my land ruined, my fences cut, my wife hurt . . . or my baby."

"Baby? You have children, Sam?"

"I will soon. Becky's with child."

I turned to look at her. She gazed modestly at the floor as I took note of the slight swell of her belly. I hadn't noticed it before.

I turned again to Sam, silent. He looked at me with the same cold, dogmatic expression. "It's something we have to do, Jim. You'll be ranching yourself before too long, and then you'll see. You'll be ready to stand up to Luther Guthrie. You'll understand."

But you don't understand, I thought silently. You don't understand the way I'm beginning to feel about the pretty young lady who would certainly be caught up in the middle of the fight. You don't understand at all, Sam. I turned away.

"I have a few things to do, Jim. I'm heading into town to buy some new fence. I'd appreciate it if you stayed around here to look out for Becky. After last night I don't feel like this is a safe place."

I smiled. "I'll be glad to stay, Sam." Then he was gone.

"More coffee, Jim?" Becky asked. I shook my head. "I think I'll just look around your place awhile. I've got a lot I need to learn about setting up a spread."

I looked closely at the cabin Sam had built. It looked rough from the outside, but the interior was actually pleasant. The table at which we had sat was rough, but well constructed and large. Around it sat several three-legged stools, not pretty but very serviceable.

The kitchen occupied one corner of the main room, consisting of a box like one might find on the back of a chuckwagon, with shelves and little nooks where cooking utensils could be stored. There was a cover on the box, which when folded down could serve as a kind of counter. Beside it sat a three-legged stove of black iron, with a large supply of wood stacked behind it.

The furniture was sparse, much of it homemade, but there was a large oak cabinet against the opposite wall that Sam had hauled in from who knows where that added a real domestic touch to the place. I felt sure that Becky was proud to own it.

The inside walls were white, the logs hewed off flat and covered with muslin. The muslin was white-washed with a substance I couldn't identify. Becky told me it was a mixture of crushed white shale and water. The south end of the cabin was papered with old newspapers, several layers thick.

There was a narrow straw mattress on a handmade bed against that wall. It looked new. Becky saw me looking at it and smiled.

"When Sam heard we were going to have a child he got so excited that he started building all sorts of things for the baby. He made that bed and tick just last week. Of course when the baby comes we'll have to restuff that mattress, it will be so old, but Sam was too happy to listen to reason. Of course it worked out good that he made it, 'cause now you'll have a place to sleep tonight."

I moved outside, looking over the structure of the cabin. Sam had done a good job, hewing the logs to uniform size. I checked out the notches. They were of the dovetail variety, tight-fitting and strong. He had chinked the cabin with clay. Some in this area used cow manure.

There was an outbuilding made of sod not far away, and I walked over to it. It was the first time I had had a chance to look closely at a sod building. I pecked on the wall with my fist. It was rock hard, with a hollow sound to it. After closer examination I understood the reason for that sound. Sam had built this house with two layers of sod, leaving a foot-wide air-space between the walls. That foot of dead air would keep this building snug and warm all winter and cool in the summer. Sam had done good work.

I entered and looked at the shelves that lined the walls. They were filled with jars, sacks, cans. Becky had done a lot of canning, it seemed, for there was a good supply of jelly, apparently made from wild plums. There was dried fruit, two large sacks of beans, and a huge can of molasses. There were storebought cans of different foods, along with a can of syrup. A side of bacon hung from the ceiling, and a tarpaulin was slung across the room with something bulky and heavy inside. I looked in it—there was a young beef, slaughtered and slung inside the tarpaulin. I had heard of this procedure before. Beef would not spoil very quickly when stored this way, unless it was left for a great length of time. Hot weather could turn such a system into a disaster, though.

I moved back outside and shut the door. Sam's garden stretched away behind the sod house and filled most of the area between it and the cabin. I walked toward the garden, frightening a jackrabbit from its hiding place and sending it scurrying away at top speed.

I stood in the shade of the cabin and thought about my own home. Where would it be? I hoped I could find a place not too far from Sam, but that might be difficult. With new settlers beginning to come in, the land was being taken up. The railroad had control of alternate tracts of land in a checkerboard pattern for miles on either side of the rails, and it even managed to control many of the tracts not specifically granted to it because of various legal questions which made it uncertain just

who owned them. The railroad was in no hurry to re-
solve the questions, for as long as there was doubt most
folks just assumed the railroad was the owner and left
it at that. So rather than try to claim free land I would
have to go to the railroad land office and buy my spread,
using the money from the sale of the farm back in Tennessee.

It would be lonely when I moved out alone to my
new home, wherever it would be. I was used to loneliness, so it didn't frighten me, but still I couldn't help
but think it would be so much nicer if I had a wife to
share it all with me, somebody like Jennifer Guthrie . . .
I cut the thought short, amazed that it had even risen in
my mind. I hardly knew Jennifer Guthrie, and after my
very undignified exit from her home it was unlikely I
would see her again for quite a long time. It was absurd
to even think of such a thing as marriage to the daughter
of a man as wealthy as Luther Guthrie—a man who just
happened to dislike me, too.

I smiled ironically. What would be Luther Guthrie's
reaction if his daughter married an upstart like me?
Likely he would go off like a box of dynamite. He
would probably sooner have his girl elope with a grizzly
as to marry Jim Hartford.

Sam got back about sunset with a load of wire. I
helped him unload the rolls and stack them inside one
of his outbuildings. We went back inside the cabin and
sat down to a delicious supper of beef and sourdough
bread, along with more coffee, then we sat talking of
old times until Sam and Becky retired to the single bedroom built off the back of the cabin, and I laid down
in the narrow bed in the front room. The fresh hay
smelled sweet.

It was later that night that the riders came.

CHAPTER 5

LIKE ghosts through the night they came, the faint noise of their horses' hooves being my first indication of their approach. As the quiet noise became louder, I first sat up in my bed, then rose and went for my Winchester that sat against the wall beside the door. Sam came up behind me, his face fearful and his Sharps in his hands. Neither of us spoke.

Directly in front of the cabin they rode, then there was the sudden blasting of rifles in tandem with the crashing of a glass pane. Sam gave a low cry in his throat and moved to the front door, throwing it open and sending a quick and useless shot out into the darkness. Then they were gone, riding into the thick, black night. Above us the moon swam in a pool of murky clouds.

Still neither my brother nor I spoke. Sam stood in the doorway, staring after the riders, his face invisible to me but his rage and tension filling the air like electricity. I moved over to where a stone, wrapped in paper, lay on the dirt floor. I picked it up, noting with irritation the trembling of my fingers, and removed the wadded paper.

Another threat, another warning of "death for fence-stringers" if the fences weren't removed. I handed it to Sam; he read it and tossed it aside.

"I can't understand it, Jim. It makes no sense. If I were fencing in a water hole, if I were blocking good grazing land, then I might understand. But I've been here for years, Jim, and I've hardly had any trouble with anyone in all that time. Now, all at once, it seems like someone around here has got it in for settlers. But why . . . why now, like this?"

I couldn't answer him. I pulled on my pants and threw on my shirt. He looked at me curiously, then Becky slowly walked into the room and put her arm around her husband's waist. I could see the fear in her eyes. She too eyed my preparations inquisitively.

"I'm going after them, Sam. Don't worry . . . I'm not planning to try anything—I'm not such a fool as that—but if I can get their trail, then maybe we can find out once and for all who is behind all of this. Hand me my gun . . . I'll be careful. I expect I'll see you around sunup."

And then I was gone, moving out to saddle my horse. Then into the blackness I rode, looking far ahead of me on the trail for some sign of them. My eyes scanned the trail. It was no use—in the darkness I could not make out any tracks. I would have to come within eyeshot of them if I planned to follow them. It would be dangerous, but I felt a reckless courage in me, from what source I do not know, and I plunged on fearlessly. This was to be my home, this territory, and I had no intention of beginning my life as a plainsman in a land terrorized by such trash as this.

They had gained a good lead on me, and to be honest I was riding blind, guessing at what direction they might have taken. I followed the road, assuming they had done the same, though they might have turned off it to cut across the plains at almost any point. I realized that my rapid pace was tiring my mount, so with reluctance I slowed down, then stopped. I listened, hoping my ears could do what my eyes could not.

Faint in the distance, it seemed, I could hear the noise of horses running—a muffled sound, as if they were on grassland. I looked to my left, scanning the open plain. The moon emerged from a bank of clouds for one moment, but in that moment I saw them.

How many there were I could not tell, but they were moving away from me, heading east. East . . . in the direction of Muster Creek and the Guthrie ranch. I felt a sharp pain inside me. Maybe Sam was right. Maybe Guthrie was the one behind this. Again I thought of Jennifer.

I moved off after them, aware that I would have to keep a good distance if I wanted to avoid detection. That would be fatal beyond any doubt. Intermittently the moon moved into clear areas in the sky, flooding the land with light. In those periods I could see them, moving slower now, still heading east. There appeared to be eight or nine of them, riding abreast of each other.

I do not know how long we continued moving, for it seemed endless, but in a short while I realized that they did not have the look of men bent on doing any more of their destructive work tonight. They were finished, and obviously felt safe, for they moved slowly but steadily, heading for what I hoped would be their camp and base of operations. Still we moved toward Muster Creek.

The land was flat, seeming almost barren in the sporadic moonlight. But before us rose up a large bank of hills—large at least for the flatlands of Montana—and something like recognition played at the corners of my mind. There was something familiar about those hills. And then I remembered.

There were hills directly behind the Guthrie spread. Barren hills, like the ones before us. And judging from the direction we had come and the time we had ridden, I guessed that what I saw before me was the back side of the same hills I had seen before my unfortunate run-in with Luther Guthrie. On the other side of that bank of hills was his ranch. It had to be.

I stopped. The riders far ahead of me had reached the hills and were moving into them. It was there, I guessed, that they made their camp. Sam had been right. It was Luther Guthrie who was leading this reign of terror. I felt deeply sad and faintly sick.

I sat in indecision for a long moment. Somehow I wanted to get closer to those men, maybe even see a few faces. But the danger of that would be overwhelming, and I doubted whether anything I could learn would be worth the risk. For a full five minutes I debated with myself. Finally the decision was made. Better to be alive with what little information I had than to gain more and quite possibly be killed in the process. I would be of more service to myself and the other terrorized ranchers if I proceeded carefully in all of this. I turned my horse and headed back toward Sam's ranch house.

In a few moments I realized the wisdom of my decision, for I detected a faint light about me. Then sometime later the sun rose in full glory behind me. I turned and looked back at the hills.

Streams of light poured over their slopes, silhouetting them against a blue and gold background, shining out across the wide grasslands, the misty scent of morning all around. Beautiful, this land . . . very beautiful. Even with the threat of the night riders, the danger in which all of the settlers now lived, I realized that I was glad I had come to this place. I had made the right decision. Since the beginning of my journey I had been plagued with occasional doubts about the wisdom of risking what little I had left and coming to the Montana Territory, but at this moment in the glorious light of morning, those doubts faded away, never to return. It was here that my destiny lay. It was here I would live and die, right here on these plains. The sunlight beamed against my face, warming it, and I smiled.

I did not tarry long, for I had promised Sam that I would return at sunrise. Already I was a little late, and it would not have surprised me in the least to see him come galloping across the plains in search of me. I goaded my horse to greater speed. This had been my first real chance to test the capabilities of the animal, and I was pleased with the purchase I had made.

I found Sam waiting on the front step of the cabin, his rifle across his knees. His face looked ashen. I could tell that the torment the riders were putting him through was beginning to wear on his nerves. I felt a strong pang of concern not only for his safety but also for his health.

He looked up at me. "Well?"

Something in me rebelled at telling him what I had seen. I had actually prayed that Guthrie had not been the mastermind of the night riders, hoped with all my soul that he was not involved simply for the sake of Jennifer. It was painful to have to admit that those prayers and hopes had been in vain. But Sam had a right to know, and I told him all I had seen.

He nodded grimly. "I thought so. It makes sense. I still can't understand why I'm being threatened, for I've never caused a bit of trouble for Luther Guthrie or any other cattlemen. But I'm getting tired of this . . . really tired. This just can't go on without something being done."

We went inside the cabin and had a breakfast of bacon, bread, jelly, and coffee. Although I was hungry, I could eat little, for my stomach was in a knot of tension. Sam apparently suffered from the same affliction, for he merely played with his food, hardly eating a bite. Becky was silent, but from the hurried glances she sent toward her husband, I could tell that she was worried about him. I didn't blame her. Sam's eyes were flashing with a strange anger that at times made him appear almost a madman deep in contemplation. I had seen his temper exploding at full force only a few times before, but from the looks of things it would not be long before that storm of fury erupted again.

Sam and I spent the morning in work, half-heartedly going through the motions of running the ranch. Close to noon we heard the sound of a horseman approaching, and with some apprehension we moved out to meet him.

I didn't know the fellow, though Sam apparently did, for he greeted him cordially and with some relief. I think he had expected more trouble.

The rider was young, hardly more than a boy. He had obviously been in the saddle all morning, for he seemed very weary. Sam invited him inside for a cup of coffee, and the breathless youth accepted gratefully.

Seated at the table with the mug of steaming coffee before him, he looked more relaxed. But the news he carried did nothing to calm the nerves of the rest of us.

"There was a man killed last night," he said. "And from the looks of it all it was them riders that done it. He was shot through the head and the chest, and all his fences was cut."

Sam tensed, his fist closing until the knuckles were white against the bone. "Who?"

"Jasper Maddux, from southeast of town."

I cried out without warning, and the youth jumped, startled. Sam said nothing, but his ashen face clouded with despair and he looked down at the table. Then he shook his head and said:

"Jasper . . . he's been here as long as I have. I've hardly seen him in the last year or so. The old fool . . . he wasn't even a legitimate rancher and had no need for fencing, but he strung some up anyway when the trouble started just to spite the riders. Old fool . . .''

The boy spoke quietly. "He didn't even have his gun on him when they found him. And he was tied up. It was murder outright."

Sam looked at the boy. "How far have you spread the news? Do all the ranchers know?"

"I've hit every spread I could reach this mornin'," he said. "And there's plans for a big meetin' in town tomorrow at noon. All the ranchers that can get there are gonna come, ones that have been bothered by them riders. We'll meet in Shorty Myers' big barn there in town. Luke McDonald is the man behind the meetin', and he's talked of everybody takin' up arms against whoever had hired them riders."

Sam nodded, his mouth set firmly. "Good. It might be necessary for us to do that. I had my house shot on last night, and got another threat. I'll not sit by anymore. And you can count on me being at that meeting."

After the boy left I approached Sam. "Do you think people are ready to take up arms about this? If it finally comes down to a range war, there might be a lot more people killed than it's worth."

Sam looked at me sharply. "Better to be killed fighting for something that is rightfully yours than to be murdered in the night like some dog," he said. "Jasper's murder shows that those threats aren't something to be scoffed at. It's not a matter of us starting a war— the war has already begun."

We passed the rest of the day in silence, working on replacing the fences that had been cut. All through the afternoon I thought of Jennifer, and it made me feel sad. What would be her place in all of this? How badly would she be hurt?

We were up before dawn the next morning and on the road to Miles City shortly after that. Sam carried his

Sharps, I had my Colt and shining new Winchester. It was a strange thought, realizing that the gun I had bought to kill game might end up being used against a man. I had never killed a man before, nor even aimed a gun at another human being. I didn't feel any desire to do so now.

On the trail we met others heading for town, all of them armed, the same light of fear burning in every eye. All words spoken sounded like those of men under siege.

"Did you leave your wife with a gun?"

"She's with Mrs. Ford on down the creek. Both of 'em have rifles. The children are there too."

"You had any fences cut?"

"Several times. The other night they even shot my milk cow. Don't know why."

"You think there's some big-time cattleman behind this?"

"Who else?"

By the time we reached Miles City there was a large band of us, some fifteen altogether. We drew a lot of attention when we rode down the main street. I could see faces peering around lacy curtains from the houses and merchants watching us from the porches of their businesses. No one asked us what we were doing. Everyone knew.

Some of the horsemen made a real show of their weapons, as if they were a gang of outlaws riding in to take over the town. It bothered me, for I sensed the beginning of that kind of unbridled rage that always injures more than it helps. There would be fighting before this affair was settled. I felt almost ashamed to be riding in the midst of the crowd of angry men, their rifles drawn and their handguns slung high on their hips. I realized why they were so angry, and I sympathized with their plight, but still I felt that our group had almost

a pitiful quality to it, and I felt like hanging my head.
I didn't want any part of mass hysteria, for a clear mind
was something which I prized highly.

We found some men already there and waiting for
us. Sam pointed out Luke McDonald, the organizer of
this meeting. He was a hefty man with a belly that hung
out like a sack of lard over his belt, and his pants hung
low about his hips. It was beyond me what kind of
magic kept them from falling around his feet. He stood
in the street before the barn where we were to meet, his
hands on his hips and his jaw jutted out in a pseudo-
military fashion. I didn't like the look of him. There
was too much of the glory-seeker about him, and he had
the air of a man with more pride than brain.

It was still some time before the meeting was to begin, and I left my rifle with Sam and walked down the
street, hoping to pass the time by loitering in the stores.
I went into the same general merchandise business that
Jennifer had entered the other day and began poking
about, examining items, trying to think of things that I
might need when I set up my own spread. I found it
hard to concentrate, though, for I was worried about
what might come out of this meeting. Suddenly I felt a
hand on my shoulder.

I turned to see McCuen standing there, a troubled
look about him. I greeted him and shook his hand.

"Mr. Hartford, just what is this all about?" he said.
"I saw your group riding in. Is this about the wire cutting?"

I nodded. Briefly I told him what had occurred, of
the death of Jasper Maddux and the hysteria that was
gripping the angry men. I told him of my fears about
what might occur.

He shook his head slowly. "I was afraid of this. It
has happened all over the west, and now it's happening
here. If only we could get this thing stopped before

there's violence! But I don't know who to go to, nor what to do . . .''

I looked at him closely. He looked trustworthy, and I had personal evidence of his honesty based on my experience with my stolen bag. I needed a good, clear-headed man like him to help me if I was going to do anything to stop the carnage that seemed so inevitable.

"Mr. McCuen, I think I might know who we need to talk to about this," I said. "I think I know who is behind this wire cutting business."

He looked at me with sudden interest. "Who? How do you know?"

I told him about having followed the riders during the night, and of where they had gone. He nodded all the while.

"Luther Guthrie, you say? You know, it makes sense. From what I've heard of him he's just the type of fellow that would do something like this. If we could only talk to him, reason with him . . ." Suddenly he stopped short, and a grin spread slowly over his face. "You know, I think I might know just the thing to do. I think I might know someone who can go with us to talk to Guthrie. Would you be willing to go along with me on this?"

"I'll do anything to keep a range war from beginning," I said. "What do you have in mind?"

"I know a rancher by the name of Jedediah Bacon, a younger rancher than most, and a good man. I was acquainted with him in the east—Boston—and I've had every intention of going to see him now that I'm here where he settled. He's a far thinking fellow, one that doesn't cling to something just because it's old. And he's been using barbed wire for years, holding his cattle where he wants them, breeding them for weight. He's living proof of what the proper use of the wire can lead to. Maybe he can talk some sense into Guthrie's head and get him to call off his men before this thing gets out of hand.''

If he could do a thing like that, I thought, then he must be a remarkable fellow indeed. But I wanted to try, for obviously the approach now being taken by the men in town was bound to end in tragedy for many families. I assented to McCuen's idea.

"Let's not waste any time about it," I said. "Let Sam stay for the meeting—I'm going with you. Once those folks get themselves worked up into a frenzy there's no telling what might happen.''

We moved back into the sun-lit street. More armed men approached. The sun was climbing toward the center of the sky. Soon the meeting would begin.

I didn't bother to tell Sam of my plans, for I feared he would only try to talk me out of it. I mounted my horse, and McCuen headed to the livery to get his own mount. When he returned we headed out of town and toward the south. McCuen talked further about his friend all the while.

"I've written to Jed over the years," he said, "and he's sent back some good reports about his use of barbed wire. Of course a lot of the really successful ranchers are slow to change their ways, at least in these parts. But he's a persuasive young fellow, and if anyone can knock some sense into Guthrie it will be him.''

McCuen talked on, but I didn't listen. I was thinking of someone else, someone with beautiful eyes and auburn hair that shimmered like nothing I had ever seen. Jennifer . . . she would be there, at the Guthrie ranch. And when we went to reason with her father, perhaps I would see her . . .

I cut short the thought. I knew it would be impossible for me to accompany McCuen and his friend to the ranch, for Guthrie would throw us off as soon as he saw me. I couldn't let my bad standing with Guthrie thwart

McCuen's mission and perhaps end up costing lives. I would have to stay behind when they went to the Guthrie ranch.

And so at least this time I would not see Jennifer. Not this time. But later . . .

CHAPTER 6

———•◦•———

JEDEDIAH Bacon's spread was typical in many ways, yet it was more orderly than most of the ranches I had seen before. It was obviously set up in a logical fashion, every fence and building in just the proper place. And so I wasn't surprised to find that Bacon himself was a neat man, not fancily dressed but nevertheless well groomed and clean. And he was young, obviously not much more than thirty. He greeted McCuen warmly and seemed quite glad to meet me. He was a jolly fellow, and very likeable. I felt relaxed in his presence and impressed by his calm and self-confident bearing.

McCuen wasted little time in telling Bacon why we had come. The young rancher had heard of the riders and their terrorist actions, but the murder of Jasper Maddux was news to him. He seemed troubled when McCuen told him of it.

"It's ridiculous, this business of riders and murder. Why can't some cattlemen accept the fact that the plains are changing, and we're going to have to adapt to those changes? The old ways aren't necessarily the best ways, but still people seem to want to cling to them no matter what the consequences. I'm acquainted with Guthrie through the cattlemen's association—and a more stubborn old fellow you couldn't find within five hundred miles. He's opposed every new idea, every hint of acceptance of the fact that new times are here to stay. A lot of ranchers are becoming convinced that running cattle on enclosed pasture rather than open range is the best way, but Guthrie is among the old school, those who still think the long drives and open land are the only way to raise cattle. But I'm surprised that he would go so far as to hire fence cutters. And murder . . . well, I think that's unbelievable. I'll be glad to go with you and talk to him, though I figure he won't really listen. And Mr. Hartford, I don't think Guthrie would take too kindly to a Tennessee farmer new to the territory coming into his home to tell him what to do. I suggest you stay off the ranch itself. No offense intended—I just think it would be the best way.''

That was a suggestion I readily consented to. There would be no quicker way for us to find ourselves kicked off Guthrie's land than for me to waltz into his house. It was almost comical to think of how the rancher would react to such brashness.

We headed toward the Guthrie ranch without hesitation. McCuen and Bacon talked of the old times they had spent together, and I discovered the surprising fact that Bacon had attended Yale. I asked him about that, and why he had come from a career as a lawyer to raise cattle in Montana. He laughed at the question.

"I started reading every book I could on striking it rich on the plains through the cattle business. Believe me, there was plenty of that kind of propaganda floating around! I couldn't resist the idea of quick wealth. It didn't work out like I planned—I'm a long way from being rich—but still I haven't been a failure, either. I don't regret coming out here. I wouldn't be elsewhere, now.''

I was impressed with Bacon, and hoped Guthrie would be as well. After all, he was proof that ranching by new methods could be a success. I asked Bacon how his method of ranching differed from Guthrie's.

"Well, there's several things I do differently," he said. "Not all of them are in any way easier than Guthrie's methods, but as the land changes I'll be able to continue with my style of ranching while he will have to adapt his.

"Guthrie still runs his cattle on the unfenced range for the most part. Some of the land is his, most is still public domain. With every new settler a little more of that land is taken from him. Someday it will be gone, and then where will Luther Guthrie be?

"I use less land, all legally mine, and I have it fenced in with plenty of Aaron's barbed wire. My cattle aren't the hit-and-miss type of breed that results from free-roaming and interbreeding cattle out on the plains. My stock is fatter, with more meat, and while I'll admit that my stock isn't as hardy as those running on the open range, they'll bring a better price at market. And there's not really as much need for them to be hardy, 'cause they're confined where I can keep a close eye on them for disease and so on. Of course, I have to raise hay to get them through the winter and sink wells for water, but I think it's definitely worth the trouble. I don't know if you noticed the windmill out on my spread—that's how I pump water for my cattle. Guthrie's system is dying; mine is just being born."

It made sense. Guthrie's method had definite advantages, I was sure, but obviously Bacon would be able to run his business over the years without the major changes that Guthrie would have to make. I knew that raising cattle in fenced-in pastures had its disadvantages, too, for I had read of cattle freezing in blizzards when fences kept them from getting to shelter. I had heard of the huge piles of rotting corpses found piled up against fences when the spring thaw came. But all in all, it seemed to me that Bacon was operating the system of the future. Just as cattle on the open plains had to adapt to changes in their environment or die, so also would the cattlemen have to adapt to the changing west. Luther Guthrie was fighting a war doomed to fail for methods that were outdated.

When at last we reached the Guthrie spread, I hung back just within view of the house. My humiliation of my only encounter with Guthrie came back to me, and I sat glumly in the saddle, biting my lip in anger. But thoughts of that embarrassment were quickly replaced by thoughts of Jennifer Guthrie, who was no doubt somewhere down there in that ranch house. I wished I could see her.

As McCuen and Bacon rode on down to the house, I dismounted and tethered my horse to a low bush in a grassy area. I began to roam about the general vicinity, realizing my wait might be a long one. I worried a bit about my not telling Sam of my plans, for he might well be concerned about my absence from the meeting. But I couldn't let that bother me—I was a grown man, in control of my own actions, and I felt that the course being followed by me and my two companions down there in Guthrie's house was by far a superior one to the hot-headed reactions of angry ranchers. Better to fight long and hard with words and logic than to turn to bullets. I hoped that the angry men in town would not be such fools as to ride in on Guthrie's ranch like an army and perhaps wind up filling graves.

"Mr. Hartford?" The voice was unmistakable. I wheeled around.

"Jenni . . . Miss Guthrie!" I'm afraid my excitement to see her so unexpectedly was clearly evident in my tone. I couldn't believe that she was actually here; I had convinced myself that I would not see her today.

"Don't worry about the 'Miss Guthrie,' Jennifer is fine," she said. "I was walking around the place—it's a habit I have—and I saw you and your friends riding up. That was Jed Bacon with you, wasn't it?''

"Yes . . . and Aaron McCuen, the man who returned the bag that was stolen from me on the train.''

"Is it some sort of business visit?''

"Yes.'' I said nothing more about it, for I didn't want her to know the exact nature of what my two companions were even now discussing with her father. For a moment after that there was a rather uncomfortable silence, and I smiled at her in a way which I later realized probably made me look like a half-wit.

Jennifer paced about nervously, obviously looking for words.

"I'm very sorry about the reception my father gave you the other evening,'' she said. "He's very protective of me, and his temper often gets the best of him. I hope you weren't too insulted.''

I shook my head. "Don't worry about it. I'm just sorry he treated you like he did.'' I realized that the last part of my comment might have been offensive to her, and I quickly added: "I'm sorry if I shouldn't have said that . . . your family business is none of my affair. I could tell you were unhappy, though.''

"I have to admit you're right about that. Father often forgets that I'm a grown woman. To him I'm still the same little girl that he trotted on his knee years ago. I think that he will always feel that way.''

"I'm sure you were a very pretty little girl, if your appearance now is any indication,'' I said. She blushed and smiled.

"Thank you, Mr. Hartford. You're very flattering.''

"If I'm to call you Jennifer, then it only seems appropriate that you call me Jim,'' I said. "And I hope that in spite of the rather uncomfortable experience we had the other night that you will consider me your friend. Lord knows, as new as I am to this territory, I need all the friends I can get.''

She laughed—a beautiful, ringing, musical sound—and I felt a warmth steal over me. ''Of course I consider you my friend,'' she said. ''I certainly don't give buggy rides to strangers unless I feel they are the kind of people that can be trusted. I guess that I was rather careless to pick you up like that, but you certainly didn't look threatening with that big spot of mud and grass stain on the seat of your pants.'' It was now my turn to blush. I guessed that I had picked up the stain when I fell off the railroad car.

''I suppose I was a long way from being a dashing figure,'' I conceded. ''You can't imagine how much I appreciated the ride.''

For quite some time we talked, chatting of trivial matters, and yet I hung on her every word as if our discussion was of profound importance. And, wonder of wonders, she seemed to be doing the same with me, as if my presence gave her pleasure. I felt as if I were floating in a dream world, a kind of paradise. Our time together was at most fifteen minutes, but when at last I saw my two companions emerge from the house on down the road, it seemed that those short minutes were even shorter, reduced to mere moments. I was deeply sorry when she turned to see McCuen and Bacon approaching.

''Your friends are coming back,'' she said. ''I'll slip on away. It's been very good to talk to you. Perhaps I'll see you again soon.''

''I would like that very much,'' I said.

She turned to leave, and from some untapped reserve of courage I suddenly found the power to speak words which surprised even me as soon as I had said them. ''Jennifer . . . if you take another walk tomorrow, do . . . do you think I might accompany you?''

She looked first surprised, then pleased. "Why, I would find that very pleasant, Jim. I'll meet you here at one sharp." Then she turned and was gone, moments before McCuen and Bacon came riding up. Such was my elation that I actually forgot for a moment the purpose of our trip, and it was a long wait before I gathered my wits enough to ask them how things had gone with Guthrie.

McCuen looked a bit disgusted. "As well as could be expected, I imagine, but not nearly as well as I would have liked. He listened to us, then got indignant when we hinted that he was the man behind the riders. He scoffed at the meeting going on in town, calling it a convention of 'fools and idiots.' But when Bacon mentioned the murder of Jasper Maddux he looked sincerely shocked. It was obvious that it was the first he had heard of it. After that he told us to leave—that's why we're back so quickly."

"So things are standing pretty much as they were," I said. "At least we tried. Maybe your talk to him did more good than he would lead you to think. Maybe he'll call off his hounds for awhile."

"I hope so," said Bacon. "One thing I believe for certain: Guthrie didn't order the death of Jasper Maddux. Apparently that was something his riders did on their own, 'cause that was sure no pretended shock that he put on. He really didn't know about it until we told him. It really threw him, too."

McCuen accompanied Bacon back to his ranch, and I left them in Miles City. I found Sam waiting for me on the boardwalk in front of the Chinese laundry.

"Where have you been? Why didn't you come to the meeting?"

I saw no harm in telling him what we had done, so I did just that. He didn't react except to nod when I told him that our trip had apparently done little good.

"It was a good idea," he said, "but trying to argue
with someone like Luther Guthrie is about as useless as
telling a dog not to scratch his fleas."

I was anxious to hear the outcome of the meeting.
Sam didn't look too happy when I asked him about it.

"It was a joke, Jim, a joke. Nobody could get together on anything, it seemed. There were those like
Luke McDonald who were ready to go in and shoot
whoever is behind those riders—they didn't know that
it's Guthrie, and I didn't tell 'em for fear that they
would do something drastic and get themselves killed.
The rest of us were more moderate and wanted to stay
on the defensive awhile longer before we switch to the
offensive. Some of 'em were talking lynching or shooting for any rancher that made any kind of threatening
move against any of us. It was all complete tomfoolery,
all of it. The only thing good that came out of the whole
thing was that all of us are more organized now, in case
there's more trouble."

I was pleased at the moderate stance Sam was taking
about the riders. From the look in his eye the last couple
of days, and from the way he had talked, I had expected
him to be right in the middle of those who were ready
to make a drastic move against the riders right away.
But apparently Sam had not only grown older over the
years since I had seen him last—he had grown wiser,
too. I felt a tremendous sense of relief. Maybe things
weren't as desperate as I thought. I could tell that in
looking at the other ranchers he had been able to see
how irrational was the wild plan for attack against the
riders. That same irrationality had been in Sam himself
earlier, but even since morning it had faded. I felt proud
of him.

"As long as I'm in town I think I'll buy a few things
I need," Sam said. "Becky's had her heart set on some
cloth down in the general store for the longest time now,

and I think I'll buy her some. I've got a few extra dollars right now, and it's been ages since she's had anything new." He started down the street, then turned. "Don't feel like you have to wait on me," he said. "Go on if you want. I'll just be a few minutes."

"I'm in no hurry. I'll wait," I responded.

I noticed a clump of men loitering around in front of the livery. Most of them were ranchers, apparently the residue of the meeting. Among them I recognized Luke McDonald. He stood in the center of the group, and though I could not hear his words he seemed to be delivering some sort of passionate tirade. I moved over and joined the group.

". . . and we can't afford to sit around and wait until something happens again. There's been one of us killed already. How many more might there be later? I'm disappointed in how this meetin' turned out—we should have made ourselves into a regular vigilante army and showed these riders that we ain't gonna take no more off of 'em. Now I figure that it's some big cattleman that's hired 'em out against us smaller ranchers. Some of 'em figure they should have the run of every inch of grazin' land in the territory, and when somebody throws up a fence it's like spittin' in their eye. And the local law ain't done one thing to check this out and I don't believe they're going to start. It's going to be us that has to protect our homes and land. And when I find out who's behind these riders I reckon that's gonna be the end of his hirin' any more guns, even if it takes killin' him and burnin' his ranch . . ."

With those words a cold chill shivered down my spine, like a winter wind coming from nowhere. Luke McDonald was not going to be content to punish merely the man behind the night riders—he would have to burn his home and probably threaten his family as well. And in this case Jennifer would be endangered. I wouldn't let him do it. I'd kill him first . . .

I felt a disgust for myself at that thought. Moments before I had been condemning McDonald and his kind, men who thought violent action was the way to correct all wrongs. And now I was ready to do exactly the same thing. The tension and anger inherent in this situation were beginning to get to me.

I looked around me at the dispersing men. All of them were family men, ones who would kill or die themselves to protect those they loved. Love. It was a frightening thing, in a way, for it could lead men to do things they wouldn't otherwise contemplate. Did I love Jennifer? I wasn't sure . . . or so I told myself. But in my heart I knew I would be just as irrational as Luke McDonald if it came to protecting Jennifer's safety.

Sam returned and headed back to the horses, and I followed. We rode to the ranch house with Sam carrying the cloth he had bought for Becky in a sack before him on the saddle. I felt slightly envious. I wished there was something I could do for Jennifer that would make her smile like Becky surely would when she saw that cloth. Jennifer had a pretty smile, prettier than any I had ever seen.

I thought of our planned meeting tomorrow. I was anxious to see her again, maybe this time for a bit longer than I had today. My feelings for her had sprung up uninvited, and they seemed to thrive and grow each time I thought of her.

She was on my mind when we reached the house, and she was still on my mind when I retired that evening. And when I slept I dreamed of her.

But at the borders of my mind I saw the image of Luke McDonald, standing with rifle in hand, and I tossed restlessly on my bed.

CHAPTER 7

I arose early the next morning and enjoyed one of Becky's fine breakfasts once more. I was happy, not only because another night had passed without an attack by Guthrie's riders, but also because of the one o'clock appointment which I so eagerly anticipated. The morning would be long, a tantalizing wait until the time I could be with Jennifer again. The whole thing seemed unreal, like a dream. It was a dream I wanted more of.

Sam wasn't sharing my good spirits. He sat glumly through his breakfast, hardly speaking. I assumed he was still disgusted at the travesty of yesterday's meeting in Miles City.

I planned to spend the morning looking over land, so I asked Sam if he knew of any good areas nearby that were still available. I was surprised when he told me that much of the land between his own ranch and the Guthrie spread was still up for sale by the railroad. It was good grazing land, land used mostly by Guthrie, and it was because of his prestige, Sam figured, that people shied away from buying the property.

"I think I'll take a look at it," I said. "I might be just the one to buy it."

Sam looked at me as if I was a fool. "Don't you think that's a little risky, with Guthrie being right across the way with his riders?"

"I think I can take care of myself," I said. I was feeling cocky and proud this morning, more than I had a right to. But knowing that Jennifer was interested in me was puffing me up like a proud preacher at a camp meeting.

Sam looked at me and slowly shook his head, apparently sensing there was no point in trying to talk sense into me. He knew me well, and was quite closely acquainted with the stubborn streak that I had possessed since infancy.

After breakfast I rode out to the area we had talked about and looked it over. It was good land, level and rich, and a stream ran through the midst of it. In my mind I began mapping out a spread. I would put my house here, by the stream, a corral over there, a sod storage building there, a chicken coop yonder . . .

I began to feel an urgent excitement. I could sense that this time I would make it. The failures of the past were truly behind me now. This was a new land for me, and a new chance. Who knows? Maybe I would even have Jennifer with me.

I had to pull my thoughts up short. I tried to tell myself that notions of Jennifer and me getting married were just too premature to consider. Best to listen to reason instead of wild fantasies.

I rode in a wide circle around the area, trying to decide just how much of the land to buy. And I wondered how Guthrie would react when he found that some of his best grazing land was being taken over by the very fellow he ran off his property not long before.

I didn't worry about him. He had neglected to make any legal arrangements for this land, apparently counting on his prominent name to keep any settler off. Let him take the consequences of his negligence. It was his problem, not mine.

I saw a rider approaching from the south. I felt faintly

apprehensive, but when he had approached within clear view I recognized him as Jack Tatum, the buffalo hunter. He had his rifle slung in a scabbard on the side of his saddle. He was riding a black.

"Howdy, Hartford," he said. "Didn't expect to run into you out here."

"Good to see you, Tatum. Your sorrel didn't make it, huh?"

He shook his head rather sadly. "Leg was just about broke clean through. Doc shot it for me."

"Sorry."

"Yeah. Got me another horse, though. It's a good one." He was right. The animal appeared spirited and strong.

Tatum glanced toward the east. "I reckon you heard about what happened over yonder last night, didn't you?"

I shook my head, tensing. "Over where?"

"Over them hills at the Guthrie ranch."

"No . . . what happened?"

"Some riders rode up on his house and fired a few shots. Nobody got hurt, I don't reckon. Killed his dog, though."

I felt weak. The image of Luke McDonald came immediately to mind.

"Some of the small ranchers? Fence-stringers?"

He nodded. "So I figure. I hear Guthrie's mad. There's been rumors that he's the man who hired the night riders. If he is then I think we can look for more trouble. He's not going to stand for folks attackin' his ranch like that. He ain't the kind to be patient and understandin'."

I felt almost sick. Luke McDonald—the old, simple-minded fool! He had done the very thing I hoped the enraged ranchers would avoid. And I doubted that he would be able to stand up to the consequences.

"You say nobody was hurt?" I asked.

"Not that I heard of."

"Good." A simple word, one totally insufficient to express my thankfulness that Jennifer was unhurt. But at the same time I wondered how she might feel toward me when she learned that my brother was a fence-stringer, and that soon I would be too, right on land her father used for grazing his herd. The prospect of buying the property seemed suddenly less appealing.

I talked for awhile to Tatum, then he moved on, heading north. I sat glumly in the saddle for several minutes, thinking of what he had said and wondering what would happen next. My spirits sank so low that not even the thought of my upcoming meeting with Jennifer was enough to lift them.

I arrived at the meeting place far ahead of time, trying to cheer myself up to meet her. It was no use. And when I saw her approaching there was something in her stance and stride that I didn't like.

She greeted me with a blank expression and great coldness. For a long and uncomfortable time she stood looking at me as if I were less than worthy of the honor.

"Jennifer, is something wrong?"

"Shut up. Don't open your mouth to me again. Why didn't you tell me what kind of business it was you were on yesterday? You stood up here sweet-talking me while your friends were down in my home accusing my father of being little more than a murderer. How could you do such a thing?"

Her words stung. I didn't know just how to respond, so I stood in appalled silence.

"I had heard of the fence-cutters before, but I never thought of them as anything less than trash. And that's how my father feels too, I can assure you. He would never give his support to such a thing as murder, no matter how many accusations you and your lying friends make.

"And now—after you do what you did—riders come *here* and shoot at the house. Innocent people could have been killed, Hartford. I could have been killed. Is that how you people take care of your worries about the riders? Pick a scapegoat and come shooting at his house under cover at night, not even being men enough to show your faces without masks?"

"Are you trying to accuse me of being one of the ones who . . ."

"I wouldn't be at all surprised. My father told me there is a rancher named Hartford west of here—is that your kin?"

"My brother."

"I figured you were tied in some way. You fence-stringers have ruined the range for my father and other ranchers like him. You disgust me. We will see each other no more, Mr. Hartford."

And with that she turned on her heel and began striding back down the slope toward the house. I watched her leave, my shock giving way to intense anger. I thought of all the things I could have told her, how I could have asked her to take a look in the hills behind her ranch if she doubted her father was involved with the night riders. I could also have told her how beyond those hills another "fence-stringer" would set up a ranch soon. In the course of hearing her berate me I had regained my desire to purchase the land I had viewed this morning. I wanted to show the haughty young lady that I would be scared away neither by harsh words nor night riders.

I would show her. I would prove that I didn't care what she thought of me.

Even though I did. I cared more than I wanted to admit.

That afternoon I visited the office of the railroad land agent and arranged to buy the land. He looked at me as if I was insane when I put my pen to the deal. But he smiled when I paid cash on the spot.

It was after nightfall when I returned to Sam's cabin. I was dejected, sullen. When I told him of buying the land he looked almost sad, but he said nothing. I realized that he was concerned about my safety, but still it irritated me.

When I lay down to sleep I found the rest would not come. I tossed fitfully, and the emotions that ran through me filled me with shame even then, more so later.

I was determined to show Jennifer that what she had said about me and my friends was foolish. I felt a childish desire to prove myself right and flaunt it in her face. I had grown to care so much for her, and she had returned that caring with scorn. And that hurt me very badly. I felt I could easily hate her right now. My mind said that I did.

My heart said I loved her.

I remained in bed for hardly more than an hour before I rose and dressed silently. Quietly I slipped out the door, my gun in my belt and my rifle in my hand; quietly I saddled my horse and moved off swift and silent in the night.

Reason had left me. No matter what the risk, I would learn more of the night riders. I would find some definite proof to link them to Luther Guthrie. I would see faces, learn names, gather evidence. I would ride right into their camp if need be, hiding myself nearby until they returned from the raid I was sure they were conducting tonight. I was a fool, and I knew it, but I didn't care. Jennifer's rejection had shaken me to the core, and I was acting completely against my usual reserved nature.

The plains were dark; the moon was obscured by clouds, and there was the feel of moisture in the air. A storm was brewing, and the low rumble of thunder shook the plains, echoing across the flat land like the distant, grumbling voice of some ancient god. I moved rapidly through the darkness, wanting to reach the hills where the riders made their camp, knowing I would have to reach them before they returned from their raid. I tried not to think of the other possibility—that they might be there when I arrived. If so it would probably be the end of Jim Hartford.

I reached the land I had purchased. My land. But it did not yet seem mine; I would have to take care of two matters before it seemed so. One was the night riders, the other my devastated relationship with Jennifer Guthrie.

The clouds were illuminated from within by magnificent bolts of lightning now; bolts leaped occasionally from cloud to cloud, lighting the plains as if it were noonday, showing in those instantaneous flashes the rolling grasslands, whipped by the rising wind, the weird and vast clouds tumbling through the heavens in anticipation of the wild storm to come, the barren hills rising before me, the scrubby trees and brush along their slopes thrashing in the wind. The air was damp with oncoming rain; in moments the plains would be drenched. Many women would rise the next morning to fill every spare cask and jar with water from the rain barrels for a temporary respite from the hard Montana waters. If the storm was to become as severe as this violent prelude threatened, then they would have a more than adequate supply.

I reached the base of the hills just as a tremendous bolt of electricity struck the earth far to the north, the yellow flash looking for all the world like a crack in the sky. The storm was moving this way; in only a short while it would be here. If the riders were out raiding tonight, the lightning might drive them back to their camp sooner than usual. And I would be waiting.

I led my horse by its reins around toward the south slope of the hills. I guessed that the riders camped right in the heart of the small chain of hills, for I had seen them enter through the narrow gap on the night I had followed them. I didn't want to be where they would find me, but yet I needed to be close to their camp in order to see them.

So far I had no reason to believe anyone was encamped in the hills at this moment, but nevertheless I proceeded carefully, circling the base of the hills. I came around to a rather rocky slope on the south, and I tied my horse to a tree as I searched for some sort of well-hidden route to the central portion of the hills. A blast of lightning ripped into the earth not more than a mile away, and I suddenly realized that I could not risk leaving my mount tied to a tree, which might serve as a natural lightning rod. I found a slight outcrop of rock under which I tethered the horse to a bush—not good protection but much better than before. Then I began climbing up the rather steep hillside with my rifle gripped close beside me. Lightning flashed, guiding my way.

I moved through a maze of small gulleys and around rocky hillsides, not having anything to guide me and always unsure of what I would encounter around the next turn. It was pitch black, and though the lightning came with enough regularity to let me see where I was going, the contrast between brilliant light and sudden blackness made it difficult to keep my bearings.

I stopped suddenly when ahead of me, visible through a small gap in the rocks, was the faint flicker of what could only be a campfire. Either that or a natural fire started by the lightning, but I had seen no bolts striking that closely. I crouched low and moved more carefully, then the light was blocked out suddenly by a figure moving between the fire and me, and I knew the riders were already in their camp.

I began to wish I was safe back on the straw tick at Sam's cabin, tucked away and sleeping. I realized suddenly just how dangerous my position was, and I debated whether or not to slip away and head home again.

But now that I was here it seemed pointless to not at least try to see some face that I might later identify. So I crept on, hoping I wouldn't make some unexpected noise and give away my presence. As I grew nearer I could hear voices. I found a safe spot in a natural little nook overlooking the circular basin in which they camped, and I began to watch and listen.

There were nine of them, some seated, a few walking about. One man was drinking coffee, and he was a rugged-looking character, husky and with one eye covered with a patch. The rugged leather of his skin had a pitted, scarred look. He wore faded denim, and a scraggly beard covered his chin. There was something wrong in his gaze, something distorted in the sallow look of his single eye that flickered red in the firelight. He lifted his tin coffee mug to his bearded lips and took a long swallow, an amber stream running down his throat to soak unnoticed into his faded blue shirt.

"I don't like this, Jess. It scares me." The speaker was a thin man with a red beard and mustache that drooped over his lips. He had a pale face, funeral-parlor pale. And as he looked nervously toward the sky it seemed to grow even whiter. "We're gonna get struck, I tell you. Fried like bacon."

The one-eyed fellow—the one he called Jess—didn't change his expression. He took another long swallow of the coffee and belched. Then he tossed the remainder of the beverage from his mug and said, "Shut up, Jake. You'll be all right."

"I dunno, Jess. I had an uncle get struck once. He bit his tongue in two like a razor had sliced it. It scares me awful bad."

"For God's sake will you shut up?" came an exasperated voice from the midst of the group. "I'm hopin' you do get struck just so you'll shut up."

"That ain't a nice thing to say, Horace. Not nice at all."

I studied the group, looking at faces, trying to let the features sink into my mind. I wanted to be able to identify them readily, to know them by sight. I crept a bit closer to the edge of the overhang upon which I lay, straining my eyes in the darkness. Thunder cracked and a drop of rain struck my arm, then more drops began pelting me. Angry curses rolled up from the men below me.

The one-eyed fellow stood. "I'm gettin' my poncho and stayin' in it 'til it's over. I hope I can keep my cigar dry." And at that moment my hand struck a piece of loose stone that clattered loudly down the slope to the camp below. My breath cut short and my heart pounded like a hammer on an anvil.

Just as the rain erupted in a drenching torrent every man in the camp was on his feet, all of them staring toward the spot where I lay hidden. I couldn't help but stare at the guns in their hands.

The leader spoke. "Get up there, Bill. Check it out."

A man moved toward me, gun in hand. I lay there, knowing full well I stood not a half a chance against the lot of them, and wondered if I should try to kill as many of them as possible before I took the inevitable bullet.

Then, with a tremendous roar and grating, skull-jarring shock, the world became an explosion of color and intense pain. I felt a sensation like I had never imagined possible, and every nerve in my body turned inside out.

CHAPTER 8

WITH an overwhelming jolt and a crushing sensation in my chest I was thrown backward, how far I could not tell. Then the world shimmered, faded away, returned, then began to fade again. I could hear voices growing steadily fainter as I lapsed toward unconsciousness.

"... nobody there ... Bill's hurt ... move ... forget about it ... to Guthrie's barn, now ..."

Then I was out, senseless.

I awoke to full morning light and a clear sky. All about me was water, almost over me at places. Everything was quiet. I tried to move, and it hurt.

For how long I lay there I did not know, for nothing seemed to make sense. I could not recall where I was, and at times even my own identity seemed a mystery. I lay confused and blinking, staring at the blue morning until the sun was high overhead. Then again I tried to move, and with considerable pain I managed to rise.

I was drenched, and the morning breeze was cold against my body. I looked about me, trying to piece together the mystery of the immediate past, and as I came to vaguely realize my location, my memory started to return again.

I struggled to my feet and moved carefully over toward the place where the riders had camped. Through the bushes I looked, and there was nothing but the charred remains of their fire, some scattered and soaked articles of clothing, and bits and pieces of trash and broken branches. They were gone. The mention of Guthrie's barn returned to me.

I rubbed my head, trying to get rid of the horrid pounding there. Every muscle in me ached severely, as if the shock of the lightning had stretched them to the breaking point. Had I been struck directly? I looked about on the ground and found a large blackened spot not far from the campfire, and I realized that the lightning had struck the earth at that point, the electricity of the bolt traveling through the ground to reach me. If it had struck a few feet closer I might well be dead.

It seemed I could not stop shuddering. Partly it was because of the wind against my wet clothing, but it went beyond that. How much damage the lightning had done to me I could not tell, but I knew that I felt worse than I had ever felt before, and my head swam in a swirling sea of confusion and my stomach turned slowly over again and again, spasms of nausea welling through me each time.

I tried to remember where I had tethered my horse, and it took a long time. I found the animal standing drenched and impatient, and with an intense, gut-wrenching effort I managed to mount it. Then I turned toward home and headed across the plains with my body slumped forward, moving at a moderate speed.

The jolts of my horse's hooves were an endless pounding that kept me from going senseless again. Occasionally I managed to raise my head and look through bloodshot eyes across the land. The miles stretched to three times their normal length, and it seemed I would never reach the cabin. Then my sense of time slowly faded, and I dropped into a half-conscious swoon.

I was conscious only of Sam's hands helping me

from the saddle, guiding me into the house, and helping me get out of my filthy clothing before I collapsed into the warmth of the straw tick and fell at once into a deep slumber.

I think that for many hours I did not dream as I lay there, but sometime later the fitful imaginations began, all of them disturbing, most confusing. Mostly it was images of faces—Sam, Becky, my parents—and others, too. One in particular kept returning; the face of the one-eyed man I had seen in the camp. There was something about him that I was supposed to recall . . . something . . . but what?

I woke long enough to see Sam's face above me, illuminated by the flickering light of a coal oil lamp. I said something to him, something I couldn't understand, then again I dropped into fitful slumber.

I awoke wet with sweat and very weary. It was light, I could tell that much, and the hurting in my brain was gone. Slowly I opened my eyes, and the light hurt them. I squinted and looked over toward my bedside. Sam was there.

"Hey there, brother!" he grinned. "I was gettin' a bit worried about you!"

I managed to smile. It was good to see my brother, the light, the cabin. I felt like a man who had just escaped some devilish torment.

"Sam . . . could I have some water?" He rose quickly and supplied me with a tin dipper brimming over with cold water. I think that until that time I never really appreciated how refreshing and delicious water could be.

"How long, Sam?"

He shrugged. "Long enough. Don't worry about it now. You still need a lot of rest."

I lay back, but I didn't close my eyes, for it was good to be awake and thinking once more. Perhaps I had been in a stupor for days. Apparently it had been for quite some time that I had been in this bed, or else Sam would not have evaded my question. I began to realize the seriousness of what might have happened. That had been a wicked jolt that had ripped through me. I was lucky to be alive, and I whispered a prayer of thanks.

Sam's eyes were tired and red-rimmed. He had sat up with me for many hours, I was sure. I realized with admiration what a good and strong man was my brother.

For a long time my mind did not return to thoughts of the riders or Luther Guthrie or Jennifer. The pain of Jennifer's last words to me was still with me, and I did not let myself think much about it. I think her scorn had burned even deeper than that powerful bolt of lightning.

But I did think of Luther Guthrie and his riders, particularly the pitted one, the one-eyed man that seemed to be giving the orders. From the first time I had seen him there had been something that stirred a hint of memory in me. I had seen him before—seen him, or perhaps heard of him. But where? Back in the valley in Tennessee? He looked like no one that I could recall from there. But still the conviction that he was in some way familiar lingered with me.

Becky's face appeared above me, in her hands a cup of steaming coffee. She helped me rise, then propped me up on pillows until I was almost sitting. I took the coffee gratefully. It was hot and delicious, and the warmness of the mug was pleasant on my hands.

It was only after several hours that Sam at last told me how long I had been in a stupor. Two days! I could hardly believe it. Becky told me of how Sam had ridden in search of the doctor as soon as I had arrived half-conscious back at the cabin, and of how he had been unable to find him. They had both lost much sleep, and Sam much work, caring for me. I felt a tremendous sense of gratitude.

I managed to make it to the table for supper that night. It was delicious—the first real food I had consumed in some time. I was thinner, and so weak that I trembled as I stood. But the meal put new strength in me.

Becky was cleaning up the dishes and I had just settled myself down in my bed when Sam came over to me. He sat on a stool beside my bed and leaned forward, speaking in a low whisper.

"Jim, tell me what you saw when you saw the riders. Faces, I mean." There was an urgency in his question that I could not understand.

"Well, I saw only one face clearly. There were nine of them in all, and it was only for a few moments that I was there. The one I saw was apparently the leader of the group. He was a one-eyed fellow, with marks on his face like he had once had smallpox or something. I heard one of the others call him Jess, I think."

Sam leaned back, frowning and looking somehow dissatisfied. I grew curious. "Sam, do you know him?"

He looked at me quickly, then shook his head. "No . . . I just wanted a description. I don't know anyone that looks like that." Then he stood quickly and moved away.

Now that was mighty strange, I thought. Why was Sam so curious about what I had seen? I could understand him wanting to know all he could about the riders that were threatening his life and property, but his question had a strange intensity and his expression was confusing.

I couldn't make sense of it, so I didn't try. I closed my eyes and settled back. The tick was soft, warm. Soon I was asleep.

In the days that followed I recovered rather slowly. Sam went back to his work, but he seemed always to be brooding about something. Several times in the evenings I would see him seated in a corner, a frown on his face.

For days there had been no trouble from the riding gunmen, nor any reports of such trouble from other ranchers, and that was to me a comfort. But I think Sam looked on it as a lull in the storm, a respite that was as impermanent as it was welcome.

I regained my strength and began helping Sam with his work. The sod building needed repair, and as we worked on it he struck a deal with me. If for this year I would work with him around the ranch and help him sell his stock, he would in turn help me build a cabin on my land, and next year would share his stock with me until my own herd could be built up. I liked the idea and quickly accepted. I needed some way of learning the ranching business before trying it myself, and working with Sam would be the ideal way.

And I would have time to build a good, solid cabin. I was determined to have a nice home, no matter how much work it took. Trees were not easy to come by in this country, but on Sam's spread was a creek lined by a good stand of trees, and there were several good trees on my own land, so I didn't worry. I spent an evening planning out the design of my cabin, as well as some smaller outbuildings, and the next day Sam and I set out for the creek, taking two good axes and some chains, along with my horse and his mule.

For a day we worked, chopping trees, trimming branches, then with the help of the horse, mule, and chains, snaking the logs to not far from Sam's cabin and laying them in a pile. The work was long and hard, but I was very well accustomed to gruelling labor, and before the day was through we had a good stack of logs. Not nearly enough for a cabin, but still a good supply.

The next day was spent in snaking the logs to my land, and in scouting out trees to be cut from my own property. I was happy, for idleness did not please me for very long, and it had been some time since I had done any real, satisfying labor. It was with real pride that I built up the stack of logs.

I gathered large, flat stones from the creek for use in the foundation. I planned on building a floor for my cabin, and designing the structure so that rooms could be added with no trouble. I found the work a challenge, a pleasure. It was with real sadness that I saw the day end, and Sam and I mounted and rode back to his cabin and another good supper of bacon, biscuits, and eggs.

The next day it rained again, all day. There was nothing to be done but make plans, and I was itching for work. But the water pounded incessantly on the roof without a minute's respite until sundown. Then the rain stopped, the sky cleared, and the stars shone down through cloudless heavens.

Sam, Becky, and I moved out into the yard in the evening, drawn by the beauty of the night. All was peaceful, still, calm.

We talked of quiet things, simple things. Becky had a look of contentment beyond any I had yet seen her show, and I smiled when I noticed her hand patting gently on her stomach, sending love to the young, developing life within. Sam saw it too, and a happy look came into his eye.

I talked to him of my cabin, and he gave me suggestions based on his experience with log buildings. Sam was an excellent craftsman, a fine builder, and I coveted his knowledge.

"Build your foundation high, Jim. I wish I had laid a good board floor in my own cabin, but in those days I hardly had the time to get a roof over our heads. That's why it's good you're working for me this year. You'll have time to build a home like it should be done. You've got enough money left over from buying that property to hold you for awhile, and what with vegetables from our garden and rabbits and such from hunting, you should be able to do just fine. You're lucky, brother. You'll make it good out here.''

I hoped so. I hoped so with all my heart. I was happier here with what was left of my family than I had been in years, and I wanted that happiness to continue, even increase. Yet at heart there was an intense sadness, for I knew that Jennifer no linger cared for me. I had known her only days, yet in that time I had come to love her dearly, and knowing we were now together no more was intensely painful.

We sat there in the beautiful and clear night far beyond the time we normally retired, and it was only with reluctance that we at last rose and went to our beds. Soon, I thought, I would be sleeping in my own bed, in my own cabin, built by my own hands. It was a good thought. I rolled it over in my mind.

I laid down and slept, and in my dreams I was hewing logs, happily working, feeling the wood in my hands, moving my ax with careful and sure strokes, watching the wood chip away until the log was smooth and square. Then I cut notches, slanting dovetail notches, and with an auger drilled holes for pegs. It was a good dream. Soon it would be reality.

I woke to a sudden roar and the feeling of wood chips striking my face, stinging. I leaped up with a cry, and instinctively I dove for my rifle against the wall. Then I rolled over on my back and realized what was happening just as Becky cried out in the back room and Sam rushed to the door in his longjohns, his rifle in his hands, bullet pouch over his shoulder, and a wild expression on his face.

The roar came again, then another, then many others. The roars of rifles, the smacking of high-caliber slugs into the walls, and the shattering of shutters as the bullets tore through them to smash into the walls and shelves in the back of the room. One ripped right past Sam's head to embed itself in the wall of his bedroom.

"No!" he screamed, almost out of his mind in rage. "No more!"

"Sam, no . . ."

My cry did no good, for without hesitation or thought to safety he threw open the door and dashed out into the night, firing and reloading as he ran, screaming in the darkness, weeping, cursing . . .

There were answering blasts from the riders, and even as I ran out after him I saw the dirt being torn up about his feet. Yet he made no effort to run, but stood fast, firing at the moving figures, all the while his voice crying out in desperation for them to stop.

He was firing too carelessly, too angry to realize that when his ammunition was gone he would be a helpless target. I moved behind the post of the cabin porch and fired two quick shots at the nearest rider. I didn't hit him, but I could tell my shots worried him, for he moved quickly away in the darkness.

"Sam! Come back! You're a clear target!"

He didn't hear, or didn't heed, at least. He continued his spasmodic fire at the dark figures that circled the cabin and rode in the fields directly before it. I shot at them, and I think it was only the peppering shots of my Winchester that kept them from drawing close enough to my brother to drop him where he stood.

I could hear Becky screaming in the room behind me, crying in hysteria as she looked over me where I crouched on the porch and saw her husband so insanely risking his life. I knew I had to get him and drag him back by sheer force if need be, before he was dropped by a slug in full view of his wife. I raised up from my crouched position and began to run.

The rider approached just as I darted forward, and the slug that ripped close by my head stopped me in my tracks. I saw him clearly, heading straight for Sam, a pistol aimed at his head, his finger ready to squeeze off the shot that would end Sam's life.

Sam's Sharps barked, and the figure was literally knocked into the air, flipping backwards over his saddle, landing with a loud grunt in the dirt while his horse wheeled and headed back into the night. And it seemed then that Sam's mind cleared of its rage, and he darted back toward the cabin. Together we moved back inside, Becky crying all the while, obviously profoundly grateful that her husband had returned to safety at least for the moment.

Sam slammed the heavy door shut, dropping the bar in place. Then he moved over to a place that somehow I had never noticed before—a place on the wall where a small opening was drilled, narrow from the outside, but flaring out wide on the inside to give a gunner a good sweep with his weapon. Sam had made the opening as a defense against Indians back in the earlier days, I guessed. I don't know why I had never noticed it.

I moved over to the window with the shattered shutter that had thrown splinters into my face while I lay sleeping. Carefully I peeped out toward the riders in the darkness.

They were moving, slowly, almost like phantoms, all in a line, and all deathly silent. They were coming toward the spot where their comrade lay dead on the ground, an ugly hole in his chest and his mouth and eyes open in a frightening, frozen expression of shock. They approached until they were right upon him, and I saw one of the group climb down from his horse to kneel beside the body. It was the one-eyed man I had noticed in the camp.

For a long time he knelt beside the body, then he stood and shook his head. He picked up the limp form and draped it over the saddle from which he had fallen when Sam's bullet struck him. Then he looked up at the cabin.

"You'll pay, damn you! You'll pay with your miserable lives!" He had a sort of rough voice, like gravels scraping together on a rusted shovel. And from his tone I could tell that he meant every word that he said.

Then he mounted and moved away with the rest of his men, riding openly and without any apparent fear of our weapons. I felt a murderous impulse to shoot them in the back, as many of them as I could hit before they moved out of range. But I fought off the feeling. Then Sam cried out with a loud voice and I jumped in surprise.

"Madison! Colonel Josiah Madison! It seems your murdering days aren't over yet, are they!"

One of the horses stopped suddenly, and a figure turned to stare back at the cabin. It was the one-eyed leader of the group. And at that moment I understood why his face had plagued me so. Stories came back to me, stories that Sam had told me, stories that had been the substance of many nightmares for many years.

"Sam, is that . . ."

"Yes, Jim, that man is Colonel Josiah Jefferson Madison, the very one who is wanted by the federal government for the atrocities that he committed when he was in charge of the Bryant Federal Detention Camp during the war. That was the man who took delight in seeing me and my friends tortured. He's a murderer, Jim, and now he has a grudge against me. Before this is over, someone is going to be dead."

He turned and strode back toward his bedroom, and I leaned my rifle against the wall and felt I might vomit.

CHAPTER 9

———◆———

I couldn't believe what I had heard. I moved quickly back to where Sam leaned against the wall in the back room.

"Are they gone?" he asked.

"Yes. They rode off. But now I'm not sure they won't be back very soon. Especially if what you said is true."

"It's true. You can be sure of that."

I shook my head. "But Sam, how can you be so certain? You've only seen him across the distance in the dark. How do you know that it's Madison?"

"I know. You don't see a man torture your best friend to death and then not recognize him later. That's Madison, with an eye patch now, but still the same face. His eye was diseased during the war. It seems he must have lost it."

"Are you sure it was wise to let him know that you recognized him? He'll be after you for sure now. He's wanted, and anyone that can identify him he won't let live, and you know it."

"I know, Jim. But I promised myself all these years that if ever I saw Josiah Madison again I would not back down, I wouldn't try to hide from him. And I won't do that now."

I knew that there was no point in trying to convince

him of anything. His mind was made up. And now we had a real problem, for no longer was this cabin the home of just another fence-stringer. It was the home of men that could identify a wanted man to the law.

Sam had told me many stories about Colonel Josiah Madison, and even from merely hearing about the horrors that went on in the prison camp that he controlled I had understood why Sam had such a hate for the man. A sudden thought struck me.

"Sam . . . you asked about the man just awhile after I woke up the other day. Why?"

"You were raving in your sleep, babbling about a man with smallpox scars and a bad eye. That made me think about Madison, and when I saw him just now I knew that's who it was."

Sam walked over to his bed and sat down. Becky was beside him, and she put her hand on his shoulder. "What now, Sam?"

"What I should have done the last time this happened. Listened to sense and fought back."

Those words chilled me. I saw the same madman rage burning in Sam that had been there several days ago. That rage had disappeared after the meeting with the other ranchers, but now it had revived again and with greater fervor. I began to fear that Sam would not react so reasonably this time.

"Just what does that mean, Sam?" I asked.

He looked at me sharply, almost in anger. "It means that tomorrow I'm taking Becky up the creek to the Ledbetter place and leaving her for safekeeping. Then I'm riding out to find Luke McDonald and tell him just who the leader of those riders is. And then you can probably guess what will happen."

I could. The ranchers would grow angry, arm themselves, and then there would be another attack on the Guthrie spread. And this time the occupants of that ranch might not come out alive. Jennifer . . .

At once a fiery rage welled up within me. Sam suddenly became my enemy, and I lashed out at him harshly.

"How can you do that? How can you become the very thing you're trying to fight? To shoot, murder . . ."

Sam looked at me coldly. My words did not cut him at all. He had determined his course, and nothing I could say would stop him.

I waited out the night on the front step of the house, my rifle across my knees and wild thoughts racing through my mind. When the morning came I again entered the house and glumly ate my breakfast. Sam and I said little to each other.

He left with Becky as soon as he had saddled his horse and hitched up the wagon for her. I watched them ride off, knowing full well that with the news Sam carried it would be only a few hours before a bloodthirsty army of ranchers would descend in force on Luther Guthrie's spread. I expected violence before the day was over.

I had to do something to keep Jennifer safe. I thought I didn't care for her anymore—perhaps I didn't—but still I would not let her be murdered. That I couldn't bear.

But what could I do? How could I get her away from the ranch? I certainly couldn't walk up and knock on the door and politely tell Luther Guthrie that a massacre was about to take place and I wanted to remove his daughter from the premises. And Jennifer would certainly not see me willingly even if I should manage to reach the house without being shot. No, there would have to be another way.

And the only way I could think of was to steal her away, to take her against her will and for her own good. That would be dangerous, for sure, but what other course was there? And with that thought I nodded my head firmly and moved back toward the cabin for my rifle.

I was out again quickly when I heard the noise of an oncoming horse. Who could be approaching the cabin at this early hour? I cocked my Winchester and cautiously stepped out to meet whoever it was.

It was Aaron McCuen, and from the looks of him he had been riding hard since before daylight. He was unshaven and bleary-eyed, and he rode almost up to the door at a full gallop.

Scarcely had I greeted him, laying my rifle aside, before he was talking at a fast pace. He was obviously worried, and very tense.

"Hartford, things are getting bad—real bad," he gasped. "There was more trouble from the riders last night, the first in days. And a little girl was shot when they fired at a cabin not too far up the river from here. It wasn't far past midnight when somebody came riding into town shouting the news. It woke up everyone. They fear the girl might die. People are worked up, Hartford, and there's blood about to be spilt. I can feel it. I didn't know how it will end. I felt like maybe we could do something, though I don't know what. I've heard that the sheriff is up in these parts, but I haven't been able to find him."

"It doesn't matter. What could the sheriff do? The riders were here last night, and they fired on us. We killed one of them."

McCuen's eyes grew large. "No! Are you sure you killed him?"

"I'm sure. But that's not the big news." I told him then about my trip out to the riders' camp and the man I had seen. And I told him of Sam's conviction that he was none other than the infamous Josiah Madison.

McCuen shook his head as if the news was too much to take in one dose.

"If that's true, then those men will surely be out for blood even more than they are now," he said. "I'm afraid that before the sun sets again there will be blood on the land around Luther Guthrie's ranch. A lot of it."

I had no trouble in agreeing with that conviction. "I've got to ride out there," I said. "I've got to get there before those ranchers have a chance to get organized." McCuen looked at me strangely. I felt a kind of embarrassment. How could I tell him my reason for wanting to go? How could I tell him how I felt about Jennifer Guthrie? I looked at him blankly.

"What do you plan to do when you get there?" he said. "What good will a trip out there do? I was thinking that you and I could . . ."

"I'm sorry. I can't explain, but I have to go. I have to. What are you going to do?"

McCuen rubbed his chin, and there was distress in his eyes. "I hoped to find some sort of lawman, but that hasn't worked out. I don't know what to do . . . I think I'll head for Bacon's ranch. He'll want to know about this. Can I meet you at Muster Creek?"

"Yes . . . meet me in the badlands straight across from Guthrie's ranch house," I said. "Up in the hills, the ones that look down on his spread. I don't know when I'll be there . . . if I'm not there when you arrive, then wait awhile. I'll wait for you if need be."

"Agreed. I can't imagine what any of us will do to stop this ridiculous business, but I'll meet you there. Maybe Bacon will be able to think of something."

"I hope so. I'll see you in a few hours."

McCuen left then, moving off swiftly, running his horse hard. The animal would be exhausted when it reached Bacon's ranch, no doubt. McCuen had already taxed the animal severely.

As I saddled my horse I felt helpless and fearful. This whole thing was beyond the control of any one person, and I suspected that no mind, not even one as keen as Jedediah Bacon's, could think of a way to stop the mindless slaughter that was approaching. And I for one was not particularly concerned with stopping it; there was no point in attempting the impossible. But one thing I did intend to do, and that was to get Jennifer safely out of the way before those enraged gunmen arrived to shoot up the ranch. I would force her away at gunpoint if I had to, I would kill anyone that stood in my way if it came to that. I would even die myself before I would see her harmed. I was surprised at the intensity of my feelings. For a long while I had thought very little of Jennifer, but now that she was in danger I found that my feelings were as strong as ever toward her. In haste I pulled the girth tight around my horse's belly and mounted.

I moved quickly across the land, now very familiar. There was a cool breeze blowing, and the wind felt good against my skin. But I could not enjoy the ride, for every second I worried that perhaps the ranchers might mobilize more quickly than I expected and reach the Guthrie ranch before I could get Jennifer away. It was ironic, being against my own brother in this, but I knew I could not do otherwise. Jennifer's safety was of paramount importance.

I slowed my horse down when I saw that the rapid pace was wearing him out. After a time I passed the area I had purchased for my ranch. Halfway I dreaded to look at my stack of logs, for I feared what the riders might have done to them. So I was mildly surprised and very pleased when I found them stacked in perfect shape, apparently untouched. It was the first pleasant discovery of the day. And maybe, I feared, the last.

Onward I moved, never stopping, never resting. Soon

the hills loomed before me large, and I guided my horse to the south to cut around the same part of the hills where I had hidden not many nights before. If the riders were in those hills again I had no desire for them to see me. I passed around the south base of the slopes with no sign of life presenting itself.

I stopped, unsure of what to do. Were the riders hidden in the same area as before? Or had they moved down to the Guthrie ranch? I needed to know; it could be fatal to walk right into the midst of them. I tethered my horse to the same spot as before and crawled up into the same gully.

There was no sound, no movement anywhere before me. I crept slowly and carefully nonetheless, for it was possible, even likely, that if the riders were there they would be asleep. They had gone through a very busy night not long before.

But as I moved forward it all seemed utterly dead and empty. I carefully moved aside the brush that blocked my view into the little hollow where the riders' camp lay. I looked in. It was empty.

I stood and leaped down into the hollow. There were tracks, seemingly not too old, and the blackened remains of a fire. But there was no trace of any supplies, blankets, bags, or anything else to indicate that anyone now lived here. There were empty cans, old cigarette butts, and old chewed-out wads of tobacco, but nothing else. Obviously the riders had gone. I felt weak. There was nowhere else they could be but down there at the Guthrie ranch, just where the coming gunmen would expect them. That meant that the ranch itself would become a battleground, and with the riders down there with Jennifer, my chances for getting her safely away seemed remote.

It might be suicide to go down there. Was it worth it? Should I risk my life to save someone who would probably scorn my help and curse me even as I saved her?

Of course it was worth it. It was Jennifer. I didn't care what happened to Luther Guthrie or anyone else except to the extent that it concerned Jennifer. She was the only one I wanted to get away from that ranch before violence erupted. Of course, it bothered me to think of Sam being down there in the midst of the battle, but he was a grown man who had made his decision. He would be there by choice. Jennifer wasn't being given an option.

Getting her away from there was going to be a real problem, but that would come later. First I had to get down there to the ranch without being seen. And with the regular ranch hands there along with the riders, there were a lot of eyes to watch me approach. I had a lot of open ground to cover without being seen.

I moved toward the top of the slope that looked down on the house. I crouched down beside the trunk of a scraggly tree and looked over the terrain.

The house was not very far, but it was a long slope that I would have to descend. Many were the windows all along the back of the house, and the entire slope of the hill was in plain view of almost every point on the ranch.

I looked toward the south. The hill sloped down in that direction too, though not as steep. And I could descend it without being seen from the ranch or the house. But when I reached the base I would have to approach the house again, and I would be in clear view of the windows. But the house might hide me from the rest of the ranch grounds. I would have to count on my luck to ensure that I wouldn't be spotted from the house. It was the only way I could approach and have any hope of making it safely.

A man strode from a barn across the lot and toward

the main house. I looked at him closely. Maybe he was one of the regular hands, maybe one of the riders. A realization came to me. If the riders were now openly living on the very ranch itself, then Jennifer would have proof that the accusations I and my friends had made toward her father were accurate. How she would react to that I could not guess.

· I moved back down the slope again. I tried not to think too much about the tremendous task facing me. I had so far only come up with a plan to reach the house, and a weak plan at that. How I would get in the house without being spotted, how I would find Jennifer and convince her to leave without betraying my presence . . . none of those matters had been solved. I was a fool, and I knew it. No sane person would try what I was about to do. Yet I felt I had no choice.

I reached the place where my horse was tethered. I loosened the halter and mounted. I certainly could not ride around to the house, but I could tie my horse a little closer to save some distance on the return trip. That is, if there was a return trip.

I·found a good place where my horse could graze and remain hidden. Leaving it there, I hefted my Winchester close to me and headed around the base of the slope.

I paused when I reached the point where I could see the house. The rest of the ranch was hidden from me, and that was comforting. If I were spotted, it would be through the windows. If I was lucky, no one would be looking.

I paused for a moment to gather my wits and breathe a quick prayer. I knew that my best bet would be to move as fast as I could toward the house and hide directly beneath a window. The slower I moved the longer I would be exposed to view. Taking a deep breath, I darted from my hiding place and moved in a crouch straight toward the log structure.

It couldn't have been for more than thirty seconds that I ran, yet it seemed many minutes. And though I tried to scurry along without much noise, I felt like a crashing buffalo. I cast up all hope. Surely someone had seen me, or at least heard me. Any minute there would come cries, rifle fire, and I would be down and bleeding.

But it never happened. I reached the house and leaned panting up against the wall, sincerely surprised and very pleased to find myself still breathing. I felt like patting myself on the back. The first part of my mission, at least, had been successful.

But now I had to get inside, and what's more, get inside without being seen. It bothered me to realize that when she laid eyes on me Jennifer would probably scream or call for her father, and all of my careful plans would be rendered pointless. But I had come this far, and I certainly couldn't stop now.

Which room would Jennifer be in? The very real possibility that she was not in the house at all occurred to me only then. That would be one fine mess—to risk my neck getting down here and pulling off the impossible feat of getting into the house only to discover that she was not even there. Were it not for the fact that I would probably get my head blown off, there would be something humorous in it.

There was a window beside me, and carefully I looked into it. It was my first real glimpse of the interior of Guthrie's home, and I was impressed with the fine way it was outfitted. Not the typical rancher's home, this place! There were real lace curtains on the windows, and paintings on the walls. The furniture was finely-made stuff, not the rough, knocked-together mess that one usually found in this part of the country. Guthrie's wife was dead, I knew, but apparently he had done

his best during her lifetime to give her a home of which
she could be proud. And now he was surely doing the
same for Jennifer. I had to admire that in him. A man
who cared for his family like he did could not be a
totally bad man.

The room was empty. Maybe it would be worthwhile
to try and get in through the window. Carefully I looked
all about me, listening for the sound of approaching
feet. There was only silence. All it would take to end
the whole affair would be for someone to walk unexpectedly around the house.

Again I looked through the window. The room still
was empty. I reached out to try the window, wondering
if I could force it open. In the walkway past the open
door of the room I saw a figure pass.

It was a man, I could tell, though I saw nothing of
his face. Luther Guthrie, perhaps? Possibly, though my
short glance had given me the impression that this was
a smaller fellow. I would have to be careful. He hadn't
seen me, but my luck might not hold for long.

I tried the window, afraid to push hard for fear it
would open suddenly and loudly, as stubborn windows
are prone to do. Several times I pushed, but it was no
use. The window would not budge.

There was another window to my right. I tried it also,
but it too was either locked or jammed. It seemed that
I wasn't going to get in at all from this side of the house.

Suddenly I heard it—a man whistling, moving toward this end of the house from across the ranch
grounds. Had he not whistled I don't think I would have
heard him at all.

There was nothing to do but dart around the back of
the house. That I did, making far more noise than I
would have liked, and becoming suddenly aware that I
was in danger of discovery by the whistler.

What could I do . . . where could I go? There was

someone in the house, but if I stayed outside I was certain to be found out. When I heard the whistling man turn the corner of the house and head toward the rear, I did the only thing possible.

I found a window, threw it open—this one, thank heavens, wasn't jammed—and half crawled, half leaped through. I hadn't even had time to see if the room I was entering was unoccupied. I turned and looked around me as I pulled my Winchester through the window after me.

Jennifer stood across the room, her hair disheveled and her eyes red and swollen as if she had been crying. I stared at her in surprise, not knowing what to say, and sensing that something was wrong here in this house. Something out of the ordinary was happening, and I had walked into the midst of it.

"Jennifer?" My voice sounded weak when I spoke her name.

"Jim!" Her words were choked, as if with fear. "Don't make any noise . . . there's a guard just outside the door, and if he finds you here, he'll kill you!"

CHAPTER 10

FOR a long moment I stood staring at Jennifer with an open mouth. The sudden sight of her had startled me and left me speechless. The significance of what she had said did not sink in at once, but when it did I felt a chilling dread creep over me.

"Guard? But who . . ."

I could sense from the look in her eye that she couldn't figure out just why I was here. And also from her look I knew that somehow she didn't hate me anymore, and even in the midst of my tension and fear it came as an overwhelming relief to me.

"Jennifer, have the riders taken over this ranch? Are they the ones that are guarding this door?" I kept my voice at a low whisper, conscious of the sound of boots on the floor just outside the door. Jennifer answered with a tense nod.

"Yes . . . they rode in very early this morning and burst into the house. I didn't know what to think . . . I thought they were more of those same riders that attacked earlier. I had no idea that they were the so-called 'night-riders' that everyone has been talking about for weeks." She paused with obvious discomfort. "I . . . I owe you an apology, I guess. You were right, you and your friends. My father is the one who hired those men to terrorize the fence builders. I didn't know it until this

morning. But he isn't in control of them anymore . . .
they've taken over everything, and that horrible man
that leads them is demanding that Father sign over the
ranch to him.''

"Sign over the ranch? You mean he wants control
of the Muster Creek Cattle Company? But that's unbelievable!''

"Maybe so,'' she said, "but that's just what he
wants. I heard it all . . . he came into the house this
morning, even before it was light, and literally dragged
my father from his bed. He said that one of his men
had been killed, and that things were getting too dangerous for the pay my father was giving them. Father
grew very angry, and demanded that he leave, saying
that he no longer worked for him. The man just laughed,
and it was a horrible laugh, just horrible. He said that
unless my father signed over the ranch to him he would
say that the murders he and his men had committed,
murders my father did not order, Jim, had been carried
out at Father's command. There was nothing my father
could do. The man even . . . even threatened me . . .''
Her voice choked off, and I felt a profound pity for her.

Yet deep inside I couldn't help but feel that Luther
Guthrie's predicament was not undeserved. He had
called in cruel men to spread fear among innocent people, and now that the situation was reversed it seemed
nothing but just.

But still I knew that I would have to help him. Not
for his own sake, but only for that of his daughter. And
there was another reason, too: a man like Josiah Madison should not be running free in any civilized territory.
His crimes deserved punishment, and I aimed to do my
part to see that he received his just deserts.

It seemed that only then did Jennifer realize the
strangeness of my presence and mode of entry. "Jim
. . . just why is it that you came here? And why did you

break in instead of just walking up to the door? I'm glad you didn't, for you would have been shot, but how did you know?''

"I came from the west and circled around the hills just behind us," I said. "I knew the riders were making camp in those hills, but when I checked they were gone. I knew they must have come here, so naturally I was careful. I didn't know you were in this room when I came in . . . I was just going through the first convenient entrance to avoid being seen by anyone. But I'm glad you're here. I came because everyone on this ranch is in great danger right now. There's going to be another attack in the next few hours, I believe. Those riders out there shot a young girl last night, and the whole territory is up in arms. Of course they believe your father was behind the whole thing, and there's no telling how much blood might be shed once they get here. I came to take you away.'' I wanted to explain about Madison, too, but there was not time. I was growing nervous, conscious that at almost any time the angry ranchers might arrive and the battle would begin. I had to get Jennifer away, and quickly. But how? With the ranch crawling with riders there was almost no way to escape unseen. And if she wanted me to help her father also, as I knew she did, then the task would be doubly difficult.

Jennifer's eyes filled with fear, and she spoke in a whisper of despair: "Jim, how can we escape? And how can we get Father away before they arrive? They'll kill him if we leave him behind.''

I couldn't argue with that. Luther Guthrie would be one of the attacking group's primary targets. Protecting him from those angry ranchers, not to mention the riders controlling the ranch, was sure to be just short of impossible, and that was looking at it optimistically.

I let out an exasperated sigh. "Where is your father, Jennifer?''

"I'm not absolutely sure," she said. "I heard some-one talking about the little log house on down the slope not long ago. I think that's where they're holding him. But there're guards all over this ranch, Jim. I'm sure that they'll have the house locked up and a man at the door with a gun."

My spirits sank as she talked. Not only would we have to get out of this house without being seen, we would also have to move across open land with guards everywhere, get into a locked building, and move out with Luther Guthrie and still hope to draw no attention. A conviction began to grow in me that this was the day I would die.

"My God, Jennifer, I can't work miracles! How can I get him away from here without getting all of us killed?" My voice was harsh, I realized, but now was not the time to dwell on niceties. But immediately I regretted my tone, for she again began to cry. I looked at her without knowing what to say.

"You mean you just want to leave him here to die? You think I can run out on my own father at a time like this?"

I sighed once more, and slowly shook my head. "Of course not, Jennifer. Of course not. Don't worry . . . we'll get your father away from here." I might as well have promised her the world in a burlap sack, for all the confidence I felt in what I was saying. But she looked up at me with an expression that somehow made it all worthwhile. I turned my thoughts to the immediate problem of escaping from the room.

The most obvious solution seemed to be to simply move on out the window in just the same way I had entered. If we could move quietly, then we should be able to do it without drawing the attention of the guard outside the door. I said as much to Jennifer, and she agreed.

But even as we moved toward the window a new thought came to me. The guard outside had a gun, one that would be turned against the ranchers when they arrived . . . one that just might be turned against my own brother, perhaps. If I could eliminate the threat of that gun, then the odds of Sam's survival would be increased at least a small bit. I grasped Jennifer's arm.

"Wait. There might be a better way." I explained to her the idea that was forming in my mind. She looked troubled.

"But why take the risk? What if it doesn't work?"

I told her of Sam, and how I couldn't miss the chance to help him, even if I didn't agree with what he was doing. "I'll help out your father, Jennifer, but I can't ignore the safety of my own kin any more than you can ignore the safety of yours." That seemed to convince her, and as I took up a heavy bottle of some sort of cologne and hid against the wall beside the door, she moved to the doorway and cleared her throat before speaking in a clear, loud voice.

"Mister . . . come in here. I need help."

There was the sound of movement just on the other side of the doorway, and a rough voice came back: "What? What's your problem?"

"Please . . . I need help right now." Jennifer put a real tone of despair into her voice. She was doing a convincing bit of acting.

There was a moment of hesitation. "I don't know, miss . . . the boss said . . ."

"But mister, I need help . . . please . . ."

Again a time of hesitation. Then, "Oh, alright. Just a blasted minute." I heard the noise of his hands fumbling with the latch, and suddenly the door was opening and his head was poking through.

Down came the bottle, as hard as I could move it. The glass shattered, and with a groan and a shudder the man dropped to the floor. His eyes glazed over and closed, and for a moment I thought I had killed him. Jennifer stood back and stared down at him with a horrified expression.

I felt weak. I had never done such a thing to another human being before, and I didn't like it. But even then I knew it had been necessary, and I felt a kind of relief. "There's one that won't be giving anyone any trouble for quite awhile," I said.

We moved into the main room of the ranch house then, for there was no longer any need to sneak out the window. The guard had been alone in the house, so at the moment we were in no danger of detection. I headed for a window to look out over the grounds in hope of getting some sort of plan in mind about the rescue of Luther Guthrie. My hand bumped against the butt of my pistol thrust in my belt, and after a moment's thought I drew it out and handed it to Jennifer.

"Here. You might need this. Do you know how to use it?"

I think my question offended her, if the look on her face was any indication. She took the gun. "Of course I can use it. A girl doesn't grow up in this territory without knowing how to use a gun."

"That's good," I said. Then I looked out the window.

I saw two men moving back some distance from the corral, heading for the bunkhouse. Apparently they were holed up there. I wondered if any of the regular hired hands were being held prisoner, or if they had joined ranks with the riders. I asked Jennifer.

"I can't say for sure," she responded. "My father had many regular hands for many years, men that would remain loyal to him no matter what. But through the years they have drifted off, a couple have died, and so on. The men that work for him now are drifters, not the quality that he likes to work with. But he takes what he can get. I'm afraid that they might have joined up with the riders, as you call them. I wouldn't be able to say for sure, of course.''

''I'd say you are probably right,'' I said. ''We'll have to assume that they'll have sided against your father.''

There was a large expanse of open ground between us and the log house where Jennifer suspected her father was being held. I noticed an armed man seated beside the door of the rough little building, and that served to convince me that Jennifer was right about where her father was.

The guard didn't look any too alert—he was nodding at his post—but still he presented a formidable obstacle to any plan I could dream up. I looked closely at the structure. There were no windows in the front nor on the side that I could see, and the door appeared to be of thick oak or some other strong wood. Looking closely I could see a padlock on the latch. The ground sloped up into a kind of hill behind the building, and the foundation was dug right into the hill, making the building appear to be sinking into the earth. I turned over plan after plan in my mind, only to reject each one in the light of logic. I shook my head. ''Jennifer, I can't think of any way to reach that building, much less let out your father, without tipping our hand to the guard. He'll see us no matter what.''

Jennifer looked at me with a firm expression. ''Then the only thing to do is get rid of that guard.'' I looked at her in shock.

''What do you mean?''

She had a cold look in her eye that bothered me. ''I mean if we're going to help my father, then we'll have to get rid of that guard outside. It's the only way.''

I found myself shaking. I was still hardly over having to strike the other fellow in the head and now Jennifer was talking about something that sounded disturbingly like killing. I had never been a violent person, and quite frankly not a brave one either. My mind rebelled at the thought of having to actually try to kill someone. I couldn't do it.

"Jennifer, you mean we should *kill* that fellow out there? Is that what you mean?"

She hung her head a bit, but still she had the determined look in her eye. "Jim, those men won't hesitate to kill my father, and neither will your fence-stringing friends that are coming. I don't like the idea of killing anyone, but what other way is there? I can't let my father die just because I couldn't bring myself to do something like that. You have to understand."

And though it bothered me to my very soul, I had to admit that she was right. If that was one of my kin locked away in that log shack, I wouldn't hesitate to do whatever was necessary to rescue him. And there was certainly no way we could get to Luther Guthrie if that guard was still alive.

"There's just one problem, though, Jennifer," I said. "How can we . . . how can we go about it? If we shoot him they'll hear us, and that would be the end of it all. And we can't just prance out there and knock him in the head."

I hoped that she could find no answer. But she pursed her lips and wrinkled her brow, and in a moment she spoke. "Jim, have you ever done any shooting with a bow and arrow?"

"Not much . . . why?"

"My father befriended a Cheyenne warrior at one time. He made a gift of a bow and a few arrows to my father. He's used it as a decoration in his room for years. It's old, but I think it is still strong. Maybe . . . maybe we could shoot that man from the house here and no one would know. It wouldn't make any noise . . ."

"That wouldn't keep the fellow from hollering if we were lucky enough to hit him from this distance," I said, glowering out the window. "And I'm not by any means a good shot with an arrow. I'm sorry. It just won't work."

Jennifer looked at me as if she were deeply disappointed. Then she looked out the window at the log shack and its lone guard. Then huge tears welled up in her eyes and rolled down her cheeks to splash onto her dress.

That did it. I couldn't stand to see her cry. "Jennifer . . . I'm sorry. Give me the bow. I'll do my best."

Jennifer hugged me then, and it made it seem worthwhile. But as she moved back to her father's room to get the weapon, I wondered if I was doing the right thing. I was risking my life to help a man who had hired riders to threaten the lives and welfare of my own friends and family, even of myself. Was I right? I didn't know. All I knew was that I wouldn't betray Jennifer. I would do for her whatever she wanted, even if I died in doing it. I hadn't even fully realized until then just how much I cared for her.

When she returned and put the bow in my hand I was ashamed of how badly I was shaking. I took an arrow with numb fingers and notched it on the bowstring. Jennifer watched me, and I know she could tell I was scared. And though she appeared calm, in her eyes I could see that she was as frightened as I was.

"Where should I shoot from?" I asked in a cracking voice. "The window?"

Jennifer shook her head. "I don't know . . . maybe the door would be better. Whatever you think." I clutched the bow tightly, feeling as if the whole thing was some sort of horrible dream. "I think I'll shoot from the door. I'll have more room."

I moved over to the front door and carefully opened

the latch with a shaking hand. Slowly I opened it, trying to make sure that no one from the outside noticed. I opened it only as far as was necessary to give me a clear shot, then slowly I raised the bow. The man in front of the shack was rolling a cigarette. If I hit him he would never know what had happened. My arms wouldn't stop trembling.

Carefully I took aim and pulled back the string. I was shaking so that I didn't think I could possibly hit the man.

"Jim . . ." Jennifer's voice was weak and shaking. "I can't ask you to do this . . . I'm sorry . . ."

"No," I said. "I'll do it."

And then I shot the arrow. I didn't realize until it was all over that my eyes had been shut when I released the string. As soon as I had fired my body went numb, and the bow dropped from my hands to clatter to my feet. Then I forced myself to look at what I had done.

The man was leaning forward, clutching at the arrow. It was stuck square through the middle of his chest. Even from across the distance I could tell he was dead. If I hadn't felt so numb I think I would have been sick.

Jennifer whispered in a voice with no expression. "You got him, Jim. You got him on the first shot."

Suddenly I knew I had to move. I had to run, to leave behind this building. Quickly I looked around. There was no sign of life anywhere on the ranch grounds. I grabbed up my Winchester in one hand and grasped Jennifer's arm with the other. "C'mon. Let's go."

We darted out of the house, moving at a dead run across the open land until we reached the log house. I tried not to look at the dead man, but somehow I couldn't take my eyes from him. He looked almost as if he were asleep, or maybe looking for something on the ground. I realized that he looked rather suspicious, so with great reluctance I pushed him back up to an upright position. His face was pale and his eyes were open and glazed. I looked away.

Jennifer was jerking on the padlock, pounding on the door. "Father . . . can you hear me? We're here to get you out!" Then I saw a figure walk around an outbuilding on down the slope, and by instinct I grabbed Jennifer and pulled her around to the side of the building and out of sight.

I could hear movement inside the shack, but there was no good chance to try to talk to Guthrie with the other man approaching. I wondered if he would notice how strangely quiet was the guard at the front door. I felt a chill of horror when the thought came that perhaps he was coming to relieve the man at watch. What would happen then?

But to my relief the man walked on past the shed, never even glancing toward us, and then he was gone. Jennifer and I scurried quickly around to the back of the shack, where we crouched low. I noticed then the small window just above us in the wall. Jennifer stood to a half-crouched position and looked inside.

"Father?"

Guthrie's voice sounded weak as he responded. "Jennifer . . . you'll get yourself killed!" It was quite apparent from the straining of his voice that he was in pain. I remembered then the stories I had heard from Sam about Madison's skill at torture, and I pitied Luther Guthrie for what he must have suffered.

"Father, we're going to get you out," she whispered. "I don't know how, but we're going to get you out."

"Jennifer, please be careful," he moaned. "Please . . . if they find you out here they'll kill you. I'm hurt bad . . . they made me sign over the ranch to them. There was nothing I could do . . ."

"I know, Father, I know," she said. "Can you push on the door? Maybe we can force the hinges apart."

My hand grabbed at Jennifer's arm. My voice failed me, and I pointed to the road that led down toward the main house.

On that road were riders, how many I could not tell. They were armed, and at their lead was a man who could be no other than Luke McDonald. And beside him was Sam.

This was it. The attack had begun, and we were caught right in the middle of it.

CHAPTER 11

THERE was nothing to do but move and move quickly. I had resigned myself to whatever fate would befall me, and I was prepared to risk my very life to keep my word to Jennifer to save her father. Now, with the enraged ranchers on the verge of attack and the ranch just seconds away from becoming a battleground, the only thing I could do was expose myself, to throw secrecy to the wind and blast Guthrie out of that shack. Pushing Jennifer down to protect her from the gunfire I expected momentarily, I dashed around the front of the little building. I knew that I was seen by the ranchers, maybe the men in the bunkhouse too, but that didn't matter. I had but a few seconds to get Guthrie out, and there was only one way to do that. I threw the lever on my Winchester and sent a slug straight into the lock, blasting it open. I grabbed at the latch and threw open the heavy door. Luther Guthrie stared back at me, pale and scared.

I didn't waste time with explanations. I moved in just long enough to grab his arm and drag him back toward the door. I expected shooting to begin at any minute. When I pulled on Guthrie's arm, he winced as if in pain, and held back.

"You . . . what are you doing here? What are you trying to do?"

"I'm trying to get you out of here alive, along with your daughter, before this ranch turns into a bloodbath. Now shut up and run!"

But even as I pulled him out into the sunlight I knew that running was something that Luther Guthrie would not be able to do. I noticed a spot of blood on his thigh, and every time he put his weight on the injured leg he grimaced in pain. I didn't have to ask what—or who— had caused the wound. I knew it had been part of Josiah Madison's work on the man, a bit of his persuasive technique aimed at getting Guthrie to sign over his ranch.

"Why should I go with you . . . why should I trust you . . ."

A shot sounded and a bullet smacked into the wall just beside us, and Guthrie's complaints were cut short. The shot had come from the bunkhouse. It would be only moments before the battle was on.

"Move, Guthrie!" I commanded. "Your daughter is waiting, and I intend to get her away from here no matter what happens to you. Now get moving! Around the back of the building, then up the slope."

He obeyed then, moving as best he could on his injured leg. We rounded the back of the building as bullets began to smack close around us. Jennifer threw her arms around her father and kissed him. She looked with deep concern at the crimson spot on his thigh. "Father, did that man do this to you?"

"Yes . . . this and more. But I wouldn't sign the ranch over to him, Jennifer, not until he threatened you. Then I had no choice."

"Now isn't the time," I said. "Get up the slope! You run beside us, and keep yourself so that your father and I are between you and the bunkhouse. It's a long run up that slope, and they'll be shooting. I'll try to help you along, Guthrie."

Guthrie didn't ask why I was here at the ranch just as a battle was breaking out. He didn't ask how I had managed to get his daughter safely out of the house. He simply gritted his teeth, braced his hand against his wounded leg, and began to limp up the slope as fast as he could.

I tried to help him along, but his bad leg made progress slow. I glanced over my shoulder. The army of gunmen was riding down toward the ranch now, and from the bunkhouse men were running, some moving toward the main house, others positioning themselves behind whatever cover was available. It was going to be a massacre, I could tell. Right now the mounted men had the advantage, but they were not for the most part trained gunmen and fighters, as were the men riding with Madison. How the fight would wind up I could not guess.

It was to our advantage that the ranchers had picked this moment to attack, for the men holed up in the ranch buildings were so preoccupied with facing the threat they posed to take much notice of the three figures scurrying up the slope. But not entirely preoccupied, for bullets smacked around our feet and whizzed through the air above our heads. Although I couldn't be sure, I didn't think any of the shots were coming from the direction of Sam's group. Maybe Sam had been able to stop them from firing at us. But there was no way to be sure that even my own brother knew I was one of the three runners, for he did not know that I had come here, and he certainly would not expect me to be helping out Luther Guthrie.

The top of the slope seemed distant, and Guthrie was getting slower with each step. I could tell that his leg was paining him terribly. I suspected that Madison had put a bullet in his thigh to help motivate him to sign over the ranch. Or he might have worked on him with a knife. Whatever brutal method he had used, it had certainly done plenty of damage to the rancher's leg. And now, with Guthrie's injury slowing all of us down, I began to doubt that we would make it to safety before one or all of us was cut down by gunfire.

Jennifer had just opened her mouth to say something to her father when the bullet struck him. It struck him hard, square in the back, and passed all the way through his body. I saw him go suddenly weak, a shudder ripping through him, and his lips worked together as if he were trying to say something but couldn't get it out. We reached to the top of the slope and found safety behind a large boulder seconds before he died.

I was amazed at the cold, objective way in which I watched Luther Guthrie die. In my own arms he died. And I, who had seen so little violence and had never even thought of killing a man until this day, could do nothing but stare at his limp form with a sort of numbness, a coldness within me. I looked first at his face, then at the ugly wound the bullet had made in his chest where it had come out of him, then at Jennifer. I expected tears, but in her eyes there was nothing but shock. I think the same coldness within me was also in her. We looked at each other for a long time and did not speak. The noise of gunfire from below came loud to our ears.

Gently I laid down the head of the man who we had tried so hard to save. His eyes were half open, and his lips were dry and coated with dust. It was strange to see him lying there, a moment ago alive, now as dead as the rock behind which we hid. I moved up on the boulder to look at the battle below, and Jennifer moved over to where I had been and took up the head of her father and laid it in her lap as if he were a sleeping baby. Still there were no words, no tears, only coldness. She stroked his hair gently, looking with no expression down into his face. Only then did the dull, throbbing ache begin in my heart. It was an ache of pity for the girl I loved, who had now lost the man who had raised her from the day she was born.

Below I could see the horsemen, most still unhurt, moving down hard on the main ranch house, the bunk-house, the corral. Bursts of smoke would explode from the rifles of the fighters, then the sound would reach up to us a split second later. I saw a horseman—I think I even recognized him from some earlier time—bearing down on one of the men firing from the corral, and then he killed him. Even across the long distance between us I could see that the rancher's bullet struck the man in the head. I'm sure that he was dead even before the sound of the shot reached me.

I tried to pick out Sam's form among the riding gun-men, but such was the dust and confusion that I could not. Yet I knew he was down there somewhere. There were a few bodies scattered about here and there; some moved, others lay frighteningly still. Was Sam's body among them? I looked closely, trying to remember what he had been wearing today. I couldn't recollect, and I began to worry.

The attackers were circling like Indians, their swiftly-moving horses making them difficult targets. Yet the same movement was making it difficult for them to get off any clear shots at the hidden gunmen holed up all over the ranch, and once those gunmen fired off their weapons they were in a position to get quickly under cover until they were ready to fire their next shot. The mounted fighters had no such advantage, and as the bat-tle continued I could see that it was hurting them. All too often I saw bodies falling from the horses, and each time it happened I felt a jolt of pain deep inside. Was Sam to be the next to fall? I had picked out a man who

I thought was him . . . yes! That was Sam! Still alive, still riding, still shooting. Thank God.

I followed his movements closely after I had located him, every breath a prayer for his safety. More and more riders were dropping from their horses, some to rise up clutching arms or legs to run to safety, others to land motionless in a cloud of dust. And always the continual crackle of gunfire, almost like the snapping of wood when a mighty oak strains to fall. How many men would die before this battle was finished? Was this the result that Sam and Luke McDonald wanted? Those men that lay still on the dirt down below would string no more barbed wire fences, herd no more cattle, put no more food on their families' tables. It was senseless. Senseless.

I looked back down at Jennifer again. Still she cradled her father's head in her arms, but she was looking at me. I could see that she had broken through her state of emotionless shock, for there were tears on her cheeks, flowing down profusely.

"I'm sorry, Jennifer," I said. "I'm so very sorry."

Very, very sadly she smiled. "We tried, Jim. We did our best. That was all we could do." Then she bowed her head and began to cry hard, her sobs shaking her and her tears falling on her father's cold face.

"Jim!" I recognized McCuen's voice. I had almost forgotten that he had agreed to meet me. I turned. He was approaching on horseback, and beside him was Jedediah Bacon and another man I didn't recognize. They rode up, and when he saw the dead body of Luther Guthrie, McCuen went pale.

"How, Jim? What happened?"

Briefly I told the story, and it seemed to hurt him to hear it. Jed Bacon's reaction was the same, and the unidentified man simply sat expressionless in his saddle.

He had the look of a cowboy, and I figured him to be one of Bacon's employees.

"We're too late, I see," said Bacon. "Maybe it's just as well. There's not one blasted thing we could have done to stop this. It was inevitable."

"How are things going down there?" asked McCuen. I told him how things stood as far as I could see them, and then the three men crawled up beside me on the rock to watch for themselves. Jennifer gently lay down her father's head on a mound of moss and moved up beside me on my left. Her tears were gone, as if she had cried herself empty. I wished I could put my arms around her.

"My God, my God!" exclaimed Bacon, shaking his head. "It's all so foolish, all this fighting. The work of fools."

"That's the way it always winds up, Jed," said McCuen. "Men try to reason, to talk things out, and then impatience sets in and someone tries to settle things with a gun. And sometimes it works. But most of the time it just ends up that innocent folks die, and the problem is solved not because there's some sort of answer but because there's no one left alive to argue anymore. I've seen it a hundred times."

"This is one battle that won't solve any problems," said Bacon. "Settlers will keep on coming, barbed wire will keep on going up, and the old ways will keep on changing. That's for certain, and all the fence-cutting riders in the world won't be able to change it. If only people would learn."

I looked across at Jennifer. Her eyes were focused on the battle below, and they were very sad. I knew that McCuen and Bacon were probably both wondering what Luther Guthrie's daughter was doing up here with me. I think McCuen suspected that there was something beyond the ordinary in the way I felt about Jennifer. My strong insistence on coming to the ranch earlier today, along with her presence here with me now, were both evidence of something special in the way I thought of her. If there was any question still in his mind it was answered immediately, for I reached over and took Jennifer's hand in mine and held her delicate fingers in my own callused ones. McCuen looked silently at us for a moment, then looked back toward the battle again.

More bodies were strewn about, most of them those of dead ranchers. There would be much mourning tonight, for many men were dead and more would follow soon, I was certain. I looked furtively about for Sam.

There he was . . . on the ground. A tremendous nausea welled up within me. Sam was dead . . . no . . . he moved! He had been wounded, apparently, but he was still alive. How long he would remain that way would be hard to guess. I prayed for him.

It was getting toward dusk when at last the battle ended. It did not end at once. It more or less just faded out, growing steadily weaker and more sporadic, until at last it was over. The surviving ranchers rode off over the slope and left bodies littered behind them, Sam's among them. Then for a time there was no movement but the occasional stirrings of the men that lay wounded all around the ranch buildings. Then men moved out from the house, the bunkhouse, the outbuildings, and picked up the wounded. Those that apparently were near death they shot, and it hurt me each time they pulled the triggers of their forty-fours. The ones not so bad off, Sam included, they carried back into the house. Hostages in case of another attack, I assumed.

"It's over," said Bacon. "There won't be another attack. I wonder how many men are dead."

"Too many, Jed. Way too many," said McCuen.

Then came a time of talk. I met the man that had rode in with Bacon. As I had guessed, he was one of

Bacon's employees, a man named Loftis. I told of how Jennifer and I had tried to rescue Guthrie, of how he had been tortured into signing over the ranch, and how he had taken a fatal bullet within a few feet of safety.

"I'm very sorry for you, Miss Guthrie," said McCuen. "But you need not worry about the ranch going to Madison. That deed would never stand up once it was known that the signing was forced. And besides, no one like Madison would ever be able to run an operation like that openly. The law would grab him once his identity was known."

Jennifer looked confused. "What is all this 'Madison' talk? That's not what my father called the leader of those men . . . is that who you're talking about?"

I realized that Jennifer had not been told of the true identity of the one-eyed leader of the night riders. I filled her in, and she looked dazed. "Josiah Madison . . . I've heard of him. I can't believe a man like that would be tied in with my father. Father must not have known who he was."

"I'm sure he didn't, Jennifer," I said. "But no matter about that. That most definitely is Josiah Madison down there in that house, and now he has my brother again. If he recognizes him from the prison camp and knows that Sam can identify him, then that will be it for Sam." I thought of Becky.

"Let's get Miss Guthrie on back to town," said McCuen. "Jed, maybe Mr. Loftis can take her on back. And it would be a good idea if we got Mr. Guthrie's body on back, too. I know it will be unpleasant for you, Miss Guthrie, but . . ."

"Don't worry. I'm a grown lady. I can take it." Jennifer stood tall as she spoke, and I was proud of her.

I hugged her close before she mounted on McCuen's horse and rode off with Loftis. Luther Guthrie's body was laid across the back of Loftis' horse, the arms

swinging with each step the animal took. There was no
dignity in it at all, and Jennifer gained my sincere admiration for the way she rode proudly along in spite of
the pain that must have been in her heart.

Then I was alone with McCuen and Bacon. "What
should we do?" I asked. I could think of nothing but
Sam. What might he be suffering right now at the hands
of Josiah Madison?

Try as we would, we could think of no plan. And so
we waited, for what we did not know, but still we
waited. And then, when the moon was sailing high in a
clear sky, the door of the Guthrie house opened, and
the riders emerged. Quickly they saddled horses, and
then they were gone, heading north. A deep depression
settled over me. What had they done to Sam?

We moved down the slope at a run. The ranch
seemed deserted. I passed over the bodies of horsemen
that had fallen. One of them was Luke McDonald. I
leaped over his body without even giving it more than
a glance.

"Hartford . . . Jim . . . wait a minute," McCuen
called out behind me. "Maybe I should go first. Maybe
you should hold on before you go in . . . let me go
first."

"He's right, Hartford," called Bacon.

I didn't listen. I had to know, and know right now,
what had happened to Sam. I reached the door and burst
in.

The place was a shambles. Furniture was knocked
about, the walls were pockmarked with bullet holes.
And there were bodies on the floor. I saw a man lying
face down, and with a moment of hesitation I rolled
him over on his back. I didn't recognize him. He was
dead.

And then I saw Sam. He was crumpled in a corner,
still and unbreathing. I felt my eyes begin to flood with

tears. Slowly I moved over to him, conscious of Bacon and McCuen watching me silently. With trembling hands I rolled his body over so I could see his face.

It was Sam alright. And his throat was cut. I looked at him for a long time, then I stood and walked past McCuen and Bacon on out the door. I leaned up against the wall, weak and shaken, and felt I could die myself.

CHAPTER 12

I was weary when we carried Sam's body, along with the other victims of the murdering night riders, back to Miles City. My body ached for sleep, yet my mind was darting wildly from one thought to another, alert and quick. I was horrified, almost devastated, by what had just happened, but what would come next was worse—the task of having to tell Becky of Sam's death. Becky, the quiet, gentle, loving wife that had stood by Sam through the hardest times—how would she be able to go on without him, especially with her child on the way?

We carried the bodies on crude moving conveyances made of two limbs, one on each side of our horses, with rope forming a crudely-woven support on which we strapped the bodies. The ends of the limbs dragged the ground, leaving little ruts in the dirt where the weight of the bodies pushed the wood into the earth. Bacon had learned how to construct the conveyances from an Indian friend, he said.

I had recovered my horse from the hills behind the Guthrie ranch, and I rode numbly, dreading to reach Miles City, and then later to face Becky with the dreadful news. Part of me was restless, longing to go after Madison and his band of murderers, but yet I knew that right now I could not. That would come later, after preparations had been made.

Whether or not hatred is ever justified I do not know, but I learned at that moment what it was to truly hate a human being. I longed to see Madison dead, and to make sure that with his final breath he knew he was dying. Sam had lived with that kind of hate all of his life, for he knew Josiah Madison for what he was. And then he had died by his hand, and that was the cruelest thing about it. My desire for vengeance was powerful; I wanted to destroy Madison not only for what he had done to me, but also for the sake of Becky, and most of all for Sam. Whether my feelings were good or bad I cannot say; at that moment it didn't seem to matter. My rationality was gone, and I wanted only revenge.

We said little to each other as we rode. The hour was late when at last we reached Miles City; it would not be long 'til dawn. I had not asked McCuen or Bacon what they planned to do about pursuing Madison. It didn't really matter—I would go alone if it came to it, for such was my bitterness that I hardly cared what happened to me.

The undertaker was waiting for us when we rode down the main street of the town. He had heard of the battle, for many of the wounded had already been brought into town for treatment from the local doctor. He methodically took the bodies off the conveyances behind our horses and moved them inside. It hurt me when he took Sam's limp form away.

McCuen approached me as I removed the crude litter from the back of my horse. "What now, Jim?" he asked. He sounded weary.

"Come first light I'm going after them, McCuen," I said. "I have to do it." I halfway expected him to argue with me about it, but instead he simply nodded his head.

"I understand. May I go with you? And maybe Jed too, if he wants?"

I looked at him, rather surprised. From the look in his eye I could tell that he understood that this was my fight, my mission, and he seemed in no way inclined to look at it as anything else. Sadly I smiled at him. "Sure. I'll be needing some help, I would guess."

"Alright, then. I'll talk to Jed. I'm sure he will want to come along." He paused. "Jim, do you think we should bring the military into this? They would sure be interested in getting their hands on Josiah Madison."

Firmly I shook my head. "That would take too long," I said. "Madison already has a good jump on us, and by the time the army got into this he would be hidden away somewhere where they could never find him. Besides, this isn't an army affair to me now. It's personal. It's for me and Becky and Jennifer and all the others who have lost friends and family tonight. I've got no time for the military in this." I sounded rather rude, I fear, for I spoke with such force that it no doubt sounded as if I were angry at my friend. But he paid no heed, for he understood that my anger was not truly directed at him.

"You need sleep," he said. "I'm staying at the hotel. There's room for two if you would like to stay there for the rest of the night."

"I can't, McCuen. I've got to tell Becky what happened." I had tried not to think about it too much, for giving her the news was going to be the hardest thing I had ever done. It scared me.

McCuen shook his head. "If you want to get on Madison's trail at first light, then you'd best get some rest. You know that by now those survivors are back in their homes and Becky surely knows already that Sam was taken prisoner. I'll see to it that she hears the rest from someone who will break it to her in the right way . . . a preacher, maybe. But right now you're beat, and I think you better head for that hotel before you drop. You've got a big job waiting for you tomorrow."

Suddenly, I realized how very tired I really was. I had to sleep, or surely I would "drop," just as he had said. It was of infinite importance that I be able to trail Madison quickly and with accuracy, and Becky would surely rather have me on his trail than staying around just to spare her a little pain. I agreed to McCuen's proposition, and he looked pleased.

"Make sure Becky knows that I'm going to get Madison," I said. "Tell her that he won't go unpunished for what he's done."

"I will, Jim. Now go on to the hotel . . . I'll be there a bit later. You go ahead and take the bed; there's a good couch that I can sleep on. We only have a little while 'til first light as it is, so you'd best hurry."

He handed me the key to his room, and I headed for the hotel. I was so bone-tired that I never could remember crawling into the bed and dropping into a deep sleep. The next thing I knew it was morning, and I still was tired.

I raised up in the bed. McCuen stirred over on the couch but did not wake. I rose and walked to the window and looked out onto the street.

What kind of day would this be? Would I be lucky enough to find Madison, or would he have vanished into the wilderness as he had done so many times in the past? So far no one had been able to catch him, though many had tried. It seemed foolhardy to think that a simple Tennessee farmer could do what trained government agents had failed to do for many years.

But I was determined to try. Maybe those government agents did not have the motivation I did. Surely they had never lost a brother like I had, and seen a lifetime of dreams and hard work cut short by the cruel knife of a murderer. That was why I would succeed where they had failed—I had a powerful motivation, and I would not rest until I had settled with Madison.

The street was quiet; there was no movement to be seen but that of a lone dog that wandered down the boardwalk across the road. It was still early, but even though I was still very tired I was anxious to get underway. Madison would be many miles ahead already, and in the broad grasslands he would be difficult to trail.

I heard McCuen stir awake behind me. I turned to see him yawn and stretch. "Good lands, is it morning already?" he murmured. "It seems I just laid down. Morning, Jim."

"Good morning. Sleep good?"

"Fine, but there wasn't enough of it." He rubbed his eyes and looked at me seriously. "I rousted out a preacher after you came up here last night, and he agreed to tell Becky. I don't know how she took it, but I'm sure she knows by now."

I felt rather guilty. Maybe I should have been the one to tell her, instead of some preacher she didn't know. Nevertheless it seemed more important for me to be on Madison's trail than anything else. But still I couldn't shake the vague feeling of guilt. Had I done the right thing?

I glanced out at the street again. A wagon approached. I looked closely . . . it was Becky. I felt a combination of relief and dread. I knew she had come to talk to me. Quickly I threw on my clothes and headed out of the room, telling McCuen of Becky's approach. He looked rather surprised.

I met Becky in the street. From the weary look on her face I could tell she had slept little, if at all. I didn't know what to say to her. Her eyes were red, and I could tell she had been crying. I couldn't blame her.

"I heard about your plan, Jim," she said. "The

preacher told me you were going after Madison."

"That's right. It's what Sam would have done."

"Yes, it is. And it's for that same reason that Sam is dead today. He reacted the wrong way, and it killed him. He's gone now . . . it's hard for me to believe, but it's true. Now you're going to be killed yourself if you go after Madison. I loved Sam with all my heart—you know that—and I would not say anything to slight his memory, but he was foolish to go up against Madison. He never had a decent chance, and he accomplished very little. Madison is alive, and Sam is dead. As far as I'm concerned, that means things are worse than before."

"But it was something Sam had to do, Becky," I responded. "I didn't understand that before, but I do now. A man can't stand aside while murderers like Madison run loose. It's his responsibility to see that justice is done to them. Madison has been murdering all his life. Who can say how many men he killed in that prison camp long before he ever set foot in this territory? We can't let him live any longer, especially after what he did to Sam. It's something I owe to my brother, Becky."

"And I think I owe it to my husband to make sure his brother doesn't get himself killed for nothing," Becky returned. "I don't want you to go, Jim."

I looked at her, not sure how to respond. "I'm sorry," I said at length. "I don't think I have any choice."

Her sad expression became a bit sadder, and she spoke softly. "Alright, then. I'll be going now." She turned away and climbed back into the wagon. I wanted to say something to her, but the words choked in my throat. I pitied her beyond all telling, and I knew there was nothing I could say that would lighten the burden she now bore.

I watched her drive away, then I turned again into the hotel. I found McCuen dressed and waiting for me. He still looked very tired, but also a bit more alert than before.

"Is everything alright?" he asked.

"As well as could be expected, I guess. Becky's a strong woman. Let's get some breakfast. Is Bacon coming?"

"Yes. I think he wants Madison almost as badly as you. He blames him not only for all the deaths yesterday but also for the bad feeling between the various cattlemen. I suspect that he has a little personal stake in all this."

We had breakfast at the cafe as soon as the doors opened. My food seemed tasteless, and I ate it without enjoyment. All I could think of was the task that lay before me. When I had come to the Montana Territory I had anticipated nothing like this.

Bacon met us just outside of town a couple of hours later, after we had stocked up on supplies to last us for several days out on the open range. The three of us said little as we rode back toward the Guthrie ranch. I realized that Sam would be buried today, and I would not be there to see it. No matter. What I had to do was far more important.

The morning had a misty feel to it, a kind of freshness that at a happier time I would have found invigorating. My horse stepped along with great liveliness, obviously feeling rested and strong. As the morning passed we made good time, and reached the ranch more quickly than I had expected.

From looking over the place it seemed hard to imagine that only yesterday it had been a bloody battleground. The place looked serene and peaceful, and ruggedly beautiful. Horses still grazed nearby, and far away toward the east I could see the tiny forms of distant cattle grazing on the rich grasses.

We rode down toward the house, for what reason I am not sure, for we were looking for nothing in particular. We had seen the direction the riders had taken the night before, and I certainly expected to find no one about the place now. We rode down to the front door and dismounted.

The door was still standing open as it had been when we left it last night. The bodies were gone now, but there were tell-tale stains of blood about that made me feel weak. Try as I would I could not help staring at the spot where I had found Sam's body. I couldn't stand it. I turned and went outside again, McCuen following me.

"I'll kill him, McCuen. Kill him with my own hands if it comes to that. He tortured Sam for years in that prison camp, then he came back from the past to kill him. I won't let him live after doing that. I won't let him live." So violent were my emotions that my voice choked. McCuen looked at me as if I frightened him a bit.

"Jim . . . it will be dangerous, and slow. And there's always the chance that Madison will get away where we'll never find him . . ."

"No! I'll tail him 'til his dying day or 'til he drops me," I said. "He'll not escape me, never." I think that at that moment I must have looked much as Sam did before the fateful battle. Certainly I was just as much the victim of violent hate and fear as he had been. I had lost my reason and was being driven only by the desire for vengeance.

Bacon walked up to us. "Well, we'll get nowhere just staying around here . . . whoa! What was that?"

I tensed at the tone of his voice. He was looking over toward the bunkhouse, his expression wary. I looked over and scanned the scene, but I saw nothing.

"What is it, Jed?" McCuen said, his hand creeping toward his sidearm. "Something over there?"

Bacon shook his head as if in indecision. "I'm not sure . . . I thought I saw a movement . . . hey, you over there! Freeze where you are or be shot!"

We had all seen him that time—a lanky man moving up on the other side of the building, peering around at us. I had seen something else, too: the flashing of sunlight on the barrel of a rifle. I mentioned it to McCuen.

There was no answer from the stranger for a moment, than a coarse voice called out: "Who are you? What are you doing here?"

"We might ask you the same thing, mister!" called out Bacon. "You'd best get rid of that rifle. There's three of us, and we might tend to shoot if we feel threatened. You understand me?"

Again there was a long pause, then a sudden clattering as the rifle was tossed out on the ground in our view. "The pistol, too!" called Bacon. A moment later it lay on the ground beside the rifle, and the lanky man approached with his hands high in the air. I had never seen him before.

"And who might you be?" asked Bacon, lowering his rifle after looking the fellow over. "Why are you around here today, especially after what happened yesterday?"

"The name's Bradley Sullivan," he said. "And I reckon I got a right to be here since this here ranch is where I work. I might wonder myself just who you are and why this place is deserted."

McCuen frowned, a bit confused. "You mean you weren't here yesterday? You don't know what happened?"

"Just got in this mornin'," he said. "I been on the trail for about a week, scoutin' out on the far ranges for

Guthrie. Where is Guthrie, anyhow?'' he asked, his eyes narrowing.

"He's dead," I said. "Shot by the riders he hired. This ranch is deeded over to the leader of those riders now—Josiah Madison."

He looked totally shocked. "Josiah Madi . . ." His voice failed him, trailing off to a whisper.

"This place was a battlefield yesterday," I continued. "There were a lot of men killed, and killed needlessly. Cattlemen, and your partners, too. Madison and his men rode out, and we're going after them. We aim to see him pay."

Sullivan shook his head. "Guthrie's dead—I can't believe it. It was a fool thing for him to hire those riders, and I told him so more than once. He wouldn't listen, though. Wouldn't listen."

Suddenly he looked up, a different look in his eye. "Men, I don't know who you are nor why you're interested in this, but if you're goin' after those riders I would sure like to go along. I'm good with a gun, and I'm one of the best trackers you ever seen. And I know folks all over this country that might have seen them scoundrels runnin'. What do you say? Am I with you?"

I didn't know how to respond to that. I cast a quick glance over at McCuen.

"I warned Guthrie about hiring them riders," Sullivan continued. "I knew it would come to something like this. I want to help out . . . please let me."

McCuen spoke up. "Alright, Sullivan, you're with us. It could get rough . . . I hope you know that."

Sullivan grinned, showing yellow teeth with plenty of wide gaps between them. "Rough is what I'm used to, mister. It's the way I like things."

I gave him back his gun, still a bit concerned about whether or not to trust him. He made no suspicious moves, though, and I relaxed a bit. Bacon mounted his

horse, and we did the same. Sullivan moved over to the
corral and chose a beautiful bay from the horses there.

"Always did take a shine to this animal," he said.
"I guess now that Guthrie's dead he won't be needin'
it none. C'mon, Sawbriar, let's get a saddle on you.
You're mine now."

Sullivan was a strange character. He seemed to feel
no real sadness about the slaughter that had taken place
here, and he didn't seem at all concerned that many of
his friends might have been among those who were
killed. He grinned as if the danger involved was of no
account. A very unique man, this Bradley Sullivan. I
felt a vague dislike for him—maybe it was because of
his beady black eyes or his unkempt clothes. Or maybe
it was because of his general odor that hung like a black
cloud all about him. For whatever reason, I knew he
wasn't destined to become one of my close friends.

We moved off to the northeast, following the path
the riders had taken the night before. Tracking was new
to me, and I had no idea how we would find them. The
land seemed so vast, so empty. They could lose themselves in so many places. The whole thing appeared
hopeless.

But apparently Sullivan didn't share that feeling, for
he moved out in the lead, keeping a close eye on the
trail and leading us along with assurance. He seemed to
have a keen eye for tracking, even better than Jed Bacon, for he hardly paused as he moved along, his eye
picking up hints of the riders' path that I could not see.
Even though I disliked him, I realized that it was fortunate that he was along.

We traveled for many hours, heading always north,
until to the west hills broke through the flat grassland,
rugged and tall. Bacon and Sullivan called a halt and
peered at them.

"It looks like a likely spot, Sullivan," said Bacon.

"They might hide in those hills a long time and not be found."

Sullivan shook his head. "They might be hidin' out there, but I know they ain't hidden entirely. I got a brother that tends sheep up in them hills. I ain't proud of it, but it's the truth. If they went into them hills he would know about it."

"How far is it to where he lives?" Bacon asked. Sullivan laughed.

"Well, sir, that depends on where he's livin' right now. He's got him a wagon that serves him for a house. He just rolls all over them hills and follers the sheep. I don't rightly know where he'd be at the moment."

McCuen rubbed his chin. "You think it would be worthwhile to find him, Sullivan? He might have seen them go by even if they didn't stop in the hills."

"I reckon you got a point," the cowpoke drawled. " 'Course, if them riders did hide up there, they might find us before we find him, if you get my drift."

I was getting his drift in more ways than one. I moved upwind from him and stopped beside McCuen. "If they're hidden up there, then we'll have to go into the hills to get them anyway. It seems to me it's a risk we'll have to take."

The tall man looked thoughtful, then nodded. "I agree. What about you, Bacon?"

"I don't see we have much choice."

"In that case, men, let's go find my brother!" Sullivan's ever-present grin grew brighter, and he headed toward the hills at a gallop before the rest of us had even turned our horses. We took out after him, the hills growing larger as we approached.

I looked at them with apprehension. They appeared somehow threatening. I fancied we were being watched from their slopes even now.

But we had set our course and I intended to see it

through. I pulled up beside McCuen as we slowed to a trot, and we rode silently together. The sun was moving toward the west. It would be dark when we reached the base of the hills.

CHAPTER 13

MCCUEN was craving a cigar when we made camp at the base of the hills, but the fear that Madison's riders might be within eyeshot of us made it impossible for him to smoke. For a long while he sat grumbling in the darkness until at last the desire became overwhelming, and he lit up a long cigar, keeping the glowing ember at the end hidden inside his hat. Every time he lifted up the cigar to take a puff the hat's brim hid his face while billows of smoke poured out around the sweatband. I sat and laughed at him and Sullivan shook his head while digging into his pocket for a tobacco twist.

"You can have your cigars, fellers—I say I'll take a chew over a smoke anytime." He bit off a huge chunk and settled it into his jaw, then grinned like a gaptoothed tomcat on a nightly prowl. So that was why his teeth were so yellow.

Bacon was sitting silent, staring at the hills in the dim moonlight. "Do you think he's up there?" I asked.

The rancher shook his head slowly. "Don't know, Hartford. It seems likely to me. We'll find out for sure tomorrow." Something in the way he said those words sent a chill down my spine.

McCuen extinguished his cigar and moved over beside us. I handed him a piece of jerky from my saddlebag and he began to eat.

"McCuen, there's a couple of things I haven't been able to figure out about this deal," I said. "Why would Josiah Madison do something like trying to take over ownership of Guthrie's ranch? It strikes me as ridiculous. It's like you told Jennifer . . . there's no way he could openly go into a legitimate business for fear of capture. I can't see why he wanted that ranch."

"I expect he didn't want it, Jim. Based on what I've heard about him over the years, I think the man is sick—mentally sick. Apparently he is a sadist of the worst sort, but one who seeks for some sort of pretext to justify his use of torture. Maybe it's guilt, I don't know. But during the war he justified his actions by virtue of the fact that his victims were war prisoners. I would guess that in the case of Guthrie he was torturing the man for no other reason than to satisfy his sadistic tendencies. The man probably had no desire for Guthrie's ranch—that was just an excuse, a justification for cruelty. Of course, I'm no expert on the human mind, but that's the way things appear to me."

It made sense. Madison had no doubt been infuriated by the death of the rider that Sam shot outside the cabin. Probably he took his fury out on Guthrie. It could have been Jennifer . . . thank God he had left her alone.

"Why did he kill Sam like he did, I wonder? he had taken him prisoner, I thought, to use as a hostage along with the others. But then he murdered them . . . they were no good to him dead, but he murdered them anyway. I can't really understand that."

But as soon as I had spoken I did understand. Madison must have recognized Sam from the prison camp. Even if he hadn't, he surely must have known him as the man who shot one of his underlings the night before. Sam had paid for that shooting with his life. I felt my stomach knotting within me. Madison was an animal, one that needed to be exterminated like a mad dog. I

hated him, hated him with all that was in me. I looked
up toward the hills, barren and dark in the moonlight.
If he was up there we would find him. And though I
dreaded the thought of the violence that would come,
still I craved it back in some deeper portion of my mind.

It was insane, this mission of ours. Four men, none
of us trained fighters, going up against a band of killers
that outnumbered us greatly and that would as quickly
kill us as look at us. Totally insane. But still we were
doing it, and as I pondered that fact, I was filled with a
sense of admiration for my two friends. Bacon and
McCuen might well be killed on this mission, yet they
were proceeding fearlessly by my side, and apparently
not giving it a second thought. Even Sullivan earned
some of my grudging admiration, for he had almost no
reason to be here. Yet I couldn't help but feel a little
cold toward the man, for my instinct told me that this
death mission was nothing but a sport to him. I think
he would just as quickly have teamed up with Madison's riders if the mood struck him. But he had been
helpful so far, and for that I was indebted to him.

Sullivan had been sitting quietly for some time now,
but suddenly he began to talk in a steady flow of ram-
bling oration, as if he had decided at that moment to
hook up his mouth to his brain and make his thoughts
audible. And once he started he would not stop.

"No sir, I ain't got no use for the life of a sheep
herder. I ain't a bit proud of havin' a brother that tends
woolies, but let me tell you a little secret, boys . . . there
was a time when I done the same thing myself. Yes sir
. . . herded them devils myself." A huge wad of amber
hit the ground with a splat to punctuate the remark.

"Couldn't take it for long, though, boys. Ain't
nothin' but loneliness when you herd woolies. For days
and days and days you just stand there and look over
them fuzzy round backs and wish you wuz somewheres

else, anywheres else. I did a lot of drinkin' in them days. 'Course, my brother was there with me, but that weren't no real help, since he never said nothin' but just stood off on the hill with that ugly dog of his and looked up at the sky and thought up poems. Yes sir, that's right . . . poems. He would think about 'em all day and write 'em down at night. I never read none of 'em—can't read, anyway—but he sure had a collection of 'em before I had my fill of herdin' woolies and took off on my own. And he would read all the time. Every time we would get into a town he wouldn't go off and get drunk like any sensible feller—he would head off and blow most of his cash on more books. I'd say that by now he has a durned wagonload of 'em. Reads 'em all the time and spouts pretty words to the sky. He's crazier than that Madison feller, boys, a lot crazier. Calls his dog a 'bosom companion' and a hoss a 'noble steed.' What in the livin' daylights that means I ain't got no idea. Like I say, though, he's crazy, so I guess it's to be expected . . .''

Forever the oration continued, boring and dreary, spoken in an irritating monotone and slurred voice. Sullivan looked at no one as he spoke, as if the words were as much for his own benefit as ours. After a time I rose and rolled out my bedroll and drifted off to sleep with Sullivan's voice droning in my ears. I awoke sometime later; I think I might have slept for close to an hour.

". . . and stupid, let me tell you they're stupid. They'd follow the leader of the flock right over the edge of a bluff if he went first. I ain't lyin'—I've seen it happen, They're skittish as can be, and sometimes it's all you can do to get them to head over the slope of a hill if'n they can't see what's across on the other side. Why, once it took me a good two hours just to get the flock to move on through a . . .''

I groaned and rolled over, trying to cut out the sound

of the cowboy's voice. That night I dreamed of sheep.

The next morning's breakfast was more jerky and a little water from our canteens. The sun lit the hills before us, making them sparkle as the dew reflected the light like a million diamonds scattered on the ground. My legs were stiff, and I walked around as I ate in an attempt to loosen them and ease the ache in my knees. Though the sunlight was warm I felt chilled clean through, and my clothes were damp.

In a short time we were riding into the hills. I was rather surprised to find myself unafraid, or so I thought, but when I noticed my hands trembling before me I realized that my nerves were on edge. I looked about me as I rode, fearing what I might see.

We encountered a flock of sheep after only a short ride, and Sullivan moved out into the lead, trying to see if his brother was anywhere near. I looked over to the north, and there he was, a lonely figure against the sky, a rifle in his hand and a dog beside him. The keen loneliness of such an existence became immediately clear to me, and I marveled that anyone could live like this, away from any human contact for months on end, with oftentimes even the isolated meetings that did take place short in duration and business-like in nature. Sullivan's tirade of the night before came back to me, and I suspected that while his brother might not be crazy, as he claimed, there were surely many other sheep herders that were. I was later to learn that my suspicions were true; the isolated life of the west had driven not only sheep herders but also ranchers and homesteaders literally out of their minds after a time. Often many people lived their whole lives with hardly any other companions but wind, toil, and rain. Life on the plains had a rough edge to it that often could cut right into a man or woman's mind and literally destroy them bit by bit, almost like an endless stream of water eroding a rock.

I pointed out the figure on the hillside to my partners. Sullivan squinted at the man, who was now coming down the slope with his dog running before him, and slowly he shook his head.

"It ain't my brother. I don't know this feller."

McCuen shrugged. "No matter. If he's friendly he might help us out anyway. If Madison came through here he's bound to have seen him."

The figure was close enough for me to see him well now. He was a red-bearded fellow with a wide-brimmed hat and clothes that apparently had not been washed in close to a year. His skin was ruddy and sunburned so deeply that I suspected that a year in a dark cave would not be sufficient to fade it out. He stopped well away from us and looked at us with no expression, though something like suspicion was visible in his eyes.

"Who are you?" he called at length.

"We came from Miles City," called Bacon. "We're looking for some folks you might have seen—a whole band of riders that might have come through here yesterday morning or thereabouts. The leader is a one-eyed fellow. You see them?"

Obviously this fellow wasn't about to give out any information without first knowing the reason it was desired. He asked us our business. Sullivan answered him.

"I got a brother—Elijah Sullivan—tendin' sheep up here somewheres. You know him?" He said nothing of why we were looking for the band of riders, but apparently his mention of his brother distracted the wary sheep herder from his question. He moved a little closer to look at Sullivan, apparently trying to see if he bore any resemblance to the Elijah he had mentioned.

After a pause the sheep herder spoke. "I reckon you are 'Lij's brother . . . I can see it in your face. You'd be Bradley, I reckon."

He turned and waved toward the northwest. "Your

brother's tendin' his sheep over yonder, not too far,"
he said. "There was a group of riders that come through
here yesterday, headin' in that direction. And last night
I heard what sounded like shootin' comin' from that
way. Don't know if it had anything to do with 'Lij or
them men, but I reckon they might have had some sort
of ruckus." He dropped into silence then, and we
thanked him for the information.

We rode off without hesitation. I pulled up beside
McCuen.

"So he is here, after all." My voice sounded more
choked than I would have liked. McCuen nodded.

"I guess so. And if I get my guess right, then we
won't find Sullivan's brother alive."

Sullivan was riding in the lead, and though I could
not see his face I sensed that he was concerned about
what we had just been told. If Elijah Sullivan had in
fact had a "ruckus" with Madison, then it was a sure
bet that he had come out with the worst end of the deal.

We crossed two more hills before we at last came
upon Elijah Sullivan's flock. It was smaller than the last
one we had seen, and on the other side of the sea of
wool that shifted and fluctuated as the sheep nipped at
the grass was a wagon, the home of Bradley Sullivan's
brother. There was no sign of any human presence in
the little valley.

We paused at the crest of the hill and looked down
into the valley. I glanced over at Sullivan. His brow was
creased and in his eyes worry was reflected. I knew that
he expected the worst, and in my heart I shared the
feeling.

"Sullivan, what do you make of it?" Bacon asked.
"Could he have left the flock alone for some reason?"

Sullivan shook his head. "No . . . he never has done
nothin' like that before, and I don't reckon he would
now. He should be here somewhere."

"Are you sure this is his flock?"

"Yeah . . . that's his wagon over yonder. This is the right flock."

I felt a strange caution creeping through my mind, and a sudden impulse to turn back gripped me. Yet I was ashamed to mention it to my companions for fear they would think me a coward. So I sat still in the saddle and scanned the horizon, looking for I know not what.

"I'm goin' down there. I gotta see what happened to 'Lij," Sullivan said.

"We'll be right beside you," Bacon said.

Slowly we moved on down the slope. The sheep scattered around our horses, making a pathway for us to travel. Toward the sheepwagon we moved. All was silent. Silent like death.

We found Elijah Sullivan dead on the ground not ten feet from the wagon. It was a horrible sight to behold; he had been shot in the head, apparently with a high-caliber slug, and at very close range. In his hands was gripped a Sharps, cocked and ready to fire. All around on the earth were the prints of horse hooves, mixed with the smaller marks where the sheep had meandered about the body.

"My God," moaned Sullivan. "Elijah . . . my God."

I noted another still, dead form close by. It was his dog, shot several times through the head and body, its brown fur matted with dried blood and its tongue hanging grotesquely from its dead jaws. Obviously the animal had tried to help its wounded master. Or had it been the other way around? Had Madison—for I was certain he was the man behind this little massacre—tried to hurt the dog, arousing Elijah Sullivan to try to protect it, thus getting both the dog and himself killed? That was a mystery that was to remain unanswered.

"I'm sorry, Sullivan," said McCuen. "It looks like Josiah Madison has done his work here, too."

''He'll die, Mr. McCuen. He'll die by my gun . . . or by my hands, if I can get them around his neck. Poor ol' Elijah . . . he never would have hurt nobody, not unless they were tryin' to hurt his sheep or his dog. There ain't no reason why this should have happened.''

With those words there was a thudding sound, followed by a spurting geyser of blood erupting from Sullivan's suddenly shattered forehead. He pitched forward from the saddle just as the noise of rifle fire reached us, a fractional second slower than the bullet itself. Sullivan was dead beside his brother before any of us had made sense of the unexpected occurrence. There was the sound of lead whizzing past our heads and thumping into the ground around our horses' hooves, mixed with McCuen's voice exclaiming with astounding casualness.

''My Lord . . . we're being shot at.''

He grunted then, and grabbed at his leg. I knew he had been hit, and I knew from where the shot had been fired, too, for I had seen the white puff of smoke that had materialized from behind a boulder on the ridge behind us only a second before the bullet and the noise of the shot reached us.

I yanked my Colt from its holster and fired in the general direction of the enemy—a futile gesture, for I could see no one, and the hope of hitting anyone at that distance with a pistol held in a numb and shaking hand was so small as to be nonexistent. But I emptied the cylinder with a mechanical action, firing slowly and regularly as if there was some purpose in doing it.

''Let's move!''

Bacon's voice was almost sufficient to pull me out of my dream world of surprise and shock into reality once more. I realized the danger we were in, and my heels dug into my horse's flesh, goading him forward after the others. I slipped my pistol back into the holster, alternately staring at the land before me and the thin trickle of red staining McCuen's trouser leg. His hand would grip the reins as he rode, then move down to rub the wounded leg, then back up to the reins again, over and over. I could hear gunfire continuing from the ridge, and lead whistled close by my head like the singing of some insect.

I crouched low in the saddle and moved swiftly, the wind whipping my face and roaring in my ears. I glanced back over my shoulder. Men had revealed themselves from behind rocks and brush on the ridge, firing steadily at us. But the shots were futile, for we had moved out of range. The men showed no inclination to pursue us. But we ran hard, just as if they were on our tails.

I was scared. More scared than I had ever been before, more scared than I had imagined possible. My breath came in short, shallow pants, fast, panicked. Before I had burned with a rage against Madison, yet now I felt no anger, none at all. In its place was only fear, blind, stomach-turning fear. I wanted nothing else but to be away from the hills, back on the grasslands, running as fast as my horse could carry me back to Miles City.

We ran for a long time until our mounts could carry us no further without a rest. There was still no sign of pursuit. Madison had apparently been satisfied by the death of Sullivan and the sight of our hasty retreat. We rested for a long time without words, letting the horrible events of the past moments play through our minds again and again.

McCuen's leg was bleeding badly, and he looked pale. Bacon examined his wound and pronounced it not too serious, but still it was something that could not be ignored.

"I'll have to dig it out, Aaron," he said. "You're lucky. If that bullet had entered an inch over it might have severed your artery. As it is I think you'll be all right once we get the slug out and get you back to Miles City."

"Do whatever you need to do, Jed. There's a bottle of whiskey in my saddlebag."

I fetched the whiskey, and Bacon poured a liberal portion right onto McCuen's wound. The man howled in pain as the alcohol made contact with the raw flesh, and with me holding McCuen down Bacon began to probe for the bullet. McCuen cried and sweated and gritted his teeth, and all the while I looked not at him but at the hills from which we had come, wondering if Madison's horsemen would show themselves and approach us before we could escape. I was shaking and weak.

When the operation was over McCuen was pale and clammy. It was clear he would require some rest before we could go on, yet it seemed dangerous to me to remain here, still so close to the hills and to Madison. I felt a hot anger against McCuen, irrational though it was. It was because of him that we were being forced to loiter here. If Madison pursued us, it would be because of this delay that he would find us and surely kill us. It was McCuen's fault, and I hated him for it.

The inhuman nature of my feelings struck me suddenly, sickening me. I was blaming an innocent man for something he could not help. I was letting my own panic steal my rationality, just like a scared rabbit that runs right into the jaws of a snake.

When at last we were again mounted and moving south toward Miles City, I lagged behind. I examined my mind, my feelings. And what I found made me intensely ashamed.

I was a coward. How else could I explain the way I had acted, the way I had cursed McCuen so unjustly? I had never suffered from the delusion that I was a brave man. I had never sought to be a hero. But a coward? Could it be that I was no more than a coward?

Never before in my life had such a feeling plagued me. Yet now it was tearing through me like a hungry rat eating away my insides, and nothing I could do could squelch it.

Coward. Coward. The word ran through my brain, as steady as a tune. After a time it ceased to be a suspicion and became a certainty.

I was a coward. A sniveling, scared coward. I could almost have wished I had stayed and starved back on the farm in Tennessee.

CHAPTER 14

WE rode steadily all day, until our horses were panting and dripping with sweat and lather. I think they could have not gone a mile farther when at last Miles City loomed up before us and we rode into the dusty streets. It was deep night; we had ridden far past sunset.

The doctor was asleep in his small room behind his upstairs office, but we roused him, and he went to work on McCuen, grumbling and wheezing all the while because his rest had been disturbed. I recalled that Sam had been unable to find this fellow when I was suffering from the effects of the lightning bolt; it was probably just as well . . . he would never have come all the way out to the cabin to look me over, if his attitude toward all his work was similar to the one he now was displaying. But still he did good work, giving McCuen medication to ease his pain and bring on sleep.

"He'll have to stay here for a while, maybe a couple of days," he said. "That leg don't look any too good. Infection might set in."

The news did nothing to lift my spirits, to say the least. I worried about McCuen; he had become over the past few days a very close friend who had proven himself worthy of comradeship and respect. The thought crossed my mind that he might have to lose that leg if worse came to worst. And all because he took a bullet while trying to help me revenge myself against Madison. Unselfish, this man. And immensely courageous.

Bacon and I were weary, almost exhausted, both physically and mentally. I took the liberty of taking McCuen's hotel key and heading for a warm bed. Bacon went along too, sleeping on the couch, for he was too tired to attempt to reach his ranch tonight.

We slept late the next morning. It was almost ten o'clock before I at last opened my eyes. I was groggy, as if I had been drugged. Dragging myself to the mirror, I looked at my reflection. My beard was scraggly and rough and my hair disheveled, and I looked at the world through bleary, bloodshot eyes. I looked like I had either been very sick or very drunk for about a week, or perhaps had crawled out of an undertaker's back room. Even after my long sleep my nerves were on edge. All of this was getting to be too much. Things couldn't go on like this much longer without me losing what little sanity I had left. My courage was gone already, I felt. Maybe it didn't really matter if I lost my mind too.

Bacon awoke, looking not much better than me. We said nothing to each other as we dragged ourselves about the room, doing what we could to get ready to face the world. I felt as if I were covered with grit and dried sweat, and I wanted the feeling of a sharp razor against my face and hot water and soap scrubbing my skin.

I treated myself to a hot bath downstairs, and basked in the luxury of the steaming water. My tensions eased a bit, and for the first time in two days I felt truly relaxed. Yet even then I sensed it was to be a short-lived relaxation, for there were still things to think about, to ponder. And one question that must be answered: was I in fact a coward, as I had become convinced yesterday?

With the thought I felt my muscles tensing and I

began to worry once more. A vague sort of contempt for myself swept over me. Coward. Nothing could convince me otherwise. I felt a growing depression. I knew that today I must surely face Becky. After all of my grand declarations of my intention to capture Madison, all my lofty discourses on duty, how could I come crawling back to her like a whipped and frightened puppy?

I thought back on yesterday's nightmare out there in the hills. The horrible way that Sullivan's head had shattered after the bullet had struck it, the way that fear had gripped me, panicked me, the way we had run . . . it sent a thrill of terror through me, and shame. How could I look into Becky's eyes now—but even worse, how could I look into Jennifer's?

Jennifer. I had hardly thought of her, at least in my conscious mind, yet I think there had not been a moment when she had not been hovering somewhere below the surface of my thoughts, back in some deep corner of my brain. I had determined to get Madison primarily to revenge Sam's murder, yet also I had been acting on Jennifer's behalf. She had seen her father die by a bullet from Madison or one of his riders, and the pain it had caused her had been shared by me. And so this failure, this joke of a mission which we had botched so completely, would surely arouse her contempt. And justly so, I mused. I wondered if she would want to see me again after what had happened.

I rose up from the tub, the water now tepid, for I had lay there musing for a long while. I shook myself dry like a dog, then rubbed myself with a rough towel. Pulling on a clean pair of pants and a freshly-laundered shirt, I felt a good bit better. I stretched my muscles and enjoyed the feeling of it.

But now it was time to face the world once more, and I dreaded that prospect. Yet it must be done. I steeled myself for the task that lay before me, and walked outside determined to find Becky.

The day was clear and bright, and the air had a freshness to it that tasted good. The sky was brilliant blue, and high above floated massive, fluffy clouds that looked like heaps of wool piled up after a shearing. And all around was the land, the level, rolling land that was at places flat as a billiard table and at other spots smoothly rounded, rippling with low hills. And all so green, filled with the life of summer, waving in the breeze. This was a huge territory, a vast one. The buildings all around me appeared squatty and drab as I viewed the sky. But beautiful though it was, I could not appreciate it, for I was full of dread. I dropped my eyes from the clouds and looked across the street.

Jennifer was approaching. I gasped and went pale. I was not yet ready to see her, not yet. But on she came, dressed more beautifully than I had ever seen her before, her hair pinned back in a way that emphasized her loveliness. My Lord, she was more breathtaking than the scenery! I finger-combed my hair into place. As she approached me I managed to force out a smile.

"Hello, Jennifer." A dull greeting, to be sure, but I could manage nothing better.

"Hello, Jim. It . . . it's good to see you." She paused, searching for words, and I realized that she was every bit as uncomfortable as me.

"I heard . . . about what happened. I heard Mr. McCuen was injured. Is he alright?"

"He seemed to be doing well when we left him last night," I replied, avoiding her eyes. "He was shot in the leg—nothing too serious; I don't think he'll be laid up too long."

"I was very sorry to hear he had been hurt."

"Jennifer . . . there was a man killed, a man who

worked for your father. Perhaps you knew him ...
Bradley Sullivan.''

She shook her head. "No. I had heard the name mentioned a time or two, but I never really met the fellow.
I don't think Father liked him too much.''

There came a very unpleasant pause, then, and both
of us scuffled our feet in the dust and refused to
exchange even the smallest glance.

"Jennifer, I'm very sorry. I know that doesn't help,
but I'm sorry. There was just no way we could stand
up to them, not at the time. And when McCuen was
hurt we had to get back to Miles City for his sake. I
never intended for anything like that to happen ... I
didn't mean for Madison to escape.''

Jennifer looked at me then, and her eyes were faintly
misted. "It's alright, Jim ... I worried about you the
whole time you were gone. I hate Madison as much as
you, but I don't know what to do about it. Maybe it's
best that we leave him alone ... let the authorities take
care of him.''

"The authorities have done nothing for years. He has
been wanted since Reconstruction for the things he did
at the prison camp during the war. But no one has ever
brought him in. Sometimes I think no one ever will,
unless it's someone like me that does it. But it looks
like I failed completely. I feared that you wouldn't want
to see me again, that you might feel contemptuously
toward me.''

Jennifer looked at me tenderly. "No, Jim. I would
never do that. You are a brave man, and you need never
worry that I will ever think differently of you, no matter
where I might be.''

How quickly did relief arise within me, and how
quickly again did it fade when I heard her last phrase!
There was something final in her tone, something that
hinted she wouldn't be around in the future. And that

was a prospect I couldn't bear to consider.

"Jennifer, what do you mean? Are you going somewhere?" I looked again at her fine dress and immaculately styled hair, and suddenly I understood that she was not dressed in such a manner for no reason—she was preparing for a journey.

Rather sadly she shook her head. "I can't stay, Jim, I can't. After what happened with Father every building, every rock, every tree makes me think of him. This place holds too many bad memories. I just can't take it anymore . . . I have to get away, at least for a time, maybe permanently. I'm catching the train this afternoon."

I felt a growing coldness within my chest. Jennifer was leaving. It was unbelievable.

"Where, Jennifer? Where will you be?"

"Helena. I have an uncle, a widower, who is a merchant there. He's agreed to let me stay at his home for as long as I would like. I may go to work for him if I decide to make it permanent. I have to go, Jim. I hope you understand. I'm going to miss you. I . . . I really like you—I think maybe you knew that already."

I stood looking at her in silence. "Like," she had said. What an insignificant word, so utterly incapable of expressing even half of what I felt for her! Yet I could not tell her—the time was not right, and my voice was choked in my throat from the thought of being without her.

"May I see you to the train, Jennifer? I would like to do that very much." I tried to restrain the quiver in my voice, though with little success.

She smiled—it hurt somehow, knowing that I would see that smile no longer—and then she nodded. "I would like to have you along. I would find the company pleasant."

"Will you share a meal with me?"

"Certainly." She slipped her arm into mine, and together we walked over to the café. I relished every moment of her touch, and realized how fleeting were these final moments with her.

I could not keep my eyes from her as I ate my meal. We talked quietly, and with every tick of the clock standing in the corner I grew a bit sadder. The afternoon came quickly, and I found myself standing at the depot south of town, watching Jennifer's baggage being loaded onto the train.

Our parting was brief, for I could not stand to lengthen it. How I longed to kiss her! But I couldn't. Perhaps I never would.

I touched her hand as she boarded, and watched her through the window of the passenger coach. She looked back at me, and smiled, though I fancied there was something very sad in her look. The noise of the locomotive increased, and the air was filled with smoke, the smell of cinders, and faint sparks expelled by the smokestack to drift all around the train and sting sharply as they settled on the skin and clothing of nearby watchers. Then the train slowly chugged onward, increasing speed steadily. I watched it disappear, my eyes bloodshot and straining to hold back tears. When I reached the main portion of town again, there were many people going about their business, filling the street and stores. Yet the place seemed so very empty. She was gone.

It was with a heavy heart that I saddled and mounted my horse and headed back toward Sam's spread. Becky would be waiting there, I felt sure. I really couldn't anticipate how she would greet me. Even though she had spoken against my pursuing Madison, the very humbling nature of my return might draw her contempt nonetheless. No matter. With Jennifer suddenly gone it all seemed of little consequence. Let her think and say what she would.

I approached the cabin slowly, for there was nothing to inspire haste. I looked over the wide and rolling land, in the distance seeing a handful of cattle grazing lazily on a wide slope. I noticed the rich color of the grasses that grew thick on that low slope. It would be a good year for cattlemen—those that had lived through the fight at Muster Creek—and I felt I myself had a good future here, a good chance for success. Strange how that didn't seem to matter anymore.

The house looked strangely dark and empty as I approached. Puzzled, I dismounted and walked to the front of the cabin, looking for Becky. No sign of her. I wondered if she had gone down the creek to see one of her neighbors, maybe to share her grief with one of the other newly-widowed ladies in this country. After the battle at Guthrie's ranch there were about enough widows to make an army.

The interior of the cabin looked much the same as always, but I noticed some items were missing. I walked back into Sam and Becky's bedroom. The linens were stripped from the bed; the hand-made wardrobe was empty. Becky was gone.

I found a note left for me on the table in the main room.

Becky was gone east, the note said, back to her home in Duluth and her relatives that still lived there. With Sam gone there was nothing to hold her to the Montana plains. She wanted her baby to grow up amid more than wind and work, alone with a widowed bride who could never begin to take care of the ranch alone. The cattle and land were mine, she said, she herself requesting only half of the year's profits. She was gone to not return. Only after death would she make the trip back to Montana, to be buried beside Sam in the grave in the back yard, beneath a tree, deep in the land he had loved so dearly throughout his short life.

I cast the letter down and walked back outside and around to the grave. I had not seen it before.

The newness of the grave was obvious. Only a single wooden cross served as a marker, though rocks had been heaped upon the fresh dirt of the grave to keep out burrowing animals. On the cross were painted letters, letters that would rapidly fade away beneath sun and rain as the years went by. They said:

HERE LIES
SAMUEL ADAMS HARTFORD
BORN 1844
DIED 1884

I read the simple inscription over and over again until the tears blurred my vision and I could read it no more. I turned and went back into the cabin and wept like an abandoned child, images of Sam flashing through my mind—Sam and I together, as children, working, playing, laughing. It would never be again, never again.

The next two days were ones of profound loneliness. I stayed in the cabin not coming out, hardly eating, hardly wanting to live. My own fears of cowardice had faded when Jennifer had assured me she did not think of me as such, yet in my anguished mental state the same fears returned, growing to overwhelming proportions in my mind. All my waking hours were spent in pacing about the cabin, letting my fear of Josiah Madison grow and eat away at my self-respect, and my dreams were of him also. I saw him striking me, stabbing me, wounding me and those I love while I made no effort to stop him save for childish babbling. The dream recurred again and again, and each time I would wake up in a cold sweat.

On the morning of the third day I knew I had to escape the cabin or go mad. I had not shaved or cleaned

myself since I had returned, and after I had taken care
of that I felt much better. I dressed myself as neatly as
I could and began riding back to Miles City again. I left
the cabin behind me, dark and empty. I knew that no
matter what I would never spend another night there. It
had become almost a symbol of my own self-doubts.
And also I understood in some obscure pocket of rationality hidden away in the back of my mind that if I
remained there it would rob me of my sanity. As the
miles dropped away behind me, I felt immensely better,
almost happy.

I went into Miles City with no clear purpose. More
than anything I was trying to escape the hours of self-
condemnation the last two days had brought me. I
wanted to do something—anything—just for the sake
of doing it. McCuen crossed my mind. I did not know
how well he was recovering from his wound, nor if the
doctor had let him leave the bed in the back room of
the office yet. I headed for the office to find out.

McCuen was still confined to the bed in the back
room, and I was hardly through the door before he was
declaring to me that there was absolutely no reason for
it, he was fine, and the fool doctor only wanted to keep
him there to run up a bigger bill. By heaven, he declared
he was ready to pay him double just to let him escape.
I sat and listened to his complaints, and it cheered me
greatly. I smiled for the first time in two days, and it
was like medicine for my darkened spirits.

McCuen continued his tirade for some time, then
paused for breath. During the pause he looked at me,
and a frown crossed his face, creating small wrinkles
beneath the scruffy growth of beard on his jaws.

"Jim, you don't look too good. Way too pale. Has
Becky been taking things rough, wearing you down a
little?"

"Becky's gone," I said. "Gone back to Duluth and a sister that lives there. I've been alone."

He settled back down into the bed. "I can't say I blame her for wanting to get away. She's been through pure hell, there's no denying. Is she coming back?"

I shook my head. "I don't think so, McCuen. She left a letter and said as much. I believe her."

"What about Jennifer Guthrie? Have you seen her?"

I felt a pang of sorrow. "She's gone too, west to Helena. She has an uncle, a merchant of some sort, who is letting her live with him as long as she wants. Whether she will come back or not I don't know."

McCuen looked at me very seriously. He spoke in a quiet voice.

"You feel something pretty special for that girl, don't you, Jim?" he said. "It's pretty apparent, if you don't mind me being so blunt."

I looked at my friend, and I could tell he understood my feelings. I was struck with a sudden desire to admit my love for Jennifer, for love it surely was. I was sick of keeping it to myself. I poured out my feelings, telling how I had met her, what had happened between us, how for two days I had been on the verge of losing my mind out of loneliness for her and the fear that I was a coward. It was a good feeling to let it all out.

"Love is a rough thing at times," McCuen said. "I was a married man at one time. She left me, and for a long time I did nothing but mourn and drink and cry. And I discovered something in all that—there's no pat answer, no tricks or gimmicks that can ease the pain that loving someone can cause. And there can be real pain, I can tell you, and you know that anyway. Loving someone is a bit like gambling—you lay your heart and feelings out before them, and sometimes you win. And sometimes you don't. And that can hurt. It's a gamble, for sure. You can't win without putting something on the line, without taking a risk.

"There's no reason to give up on Jennifer yet. She's been through a lot, and she needs time to think, just like you, just like all of us. If she cares for you she'll come back. If she doesn't . . . then you'll know you never really had any hold on her in the first place.

"And as for your feeling about being a coward—well, I'm not even going to try to answer that. I can't. That's something a man can only answer for himself, something only he can decide. But I will tell you this: I see no reason to think you are anything less than a brave man. And I think with time you'll realize that I'm right. But I'm not the sort to hand out advice very much, for there's not anything much more useless, and so I think I'll just shut up."

I wanted to say something to him, to thank him for his words, but I didn't get the chance, for the door opened and in walked Jed Bacon. With him was a stranger, a tall man with dark hair and eyes. Both of the men looked very serious.

CHAPTER 15

THE stranger's name was Nathan Thorne. Bacon informed us that Thorne was an agent of the United States Secret Service.

"I came to Mr. Bacon only last night," said Thorne. "As you might have already guessed, I'm coming to you in connection with Josiah Madison. I've been on his trail for years, along with half a dozen other government agents. He's evaded us all along, just like a slippery snake. From what I understand, you men have had the most recent contact with our friend Madison. I'm glad I found you here, Mr. Hartford. It makes things much more convenient."

"What can we tell you about Madison that you don't know already?" asked McCuen. "About the closest contact I've had with the man is when he or one of his men put this hole in my leg. I'll tell you everything I know, though."

Thorne produced a pad and pencil and sat down in the corner. McCuen told his version of the events of the recent past, then I did the same. Bacon had already talked to the man prior to their coming to the office. As Thorne took notes he nodded and frowned, grunting whenever something was said that he found particularly interesting. Something in his bearing made me careful of what I said, made me conscious of detail in the story, made me want to be as accurate as possible in every way. Thorne had a professional air about him, a no-nonsense approach to his work that let all of us know that he meant business when it came to capturing Josiah Madison.

That was a good thing to know. I was sincerely glad that someone was on the trail of the man who I loathed so much, not only for what he had done to my loved ones but also for making me look on myself as a coward. I looked at the tall, handsome Thorne. He was so unlike me, not the kind to turn his back on duty just because things got tight. I envied him.

I forced the thought away, reminding myself that I had just met Nathan Thorne; I had no evidence to prove that he was such a better man than me. It was only my depressed state that caused me to see him, and everyone else, as being my better. I felt a bit angry at myself. Self-condemnation had become a habit in the last two or three days, and I was growing weary of it, blasted weary.

"If you want to find Madison, look north of here," said Bacon. "I expect he's still in that general area. But I wouldn't advise you to go after him unless you're prepared to take on a little army single-handed. We were fools enough to go against him with only four men—there would be nothing to expect but death if you went after him alone."

Thorne stood and shook his head. "Don't worry. I have no intention of going against Madison alone. No intention at all."

"You have men with you?" McCuen asked.

Thorne responded with a look that conveyed its meaning perfectly: Official business—confidential. He pocketed his pad and pencil and shook each of our hands in turn.

"Thank you, gentlemen. You've been very helpful.

I make it my business to talk to any person that has
contact with Madison, no matter how slight. The information you have given me will go on record in Wash-
ington. I should tell you, I suppose, that if we manage
to get Madison to trial you might be called to testify.
He has a string of crimes to his name that couldn't be
printed in a dozen books, and your wound, Mr. Mc-
Cuen, is just a minor affair compared to what he has
done to other men. He's a beast, and I plan to catch
him. You will, of course, keep all we have said in confidence.''

Thorne slammed his hand hard against his hip to
punctuate his little speech, then turned on his heel and
walked out of the room. If I hadn't been so overwhelmed by his rather pretentious bearing, I might have
laughed at the almost military way in which he walked.
But comical though some of his traits might be, I sensed
that he was deadly serious in his intent to capture Madison. And if there was any man that could do it, it would
surely be someone like Thorne.

"Well, there goes a character," said Bacon, moving
over to the window. "But I guess it will take a man
like that, dedicated to his work, to ever bring in Madison."

I moved over beside Bacon. Thorne was walking
across the street toward the hotel, his shoulders straight
and his head held high. He was wearing a light gray hat
tipped to the side on his head. Very sharp.

"Pretty secretive about things, wasn't he?" I commented. "I wonder how much he knows that we don't.
He didn't seem too impressed when you told him to
look to the north for Madison. Maybe the one-eyed devil has moved on."

"Could be," said Bacon. "He could have covered a
lot of ground since we saw him last."

I asked McCuen if he minded my staying in his hotel

room until he was back on his feet. I would take care of expenses, of course. He seemed happy to agree.

"I've still got most of my stuff over there," he said. "Keep an eye on it, would you?"

After I left Bacon with McCuen I still felt the urge to roam. Being cooped up for the last two days inside Sam's little cabin had created a desire for open spaces and blue sky, and now seemed just the time to get a good dose of both. I headed south to the railroad depot and then eastward along the track. It felt good to walk and feel my blood pumping.

The air was fresh and pure, and it seemed to fill my lungs with an energy and vigor that then spread through my bloodstream. My legs grew slightly sore, for I had gotten little exercise in the past two days, yet it was a pleasant soreness, one that made me feel alive and well once more. I walked rapidly along the rails, taking in the scenery and remembering another time when I walked alongside the track—the time I met Jasper Maddux and then Jennifer.

The track appeared endless, stretching as far as my eye could see across the plains. Railroads fascinated me, and I had read of them as long as there had been talk of transcontinental rail service. Controversy had clouded their history from almost the earliest times, and greed had been the primary moving force that led to their creation. This particular line, the Northern Pacific, had only been complete since last year, but it had touched the whole nation in another way a decade before when a government loan had failed to come through to the financier of the line. The subsequent collapse of that financier had led the whole country into a five-year depression.

That had been about the same time that my own little farming empire in Tennessee had been steadily failing. Now, suddenly, there was hope once more. I had land now, even a herd of good cattle since Becky had left Sam's ranch in my hands. I hoped I could manage to give her more than half the profits. If I could simply get by this year I would be happy; she deserved much for what she had suffered.

With every step my mind grew clearer, my soul rose higher. Still the same fears plagued me—fears of cowardice, fear that I might lose Jennifer—but no longer did they overwhelm me. I felt something like happiness again.

It was then I saw, further down the track, a straggler, apparently very drunk, for he was weaving about as he stumbled along. He wore no hat and carried nothing with him. I stopped and watched him, debating whether or not to continue, for I had no desire to be hounded for money or a drink. He must have been *very* drunk, for it seemed it was almost impossible for him to stand at all. He would rise, then progress a few halting steps before collapsing onto his hands and knees, pushing himself up, then going through the same procedure again. As I drew nearer a suspicion began to plague me. Maybe this man wasn't drunk . . . maybe he was hurt in some way. It could be that he had fallen off the train. I knew from personal experience that such an occurrence could happen far more easily than most might think.

There was only one way to check out this character, and that was face to face. I trotted along quickly. I reached him only seconds after he fell for one last time, now apparently unable to push himself up at all. I knelt beside him and immediately saw what his problem was.

There was a tremendous knot on the back of his skull. This man had been struck by some very hard object, for the skin was laid open and blood trickled down the back of his neck. Gently I rolled him over onto his back. His eyes were still open, though they seemed quite dull and glazed. His tongue and lips were moving, as if he was trying to speak, but no words would form and only faint grunts emerged from his throat. This fellow was in bad shape, very bad.

"Easy, mister, easy," I said. "I'll get you into town so the doctor can take care of you. First thing to do, though, is get you off this track. Can you stand up if I help you?"

I wasn't at all sure that he understood anything I said, but it seemed to me that he nodded slightly. So with great effort I pulled him to his feet. He leaned against me, moaning, and his feet seemed to be like weights of lead at the end of weak, quivering legs. Still, though, I managed to get him far off the track and into the shade of some low, scrubby bushes that grew on the crest of a little bank of dirt.

I made him as comfortable as possible, speaking words of comfort and trying to position him so that no pressure was placed against his ugly head wound. Obviously he had been either struck by some very vicious person, or else he had pounded his head against the track after a fall from the train. Either way, I felt absolutely no assurance that he would live for even the next few minutes.

I estimated I had walked about two miles from town. Obviously I could not carry this man back on my shoulders, and I had no horse or wagon. The only thing to do was to get to the road and try to wave down a passing wagon or buckboard and persuade the driver to carry this man into town.

Leaving him alone, I ran to the main road. There was no traffic for a long time, until at last a buggy approached. The driver was a very unpleasant-looking old man, and he ran right past me, cursing as I tried to wave him down. Angry, I kicked a stone after him as the buggy creaked on down the road.

There was no other passerby for almost an hour, and

I began to worry about the wounded man, lying there alone on the hard ground. How long he had been wandering down the track I could not guess; he might be terribly thirsty and weak. I was just starting back to check on him when a wagon approached. This time the driver was not so crabby, and when I explained the situation to him he seemed glad to help.

Together we went to the wounded man and carried him carefully back to the wagon. We made him as comfortable a possible, laying him atop some empty cloth sacks and resting the back of his neck on a little pillow made with sacks stuffed inside a burlap bag. The driver urged the two horses on at full speed, and we reached Miles City in what I guessed was record time.

It took another thirty minutes to locate the doctor, who was drinking alone in the corner of a saloon. As I expected, he acted as if my request for him to treat the injured man was an intrusion into his privacy. But with considerable complaining he at last came along.

I think McCuen could have broken into a dance routine in spite of his wounded leg when the doctor informed him that he was going to at last be evicted from the bed in the office. Apparently the man I had brought in needed more immediate care than McCuen in the good doctor's opinion, so at last my friend was being set free from his upstairs prison. He wasted no time in getting across to the hotel for a bath and shave, smiling in spite of the soreness of his leg.

I loitered around the office long enough to hear the doctor's verdict.

"He took a hard blow. If my guess is right, it wasn't the result of falling off a train—that man was struck deliberately by someone who didn't care how much damage he did. But I don't think the man will die. He might be unconscious for a day or so, but then I expect he'll come around. He didn't have no wallet nor money nor name anywhere on him. I reckon if he does die I'll have to come to you for the bill.''

Fool doctor, I thought. Blasted money-hoarding old billy goat. All he apparently thought of was hard cash. But he was the best the town had at the moment. I agreed to pay the bill if the man didn't survive, then left in a huff.

I saw Nathan Thorne emerging from the hotel just as I descended the stairs. He was dressed roughly, looking a good deal more like a cowboy than a government agent. For some reason I felt rather surprised to see him decked out as he was in denim pants, home-spun shirt, vest, and gunbelt. In his hands was a bag, which I guessed held his possessions. He moved on across the street and toward the depot. The whistle of an approaching train carried across in the summer breeze, and I wondered if he was preparing to leave.

And where he was going must surely be where Madison was. I was intrigued. The train was approaching from the east, so surely Thorne was preparing to go west. Could Madison have moved in that direction? He had been on the run for days now. In that time he could have reached Billings, Bozeman, even—the thought brought me up short and sent a chill through me—even Helena. What if Madison had gone to Helena, the very place Jennifer now lived?

It didn't take much thought to realize the consequences such a move might entail. If Madison saw Jennifer he would surely try to kill her, for clearly he would want no one alive who could so readily identify him. If Madison had gone to Helena, Jennifer would have no knowledge of the danger she was in. Madison could reach her, even kill her, before she had any idea of what was happening.

Thorne was still moving toward the depot. On impulse I followed him. Maybe he wasn't going to catch the train after all. Maybe he was just going to meet someone. I prayed that it was true. If he boarded that train and headed west, then my fears would surely be confirmed. I tried to remind myself that there were many places west of Miles City other than Helena, and that there was no reason to suppose that Madison would pick out that particular spot among all the possibilities open to him. He might have gone into the mountains to avoid capture. But still . . .

I stayed out of view of Thorne until we reached the depot. There I loitered just around the corner from him, within earshot of his low whistling, and waited. The train pulled up to a stop, and within minutes passengers began to emerge, while a handful of waiting people on the station porch gathered up bags and prepared to board. I breathed a little easier when I saw that Thorne was not among them.

A man dressed in dirty riding clothes stepped off the train and looked across the crowd. Upon seeing Thorne he moved quickly over to him. I tried not to breathe, wanting to hear what was said.

"Hello. Have you learned anything?" The man had a soft, whisper-like voice.

"A little. Nothing to really help. Here . . . take this and get rid of it in Billings. I'll leave tomorrow. Wait for me in Livingston.

"Something has come up, something I'll have to take care of. I thought our friend was out of the way, but I was wrong. They brought him into the doctor's office just awhile ago. It could be trouble for us if he talks. I'll have to eliminate that problem as soon as I can."

The shock that crept over me as I listened to those words was intense. Thorne was talking about the man I had carried into town, the one who might even now be dying in the doctor's office! Could it have been Thorne that opened up that hideous gash in the man's head? But why?

Thorne talked for a bit longer with the stranger, but the words were so quietly spoken that I could not hear enough to understand. My curiosity was aroused along with a feeling of repulsion. Judging from what Thorne had said I suspected that he had murder in mind. Murder! The thought was enough to make me shudder. I began to doubt the validity of Thorne's claim to work with the government. Something was going on here that I didn't understand. What secret did the man lying in the doctor's office hold that Thorne did not want revealed?

The man talking to Thorne boarded the train again, taking the bag with him. Thorne turned to walk around the corner and back to town, and I escaped detection only by slipping into a side doorway just as he passed. I watched him moving back toward town, and being careful to remain inconspicuous, I slipped out to follow him.

He walked past the doctor's office without stopping, though he glanced up the staircase. I fancied I could read the thoughts racing through his mind.

I had no idea what information the unidentified victim inside the office held, but I was determined to find out. Obviously there was some connection with Madison, and that made it of great interest to me. Thorne, whoever he might be, had come to Miles City impersonating an agent of the Secret Service, asked questions about Josiah Madison, putting on quite an act. Now, by sheer accident, I had discovered his involvement in what was at least attempted murder. And if his words to his strange companion at the depot were any indication, there would be another attempt later.

I paused on the street after Thorne again entered the hotel. What to do? Should I tell McCuen or Bacon what

I had seen and heard? A dreadful possibility crossed my mind. What if Thorne was, as he claimed, a Secret Service agent? I had never thought that any government representative would ever sanction or take part in murder, but then I had no way to prove that conviction was accurate. Yet I could not shake the feeling that Thorne was an imposter. Anything I did would have to be based on that assumption.

I decided to let McCuen in on this, for I could think of no clear course of action. I climbed the stairs and found McCuen fumbling with his tie. He had only just finished bathing and dressing. With his beard gone and his hair washed and combed he looked like a new man.

When I told him what had happened he appeared a bit confused. The story sounded wild, I realized, yet I knew it to be accurate, for I had heard Thorne's conversation myself. McCuen sat down on the edge of his bed and frowned.

"This whole affair gets more unbelievable as things go on," he muttered. "But if what you say is true I think you are right in expecting something to happen. If Thorne plans to finish off the man you brought in I expect he would do it tonight. Things would be much too risky in the daylight. Let's get back over to the office and see how the man is. Maybe he's come around and can tell us something to give us a clue."

We crossed the street and climbed up the stairs. McCuen limped noticeably, though he tried to pretend his leg was alright. We met the doctor coming out as we reached the top of the stairs.

"Ain't no point in goin' in there," he said. "Your friend died a few minutes ago."

Now that was a shock. It threw everything into a new light. And it knocked out our chance to find out what Thorne was up to.

McCuen touched the doctor's shoulder. "Doc, if you

don't mind, you could do us a mighty big favor. Are you heading out to get the undertaker?''

"Yes.''

"I would rather you hold off on that right now. I have reason to believe that a murder attempt has been planned against the man in there.''

"Murder attempt? But that ridiculous. He's dead already!''

"I know that, but the murderer does not. Doctor, I'm taking you into my confidence on this. I'm a Secret Service agent, and that man who just died was one of my partners. This is serious government business, Doctor, and we need your cooperation.''

I almost laughed at the serious way in which McCuen bluffed the doctor, but apparently his story was believed, for the grizzled old fellow's eyes widened and his breath came quickly.

"No! Are you serious? You're a government agent?''

McCuen nodded. "Yes. And this is my partner. We're traveling anonymously, so we'll have to trust to your strict silence in this matter.''

The doctor nodded and grinned. For the first time I noticed he didn't have any teeth.

"You got it, mister. What do you want me to do?''

McCuen pulled a few bills from his pocket and placed them in the man's hand. "Go over to the hotel and check into a room. Buy yourself a hot meal, a few drinks, anything you want. But leave the office just as it is. If there's to be any murder attempt we don't want the killer to know his victim is already dead. But remember—you must never say a word of this to anyone. Do you understand?''

The white-haired old man grinned and winked. "You betcha. Thanks a lot, partner.'' He started down the stairs, then turned suddenly. "What about the bill for that feller?'' he asked. "You gonna pay it?''

It was my turn to bluff this time around. "You'll receive full payment and more from the federal government within two weeks," I said. That seemed to please him, for he grinned once more and headed on down the street to the nearest saloon. I expected he would blow most or all of what McCuen had given him on liquor.

"What now, McCuen?"

"We wait. And we watch. I expect that our friend Thorne will make his move tonight, if what you suspect about him is accurate. And I would be willing to bet that it is. I don't believe Thorne is any more a Secret Service agent than I am."

CHAPTER 16

IT happened largely as we expected. It was well after dark when Thorne emerged from the hotel. McCuen and I stood in the doorway of a deserted building, nothing more than a rickety shack, and watched him move slowly across toward the doctor's office. Very calm he was, doing nothing that would draw attention. He did not mount the stairs immediately, but instead stood at the end of the boardwalk, smoking and watching people pass, listening to the music from the saloons that lit up the street with the glow spilling from their crowded interiors. Then, as if he were doing nothing out of the ordinary, he crushed out his cigar and slowly began moving up the stairs. McCuen and I shifted our positions to make sure we could see everything.

Thorne knocked on the door and waited, then knocked again, this time with more force. When he was satisfied that the doctor was not inside, he produced something from his vest pocket—though I was too far away to be certain, I took it to be a file—and began prying at the lock. In only moments he had forced the door open and was inside.

He must have remained in the office for no more than a minute before he again emerged, this time trotting down the steps gingerly, whistling a tune. It made me shudder, knowing that he rejoiced over the death of a

man. I'm sure he had stabbed him before even checking
to see if he was awake, for I noticed a large knife
strapped to his belt. Obviously he had fired no shots, so
the blade must have been the weapon. I doubted that he
had noticed his victim was already dead.

He headed for the livery stable then, and within moments had emerged, mounted on a white horse. Where
he had got the animal I couldn't guess; he had ridden
the train into Miles City, I assumed. Probably he had
bought the horse earlier today, maybe even stolen it.
But wherever the animal had come from, it was rapidly
carrying its rider out of town—toward the west, I noted.

It was what we had expected, and we were ready for
it. We moved to where our own horses were hidden,
already saddled and ready, and then we were after him,
moving swiftly along his trail. McCuen was having a
hard time of it, I could tell, for the jolts of his horse
made his leg painful, but still he kept up with me, moving rapidly and surely. Where Nathan Thorne went we
would go.

We left Miles City and the light of the saloons and
brothels, and moved into the darker plains. It would be
tricky, following Thorne in this darkness without drawing too near, but we managed to do it. Occasionally we
would lose sight of his faint, small form far ahead of
us on the grasslands, but always we would find him
again. Where he was going I could not tell. I supposed
that his main purpose was to simply get away from town
to avoid suspicion in the death of the stranger in the
doctor's office.

We were following the railroad, moving rapidly until
we were well away from town. Then Thorne slowed,
and we watched him move into an area of scrubby brush
and low hills like shallow, rounded bumps on the land.
And it was then that we lost him.

How he managed to disappear so totally I never was

able to figure out. Partly it was an unexpected surge of darkness that came when clouds obscured the moon; partly it was because the man obviously was accustomed to life on the plains and knew very well how to take care of himself. I don't think he had any notion that he was being followed; probably he pulled whatever magical evasive action that had let him escape simply as a routine gesture. But one thing was beyond doubt: he was gone, and we would not find him.

"Well, if that doesn't beat all!" exclaimed McCuen. "All of this for nothing. But he is heading west, just like his partner earlier today. Madison must be in that area."

That was a conviction I shared. Again I reminded myself that just because he had moved west was no reason to believe he was going to wind up in Helena. But again there was always the possibility that he would. And then, what of Jennifer?

"Let's go back to Miles City," I said. "There's things I need to do."

"Don't tell me . . . you're going to Helena, aren't you?"

"Yes. This time I'm not running from Madison. I'm tired of thinking of myself as a coward, and it's high time I proved to myself that I'm not. C'mon. We're wasting time."

There really was no hurry about our getting back, but I was filled with determination and wanted to get things underway. I would go to Helena and find Jennifer. If Madison showed up I would do whatever was necessary to protect her from him, and I would bring her back where she belonged. That was most important—to get her back with me again. And if she wouldn't return, then I was ready to throw my previous plans to the wind and live in Helena—anything to be close to her.

I got little sleep later that night, for I was gathering

my possessions and preparing for the journey. It was
really unnecessary; there would not even be a train
through until the day after tomorrow. But I was too
excited to wait. If I couldn't go tomorrow I could at
least make preparations.

The next day seemed endless. All I could think of
was Jennifer. I went to bed early to prepare myself. I
would need all of my energy for the trip.

McCuen saw me to the station, and I was off for
Helena. I rode third class.

The coach was full of every breed of humanity, all
crowded into an oblong car and seated on rough, narrow
benches. I looked over the group. Some were obviously
cowboys and homesteaders, some ranchers, making
short-term trips. There were many stops all along the
line, and the crowd, I knew, would fluctuate constantly.
There were other persons on board that obviously were
not part of the short-term traffic of the railroad. Some
had a look about them that told they were in a strange
land. I guessed them to be immigrants, from where I
could not know. Maybe Ireland, Germany, almost any
other place. I expected somehow that as the years went
by there would only be more and more of them, coming
from every part of the globe to try to make a success
somewhere on the plains. I could easily imagine that
what they saw out the windows of the car was not quite
what they had expected. It was no promised land. Yet
there was hope in the land, a chance for success. The
railroads provided the means of travel and also much of
the available land.

Yet in a sense the railroad was a barrier to the success
of the immigrant, for land that had before been in the
public domain, free for the taking, was now being held
by the railroad as a result of the immense land grants
given by the government to finance the building of the
line. So the penniless and destitute couldn't make claims

of free land as they could a few years ago. It was now a matter of paying anywhere from two to five dollars an acre for railroad property.

Many of those coming to Montana came, like me, to get into the cattle business. Others came to try their hand at farming the plains. I had considered that myself, but I knew enough to realize that it would take far more land to make a go of it in this country than it did in the east. A handful of farmers managed to eke out a living in the more fertile portions of the state, but in most of Montana it was cattle ranching that was the basis of the territory's economy.

The car was filled with smoke from numerous pipes and cigars, and most people were sitting silently, with a few obnoxious exceptions. Two women, one with a mouth well-stuffed with snuff and the other with a horrid-smelling pipeful of tobacco, sat talking in loud and coarse voices toward the front of the coach. Their language would have embarrassed a sailor, and I saw many young mothers holding the ears of their children beneath cupped palms to block out the voices. This, naturally, only made the children all the more interested in hearing what the old ladies were saying. As always, the forbidden fruit was the most desired.

The car rode roughly, rocking from side to side far more than I would have liked, and my palms were moist with sweat. I shifted constantly in my seat, for the hard wood of the bench was uncomfortable. At last a conductor came wandering down the aisle, selling small, straw-stuffed pillows at a ridiculously high price. Though it hurt me to do it, I bought one. It was a relief for awhile, but then the dry straw became matted and hard and I might as well have thrown the blasted thing out the window for all the good it was doing me. All the bad memories of my train ride to the Montana Territory came rushing back.

We stopped in Hathaway to pick up new passengers, and a few people got off. I was among them, for I was very hungry, and I saw a lady hawking biscuits and ham on the station platform. I purchased three of the delights, along with a tin of milk (rather warm but still satisfying), and climbed back onto the train just in time. Engineers wasted little time at stops; they often did not give passengers more than twenty or thirty minutes to eat lunch.

I walked down the narrow aisle back toward my bench, doing my best to avoid trodding on feet that stuck out into the aisle while at the same time balancing my food and milk. I was taken aback when I discovered that one of the men who had just come aboard the train—a bearded man with very dark hair and a black suit and hat—had seated himself in the very spot I had vacated to buy my meal. I looked at him for a moment, unsure of whether or not I should ask him to move or simply look for a seat elsewhere.

"Oh, I beg your pardon—this was your seat, sir?" He was a polite enough fellow, at least.

"Well, yes . . . but keep it. I can sit over here."

"I think we might both have room if I move over . . . there. If you would like some company I would be glad to provide it. I know few people around here. It gets rather lonesome."

Whether or not I should trust the fellow I did not know, but after a moment's thought I gave a shrug and sat down. I said nothing as I began to munch my meat and biscuit and sip my milk. After a moment I noticed he was watching me eat from the corner of his eye. Letting out a sigh that was louder than I intended, I asked him if he would like one of the biscuits. Of course it was simply a polite gesture, and I knew he would not accept. Or thought I knew, for he smiled and grabbed the largest of the biscuits and began to gobble it down.

I was greatly irritated, but tried not to show it. After all,
I *had* offered it to him.

"Thank you so much, sir . . . I hadn't eaten since
early yesterday evening." He extended a hand covered
with biscuit crumbs, but before I could take it he with-
drew it and began picking off the crumbs and popping
them in his mouth. This fellow didn't intend to waste a
bit of his free lunch.

"Barnabas Runyon," he said. "Man of the west,
womanizer, occasional preacher, and mostly gambler—
that's what I am. And you?"

I really didn't want to talk to Runyon, but I knew no
way to get out of it. "Jim Hartford. I live north of Miles
City."

"Ah, yes! Miles City is one of my favorite spots on
God's green earth. I won over two thousand dollars
there in one evening at a game of stud poker. If I hadn't
stolen a horse and took off at top speed I would be
moldering in a grave with rope burns around my neck.
Folks don't often take kindly to losing all they own to
a stranger. But that's how it goes, the way I look at it.
Don't sit down at the table if you aren't willing to lose.
Lord knows I've lost enough myself."

"That's how it goes." I had no desire to continue
the conversation, and I did my best to end it. But no
matter. Barnabas Runyon was in a mood to talk.

"I'm heading for Helena," he volunteered, and the
news was not welcome. "Are you getting off there or
going on through?"

"I'm getting off. I'll be looking up some friends
there." I deliberately tried to sound glum and un-
friendly, hoping he would realize that I was looking
neither for conversation or companionship. It didn't
work.

"Great! Perhaps we'll run into each other. If you
spend any time in the saloons I'll guarantee you'll see

me. I intend to leave Helena a wealthy man, Mr. Hartford. I'm broke down to my last dollar at the moment. That's why I'm riding a third-class immigrant coach instead of the first-class car. I've won many a dollar hustling the high and mighty that ride in the first-class coaches. If we were both sitting in one of them right now I wouldn't be telling you all this about myself. Instead I would be doing my best to get you into a friendly game of chance. And chances are I would walk away with every cent you had on you. Yes sir. I'm a gambler, and a fine one.''

And a braggart and a loud mouth buffoon, I added mentally. This man was almost as irritating in his continual blabbing as was Bradley Sullivan when he talked about sheep herding. It was only with great effort that I managed to remain polite.

"Helena is a wonderful city in many ways, yet it can be a rough one, too. It started as a mining town, and after that it did nothing but grow and thrive, even after the gold ran out. But it didn't run out until nineteen million dollars' worth of the stuff had been dug out. Nineteen million! It's enough to make my mouth water. I got my hands on a little of it myself—not digging it out, mind you, but winning it off of miners at the poker table. Last Chance Gulch, they called it when it first opened up. It was the richest strike north of Virginia City. Helena was a wonderful town in those days.

"But a man had to watch his step mighty close, or he might wind up swinging from a tree limb somewhere. There wasn't any real law to speak of in the mining days, so folks pretty much had to provide their own. A man guilty of a crime didn't have much chance around Helena—nor an innocent one, if he stood too close to a guilty one. If in doubt, string 'em up. That was pretty much the way folks looked at it back then. Had a tree in town—the 'Hanging Tree,' they called it—

and folks didn't waste much time on trials. Yes sir. A man had to watch his step in Helena.''

Runyon talked some more, and after a while I quit listening. I nodded occasionally, and grunted every now and then as if I was listening closely to what he said, but on my mind was a face, a lovely face, the face of Jennifer. It made me feel warm inside to know that with every mile I grew closer to where she was.

I had come to the Montana Territory with a dream, a dream of success. Yet now it had changed, altered somehow. It had divided in two, making room for another besides myself. I looked past Runyon and on out across the grassland. It was alien, a strange world. But I could conquer it—me, a misplaced Tennessee farmer, if she was beside me. If she wasn't, then I had no desire to even fight. Never, never had I met anyone like her. Never before had I even imagined I could feel about someone the way I felt about Jennifer.

My mind drifted to Madison. Where was he? All the evidence indicated that he was in the western portion of the territory. But that was a large region, and very rugged. Even if by chance Madison did come to Helena, it would only be a slight possibility that he would encounter either me or Jennifer. But something was pulling me on—the desire to protect Jennifer even against such a remote threat as Madison, the desire to prove to myself that I would not run. I would not act a coward this time if I should meet my enemy.

Runyon had talked himself to sleep, and for that I was grateful. It was going to be hard to get any rest on this hard bench, and with Runyon dozing beside me I found it almost impossible to position myself into anything resembling a comfortable position. I could have shaken him awake and had him move, but I was not about to do anything that might set that talking machine in action again. So I shifted and turned, and at last dozed off.

I awoke when the train lurched to a stop. We had pulled up to one of the innumerable stations along the way. Again there was a change in the population of the coach, and then once more we were on our way. The two foul-mouthed ladies got off at this stop, which made me very happy, but Runyon came awake again, and once more I was listening to a seemingly endless discourse.

Night fell, and I traded seats with Runyon. I wanted to look out across the vastness of Montana, to see the rugged land, and mostly to dream of Jennifer. And that I did, even after I had drifted off to sleep.

CHAPTER 17

I stood on the street in Helena with my bag in my hand, realizing that I did not even know the name of Jennifer's uncle nor where his store was located. Runyon was beside me, grinning broadly and breathing in the fresh air with loud sniffs of satisfaction.

"Ah, Helena, you're even better than I remembered you!" he exclaimed. "You're a town of gold, and I intend to take a good chunk of you away with me!"

I found Runyon's cheerfulness to be a little irritating, for I was pondering a problem. Where should I go? I looked at the row of stores and saloons lining the street. Jennifer was probably in one of the those stores, though I had no idea which one. All I knew what that her uncle was a merchant, and that was a feeble clue. Only his relationship to the famous Luther Guthrie might help me find him.

"Well, are we going to stand here all day or are we going to look for a place to stay?" Runyon said. Apparently, I realized, he intended for us to stay together. At first I started to protest, but then I thought better of it. I knew no one here. A companion who was familiar with Helena might come in handy, and Runyon might be able to help me find Jennifer's uncle.

"There's a hotel over there," I pointed out. "How about us checking in there?"

Runyon frowned. ''You haven't seen their prices. They'll charge you an arm and leg for a bed and more for any extras. Down the street a little further is some other rooms—see the sign? Twenty-five cents a night. It isn't fancy, but it's cheap.''

So to the little weatherboarded building we went. I didn't really like the look of the place, and when I entered the tiny room I was given I felt even more negatively inclined toward it. The bed was dusty, and I suspected several people had slept on the sheets now on it since it was last changed. I noticed the legs of the bed were sitting in little tins of some sort of liquid. I knelt down to smell it. Kerosene. I knew the purpose of it; this room was infested with bedbugs, and the containers of kerosene were there to keep them out of the bed. But when I plopped my bag down on the sagging mattress I saw one of the loathsome creatures scurry off to safety. I was almost itching already, just anticipating the night to come.

I was so hungry that I couldn't even think of beginning to look for Jennifer until I had eaten a good meal. I headed back outside to my companion, who had already dumped his few possessions in the next room.

''Well, Hartford, let's grab a meal somewhere. I'm as empty as a church house on Saturday night.''

We found a pleasant-looking cafe immediately, and I turned to go inside. Runyon held back.

''I think I'll go on down a little further to the saloon. The food won't be too great, I expect, but maybe I can get into a little poker game and win some cash.''

I nodded and went on in. The interior was dark and cool, and I removed my hat and enjoyed the coolness against my forehead. I sat down at a table and ordered a meal from the plump, friendly-looking woman who was hustling about the place, seemingly doing ten things at once. Let Runyon have his saloon and gambling table; I would stick to the simpler pleasures of a hot meal and a good cup of coffee.

I looked out into the street as I ate, watching people passing, wondering what it must have been like in the days when the strikes were pouring out gold like an endless stream. Surely there had been a tremendous excitement in those days—there must have been—an excitement that might never again be experienced in the history of the nation. To think of a town springing up within a few days in a spot that had before been only wilderness—Lord, that was something amazing. And it had happened all over the west, anywhere where some lonely prospector had turned up a chunk of shiny gold in his pan. Sam had been a part of that years before, back in Confederate Gulch, right after the war, when the rich deposits there turned out somewhere between ten and thirty million dollars' worth of gold. There had been a time when almost ten thousand people had swarmed around the region east of Helena, named Confederate Gulch in honor of the four men from Georgia that had first discovered the wealth buried in the land. It must have been quite a time! New towns rising up quickly to die as fast when the gold ran out or when fire ravaged the tinderbox buildings; men walking the streets with pockets heavy with gold dust; women calling out from tents and buildings along the way, offering themselves for that same gold; men like Runyon seated around tables in the saloons, trying to strike it rich in their own way without putting a hand to a pick or shovel. It must have been a time worth seeing. Certainly it was a time that would never come again.

I finished my meal and paid the bill. I moved back outside, squinting in the sunlight until my eyes adjusted to the brilliance. Runyon had gone into the saloon only a couple of doors down from the cafe. I decided I would find him and tell him who I was searching for. Obviously a man with a relative as famous as Luther Guthrie would be known to most of the people who had been around Helena for any length of time. Maybe Runyon could tell me just where to look.

I pushed my way into the saloon and glanced around until I saw Runyon seated at a corner table, studying his hand of cards. I headed toward him, then stopped suddenly in my tracks.

He was gambling with a man that looked terribly familiar, though I couldn't recall where I had seen him before. He was thin, with a red beard, and something about him filled me with caution. I stood transfixed for a moment, then the memory of a voice came back to me . . . a voice saying something about lightning striking and somebody's uncle biting his tongue in two.

Then I remembered. This was one of the fellows that had been hidden in the hills behind Guthrie's ranch that night, the night of the thunderstorm that had almost seared me with a flash of lightning. One of Madison's men, one of the riders. So they *were* here, they really had come to Helena, just as I feared. But where was Madison? He was not in the saloon, and the other man dealing cards with the red-bearded man and Runyon I had never seen before. I backed out through the door again, then peeped around the corner so I could keep an eye on the fellow. He was obviously unhappy about something; probably Runyon was cleaning him out with some sly deals.

That must have been the case, for suddenly the red-bearded man stood, his face growing so scarlet with apparent rage that I could hardly tell where the skin stopped and the beard began. He pushed his chair back violently and spoke in a loud voice.

"Why don't you try dealin' from the top of the deck, mister? I'm sick of your cheatin'—you'd best be prepared to take a lickin', 'cause I'm gonna take back my money right outta your skin.''

The other man gambling with the pair backed away and headed out a back door. The bartender was watching Runyon and his challenger very closely, and the air in the room prickled as if with an electrical charge. Trouble not only was coming—it was here.

Runyon looked as cool as a trout in a frozen pond, never once blinking or looking frightened. Obviously this was no new game to him; he wasn't about to be taken by surprise by anything this fellow might pull. I recalled that Madison had called him Jake.

"When you accuse a man of cheating, it's a mighty serious charge," Runyon said calmly. "Some have died for less than that."

"And plenty have died for dealin' crooked cards, too," spit back Jake. "You'd best be prepared to tangle, 'cause nobody cheats Jake Crocker and gets away with it."

Runyon was up so fast that I couldn't tell what had happened until I saw Jake Crocker standing with a derringer aimed straight at his nose, the muzzle no more than two inches away from him. For a moment he and Runyon stood there in silence, and I wondered if my gambling companion was about to resort to murder.

"Get your tail outta my sight, and don't come around me again with your lies about cheating," growled Runyon. "I ought to shoot you, but you wouldn't be worth the wasted bullet. Now clear out."

I barely had time to step out of the way before the frightened man swept past me, not looking back one time. He mounted his horse and took off at a gallop, heading south. South. Maybe that was where Madison was holed up. If only I had a horse—I could follow Jake at a distance and find out for sure.

But that was impossible. He was out of sight quickly.

I entered the saloon. Runyon was pouring a shot of whiskey and laughing for all he was worth. He raised his glass in greeting when he saw me enter.

"Mr. Hartford! You just missed the fun! Come and join me in a drink."

"No thanks. And you're wrong . . . I saw it all through the door. You do a pretty good job of taking care of yourself. But anyway, the reason I came in is I want to ask you a question. I'm looking for a local man, a merchant, who is related to Luther Guthrie. You know anyone like that?"

"Luther Guthrie . . . that's the cattleman, isn't it? I heard that he died a few days back."

"That's right. But do you know who that merchant might be?"

"I know, fella." It was the bartender speaking. "That would be Charles Cummins. He's a brother-in-law to Guthrie—Guthrie married his sister years and years ago. He runs a hardware store at the other end of town. Mighty pretty girl working with him now—Guthrie's daughter, I heard."

My heart leaped within me at the words. That was Jennifer he was talking about. She was alright, and soon I would see her.

"The other end of town—on this street?"

"No . . . next one over. You can't miss the store. It's two stories, painted white. The sign says 'Cummins Hardware.' "

I thanked the bartender and left him alone with Runyon. I headed down the street at a dead run, then turned the corner and headed toward the white building I could see at the other end of the street. I knew it was the hardware store even before I saw its sign. Halfway there I slowed, then stopped. Soon would come the meeting with Jennifer, and how she would react to my unexpected presence I had no idea. Steeling my nerves as best I could, I walked slowly toward the building.

It was a rather large place, two stories, with a multitude of plows, yokes, hoes, shovels, picks—all the things that were a part of the usual inventory of a western hardware store. And there were people about, too. Apparently Charles Cummins did a remarkable business. As I drew near I could see that the upstairs windows had lacy curtains, not the simple, functional ones like a business might have. I guessed that he lived above the store, and probably that was where Jennifer was staying.

My breath was coming rapidly as I mounted the porch, and I felt a cold sweat around my temples. Somehow I dreaded meeting Jennifer, yet I longed to see her. Probably I looked like an over-protective and over-anxious fool, running all the way from Miles City just to protect her from some vague threat, but now I knew that the move had been a wise one, for I had concrete evidence of Madison's presence in or near Helena. And besides that, I loved Jennifer, and I wanted to see her. And that, I emphasized to myself, was nothing to be ashamed of.

I looked inside before I entered, trying to find her. I didn't see anyone except a couple of men browsing about and looking over the stock of knives. A man in a canvas apron was behind the counter, figuring up a bill for a third customer. I took him to be Cummins. He finished his business and thanked the customer, then turned to greet me.

"Good day, sir. Anything I can do for you?"

Now this was a clumsy situation. I didn't know whether or not to try and explain who I was and why I was there, and for a moment I stammered unintelligibly, feeling a bit foolish.

"I beg your pardon?" he returned, frowning slightly.

"I'm looking for Jennifer Guthrie. Is she here?"

His face grew a bit cold then. He straightened up and inhaled audibly, eyeing me in quite a different manner than before.

"Why do you ask?"

I might have been offended at the question had I not understood the reason for it. Surely he knew about Madison and the threat he could pose to Jennifer should he ever find her, and his question was a protective measure.

"My name is Jim Hartford. I'm a . . . a friend of Jennifer from Miles City. Please—if she's here I'm sure she'll want to see me. May I speak to her?"

He looked doubtful, and for a time he said nothing. I felt embarrassed, but I could feel no anger toward him. Rather, I was glad that Jennifer was staying with someone who was so careful about her welfare. That's the way I wanted it.

"Sorry. There's no one here by that name. Now if there's nothing I can do for you, please excuse me. As you can see, there are customers I have to take care of."

That was that. I knew he would not let me see Jennifer no matter how persistent I might be. Feeling exasperated, I walked out of the store and back into the street.

I leaned up against the hitching post and thought the situation over. I knew Jennifer was somewhere in that store. She had not been downstairs, so obviously she must be in the upstairs living quarters. Now, if only I could get her attention somehow, without disturbing Cummins and maybe getting myself shot or run off at gunpoint . . .

I walked toward the alley between the store and the nest building, a bakery. I ducked the window to avoid being spotted by Cummins, then rounded the back corner of the building.

There was a rough, brown, unpainted shed of weath-

'ered wood built up against the back wall of the store. The roof was of old shingles, and it sloped up slightly to meet with the wall of the main building. There was a window there, leading into the upstairs portion of the store. I looked at it doubtfully, not sure whether I should try the scheme that was formulating in my mind.

But I had to see Jennifer. I hadn't come all the way to Helena to be deprived of that privilege. Looking around, I found an old barrel, half filled with stagnant water, which I overturned and emptied. A miniature brown river swirled about my feet as I positioned the barrel at the corner of the shed and stepped on top.

I got a good grip on the roof of the shed and began to heave myself upward. It was surprisingly difficult; I felt much older than I had realized. But with much grunting and straining I managed to get one foot hung over the top of the shingled roof, then with a tremendous heave I rolled over on top.

I stood carefully and dusted myself off. The roof upon which I was standing didn't look any too strong, and it was with a trembling step that I moved forward. I could see only a few feet into the darkness of the window, and from what I could tell there was no sign of anyone being inside.

I inched over to the window, grimacing as the shingles snapped and creaked under my boots. When at last I reached the window I grabbed for the sill. I wanted to lean my weight against something besides the rotting roof that was giving way at least two inches beneath my feet. I shifted my weight onto my hands and looked through the dusty glass.

The window opened into something that looked like a large closet or storage room. There were old pieces of furniture stacked in it, along with a mop and broom and a few old buckets, as well as cobweb-covered rolls

of cloth and piles of empty burlap sacks. I certainly
would not find Jennifer in there.

Now I really didn't know what to do. I thought about
trying to get the window open so I could crawl inside,
but that seemed a bit criminal. If I were seen I might
wind up in a cell instead of in Jennifer's arms. And
anyway, I didn't want to startle her by popping up from
nowhere. And to top it all off, the window was jammed.

Feeling rather ridiculous, I did the only thing possible—I tapped on the pane with my finger while softly
calling Jennifer's name. If she happened to be anywhere
near the storeroom she might hear me and let me inside.
I wanted to call out more loudly, but I couldn't risk
drawing the attention of anyone else.

For a long time I continued tapping and calling, but
with no result. It was then that I heard above me a soft
murmur, a kind of low, sustained hum that at first I
could not identify. I glanced up.

There were two cats, both toms, and they were squar-
ing off for battle right at the peak of the store's roof.
Their voices blended into a kind of weird harmony as
they looked closely at each other, every muscle stiff and
tense, the only movement being the twitching of their
whiskers and the back and forth movement of their tails.
It looked like it was going to be a humdinger of a fight.

But I didn't have time to watch a couple of brawling
animals, so I went back to tapping and calling for Jennifer. This time I did it a little more loudly, for obviously I was getting nowhere as it was. And at last I got
results, for I saw the latch of the storeroom door slowly
begin to turn, even as a sudden squalling above me her-
alded the commencement of war.

The door opened ever so slowly, and Jennifer's head
peeked around it. I grinned broadly and waved, so glad
to see her that I didn't even consider how strange the
whole situation must have appeared to her.

She looked at me in obvious disbelief, and I saw her mouth forming my name. Then she smiled, her eyes brightening, and she threw open the door and moved to the window.

"Jim!" Her voice was slightly muffled through the glass. "What in the name of heaven are you doing here . . . and out on the roof at that?"

"I can't explain right now," I returned. "If you can get this blasted window open I'll come inside. Your uncle apparently didn't think I looked very trustworthy. He wouldn't let me see you."

"Oh, I'm so glad you're here—you can't imagine how glad!" She smiled and put her palm up against the glass. "Here . . . let me see if I can get this window open . . ."

She grasped the metal grips at the base of the window and gave a strong push while I did the same from the outside. The window creaked and groaned but did not open.

"It's jammed, Jim," she said.

"I know. But I think it gave a little. Try it one more time."

We did, and this time it opened. I stood face to face with Jennifer, and it all seemed too wonderful to be true. But she reached out her hand and touched me, and I knew that it was no fantasy. All around me ceased to exist—the roof, the window, the fighting cats above— and Jennifer became the sole reality in my universe. Her touch was warm and tingled against my skin like electricity. At once the whole world glowed with magic.

I hugged her close then, and suddenly I knew I had to kiss her. I would never have thought such a thing would even cross my mind, but so happy was I to see her that nothing in the world seemed too much to expect. I looked into her eyes and drew her close. Her breath quickened and her soft lips moved close to mine . . .

Two clawing, screaming, fighting balls of hot fur struck directly atop my head. I cried out in shock and threw myself backward, forgetting that I clutched Jennifer in my arms. Right through the open window she came, and when the rotting roof gave way beneath our combined weights, she, both cats, and I all tumbled through to land in one huge heap on the floor of the shed.

Jennifer uttered a word I had no idea she had even heard before, and the two cats made a sudden peace treaty and scampered off together. I lay stunned, watching the door of the shed open and staring up into the muzzle of a Sharps and on past it to the angry and flabbergasted face of Charles Cummins.

"Jennifer . . . what . . . how . . ." He lowered the rifle and stared at his disheveled niece, and I felt like crawling away like a miserable rat.

CHAPTER 18

IT took quite a bit of time before Jennifer cooled down to the point she could convince her uncle that I wasn't a madman who had tried to carry her off. At last we got the whole confused mess cleared up, and I sat with a mug of hot coffee in my hand upstairs in Cummins' living quarters. He was seated across from me, apparently undecided about whether to like me, based on what Jennifer had told him, or to shoot me, based on what he had seen for himself. But no matter—at least he was accepting me. I had even received an invitation to move in with him and Jennifer, at least for a day or two. I would sleep on a pallet before the fireplace.

Cummins had closed the store when he heard that I had seen one of Madison's men in Helena. He had, of course, heard the story of our dealings with Madison from Jennifer, and he understood the danger the outlaw's presence posed to us. Jennifer was deeply concerned, and I myself felt quite apprehensive. "This whole situation is hard to believe. Did that Crocker fellow see you?" Cummins asked.

"No. He was too worried about his own skin to notice."

Jennifer sighed. "What are we going to do, Jim? If Madison is in Helena, then we're as bad off as before.

And if he lays eyes on either one of us . . . well, you
know what might happen.''

"I know, Jennifer. It isn't safe for either one of us
here. I don't know what you'll think about this suggestion, but I believe that we should catch the first train
back to Miles City. If Madison is here, I want to get
you away. I ran from him once—I'll never do it again,
not for my own sake. But I will take you away if it's
necessary to keep you safe.''

Cummins looked at me closely, his brow knit in
thought.

"He's right, Jennifer. You know I love you and really am glad to have you here with me, but there's no
point in staying if your life will be in danger. I think
Miles City is the place for you. And anyway, you must
realize that you own a large cattle ranch right now.
You'll have to take care of it. You can't hide forever.''

Jennifer turned on both of us, rage visible in her eyes.

"You don't understand—either one of you. I can't
go back there, not until I've had time to think, to get
used to the fact that Father is gone. The ranch is like a
sort of hell to me now—I can't turn a corner or open
my eyes in the morning without thinking of Father and
the way he died. You don't know what it's like. You've
never lost a father to a man like Josiah Madison.''

I responded quietly. "But I've lost a brother. And I
won't lose you.''

Jennifer glared at me. "What do you mean, 'lose
me'? Do you think I'm some possession of yours, something you own like a hat or a saddle? I think perhaps
you'd better think again, Mr. Hartford!''

She turned and stalked out of the room, and I felt my
face turning red. Cummins stood watching me, and that
made things not one bit easier.

I had presumed too much, it seemed. In the time I
had been away from Jennifer I had come to idolize her,

to look upon her as my own love. Now I was being forced to face the hard fact that it wasn't so. And that hurt pretty badly.

Cummins was obviously at a loss for words. The situation was a strange one for him. He had been dragged into it by chance, and he had at best only a sketchy knowledge of what was going on, in spite of the explanations he had heard from Jennifer. A sudden thought struck me: Cummins himself was not free from danger as long as Jennifer and I were near him.

"It will take her awhile to understand, Hartford," he said at length. "It must have been a hard blow, seeing her father die like he did. Luther Guthrie was not a gentle man, maybe even an unethical one, but he was always good to my sister and to Jennifer. I was truly sorry to hear of his death. I'm just glad that I was here. Jennifer needed someone to turn to."

I nodded and smiled at the man, but his words made me sad. How it would have thrilled me if Jennifer had turned to me in her time of grief! I would have loved to have been the one to dry her tears and comfort her. But that wasn't how it had been. Maybe I would just have to accept the fact that it would never be that way.

"I think we have one thing in our favor," said Cummins. "Madison has not seen either you or Jennifer around here, so obviously he won't be out looking for you. So as long as he doesn't know of your presence here you should be relatively safe."

"You said Jennifer wasn't here when I met you this afternoon," I said. "I assumed you were trying to protect her in case I was one of Madison's men. Am I right?"

"Yes, partly. I guess I just didn't like the idea of a stranger coming up unexpectedly and asking about her. Of course, I had no idea then that Madison was in these parts. And she had mentioned your name to me several times, but for some reason it slipped my mind when you introduced yourself. Sorry.''

"It's alright. I'm glad you're being careful with her. And I think it's good that you're keeping her up here away from the public eye. If Madison or one of his men came into town and saw her . . .''

"What about you? You could be just as easily recognized.''

"I know. I'll have to keep a low profile too. I think we belong in Miles City instead of here, but until Jennifer's ready to go I don't plan to force her.''

Cummins agreed. "I think you're right, Hartford. She'll go back when she's ready. Until then it will just be a matter of being careful.''

That was for sure. We would have to be darned careful.

I waited until dark before I headed back to the room I had rented. I took up my pack and headed out gladly. The bedbugs could feed on someone else tonight; I was glad to have the pallet on the floor upstairs in Cummins' store. I was out in the street before I thought of Runyon. He would be gambling half the night, probably. But still I should leave him a note so he wouldn't think my possessions had been robbed. I scribbled one quickly on the back of an envelope and tacked it to his door. I didn't say where I was, for I didn't want to chance having the wrong eyes see it and get a little too much information.

I was out the door when the proprietor of the place called me down and demanded twenty-five cents for the room. I was aghast.

"I haven't even slept in it! I'm not paying you a cent!''

"I could have rented that room to another feller earlier today, but you was in it. You done cost me twenty-five cents, and I expect you to make it up. Hand it over!''

And rather than stand and argue with him, I did.

I felt cheated as I climbed the stairs to my sleeping quarters and lay down on the pallet. Cummins was softly snoring in his own bedroom, and I could hear Jennifer softly stirring about in hers. Strange it was to be this close to her. But there was still a distance between us that made me feel helpless and alone. Maybe time would close that distance. I certainly hoped so.

The next day was spent upstairs in the soft chair beside the fireplace. Jennifer stayed with me, and I found the company quite pleasant. Her anger had passed, though she gave no indication that her opinions had changed. It was clear that she cared for me at least a little—I had abundant evidence of that from past experience. But clearly my feelings for her went far beyond anything she felt for me—or at least beyond what she allowed herself to show.

Cummins had a good library, and lately I had read little, so now I did my best to make up for it. Learning had always been a passion of mine, and the one thing I liked least about the farming life I had always led was the lack of time to study and read. I had always managed to squeeze it in between chores, but never enough to really satisfy me.

Cummins had plenty of good volumes, both from European and American writers. I noticed several volumes by Twain on his shelf. I had been delighted by the work of that humorist many times over, and I picked up some of his books and began leafing through them. The day passed by slow and drowsy as I sat in that comfortable chair reading, and I felt a sense of lazy contentment.

I looked further into Cummins' book collection. Works by Shakespeare were there, along with a volume of popular modern poetry and a few of Paine's treatises. And of course there was the inevitable Bible. Most of

the books were well-worn and dog-eared, showing tha
Cummins read as well as merely collected his books
And for that he gained my admiration, for I respecte
men of learning. I hoped someday to be one myself.

Jennifer looked restless as she wandered about th
place. I think the realization that we were pretty muc
prisoners here until the threat of Josiah Madison ha
passed was only just now beginning to strike hei
Maybe she would see the sense in my suggestion o
returning to Miles City, though I wasn't about to brin
it up. Jennifer had suffered much, and I would forc
nothing on her unless I saw there was no other choice
So I leaned back once more and again started reading

It was the middle of the afternoon when Cummin
came back upstairs, looking rather weary.

"It's blasted busy down there today," he said. "
almost wish you two were working for me. You know
Hartford, I had Jennifer at work the first day she wa
here, but then I got to thinking I shouldn't have her ou
in public. It was just kind of an instinctive thing whe
I took her off work, but I'm glad I did.

"Anyway, I came up to deliver this to you. A rail
road man brought it in a few minutes ago."

He handed me an envelope. I snatched it awa
quickly, intrigued. Who could be sending me mail here
And how did whoever it was know how to reach me?

The letter was from McCuen.

Dear Jim,

It took a lot of doing to find out where to reach you,
but I have information I thought you would like to
know. I hope this letter gets to you. I found out Mr.
Cummins' name by asking around among local folks
who know Guthrie's family.

As soon as you left for Helena I began thinking
things through. Obviously we have not done a very ef-

fective job of taking care of Madison, so I did what I now think we should have done in the first place—I went to Fort Keogh and notified the Army officials there about Madison, Thorne, and the whole business.

The reaction was predictable. While they were certainly glad to have the information, they were not at all pleased to be the last ones to find out about it. They did some checking on both Madison and Thorne. What they found out about our friend Nathan Thorne is worth knowing.

There is, in fact, a Nathan Thorne affiliated with the Secret Service. Madison's actions since the war have been considered subversive to the country, so the Secret Service has had Thorne and several other agents trying to trace the man down for years. And Thorne was scheduled to come to Miles City in response to the reports of Madison's presence here. The Fort Keogh staff knew he was coming, but his business here was unspecified to them.

The man you picked up on the railroad was checked over by the Fort Keogh doctor. Just as we thought, the man had been stabbed several times—after he was dead. And as you might suspect, checks by telegraph with Secret Service officials confirmed that the poor fellow matched the description of the true Nathan Thorne.

Which leaves some interesting questions. Why did our fraudulent Nathan Thorne take on the identity of a Secret Service agent and question us so closely about Josiah Madison? Why was he so dedicated to keeping his impersonation a secret that he was willing to murder the true Thorne? Does he have accomplices? If so, how many? Where does he get his information? Who was the man he met at the train station? And most of all, what is his interest in Josiah Madison?

There is something else you should know. Fort Ellis,

near Bozeman, has received reports that a group of armed men matching the description of Madison and his riders has been spotted southeast of Helena. How the Army plans to deal with it I don't know, but I hope you and Jennifer will be careful. In my opinion you would be well advised to return to Miles City.

I hope you are enjoying your stay in Helena. Be careful of Madison. Please send my regards to Miss Guthrie, and I shall remain:

Yours truly,
Aaron McCuen

I folded the letter and sighed. Sometimes it was hard to believe all of this was real.

"Anything we should know?" quizzed Cummins.

"Yes, I think so." I filled him in on what McCuen had found out, explaining all the details that he didn't yet understand. He looked concerned, but at the same time he expressed hope.

"I'm glad the Army is into this," he said. "Maybe they will take care of that scoundrel before anyone else is hurt. This is the sort of thing for them, not for ranchers' daughters and Tennessee farmers and hardware merchants."

The day passed without further incident, and clouds began to gather in the heavens as the last light faded. I looked out the window at the rolling masses of dark clouds high above the buildings of Helena. The city appeared stark and small in comparison to the majesty of the violent sky. I felt small, insignificant.

The darkness fell, and the wind began whipping wildly, howling around the eves and corners of the buildings like a mournful, disembodied voice. I felt the desire to step outside and feel that wind, laden with the taste and smell of the coming rain, whipping against my face and hair.

I looked up and down the street. Deserted. Even the saloons did not have the steady in and out flow of customers that usually began at this time of day. The storm promised to be a wild, rough one, and apparently the threat of its impending explosion of lightning and rain was sufficient to drive everyone to shelter. But I had been cooped up all day; I wanted to taste that moist, moving air.

Surely it was safe. I could not see any sign of another human presence anywhere in the street. I headed out the door and down the stairs, then out onto the porch of the store. The lightning had begun, illuminating the dark clouds and the bare, exposed buildings with every flash, and the rumble of thunder was almost constant. A few scattered drops of rain struck my cheek, whipped beneath the sheltering porch by the moaning, wailing wind, a herald of the downpour to come.

I glanced up and down the street, still worried that someone might see me. Madison and his men might have come into town on a night like this, for even outlaws want shelter from lightning and rain. I thought back on the time I had watched them in the hollow of the hills behind Guthrie's ranch. If Jake Crocker was out there in the wilderness near Helena, surely he was worrying himself sick again, dreading the lightning. Let him worry—a long way from me and Jennifer.

Satisfied that I was truly alone, I sat down on the edge of the porch and watched the sky. Majestic, huge, unforgettable it was. A vastness filled with clouds and energy, lit with flashes of fire like the sparks from some heavenly anvil. I became engrossed in watching it.

A searing bolt of lightning leaped across the sky, followed a moment later by a tremendous jolt of thunder that shook the very ground. The noise faded slowly, like a low rumble, diminishing into nothingness.

And in the silence I heard a new sound, one that

jerked my thoughts out of the clouds and lightning and sat them back down in the streets of Helena once more. It was a rider approaching.

The rider moved right down the middle of the street. He wore a dark, Mexican-style poncho, the hood pulled up for protection from wind and rain, and his horse plodded slowly. I could not see his face, though the glow of the burning tip of a cigarette cast a faint redness within the hood of the poncho. Whether or not he was watching me I could not tell.

It was Madison. I could sense it. Something in his stance in the saddle, the way he slumped, the way he gripped the reins . . .

He rode onward, not even glancing in my direction. The tip of the cigarette flared a brighter red as he inhaled a puff of smoke, then he was on past me, only his back visible. I shuddered.

Quickly I arose and moved back inside the building, then on up the stairs. How could I have been so foolish as to expose myself to him? I felt I should be shot.

I said nothing to Cummins or Jennifer about what had happened. They had been in the back room, not even knowing I had stepped outside, but they looked at me strangely when they reentered the room. I imagine I must have looked distressed.

Seated in the chair before the fireplace, I tried to convince myself that the man I had seen was not Madison. I hadn't even seen his face, and if he had noticed me at all he certainly hadn't shown it. It must have been some drifter passing through. I smiled to myself, relieved.

The rain had begun full force. I stood and went over to the window to watch it.

The streets were black like pitch, swept with rain. Upstairs in this secure building, warm and dry, I felt safe once more.

A lightning bolt ripped a jagged course through the sky, and for a moment the street was lit as if at noonday.

The rider was there, at the end of the street, facing the store. He sat like a statue, staring up at my window. Nothing more . . . just staring up at me as I watched him in the lightning's glow.

The light disappeared suddenly, and again the street was black. When the next flash came the rider was gone.

I cast myself down in the chair and stared at the dark window. A verse from the Book of Revelation played over and over through my mind:

". . . and I looked, and behold a pale horse: and his name that sat on him was Death, and Hell followed with him."

CHAPTER 19

THE next day I said nothing of what had happened to either Jennifer or her uncle. I didn't dare leave the security of my upstairs refuge, even though now hiding was almost pointless, and I felt like a tremendous fool for having so carelessly endangered myself and the others with me.

I spent much time staring out the window at the spot where I had seen Madison's shadowy figure the night before. It all seemed unreal; with a little self-argument I think I could have convinced myself that the whole thing had been merely a dream. But I couldn't afford to deceive myself. Josiah Madison now knew that I was here—he had obviously recognized me, and it seemed almost as certain that he would make some response to my presence.

I had never had any face-to-face contact with the man, though I had seen him indirectly more times than I liked. I could tell from his reaction to me last night that he knew me. I had been in Sam's cabin the night one of his riders had been shot, and I had been with McCuen, Bacon, and Sullivan the day we were ambushed in the hills north of town. He might have even recognized me as the man who helped spring the ill-fated Luther Guthrie from his prison on the Guthrie ranch grounds. He had been given many opportunities to become familiar with my face.

I considered telling Cummins about the incident, but something kept me from doing so—something called pride. I found it impossible to admit that through my own carelessness I had put all of us in danger. Each time I thought of breaking down and confessing, my throat constricted and my heart pounded. I couldn't do it.

And the thought of again running from Josiah Madison was repulsive to me. I had determined in my mind that never, never again would I cower before him, and I was stubbornly set on keeping that determination. True, I had told Jennifer that I would run if it was necessary to keep her safe, but now that the situation had arisen I just couldn't make the move. The wisest thing we could do right now, I knew, would be to board the first train back to Miles City and put as much distance as possible between us and this place, but I shut the thought from my mind, deliberately not letting myself think of the possible consequences. I would not run. I would not run. Again and again I repeated the determination.

Jennifer must have noticed my anxiety, for she cast repeated covert glances at me all day, a puzzled expression on her face. I pretended I didn't notice.

"Jim," she said to me in the afternoon, "is something wrong? You haven't said two words all day."

"Nothing is wrong. Can't a man have a little peace without somebody jumping all over him about it?"

Immediately I regretted my unjustified rudeness, for I saw the hurt in her eyes. She lowered her gaze from my face and turned away. I felt immensely cruel and even more foolish. I knew I should apologize, but . . . well, maybe later.

I spent the rest of the day in the chair before the

window, looking out at the clouds rolling across the sky. The town was still damp from the drenching it had received the night before, but still the sky was free of the ominous gray rain clouds that had lowered around sunset yesterday, and in their place were huge, billowed masses of snowy-white vapor floating high in the heavens. It was beautiful, but I think thunder and lightning would have better suited my mood.

I slept sporadically that night, every noise in the walls and creaking in the joists making me jump. I arose several times to go over to the window and look out on the moonlit street, searching for some sign of my enemy. Each time I returned to my pallet relieved, for there was no sign of Madison, yet paradoxically also perturbed, for the longer he waited to strike the longer I had to endure the misery of dread.

The next morning I knew that I had to head out to face the world or lose my mind. I had snapped at Jennifer again, this time bringing tears which she tried unsuccessfully to hide, and I felt the only thing that would keep me from hurting her again would be a good walk. After all, I reasoned, since Madison was already aware of my presence, was there any reason to go on hiding? And with that bit of logic spurring me onward, I picked up my hat and started out the door.

It was another beautiful day, and I enjoyed the warmth of the sun against my face. Helena was busy today, a general bustle going on in every store, wagons and buggies moving in all directions, the drivers cursing and shouting at street stragglers and other drivers, women stepping primly along the boardwalk. Children splashed the contents out of remnants of puddles, and lazy dogs basked in the sunlight, ignoring all around them. Here in the bright glow of everyday reality, Madison seemed only a vague and formless threat at most.

I stepped along with great vigor, whistling beneath my breath.

Leaned up against a hitching post, rolling a cigarette, I saw Runyon. I headed toward him, calling and waving. He lifted a finger for a moment, then licked the rice paper up and down its length before sealing it in place around the tobacco. He struck a match on the bottom of his boot, then lit the cigarette. A white cloud streamed from his nostrils to hang in the air and then be whisked away into nothingness by the draft from a passing buggy.

"Good day, Hartford! I haven't seen you around. How's Helena treating you?"

I shrugged and smiled, for that was a question I couldn't really answer. "I'm surprised to see you out in the morning. I would have figured you were dealing cards all night and sleeping in the day," I said.

"There are occasions when the day is just too beautiful to sleep away," he said. "And anyway, I only sleep when it's absolutely necessary. Too much of a bother, you know. By the way, I found the note you left for me. Nice of you. Where are you staying? The note didn't say."

I saw no harm in telling Runyon where I was. "I'm staying with a hardware merchant–friend of mine. I sleep on the floor, but it's free, so I'm not complaining."

Runyon gave a powerful drag on his cigarette that consumed at least a quarter of an inch of tobacco. "Don't reckon I'd gripe about that, either. Come over to the cafe with me and have something to drink."

"What are you doing drinking in a cafe? The strongest thing you'll get there is black coffee."

"In the morning that's plenty good for me. C'mon. I'll buy. I had a streak of luck last night—really cleaned out an old cowpoke."

We found a cafe and ordered coffee. It was strong enough to eat the rust off a crowbar, but it was good-tasting. I sipped it slowly, though, to avoid eating away my gullet.

"Well, what's been going on around here?" I asked idly. "I haven't heard much news lately."

"Only important thing I've heard is something folks were talking about around the table last night. There was some sort of vigilante action down south of town. Some soldiers from Fort Ellis found six or seven men strung up to a tree, like it had been a lynching party. I have no idea who it was. Folks were doing a lot of speculating, but in my book it doesn't amount to a hill of beans. I figure some rancher found some rustlers and just took care of them."

I looked away from Runyon, thinking. Six or seven men . . . south of town . . .

"You say you have no idea who they were?" I quizzed, perhaps a bit too eagerly. "No idea at all?"

Runyon grinned as if he were bemused a bit by my intense questioning. "You must be taking quite an interest in this, Hartford! No, I don't know who they were. Nobody else does either."

I was thinking of the man who had come to the doctor's office in Miles City claiming to be Nathan Thorne. If he had been working with others, as apparently he was, then possibly Madison's men had gotten to them and wiped them out. And of course, it might be just the opposite. Maybe one of the men hanging from a tree had been Josiah Madison, killed by the mysterious imposter of Nathan Thorne. And if that was true, then no longer was there any threat to Jennifer and me.

I stayed and talked to Runyon awhile longer, but it was only with real effort that I did so. I was almost trembling in excitement; maybe the danger now was over and I could again rest easily. I wanted to question

Runyon further about the lynching, but I feared arousing his curiosity about my interest any further, so I let it go.

Runyon at last left to crawl into his twenty-five-cent-a-night bed, and I headed back to the store. I was back up the stairs in a flash, and I think that Jennifer immediately recognized a difference in my attitude. She smiled.

I apologized for my earlier rudeness, and she laughed it off. "I think something must have been bothering you," she said. "Is everything alright now?"

"Yes. I think maybe everything is just fine." I hugged her, not even worrying about how she would respond to such a forward gesture. To my surprise she hugged back.

I didn't tell her all that Runyon had told me for fear she would only be all the more disappointed if Madison turned out to be still living. But I did tell the story to Cummins when he came up after closing the store.

"That's good," he said. "But let's not get too over-confident until we know for sure that he's dead. If one of the lynched men is Madison, then there's no way that will be kept a secret."

"You're right. That's why I didn't tell Jennifer about it. No point in building up false hopes."

"Have you had any luck in convincing Jennifer to go back to Miles City?"

"No . . . but then I haven't really tried. I can't blame her for wanting to avoid that ranch. I have no fond memories of the place myself."

"Yes, but if she doesn't decide on her own in a day or so, I think I'm going to insist. I'm certainly glad to have you two here with me, but Jennifer can't afford to let the Muster Creek Cattle Company sit in limbo like this."

Cummins was right. After some thought I told him that if he decided soon to send Jennifer back to Miles

City, even against her will, I would help him out.

Jennifer prepared a delicious supper of pork, beans, and sweet potatoes, topped by fat brown biscuits, and I ate far more than was good for me. After the dishes had been cleaned up I sat with her by the window.

"Jennifer, have you given any thought to the future? Do you plan to stay here permanently?"

"I don't know, Jim. I can't afford to neglect the ranch I've inherited. Father always expected that someday it would be in my hands, and he taught me what I need to know to run it. I expect that someday I'll go back, maybe even soon. Just don't pressure me."

"I'm sorry. Maybe it's not even my business. But I want you to let me help you in any way I can when the time comes. I hope you will."

Jennifer smiled, and her eyes looked so beautiful and soft that it was all I could do to keep from drawing her close and kissing those lovely lips. The fact that I couldn't do it made it only worse.

"You've already been plenty of help, Jim—more than you might realize. I hope you know I appreciate it."

I felt a warmth stealing over me. It was a good thing I wasn't wearing a hat—the way my head was swelling I think I would have burst the sweatband.

And I sensed that the time was right to clear the air about my ill-timed implication of romance between us that I had fostered after coming to Helena. "Jennifer . . . I'm sorry about what I said the other day, that hint that there was something, well, special between us. I had no intention of being improper. I just thought, well . . . I guess I was wrong."

She stood suddenly, moving toward her bedroom door. I felt like kicking myself in my own thick head. Clearly I had made another blunder . . .

"Jim?"

"Yes?"

"You weren't wrong." And with that she closed her door, leaving me to sit in a daze.

I slept peacefully that night, and my dreams were serene.

It was very late when I awoke, gasping for breath. My lungs were choked with hot, raw smoke. Unbearable heat struck me. In a moment it all sunk in, and I was up, calling, screaming Jennifer's name, trying to breathe, choking.

The heat was incredible, and smoke flooded every corner of the room. It was a searing, cutting smoke that ate into my lungs like hot acid. I staggered toward Jennifer's door, feeling increasingly weaker.

The latch was hot as if by a forger's flame, but I ignored the pain and threw open the door. Hot air and smoke struck me in the face like a hammer blow, and I fell back.

The air on the floor was clearer, and I gasped, filling my injured lungs with air. Then I crawled forward, through Jennifer's door, calling her name.

I could see her form crumpled before me on the floor, just beside her bed, a bed now roaring in flames. Every muscle straining, I inched toward her, the distance only a few feet, yet seemingly endless. With every movement I grew weaker, fainter.

My hand grasped hers, and I began dragging her limp body after me, moving back out into the main room again, so slowly that I thought the building would collapse about us before I made it to safety. Flames licked at the walls all around, and now even the air just above the floor was growing too hot and smoky to be breathable.

A door opened, the door to the landing and stairway that led down to the store. Cummins' voice reached me amid the sound of flaming timbers.

"Jim! Here is the door!"

I forced myself up to my feet, now not breathing at all, for the air was poison and hot. I grasped Jennifer, then lifted her up to my chest, covering her mouth and nose with my hand while struggling to see through the thick, flame-illuminated smoke that was everywhere.

I reached the landing, and Cummins was beside me.

"The stairs . . . the stairs are burning!"

He was right. Flames were shooting up the enclosed staircase, tongues of fires licking at us as if through an open door to hell.

I remembered the window, directly beside me. It was a second story window, but then it seemed the only escape.

"Hold Jennifer, quick!" I said to Cummins. He took her from me, his face red and lungs gasping.

With one kick of my bare foot the glass of the window shattered, and the flames roared up the stairs with increasing fervor. I pushed away the jagged edges of broken glass and moved my legs outside, sitting on the sill long enough to bark out an order:

"Toss her down! I'll catch her!"

Then I leaped. I struck the earth and rolled, and then I was conscious of others around me. Voices exploded all around as I struggled to my feet.

"Lord . . . here's one!"

"His pants are on fire . . . beat 'em out!"

"There's two others above . . ."

My strength faded suddenly, the world spinning and going dark. I collapsed into a senseless heap, my last thought being that Jennifer was still up there in the heat and flame, and I could not save her.

I awoke in a soft bed, a cool, damp cloth sponging my forehead. I looked up into the face of a middle-aged woman I had never seen before.

"There we are . . . back awake again. We were pretty worried about you."

"Where am I?" My mouth was filled with the taste of acrid smoke.

"You're safe, far away from the store."

"The others . . ."

"They're fine. The folks around caught Cummins and the girl when they jumped. They got out just before the stairway collapsed."

Jennifer was alright. With that assurance I drifted off to sleep, if the stupor into which I fell can justly be called that. I awoke again to brighter sunlight, feeling much stronger.

Jennifer was there, smiling down at me. She looked pale, though on her neck and arms there were red blisters. Some of her lovely auburn hair was singed, but still she was beautiful.

"Hello, Jim."

"Jennifer." I smiled, then grew solemn. "The store . . ."

"The store is burned down. We're at the home of Alex Murphy, another local merchant. And Jim . . ."

"Yes?"

"One man says he saw a fellow splashing coal oil on the porch of the store before the fire started. The witness was drunk and sleeping in an alley when he woke up and saw it."

I exhaled firmly. "Madison. He's the one, no doubt about it."

"Yes. I just wonder how he found us."

I stared at the ceiling, not answering. Then I looked again at her.

"Jennifer, we're leaving. We're going back to Miles City by the first train. Your uncle can come too, if he wants."

"He says he's staying. He says he won't let Madison beat him."

"Then you've already decided to leave?"

"Yes . . . what choice do we have?"

"It's settled, then. And Jennifer . . . we're not going to let Madison beat us, either."

CHAPTER 20

———·———

I felt intensely guilty when I saw Cummins again, for in one sense I was responsible for the loss of his store. It had been because of my carelessness that Madison had discovered my presence in Helena, and surely because of that that he had burned the hardware store. Of course, I had no proof that Madison had set the blaze, but I could think of no other culprit.

But Cummins did not know that Madison had seen me, thus he could not place the blame on me where it belonged. He simply looked on the whole thing as a mystery and let it go at that.

"I don't know how that devil found out you two were here," he said, "but I guess it isn't too surprising. Anyway, I'm just glad no one was seriously hurt. Mostly I'm grateful that we were able to get Jennifer out."

"Amen to that, Mr. Cummins," I said. "Have you checked on the railroad schedule?"

"Yes: There will be a train leaving at five this evening. I've already arranged for you and Jennifer to be on it."

Good, I thought. There won't be any wasted time. If Madison would go to the trouble of setting the fire, then surely he would check to see if his work had been com-

pleted. Once he discovered I had escaped the blaze he
would surely try again.

There was little packing to be done, for most of our
possessions had been destroyed, and we wore borrowed
clothing. More than anything I regretted the loss of my
pistol, for it had cost me good money and had been a
fine firearm. And now I was pretty much defenseless
should I encounter Madison. Perhaps it was just as well.
I could never hope to stand up to him in a gunfight.

It hurt me to see the ruined shell of a building that
was all remaining of the hardware store. Cummins had
taken a tremendous loss. I promised myself that I would
help him get back on his feet if it took every cent I
made in the next ten years. It was my duty.

Jennifer bade her uncle good-bye when we reached
the station that evening. The train awaited us, a huge
metal racing horse smoking and chugging and chomp-
ing at the bit. Jennifer had tears in her eyes as we looked
out the window of the passenger coach and waved at
Cummins.

"Do you think Madison will hurt him, Jim?"

I tried to sound confident as I assured her that her
uncle would be alright. "Madison would have no reason
to harm him," I said. "I don't really think he would
even know him. It's me and you that he's after."

I wished I hadn't made that last statement as soon as
I had done it. It didn't make Jennifer rest any easier—
or me, for that matter. But it was true, and as long as
we were in the same region as Madison we were in
danger.

Cummins had gotten us seats in the second class section of the train, a slightly more luxurious ride than the
immigrant coach, though nothing spectacular. But at
least Jennifer and I were on padded seats instead of
rough wooden benches, and the cursing, swearing, un-
cleaned folk of the wilder side of the territory were not

so close at hand. I realized that my desire to protect
Jennifer from that aspect of life was pointless, for she
had grown up on a rough-and-tumble cattle ranch and
probably had seen much more than I ever would. But a
man in love doesn't always think rationally, and if I
was anything I was most definitely a man in love.

Jennifer sat close to me, and I loved every minute of
it. I pretended to not notice, of course, and she did the
same, and we both sat enjoying and acting as if we
weren't as the miles rolled away behind us. I looked out
across the hills and watched the day ending, the sun
glowing brilliant red behind us.

I talked to her of the things I had seen, of Tennessee
and my home near Cumberland Gap. I told her of the
thousands who had traveled through the Gap when the
first doors to the west were being opened. I told her of
Gabriel Arthur, the young white servant captured by Indians and saved from death at the burning stake by a
Tomahitan chief. I told her of Dr. Walker, who named
the Gap, and of Daniel Boone, who in his life had become one of the most famous of all woodsmen. Jennifer
listened closely, enthralled, for she had never been east
in her life, nor south, and all of what I told her was
pretty much new to her.

She talked too, telling me all she had learned during
the years of watching her father develop his extensive
cattle business. She told me the stories she had heard
from him, how he had driven herds from Texas along
the Chisholm Trail before settling in Montana. She
talked of the coming of the railroad and how life was
changing as a result. She spoke of the immense growth
of the cattle business in the territory, and how it was
becoming increasingly important for ranchers to cooperate on roundups, for the overcrowded range resulted
in a huge mix-up of herds, with cattle of varied brands
running alongside each other. I had never thought of

ranching as anything other than hard labor, but now I
could see that it had its own special sort of magic, and
it could be a profession that could hook a man and not
let him go. Suddenly I understood men like Luther
Guthrie a little better. He had been in the territory for
years; it was his land, his and other men like him. No
wonder he had been reluctant to see his old way of life
vanishing, fading away bit by bit.

The darkness came, and the train became a fiery ser-
pent winding its way through dark hills. Here in the
dimly lit coach, seated beside a protecting window and
moving at high speed, the land outside seemed a bit
eerie and unreal. As the trees whipped by like phantoms,
I felt myself growing drowsy from the mesmerizing effect of it, and my chin began to drop down to my chest.
Jennifer was already asleep, curled up against my shoulder.

I don't know how long I had slept when I felt a gentle
nudge against my stomach, then another. I raised my
head, confused and groggy, and forced my eyes open.

How can a man describe what it is like to look right
into the face of death at a time when he expects it least?
How can a man put in words what it feels like to know
that what he has dreaded most is now a stark and immediate reality?

Madison sat across from me, grinning, evil, with his
single dark eye glittering in the light of the flickering
wall lamps. So intense was the shock that for a moment
I sat stiffly and stared into his face, numb and wordless.
Jennifer stirred beside me, and I heard her gasp when
she, too, saw the apparition that had apparently materialized from nowhere, now grinning in a sort of evil
triumph in the seat facing us. All hope drained from
me.

"You know me." Madison's voice was low, almost
inaudible.

"Yes. And you know me."

"I know you . . . and that you're the one behind everything that has been happening. I know that you're going to pay."

"You're going to kill us?" Jennifer's voice trembled, yet she spoke clearly and with courage.

"Of course. I can't let you live after what you've done."

"And what have either of us done to you?"

Madison's face turned a deep crimson with rage, and my heart pounded faster. "How can you look at me and tell me you don't know what you've done? You've been like a curse to me. Every time your ugly face has turned up something has gone wrong. First you show up and one of my men gets killed outside that damn ranch cabin. You turn up at Guthrie's ranch and my men almost get wiped out by those miserable ranchers. You and your friends tail me and my men into the hills. You put the Army on our tails. Carson and his riders get to my men and wipe 'em out just at the same time you show up in Helena. Everywhere I've seen you there's been trouble. You're a curse, a jinx. And you're gonna pay for it . . . you too, lady. I can't have anybody like you around to identify me to the law."

I knew his threat was not idle. But I suspected that even Josiah Madison would hesitate to pull a trigger in the midst of a filled railroad car where escape would be difficult. No . . . he probably had something different in store for us.

I was confused by his reference to "Carson and his riders," for that was a new name to me. But whoever this mysterious Carson was, he had apparently massacred Madison's men, though obviously Madison himself had escaped. So now the outlaw was alone.

Or so I thought. Something cold touched the back of my neck, and I jumped. I twisted my head to look at the man who so casually had touched the blade of a knife to my skin. It was Jake Crocker, red beard, bad smell, and all.

"Well, Jess," he said, calling Madison by his alias rather than his true name, "it looks like we got 'em where we want 'em. What are you gonna do?"

Madison smiled in a way that made my blood run cold. "You stay here and make sure nobody goes out on the back platform," he said. "Me and my friends will be taking care of a little business back there. Now get up slow, you two, and move careful and easy."

I saw the glint of a small handgun in his grasp, and I knew it was useless to defy him. Slowly I stood, and Jennifer stood with me, clutching my hand.

"Now move on to the rear of the car. We're gonna go out and get a little fresh air."

We obeyed, trembling, not knowing what was coming, though expecting certain death. People watched us, no one knowing or caring about what was taking place.

We exited through the rear door of the car and stepped out onto the platform, Madison after us.

"Your name's Hartford, ain't it?" he said to me, grinning. "I reckon that was your brother whose throat I slit. I enjoyed that, you know—and I think the same will do for you."

His left hand whipped out a long and frightening knife in one deft motion. Grinning, he lunged out at me before I expected it. Only by throwing up my hand did I keep the blade from slashing my throat open. My hand took the worst part of the cut, and blood dripped from it onto the platform floor as I moved quickly to evade his next thrust.

"God! Jim, watch out!" Jennifer cried.

Madison was laughing insanely as he again stabbed out at me, this time ripping away a portion of my shirt and scratching my skin. I wanted to leap at him, but his pistol was still gripped in his other hand and pointed at me, and I couldn't risk taking a shot at such close range. And Jennifer was there, too, so a bullet might strike her even if by some miracle it missed me.

Jennifer moved unexpectedly, throwing her entire weight against Madison, upsetting him. He fell back, cursing, and suddenly his gun hand was pinned to the wall. Jennifer held his wrist with both hands, crying out for me to grab the gun.

I saw the knife moving toward her, and at once I leaped. The blade passed deep into my thigh, and I cried out. Jennifer knocked Madison's hand hard against the wall, and the gun fell from his grasp. With one swift kick she knocked it from the platform to the ground at the foot of the grade.

Madison drew his knife back again and started to stab with it once more. But this time I managed to catch his arm and stop the blade from striking. Jennifer fell back, and Madison struggled to his feet, straining against my restraining arm, his free hand beating into my back and head.

I wrestled with his arm, but to no avail. His strength was incredible, and with the blood draining from the wound in my leg it was all but impossible to hold him back. My grip on his arm was weakening, and I knew it would be only a matter of moments before he broke free again.

"The ladder, Jennifer! Get up the ladder!"

It took her a moment to understand the meaning of my command. There was a brakeman's ladder running up the back of the coach, and now it seemed to be the only escape route for Jennifer. I expected that Madison would finish me off in only a moment, but at least Jennifer could run, even if to so poor a refuge as the top of the speeding train.

She was on the ladder, her knuckles white on the

bone as she clung to it. The rumbling of the train made it difficult for her to climb, but she managed to work her way upward, until at last she disappeared from my sight, and I knew she was on top.

Madison shoved me backward, just as the rear door of the car opened and Crocker came out.

"You want me to shoot him, Jess? Should I shoot him?"

Madison said nothing, but instead lunged at me, knife blade extended. How I managed to evade the blade I never knew, but he grunted as he fell past me to the railing, striking his head. At that moment Crocker drew his pistol.

More out of desperation than anything else I lunged at him, knocking the pistol aside and making it impossible for him to aim at me. Madison was stunned from his fall against the railing, so for the moment at least he was not a threat. Crocker was taken by surprise by my tactic, and as he stood gaping, the breath knocked out of him, I swung a hard right against his jaw, the impact of my fist shattering the bone and sending him slumping to the platform floor.

Without hesitation I swung up onto the ladder and began to climb. I reached the top of the heaving, rolling train and looked across.

Jennifer crouched down at the other end of the car, a man beside her. For a moment I was shocked to see him there, but in the moonlight I saw a light glimmer, then a lantern was lit. It was the brakeman, the man who rode atop the train in almost all kinds of weather.

"Here now, who are you?" he called.

"It's alright—it's Jim!" Jennifer said.

"Well, where are them others, the ones who was botherin' you?" he asked. Then he spoke once more to me. "Well, come on up, if that's what you plan to do, and be quick about it. Let's have a look at you."

He was obviously confused by this strange situation, and he had a right to be. But apparently Jennifer had told him of what was happening, for he was clearly looking out for her, and wasn't going to let me near her until he was sure I wasn't one of the men seeking to harm her.

"I told you, he's alright. He's my friend, the one who was helping me. Don't hurt him!"

Gasping for breath, I pulled my body prone across the top of the rumbling car. "Madison is stunned. The other fellow too. Nowhere for us to run . . ." I panted until I had caught my breath. "You got a gun, mister?"

"No sir, I don't, and if I did I don't think I would give it to you. I don't like this business of fights and climbin' up here where you ain't supposed to be. So how about you two headin' on down where you should be . . . hey, now! Who are you?"

I stood quickly, wheeling around. Crocker's head was poking up over the edge of the car, blood streaming from his broken jaw. And before I had time to gather my wits, his right hand came up, gripping his pistol. I cursed myself for having not taken it from him just as he fired a quick shot that appeared to be aimed at no one in particular.

The brakeman was caught full in the chest, and he grunted loudly as he toppled from the speeding car to land in a rolling, contorted heap at the foot of the grade. His lantern lay on top of the car, rolling from side to side, the light flickering brightly.

I grabbed the lantern just as Crocker lifted his pistol once more, and before he could squeeze off the shot that would take off the top of my head, I swung the lantern square at his face.

The lantern shattered on impact, and suddenly the man was covered with flaming liquid, glaring in the darkness like a human torch. I saw the shocked, agonized expression on his face for only an instant before he let go his grip on the ladder and fell headlong from the train, his dying wail resounding.

Even after he had landed in a silent heap on the track I saw the flames licking at his dead body. And I knew that the next man up the ladder would be Madison.

I could think of nothing to do but try to get Jennifer as far away as possible from where he would be. It would be a one-on-one battle, one which I would surely lose. I had to get Jennifer away.

I grasped her hand and began moving toward the front of the train. "C'mon!" I cried. "We're going to have to jump the cars!"

I found that running along the top of a moving train was something like riding a bucking bronco while standing on its back. But we both managed to keep our balance as we moved steadily forward, leaping from car to car, the smoke from the engine choking us, the smokestack showering us with sparks.

"If we can reach the engine—maybe we can get the attention of the engineer . . . he might have a gun . . ." I gasped out the words to Jennifer, though with the roaring of the engine and the singing of the wind in our ears I'm not sure that she heard me at all.

We were almost to the front car when I looked back over my shoulder. Madison was there, his knife gripped in his teeth, leaping over the gap between two cars, his single eye glittering with fury. I knew that in a moment he would be upon us. There was no time to try to get the engineer's attention.

"Jim! Look up ahead!"

Jennifer's cry was voiced with such urgency that I obeyed. And when I saw what had caused her to cry out I forced her down, my hand grabbing for anything at all to keep us from falling from the top of the train.

Before us on the track was a huge barricade of logs,

completely across the track. The train had rounded a bend and illuminated the huge structure with its dim forward light far too late for the engineer to do anything about it.

The impact was beyond anything I had experienced in my life, and I thought my fingers would be torn from the roots as I grasped with one hand to the edge of the car and to Jennifer's arm with the other. For a long time there was a horrible commotion of loud cries, screeching wheels, burning smoke and ash, and flying, shredded wood.

Then as suddenly as it had come, it was over. The train was motionless, miraculously not derailed, and shattered, massive logs were everywhere. Screams came from the interiors of the passenger cars below us.

It was then that men emerged from the darkness of the forest, pistols, rifles, and torches gripped in their hands.

CHAPTER 21

———

IN the glowing torchlight I recognized the man who had come to Miles City claiming to be Nathan Thorne.

"Hartford! You alright up there?" He called out as if he was concerned for my safety, but at the same time he was brandishing a pistol in my direction. I simply stared back at him, then over to Jennifer. She was shaken up considerably, but not injured. I suddenly became conscious of the pain in my leg, and when I looked down I noticed my pants were deeply stained with blood, and I could feel a scab hardening where Madison had stabbed me. I felt thankful that an artery had not been severed.

People began to move out of the train, slowly, carefully, obviously frightened by the sudden jolting stop and the crowd of men awaiting them outside.

"Is this a holdup?" a man asked.

"No sir. You haven't got a thing we want," said Carson. "If everyone will cooperate there's no reason for anybody to be hurt. Men, start gathering pistols from these good passengers."

No one tried to stop them, no one pulled a gun except to hand it over. All of the men—some fifteen in number—were heavily armed.

Jennifer and I moved down a ladder on the side of the engine and joined the other train passengers who stood in a semicircle around the gunmen. Many were the cold stares, many the expressions of fear. But few words were spoken, for the realization that this was no robbery was beginning to spread. But if not a robbery . . . then what?

I thought of Madison, and turned. He approached, apparently unhurt by the collision, but two of the gunmen held guns pressed into his back. I looked over at the handsome, fraudulent Thorne. In his eyes was an expression of triumph.

He strode toward Madison, staring at him, laughing a bit beneath his breath in a way that was rather unnerving. The leader looked at the scowling outlaw with a mixture of hatred and delight. Madison returned the gaze with a blank stare, then he looked over at me with an expression of hatred. But there was something else in his expression, too, a childish questioning, asking me why this was happening, why once more my presence had brought him disaster. I had no answer. I drew Jennifer close to me, and realized that we were both trembling.

"Well, Carson, you've got me. What now?"

Carson . . . Madison had called him Carson! So that was the answer! It had been this man and his companions that had wiped out Madison's gang south of Helena. It had been this Carson who had impersonated Nathan Thorne in Miles City after attempting to kill the true Thorne on the train, and it had been him that had gone back into the doctor's office to finish the job he thought he had botched. Carson . . . who was he, and why was he doing all of this? I was intrigued.

"It's judgment day, Madison. It's your judgment day at last. For all you have done to so many you are going to pay, for the sake of every life you've taken, every woman you've widowed, every son of the south you've tortured and maimed. It's time to make amends, after all these long years.''

Madison smiled darkly. ''And how do you propose to take care of me, Carson? How are you going to get your satisfaction?''

Carson wheeled around and faced the encircling train passengers, a crowd of mingled humanity from every level of western society. He stared at each of us in turn, and all mumbling faded, all shuffling about ceased. Every mind had its own questions about this, and clearly Carson was about to provide answers.

''Friends, you are not here to idly watch what will happen. You are witnesses of something that too often has escaped those who deserve it—justice. This, good people, is a trial. A trial of this man—Colonel Josiah Madison, the murderer of the Bryant's Fork prison camp, the creator of atrocities too numerous and too horrible to discuss in public. Yet they must be discussed, they must be brought to light. And most important of all, Josiah Madison must pay for them.''

''Are you not goin' to rob us?'' a man asked.

Carson laughed. ''No sir. I have no need of any of your possessions. All I desire of you is one thing—that each of you witness what we are going to do, so you will know that justice has been done, and that what you see will not be idle murder. You should count this as a gift, the result of Providence. Beneath God's heaven, at last a sore is going to be healed. A debt is going to be paid. Justice is going to be done.''

Jennifer leaned toward me and whispered, ''He's obsessed, Jim. Almost like Madison himself.'' She was right. Carson didn't seem my idea of a sane man.

Since hearing the name Carson my mind had been working, straining to pull some item from my memory, some special significance connected with that name. But so far I had been unable to recall just what that significance was. It seemed, though, that Sam had mentioned the name at some point.

"The court to try Colonel Josiah Madison, formerly of the United States Army, is now in session," Carson said. "The defendant will be seated. Since he has no counsel he will be allowed to speak in his own defense, but only when given permission by the man who will serve as judge—Mr. Morgan Samuel." He gestured toward one of the gunmen, a one-armed man who handed his weapon to his neighbor and seated himself on a stone.

Morgan Samuel . . . another vaguely familiar name. Again the conviction that at some point I had heard Sam speak of him. It was beginning to make sense now . . .

"Madison, here is your jury. You will recall Mr. William Myers, Mr. Amos Hodge, Mr. Tom Bradlin, Mr. Ben Carrington . . ."

As he went through the list I suddenly remembered. Sam *had* mentioned these names before—when he talked of his days in the Bryant's Fork prison camp. Lord in Heaven, could it be? Had these men, these fellow prisoners of Sam, pursued Madison all of these years? Did they hate him so much that they had followed him for all this time just for the pleasure of giving him the same hell he had given them? The evidence stood before me.

"Friends, seat yourselves where you are. You shall be our witnesses, you shall watch as Josiah Madison pays for his crimes." Carson wheeled and strolled back and forth, his hand rubbing his chin, as two gunmen wrestled Madison to the earth and forced him to sit. Clearly, Carson was going to be the prosecutor in this farce of a trial. And who was in doubt about what the verdict would be? Madison was as good as dead, and he knew it.

Since the name of Josiah Madison had been spoken,

the crowd behind me had whispered among itself and stared at the man. The name was infamous, the subject of many legends, and to actually see the man in the flesh, being tried by a court of his victims, was something beyond the wildest fantasies of any of them.

The trial got going at full swing, the list of charges being lengthy. Specific atrocities were enumerated in gory detail, and I saw many women and not a few men go pale and cover their faces with trembling hands. But still Carson continued, listing the crimes from memory without a single stammer or moment of hesitation. He had clearly gone over that list many times, pounding it into his memory until it could be called forth with ease. For almost half an hour he continued, and when he mentioned the crimes committed against the men now sitting in judgment against the defendant, shirts were pulled down and sleeves rolled up to reveal scars that served as evidence of the truth of the charges. The "judge" Morgan Samuel revealed the stump of his arm as Carson described the way Madison had chopped it off, and I felt ill. Many in the crowd seemed on the verge of fainting or losing their suppers.

Madison sat like a statue, seemingly unmoved by it all, but his fists were clenched and his arm trembled slightly. He stared at Carson throughout the oration, the moonlight and torchglow bathing the whole scene in an eerie light.

The jury looked like a congregation of phantoms, sitting very still, their faces stony. I noticed for the first time that some of them were dressed in the ragged remnants of Confederate uniforms, covered with patches and very dirty. I think it must have been somewhat of a symbolic gesture, and the effect apparently did not go unnoticed by the silent defendant, for occasionally he would cast a glance at the silent group, covering his fear with a veneer of calmness that looked increasingly thin.

Carson finished his list of charges and dropped into sudden silence, during which he looked first at Madison, then at each of the jurors, if the group deserved such a title. At last he turned again to Madison.

"How do you plead, sir? Do you deny the truth of these charges? If so, then speak your defense."

Madison stared at him, and his lip trembled slightly. But he said nothing.

"Speak, devil! Speak or let your silence serve as a guilty plea!"

Still no words.

Carson stomped his foot like an impatient child. "Speak! Or we'll pronounce sentence right now!"

Madison seemed to swell with sudden rage. And with unexpected suddenness he lurched forward and spit into Carson's face.

The man responded with a ringing slap across Madison's face. Then he backed away, pulling a handkerchief from his pocket to wipe the spittle from his face. "Judge, let the court pronounce its verdict."

The pseudo-judge turned to the line of men sitting in jury. Looking at the first he said, "Carrington?"

"Guilty." No hesitation, no change of expression. Just the dully sounded word that fell dead into the night.

"Myers?"

"Guilty."

"Bradlin?"

"Guilty."

"Hodge?"

"Guilty."

And on down the line it went, the answers predictably the same, each sounded with the same dull expression, each responded to by Madison with a desperate, almost pitiful flashing of his eye and flaring of his nostrils. He was doomed. All knew it. He knew it.

When at last the verdict was in, Carson turned to the man sitting in judgment. The very silence seemed to ring in my ears, and Jennifer moved closer to me.

"You have heard the verdict, Your Honor. What is the court's sentence?"

The "judge" stood and looked toward Madison. He looked straight into his face and said in a clear voice, "Death. By hanging, at sunrise."

The crowd seemed to break through its stupor then, and angry voices were heard, protesting the insanity of it all, horrified by all that had occurred and fearful of what was to come.

"Here, now—I won't be a witness to murder!"

"This is absurd—I insist that this man be taken to the authorities for a real trial . . ."

"This is preposterous!"

Carson whirled about, a pistol flashing torchlight in his grasp. "Shut up! All of you! There has been a trial and a verdict, and the sentence will be carried out! Ben, get a rope—it isn't long 'til dawn."

I heard a sudden rustling behind me. A lady, dressed in a fashionable and highly starched dress, had fainted into the arms of a seedy cowboy who looked at a loss as to what to do with her. I couldn't blame her for passing out, for I had no desire to see what was coming any more than she did. I almost envied her.

Strange how I found it hard to hate Madison now. I knew that he deserved exactly what he was getting, but still . . .

I looked at Carson and his men. Obsessed, maddened men, forever warped by the horrors they had seen in the war. Their lives had known one central purpose all of these years—to find and destroy Josiah Madison. And when he at last was finished, what then would they live for?

Carson. A man so obsessed with justice that he would commit any injustice to attain it. So hateful for Madison that he became just like him to destroy him. There was an irony in it I was sure he would never himself see.

A noose was tied and strung across a limb, and as it dangled menacingly in the fading night there were many murmurs of dissent. But no one could lift a finger to stop the execution, for several of the gunmen had turned their weapons on the crowd, apparently in a deliberate effort to dispel any thoughts of trying to stop what was happening.

In the east the sky lightened into a gold touched with violet, then the colors faded into the yellow of the last morning Josiah Madison would ever see.

Carson looked over at the pitiful outlaw, who now had lost his air of defiance and trembled like a whipped child. "Tie him up," Carson ordered.

The order was carried out, thongs being tied roughly around Madison's wrists behind his back. I could tell that the bonds were too tight, for Madison winced as they pulled them into hard knots that constricted his wrists so tightly that his hands reddened and seemed to swell.

Other men were dragging crates from the train and emptying the contents on the ground. Three of the large crates were dragged over to the tree and stacked atop each other beneath the rope. It was a rickety platform— and deliberately so. A ladder also taken from the train was leaned against the tree beside the crates.

"Up the ladder, Madison. Move, man! The time has come!"

Madison broke down, screaming horribly, weeping, cursing Carson and those with him. But nonetheless he was shoved forward, moved toward the makeshift gallows that stood silently in the early morning light, the noose casting an ominous shadow on the trunk of the tree.

Madison was forced up the ladder and out onto the platform of crates, and the noose was adjusted tightly around his neck. And then he was left alone on his perch, the ladder kicked away, Carson's men moving aside.

"Jim, I can't watch this . . . I can't," Jennifer said, turning and burying her face in my shoulder. I wanted to turn away too, but something kept me from doing so. I felt strangely obliged to watch what was happening.

Carson moved forward, smiling up at the doomed man on the crates.

"Josiah Madison, for crimes against innumerable innocent victims throughout the course of your miserable life, I hereby do carry out the sentence of this court. Pray, if you know how, for your life is now ending."

Madison lifted his eye to the sky as Carson moved forward, and tears streamed down his cheeks. Just as Carson's foot kicked away the bottom crate the outlaw wailed out a cry, the words indiscernible, the pitiful wailing cut sickeningly short as the rope jerked and separated the bones in Madison's neck. For a moment the body twitched, then the eye glazed, and it was over. Behind me I heard the sound of someone vomiting.

Josiah Madison was dead.

Carson's men made no noise, gave no cheer. They moved forward and grouped themselves around the silent, hanging body, staring at it almost like worshippers at a shrine. Carson's face showed at first a sort of satisfaction that then faded into a look of emptiness.

I couldn't stand to watch anymore, and I turned away. Jennifer was weeping, and I pulled her close to me. In all my life I had never felt so mortal, so aware of death.

CHAPTER 22

⎯⎯•⎯⎯

THE sun drove away the morning mist, and Carson and his riders vanished with it.

The body of Madison was cut down and placed in an empty crate from the train. With the swinging, limp form gone from the tree, it was hard to think of what had occurred as more than a dream.

To my surprise the train's engine was not too damaged to continue, and after the tracks were cleared and minor readjustments were completed the passengers boarded and the trip resumed almost as if nothing had happened. Jennifer and I sat clinging to each other, though, finding it hard to believe that it was all finally over.

After a time of silence we began to talk about what had happened. "How did Carson know Madison would be aboard that train?" she asked.

"I don't fully know," I said. "But I suspect one of his men spotted Madison in Helena, saw him board the train, and wired the information on the telegraph. Carson probably had a wiretap set up. It amazes me to see the extent to which he and his men worked just to get their hands on Madison. How could any human being hate another that much?"

Jennifer made no attempt to answer that question. I drew her close to me, and her presence strengthened me.

In that strength I found the ability to ask the question that had nagged at my mind almost since I had first met Jennifer that first day in Montana. And the answer she gave filled me with joy.

I met McCuen in the streets of Miles City the following day. He was laughing, shaking his head in disbelief.

"Marriage! That astounds me, Hartford! It's not exactly what you expected when you came to Montana, is it?"

"Not by a long shot. But I'm grateful it's happened. And I want you to come to the ceremony, of course."

"I'll be there. I wouldn't miss this for the world. And I've got just the present for you . . ."

"What's that?"

"A few rolls of barbed wire, of course."

"Thanks . . . I'll be needing it. With Sam's spread, as well as my land and that legally owned by the Muster Creek Company, we'll be stringing a lot of fences."

And so ends the story of how I came as a destitute farmer from Powell's Valley, Tennessee and married the daughter of the richest cattle baron in the Montana Territory.

VIGILANTE JUSTICE

Keller turned away and climbed back onto his horse. His heart was hammering, and he sweated like he had just finished a fast run up a steep hill. He knew what would happen now, and that once it happened, he would undeniably be the very thing he had sworn never to be. A vigilante. An Old Boy. He couldn't back out now. So be it.

Doyle Boston threw his rope over the limb and tied a noose. A couple of others in the group joined him with ropes of their own. The three horse thieves watched the process wordlessly; the first had gotten control of himself and now only whimpered a little. Keller was glad the man had stopped crying.

Keller didn't want to watch the actual hangings, but he made himself do it. Having come this far, he wouldn't falter....

BRAZOS

CAMERON JUDD

St. Martin's Paperbacks

This is a work of fiction. All of the characters, organizations and events portrayed in this novel are either products of the author's imagination or are used fictitiously.

DEVIL WIRE / BRAZOS

Devil Wire copyright © 1981 by Cameron Judd.
Brazos copyright © 1994 by Cameron Judd.
Excerpt from *Dead Man's Gold* copyright © 1999 by Cameron Judd.

For information address St. Martin's Press, 175 Fifth Avenue, New York, NY 10010.

ISBN: 0-312-94436-5
EAN: 978-0-312-94436-0

Printed in the United States of America

Devil Wire Zebra edition published 1981
Bantam Domain edition / February 1995
St. Martin's Paperbacks edition / June 1999

Brazos Bantam Domain edition / March 1994
St. Martin's Paperbacks edition / January 2000

St. Martin's Paperbacks are published by St. Martin's Press, 175 Fifth Avenue, New York, NY 10010.

10 9 8 7 6 5 4 3 2 1

"Lightnin' Les," this one's for you.

BRAZOS

1

The first man stood alone in the late winter dusk. Before him were two graves that still bore the indentations of the shovels that had dug and filled them many days before.

The graves were marked with wood crosses and lay near the place the house had stood. The house itself was now nothing but a pile of thoroughly burned, stinking timber. The fire must have raged every bit as hot as the folks in nearby Cade had declared, for the ground for several yards all around was blackened even yet, the chimney had crumbled to a rubble heap from the heat, and two nearby outbuildings had also burned to the ground. The little cookhouse and adjacent bunkhouse stood on the other side of a narrow grove of trees, out of sight and far enough away that they had been spared destruction.

Hat in hand, the mackinawed man stood by Magart Broadmore's final resting place and wondered morbidly how anyone had managed to find any human remains worthy of burial after such a conflagration.

He was a tall man in his forties, broad-shouldered and long-legged. Unlike his smooth-pated father, who had balded in his twenties, he had managed so far to keep every bit of the thick shock of hair that curled behind his ears, despite all his efforts to comb it straight. It was gray at the temples, but the rest remained black as nightshade. If not for his thoroughly weather-creased face, he might have passed for a man ten years younger than he was.

Usually he was calm and stoic. But today he was deeply shaken, and glad to be alone where no one could see the dampness and redness of his eyes. He had come to the Brazos country expecting to find a long-estranged sister. He had not come expecting to find her and her husband dead, and their ranch abandoned.

His moistened eyes shifted to the other grave, the one closest to the ruins of the house, the one marked F. R. BROADMORE—b. 1842, d. 1875. His lip curled in distaste that approached hatred. He harbored no grief for this grave's occupant. Folly Broadmore had been a sorry soul in life, and death did nothing to make the thought of him any more tolerable. The man was born no good and had lived up to his heritage. Gambler, cheat, sometime swindler, full-time loser. That was Folly Broadmore.

Too bad they were already buried when I got here, the man thought. *I never would have let them bury Magart beside him. It ain't right that she has to lie beside a man like him, even if he was her husband.*

He turned away, eyes sweeping the rolling Brazos country. He dug a hand under his coat and into his pocket to fetch out his tobacco and papers. Within a few seconds he had rolled a perfect cigarette, or quirly, as he would have called it. Snapping a phosphorus-and-sulfur match off the match block in his pocket, he struck flame on his boot heel and lit the tobacco. The smoke of it was raw against his throat, but it soothed him.

The sun, swollen and orange, was nestling its lower edge against the western horizon. The wind rose higher, carrying the scent of river and town through the chill-sharpened air. The man sniffed. Funny thing, he mused, how that lousy town seemed to have its own distinct scent, like a living thing. He could pick it out from here, a full two miles away. It was a conglomerate smell of humans, horses, dogs, pigs, cattle, timber, chimney smoke, tobacco, whiskey, and all the thousand other things that went into the mix of the ugly little farrago that had grown up in the shadow of equally ugly Fort Cade.

The man tossed down the quirly and crushed it under his heel. Putting foot to stirrup, he swung into his gelding's saddle and rode slowly by the light of the sunset back toward Cade. There was only one thing to do at a time like this: Get as drunk as possible, and stay that way as long as he could.

The second man wasn't as tall as the first, but every bit as lean, perhaps leaner. His hair was wispy, thinning on the crown of his head, and its color was that of wet sand. His skin was fair, more freckled and windburnt than tan.

He was crouched in the brush beside a curving stream that snaked between two low hills wooded with oak. Above him hung an orange and violet sunset. He held a battered carbine, already levered and cocked, and his heart thumped like a hammer. A little rivulet of blood stained his calf, coming from a superficial bullet wound suffered while he rode full tilt away from the three horsemen who had pursued him.

He hadn't recognized any of the three and hoped they hadn't recognized him. Who were they? Ranchers, cowboys . . . or range detectives? He hoped not the latter, though the possibility was there. Local ranchers were getting weary of losing stock, and drastic measures, such as hired range guards, could not be too long in coming.

He shifted his posture and winced at the pain of his wound. Glancing at it, he wondered how deep it was. The pain of it was certainly noticeable, though there was not the dull throb of a deep puncture. It had been a grazing shot, nothing more. But he would have to get rid of these bloodied trousers, for a bloodstained and bullet-torn fabric would generate some uncomfortable questions back in Cade.

He crouched where he was for the next half hour. Finally, when it was almost fully dark, he stood, grinning broadly. No pursuers had appeared; they must have gone past on the far side of the rise. He spoke to the black horse that searched for early forage behind him, down by the water and out of sight of any potential watchers from the rolling countryside beyond the oak stand. "Horse, I think we shook 'em."

He examined his wound; as he had thought, it was superficial. It had already quit bleeding on its own. The sting was gone now, leaving only a slight ache. Limping a little, he got the horse, mounted, and rode out of the thicket, heading east toward his big ranch house.

Cheerful though he was at evading capture, the experience had sobered him. He would have to be more careful in the future. He had too much going for him here in Cade to be careless. Too many plans, too many ambitions, too much to lose—and lose it all he would, if ever he was pegged as a stock thief. From here on out, he decided, he would have to leave the actual act of stock theft to his associates in crime. From now on he would play his role strictly in the background, carefully hiding the vital secret of his involvement. This would be especially important after the election was over and he was firmly ensconced in the county sheriff's office over in Cade.

On his way back to his big stone house, the man rode across the Broadmore spread. He paused there, looking toward the black rubble heap of the house. There was just enough light for him to make out the two crosses on the graves. He eyed them a moment, then rode on.

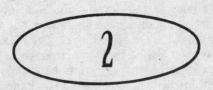

2

Two Days Later

Paco the Mex saw his beloved one drawing near. He
stirred where he lay, eyes closed, and smiled. "Bellina," he whispered worshipfully. Bellina of the mysterious darkness, Bellina of eyes and hair black as
midnight, Bellina of brown skin as cool to Paco's touch
as the bottle of whiskey that had given her the only
reality she now possessed.

"Paco . . . *hermoso, fuerte* . . ." Her voice was
musical and sweet, soothing to hear, even if only in his
imagination.

Only when Paco was drunk did Bellina come to
him, and as far as he was concerned, that provided the
best of many good reasons to get drunk as frequently as
possible. When he was sober, all life had to offer was
the squalor of this town: its dirt, poverty, heat, danger,
and a populace that looked down on him and made him
look down on himself. When he was drunk, things were
better. Intoxication gave Paco the only two luxuries he
had known for many years: escape from ugly reality,
and Bellina, a lover made of memories and dreams.

Yet now, as Bellina reached out to caress him, her

5

touch was not a phantom's, but solid, human. A thrill shivered through Paco. She was real! She was alive! "Bellina, bella Bellina . . ." He smiled broadly, reaching out to her as he opened his eyes.

Paco's body jerked upward and suddenly he was looking into a stubbled male anglo face that was certainly not that of his imagined lover. The Mexican's lip curled back over a wide gap where front teeth had been in the days when he was young and handsome and had loved a real-life Bellina, now many years in her grave. A gargling, panicked sound bubbled up from his throat.

"Bellina, eh?" the anglo said. His eyes were red and his breath heavy with whiskey. Paco was face upward, his liquor-weakened legs, all one and a half of them, sprawled out. He had removed his whittled peg leg for comfort's sake before settling down to drink; now it lay beside him. His torso was pulled half upright as the anglo held him by the collar of his ragged coat. "I'm a long way from being any Bellina, *amigo*. You're the one they call Paco the Mex?"

"*Si, si*—I am Paco. *Misericordia, señor,* mercy . . ."

"They tell me you're a cheap thief and beggar, Paco. That right?"

"No, *señor*—*no lo quiera Dios!* I am no thief. I beg you, let me go!"

"You're a pitiful excuse even for what you are, Paco. The smell of you alone is enough to make a man sick. You think any sweet Bellina would have anything to do with a skunk like you? Do you?"

"No, *señor*. No. I am a wretch, *señor. Por favor,* don't hurt me!"

"Hurt you? Why would I want to hurt you? Of course, if you decide to be uncooperative . . ."

"What do you want of me, *señor*?"

"I want you to tell me what you know about the death of Magart Broadmore."

Paco suddenly recognized the man who held him.

His tongue swiped out; his eyes grew wide, making the brown-black pupils stand out against the background of the surrounding bloodshot whites. "Keller!" he said. "You are Keller!"

"That's right, Paco. I am Keller, and before she married, Magart Broadmore was named Keller too. She was my sister, Paco. I came here to find her, and what I found instead was her grave. Now I hear whispers in the saloons that you know more about how she died than what the local rag wrote."

"No! I know nothing!"

"Only a dead man knows nothing, Paco, and if you don't talk, dead you'll be. Tell me what you know about Magart Broadmore's death!"

"The fire, she died in a fire, she and her husband!"

Keller swore and shook the Mexican. "Tell me what I don't already know! Tell me the truth!"

"*Señor, por favor,* I know nothing more! I swear it before God, before the blessed Virgin! I know nothing!"

"That's not what I hear, Paco. They tell me you talk too much when you're drunk. They tell me you say it wasn't the accident it was claimed to be!"

"Please, *Señor* Keller, believe me—if I knew anything, I would tell you!"

Keller's face became hard and ugly. He was driven by liquor and fury, a state he was unaccustomed to, and therefore could hardly control. His lips tightened to a line. "You're a liar, Paco. A liar and a scoundrel. And letting you keep on breathing is a waste of good air."

Keller drew his pistol and thrust it into Paco's face. He was thumbing back the hammer when he suddenly froze, realizing the horrible thing he was about to do. *God help me, have I sunk so low as to murder a man in an alley?*

Paco wrenched free and screamed in terror as he fell back, spreading his arms behind him to catch himself. In so doing, he chanced to put his fingers around the peg leg. He grabbed it, swung it up, and clubbed

Keller soundly in the side of the head. The pistol went off in Keller's hand, splattering a harsh powder burn across the left side of Paco's face but sending the slug into the ground beside him.

The Mexican hit Keller again, knocking him aside, then leaped to his single foot. Still yelling frightfully, he began hopping away, peg leg in hand. He bounced off around the corner of the stable behind which the encounter had occurred. Keller was on his knees, grimacing and slightly dizzy from being clouted. He picked up his pistol and held it limply. "God, I almost murdered a man!" he murmured to himself. He gingerly touched his head where Paco had struck him and found blood on his fingers when he took them away.

Keller stood waveringly, pistol dangling in hand, and heard footfalls on the side of the building opposite where Paco had just run. He turned as two wide-eyed men with identical deputy badges and almost identical faces emerged to face him. One already had his pistol drawn; the other drew his as soon as he saw Keller standing there with weapon in hand.

"Drop that pistol! Drop it!" the first man ordered. Keller had seen these lawmen before and knew they were the Polk twins, Homer and Haman, look-alike brothers who helped the county sheriff ride herd on the town of Cade and its surrounding environs. Which was Homer and which was Haman, he didn't know.

Keller stooped and laid the pistol on the ground. Standing, he lifted his hands. A thin trickle of blood edged down under his collar.

"Who were you shooting at?" the lead Polk demanded, pistol still trained on Keller.

"Nobody," Keller said. His anger had drained out, replaced by shame and desperation. He wanted badly to turn and run.

"That's a lie. I heard yelling."

"That was me," Keller said, groping for an out. "I

saw a snake, yelled, and shot at it. Snakes scare me bad."

"I heard Paco the Mex's voice back here," the second Polk said. "And I don't think no snake clouted you in the skull."

"Look, men, I'm a longtime peace officer myself, and this looks to me like a situation you ought to just let drop," Keller said, flashing what he hoped was a disarming grin.

"I reckon you would think that way," the first Polk said. He squinted. "Hey, you're that Keller fellow, ain't you? Brother of poor old Magart Broadmore?"

"I am. How do you know me?"

Polk cleared his throat, looking ill at ease. "The sheriff said you were in town. I'm sorry about what happened to your sister, Mr. Keller. I feel sorry for you and all. But I can't let you go until we know what was going on back here."

Another man came around behind the Polks. "Haman, Paco the Mex just hopped all the way down the street with one side of his face burnt red, yelling he'd been shot at. He looked drunk, but he was hopping like a dang jackrabbit."

"So that *was* Paco I heard yelling back here!" Haman Polk declared. "You lied to us, Mr. Keller. Come on. Let's go see Sheriff Cooke."

"Wait a minute . . . did you say Cooke?"

"Yeah. Till Cooke. He says he knows you. Planned to look you up while you were in town. It looks like we'll be saving him the trouble. Now come on, get moving."

Keller walked all the way to the sheriff's office with Haman Polk's pistol trained on the small of his back, his hands uplifted to shoulder level, and a stunned expression on his face. Till Cooke was the law in Cade? He hadn't known that. It was the first good thing he had heard since arriving here.

Or maybe it wasn't so good. How would Till

Cooke react to learning that a man he had trained in the ways of the law had fallen to the point of beating on peg-legged Mexicans in back alleys?

This one was going to be difficult to explain, especially to a stern law-and-order man like Till Cooke.

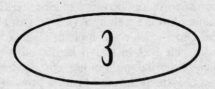

3

The Next Morning

Till Cooke had once stood five inches above six feet tall—an imposing height that had caused many a violence-prone drunk to choose discretion once faced with the towering lawman. But the years had done their work on him, arching his spine and robbing almost three inches from his stature, while adding them, plus many others, to his girth. Cooke's jowls had stretched and drooped, his hair had faded to white, and his once-erect shoulders had rounded off like weather-worn boulders.

He took a final pull on the cigar that had rested on his lip since breakfast. It had been lighted, allowed to go out, and relighted all morning, until now only an inch of it remained. Cooke flipped the butt into the belly of the stove in the corner of the office, stretched, and addressed Haman Polk, who was seated on the corner of the big paper-piled rolltop situated off center in the office.

"So old Jed's got himself arrested, huh?"

Haman Polk used his official voice, deeper and cleaner-clipped than his usual slur. He and his brother

11

were young men, recently hired, and still stood in awe of their seasoned superior. "Yes sir, Mr. Cooke. Somebody told him that Paco the Mex has been talking about the fire that killed his sister, and Keller got drunk and decided to try to scare Paco into talking. Keller swears he didn't intend to fire a shot. Says it was an accident."

"I see. Did Paco file a complaint against Keller?"

"Oh, no. He was so scared he denied it ever happened, once we started questioning him. But he was seen hopping scared down the street with a powder burn on his face, so we know it happened. Homer tracked him down. He was hiding behind the rain barrel in the alley beside the Big Dakota."

Till Cooke said, "I'm going back to talk to Keller."

"He's sleeping."

"Then I'll wake him up." He gave a snorting chuckle. "I expected to see Jed while he was in town, but I didn't expect it would be like this."

Jed Keller was asleep on his back on the cell bunk, his hands behind his head. The cell's pillow had been ripped to pieces by a drunk who had occupied this cell the previous night, and it was now nothing but cloth and feathers all over the floor. Keller had been allowed to keep his hat, and it rested on his forehead, tipped down to shade his eyes. The only other occupant of the jail was in an adjoining cell separated from Keller's by a stone wall, and he was also asleep.

Till Cooke left the cell door open and walked over to the bunk. The cell was chilly. He crossed his arms and studied the reclining prisoner. Keller moved a little, then reached up to push back the hat enough to let him see.

"Dog if it ain't really you after all, Till," Keller mumbled sleepily. "Just like them twins said. How you doing?"

"Tolerably well, Jed," the lawman said. "Keeping myself out of hot water, which is better than I can say for you."

Keller flipped the hat off onto the floor and sat up, groaning as morning-after discomforts hit him. He yawned and stretched very slowly. "I've stepped in it this time, I admit, and I'm ashamed. I was drunk. Wouldn't have done it otherwise." He froze in mid-stretch as he got his first good look at the sheriff. "Dang, Till, you're old!"

"I am, no denying. I ain't got a day younger since I seen you last. Now, why don't you scoot over and give a tired old man a chance to rest his backside, huh?"

The bunk creaked under the added weight. Till Cooke sighed, dug a new cigar from his vest pocket and bit the end off it. For the sake of his personal budget he allowed himself only two good cigars a day. If he needed smokes beyond that, he made do with the foul-smelling "short sixes" they sold for a penny in the saloons.

After he had fired up, he reached into his pocket and handed a cigar to Keller. It was one of his good ones.

"I'm sorry about Magart," Cooke said through the rich smoke. "It's a hard thing to lose kin."

"I didn't even know she was dead until I got here," Keller said. He chuckled ironically. "Funny, in a way. You come to make peace with your sister after too many years, and find out she's dead and gone. Ain't that just the way things go!"

"Unfortunately it is." Another drag and puff. "Was it because of Magart you were pestering Paco the Mex?"

"Yeah. I heard he had been talking about a secret he knew, a secret concerning the Broadmore fire."

"Where'd you hear that?"

"A gent in a saloon. He said Paco had tried to sell him the secret in exchange for a bottle. The fellow told him no sale."

"Likely that fellow was just one of Paco s many

antagonists. He's sort of the village idiot, you know. Folks like to give him a hard time."

"So you don't think Paco really knew anything?"

"Generally speaking, Paco don't know beans from bullets. He's half crazy from drinking his life away, and makes up all kinds of stories, most as wild as weeds. Folks like to pick on him, just to make him squeal so they can have a good laugh. Life is hard for that poor old Mexican." Cooke's cigar sent him into a coughing fit. He hacked into his hand, cutting off conversation a few seconds. He cleared his throat and went on, now in a more somber tone. "Jed, I wish you hadn't have shot at Paco. It makes it look like you were sure 'nough wanting to kill him."

"It was an accident. He hit me with that wooden leg and made the pistol go off. Like I said, I wouldn't have done any of it if I hadn't been drunk."

"If you'd killed him, that would have been murder. And I would have seen you prosecuted—even if you were the best Missouri deputy I ever hired."

"I know. You'd hang your own father if he stole a horse, Till."

"Speaking of fathers, how's yours?"

"He's dead, Till."

"Mark is dead? I'm sorry to hear it. How long?"

"A month or so. It was a natural death. He was just old and wore out." Jed paused. "And he never forgave Magart for marrying Folly Broadmore. Took the anger to his grave. That's the main reason I decided to come look her up. A family ought not fight amongst itself. I wanted to patch up all the old wounds with her."

"Must have been quite a kick in the gut to get here and find out what had happened to her."

"Yeah." Keller looked sidewise at Till Cooke. Now that he was past the surprise of seeing how the years had weathered the man, he seemed more like the Till Cooke he had known when he was a neophyte deputy in Missouri, and Cooke, then his boss, was still ranked among the toughest of the frontier lawmen. "What do *you* know about that fire, Till?"

Cooke shrugged. "No more than anybody else. It started around the fireplace, as most do, and burned the house to the ground with Magart and Folly still inside. Both bodies were found. Now they're buried together in the yard. It was an accidental thing, as best anybody can tell. It's mighty sad; the Broadmore ranch was turning into a good spread."

"Was Folly good to Magart?"

"I won't lie to you, Jed. He wasn't. They say he treated her pretty rough."

Keller ground his teeth and mentally cursed Folly Broadmore's name.

"Let me give you some advice, Jed, not as sheriff to prisoner, but as one old friend to another. Go ahead and grieve for Magart, go ahead and hate Folly Broadmore for being what he was to her—but then put it aside and forget about it. You can't change a thing that's happened, and you can't let yourself get into such a state that you go around Cade pulling pistols on poor old Mexicans and such. You do any more of that, and I'll have to start interfering something fierce in your life."

"Hah! You've already interfered, it appears to me. You've got me locked up, ain't you?"

"Not anymore. You're free to go—but you heed my warning, hear? Let it go. She's dead, and nothing you can do will bring her back."

Jed Keller nodded, saying nothing.

Till Cooke stood. "How long until you're moving on, Jed?"

"I'm not," Keller replied. "Folly Broadmore had no living kin to leave that ranch to. So it appears I'm in the ranching business."

Till Cooke's brows flicked. "You—a rancher?"

"That's right," Keller replied.

"That's going to be quite a rebuilding job. You got any capital to work with?"

"I sold Pap's farm, and that property of his near Liberty. I've got more money than I've ever had, and it's already in the bank." Keller paused. "Pap had written Magart out of his will, but it was my intention to divide the inheritance with her anyway. I was too late. Too blasted late."

"I wonder if you know what you're in for, getting into the cattle business at Cade."

"It don't take any more brains than I've got to run livestock, I don't reckon."

"Things ain't been the best for ranchers here the past year or so. Or for sheriffs either . . . not that I have to worry about that part of it much longer."

"What do you mean?"

"Cade is full of every kind of scoundrel, and the whole blasted territory is crawling with stock rustlers. I've had my fill of fighting it. I've already given my notice—a few more weeks and I'm out. I'm a cattleman on the side, you know. Nothing big and no full-time hands. It's a small spread a couple of miles from Fort Cade. I'm going to devote the rest of my days to minding my own business and trying to keep the thieves out of my stock. Claire's been staying there with me, by the way."

"Claire? That skinny runt niece of yours?"

"Oh, but she's no runt now. She's pretty as a Georgia peach. She's the daughter this old widower never had a chance to have. She's really brightened up things around here for me."

"How'd she come to be with you?"

"Well, she got married right after her folks died. It was sort of like Magart's case: She didn't marry well. Her husband ran around on her and finally deserted her flat out. She divorced him. It caused quite a scandal back home. I wrote her that she was welcome to come here and rest it out, and she did. It don't appear she has any plans to leave now."

"Well, I'll be! I'd sure like to see her."

"You will—I want you out for supper tomorrow night."

"Why, thank you. I'll be there. But tell me something: Who's going to be the law about Cade, once Till Cooke throws away his badge?"

"That's up to the voters. There'll be a special election." He grinned. "Maybe you ought to run, Jed."

"No," Keller said firmly. "Not me. Let somebody else keep the peace and chase the scoundrels. I'm through with all that. I'll not see another innocent person dead by my hand." And then it struck him how ironic that statement was, given that he had come so close to killing Paco the Mex. It gave him a chill.

Till Cooke lifted his brows. "So you still won't let go of that one old tragedy, huh? Even after all these years you won't quit dwelling on it?"

Keller looked away. "It ain't that I dwell on it," he said. "It's just that it won't quit dwelling on me."

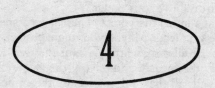

4

And that night it dwelled on him even more painfully than usual. Keller sat alone in his room in the Big Dakota Hotel, a glass and bottle of whiskey on the table before him, and played it all through his mind for what seemed the ten thousandth time.

It was an old memory, but no less stark for age. A few years ago he would have tried to block it; now he let it flow freely, knowing from experience that any other course was futile.

He had been a fledgling Missouri deputy when it happened. Till Cooke, then in his strapping prime, had hired him only a month before, and Jed Keller was still operating under a full head of pride-generated steam. He felt he cut quite the dashing figure when he strode the streets in his brand-new gun belt and badge. The badge had been well-worn from use by half a dozen previous deputies, but Keller had shined it up nicely and enjoyed catching the flash of it in the bottom of his eye when it glinted in the sunlight.

The first days on the job had been easy. Then came the first major challenge for the young peace officer: nothing less than an armed robbery of a bank. It had occurred on an autumn afternoon so quiet that at the beginning the entire thing seemed surreal. Keller remembered running with Till Cooke from the marshal's office toward the bank, holding a rifle snatched from the rack and feeling that surely this was all a jest or misunderstanding.

As Keller and Cooke came into sight of the bank, the sound of a gunshot and the appalling sight of a man's body flopping limply out a side window brought home the reality and horror of what was happening. Later inquiry would reveal that the dead man was a teller who had bolted toward the open window and took a bullet for his efforts. He had expired even as he lunged out the window onto the street.

That killing was the start of a long standoff with the robbers, who remained inside the bank, holding hostages. Cooke deputized townsmen on the spot and sent them scurrying to fetch rifles, and at length a charge against the bank was made. In the course of the foray many shots were fired on all sides, and when it was done, the three robbers were in custody, and Jed Keller stood looking down on the body of the first man he had ever killed.

He was little more than a boy. A simple fellow in his early twenties, who kept the bank swept for a few pennies a week. In the confusion Keller had mistaken him for one of the robbers and gunned him down. The moment when he realized his terrible error, an unforgettable feeling churned through him. For a long time thereafter Keller would awaken at night, reliving that same sickening burst of horror, feeling it chew through his insides like some parasitic worm.

That had been so many years ago, and still that feeling would come from time to time, making him waken covered with chilly sweat.

Only the gentle counsel of Till Cooke had stopped Jed Keller from ending his career in law enforcement right after the shooting. Things like that happen to the best of us, Cooke had told him. Someday it might happen to me, or maybe again to you. You can't let it stop your work. Where there's law to be upheld, there's always the risk of mistakes. But for every mistake you make, no matter how big it is, you'll do a score of things right. For every life wrongfully taken in the name of law, there are a score rightfully saved.

Keller had listened, and in the end decided not to resign. He had stayed on with Cooke, building his skills and rebuilding his confidence, eventually going elsewhere, to other Missouri towns and jobs, but always as a peace officer of one kind or another. He had never known anything else, except for some meager farming and cattle work on the side.

Though Till Cooke's counsel had been enough to keep him a lawman, it hadn't erased the haunting memory of the wrongful shooting at the bank. Even now, Jed Keller remembered the way that poor fellow had looked, dead and bloodied on the floor. And for the past two years, for some reason, the memory had grown even more clear and came more frequently. At the same time, Keller had found it increasingly difficult to do his job well, for every time he had to draw his pistol to quiet some rowdy cowboy or threatening drunk, he would for a second see in their features the face of that dead boy in the bank.

Keller poured another glass of whiskey and lifted it toward his lips, then in a burst of self-disgust threw it against the wall. Whiskey splattered in an amber explosion and dripped down the wallboards. *What am I trying to do,* he thought, *turn myself into a drunk? What good would that do?*

Keller decided he needed a walk and what fresh air the smelly environs of Cade had to offer. He stood, swiftly donned hat and mackinaw, and stalked out of his room, taking care to lock the door. Stowed in the wardrobe were the few personal possessions he had brought with him to Cade. Most of what he owned had been sold along with his father's holdings, for he had wanted to make a thoroughly fresh start.

Keller strode through the streets and examined the town. Since coming here he had been too distracted by his sister's death to take a close look at Cade. Now that he did, he was impressed, and not positively.

The town was ugly and haphazard, splattered across the flat below the hill on which Fort Cade stood. About every other building was a saloon, dance hall, gambling house, or liquor store. On the sagging balconies of several buildings women in bright, tight-fighting dresses postured provocatively and blew inviting kisses at the men on the street below. Keller, as a good-looking newcomer, got plenty of such attention. He ignored it. He liked women as well as any man, but not this kind of woman. He had been married once before, to a fine and beautiful young lady. Like a fool, he had let her slip away. But her memory had spoiled him. He had no use for cheap women who were bought for a night and cast aside.

He smiled ironically as he walked, thinking how odd an expectation of Cade he had held before actually seeing the town. As he had nursed his ailing father through the last months of his life, vainly urging him to put aside his animosity toward his estranged daughter, Keller had begun to think of coming to Cade to find Magart and set things right again. He had pictured Cade as a place of refuge, a quiet town that would likely be filled with flowers and beauty and peace. It was a strange and baseless way to think, but still the notion had lingered and grown into a firm and detailed illusion.

Now that he was here, the illusion was crumbling like dried mud. If Cade was a refuge at all, it was a refuge for lost souls.

True, there were a handful of tame and common institutions—a post office, jail, large general store, bakery, laundry, dress shop, feed store, and even a church house shared by the Catholics and the Presbyterians—but these were so overshadowed by the various houses of vice that they blended almost invisibly into the dingy background. This was a mud-colored town on a mud-colored, wintry landscape, and even its newest buildings managed to look old. Too many of the faces Keller saw around him on the street looked old too, even when they weren't, and gave weary evidence of lives wasted.

Cade was a haven of recreation for cowboys, buffalo hunters, freighters, and those who traveled the Brazos country with no real profession to attach to their names. It had more than its share of Indians too, mostly Tonkawas and Lipans. A group of the former were loitering on a nearby corner, passing around a bottle, gambling with a pair of dice, and hooting loudly at the outcome of each roll. Watching them with dark expressions were a few foot soldiers from Fort Cade, the stockaded enclosure that stood on the hill overlooking both the town and the wooded banks of Cade Creek, which flowed into the Brazos about two miles to the north.

The Brazos—in the older days called Brazos de Dios, the "Arms of God." Keller thought it very odd that such a seemingly vile town as Cade would lie in a country drained by a river with so grand and holy a name. Surely even the diety's arms weren't broad enough to embrace such a place as Cade.

He stopped long enough to roll a quirly, then continued down the street, trailing smoke behind him.

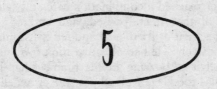

5

Being in Cade gave Keller the sense of a world apart from the rest of the nation—a nation at the moment distracted by its own approaching Centennial, the celebration of which many hoped would go far toward healing the rending wounds of a bloody war still too painfully fresh in the national memory. Keller had read in the newspapers about the big Centennial celebration up in Philadelphia and all the modern marvels it would display, and had realized that this was becoming quite an amazing world to live in. In the cities, people lighted their houses by lamps that were built right onto the wall and sent out gas jets for burning. There was talk about building suspended trains to carry people around big cities such as New York. At the same time, plans were taking shape for a canal to cut right across the Isthmus and make shipping from the east to west a far shorter and simpler affair. Keller had heard of something called a Corliss engine that supposedly ran itself with the power of a hundred horses times twenty-five . . . had heard of it, but didn't believe it, any more than he believed the even wilder story that a man in Boston had developed a machine that could send a man's voice through a wire to come out at the other end. Keller knew that wires could carry the pulses of telegraphs, but to carry an actual voice? That was too much for a born skeptic like Jed Keller to buy. Nobody was about to foist such foolishness on him!

Keller reached a combination café and saloon near the end of the street, paused, and entered when he caught the scent of fried meat and felt his stomach rumble responsively. He had already drunk too much whiskey and felt it buzzing in his brain; what he really needed was food. He walked past the crowded bar and headed for the collection of tables at the back. Sitting down, he ordered steak, biscuits, and coffee from an unshaven man who came to him with a blank pad and blanker expression. Then Keller sat back, rolled and lit another quirly, and eyed the crowd as he awaited his meal.

A man emerged from the crowd around the bar and made his way toward him, smiling pleasantly. Keller's eyes were drawn to him; he had the quick notion he knew this man from years past, but he could not place him. The fellow was dressed more fastidiously than anyone else in the place, though a closer look showed his clothes were thoroughly rumpled and dirty. Bringing his beer, the man came all the way to Keller's table, where he didn't wait for an invitation to sit down. He wordlessly scooted back the chair opposite Keller and flopped into it, his long legs sprawling out like those of a giant octopus Keller had once seen in an illustrated *Harper's Monthly* story about mysteries of the ocean.

"Hello, Jedford Keller," he said in a smooth voice. "My name is Lilly. Charles Lilly. Call me Charles, Charlie, Lilly, anything you wish, for that matter, as long as it doesn't besmirch my dear late mother."

Keller gave no answer, finding the man very odd. He was still struggling to figure out why he looked familiar.

"I hope you don't mind my intrusion into your evening," Lilly said.

Keller grunted noncommittally. He began to suspect Lilly was a gambler looking for an easy mark.

"Ah, but you're a silent man!" Lilly said. "Your sister was much the same way. Very little to say, most of the time."

Keller sat up straighter. Now Lilly had his attention. "You knew my sister?"

"Indeed I did. I was employed by her and Mr. Broadmore up until the tragedy."

Employed? Lilly certainly didn't look like a common ranch hand.

He apparently deciphered Keller's thoughts, for he chuckled and said, "I was the cook for the Broadmore ranch."

"I didn't think you looked like a cowboy. The truth is, you don't look like any ranch cook I've ever seen either."

Lilly took that as a compliment. "Why, thank you, sir. 'Praise above all—for praise prevails; heap up the measure, load the scales!' "

"What?"

"Pardon me, Mr. Keller. That was from Christopher Smart's 'A Song to David.' I often quote the great poets. It tends to annoy, I know, but it's an unbreakable habit."

Keller was thinking that Lilly was the strangest man he had ever met. He was elegant yet rumpled, scholarly yet earthy. Like a big-city schoolteacher who had been too long on holiday in the country.

"What do you want from me, Mr. Lilly?" Keller asked.

"Merely to make your acquaintance—and to offer my services to you in the cookhouse. It's my understanding you intend to operate the ranch."

"Where did you hear that?"

"From our mutual friend Till Cooke, earlier this morning."

Keller instantly felt less wary of Lilly. If he was a

friend of Cooke, he couldn't be a bad man. "To be honest, Mr. Lilly, I've not given any thought yet to hiring anyone in particular."

"You can't run a ranch that size alone—and if you'll allow me to make a suggestion, I believe you should give hastened effort to replenishing the ranch's staff of employees. Even as we speak, I'm certain Broadmore cattle are being quickly absorbed into other herds."

Keller's plate and cup arrived and were plunked down before him. The grubby waiter shuffled off, back to the bar. Keller began eating, figuring Lilly would leave. Instead, Lilly reached over, took one of the three biscuits on Keller's plate and began munching it.

"Excellent biscuits here," he said. "Except, of course, for the times you find weevils cooked in them. And they tend to be over-light on the salt and heavy on the lard."

Keller was more interested in other matters. "Is stock theft hereabouts as bad as everybody says it is?"

"Absolutely, sir. And Till Cooke, good man though he is, hasn't been able to affect it much. Not many fault him, though. The law sometimes lacks the teeth to take a big enough bite out of such things. It's one thing to arrest a horse thief and see him indicted. It's another entirely to see him remain for trial and go on through to conviction. Cooke is retiring to his ranch on good terms with the populace despite his failure to make much difference for them."

The silver-tongued Lilly dunked the usurped biscuit in his beer, took another bite, and chewed quite elegantly. At that moment the door opened and a sandy-haired man in spanking new clothes entered, limping slightly. There was an immediate reaction from those at the bar; their voices rose in simultaneous greeting. The newcomer grinned, waved at his greeters and then at everyone in general, and made his way to the bar. Following him was a stockier, flat-featured man, with brown hair that needed cutting.

"Give my friends here a fresh round of whatever they're drinking," he said in a loud voice. "And put it on my bill."

That prompted another jumble of happy exclamations as the sandy-haired man and his companion were engulfed by the already well-watered patrons.

Lilly had turned in his chair when the man came in. Turning back to Keller, he said, "Now, isn't that timely! There stands the very man who'll be taking on Till Cooke's off-cast mantle come election."

"Who is he?"

"David Ronald Weyburn. He's a local cattleman, and quite the popular man."

"Reckon he would be, buying drinks all around. Does he do that often?"

"He does. Particularly since he announced his candidacy for sheriff."

"Must be made out of money."

"He's got enough of it, and did even before he came to Cade. He now owns a ranch along Cade Creek north of town. He built himself a fine stone house, very large, though he lives alone in it except for a Mexican couple who tend house for him. He's a widower, I've heard."

"Who's that with him?"

"Floyd Fells. He lives in a little cabin on Weyburn's property, near the bunkhouse and stables and such, and runs much of the operation for Weyburn. The two come as a pair. Where you see Weyburn, you usually see Fells close behind."

"Who's running against Weyburn?"

"A drunken old soul named Jimmy Tripper. He hasn't a prayer of defeating the exalted Mr. Weyburn."

Keller remembered Till Cooke's negative comments about the man he anticipated would be the next sheriff.

He must have been referring to Weyburn. "So Weyburn's a sure bet, huh?"

"That's right . . . unless someone better soon emerges to challenge him. Which reminds me: Till Cooke tells me you are a man of the law. Perhaps you should consider—"

Keller cut him off. "Till hinted at the same. But no. Not me. From now on, I'm a cattleman, and that's all."

"Do you have experience with cattle ranching, Mr. Keller?"

"Not a lot," Keller admitted.

"All the more reason to move quickly to employ good men. I'll be glad to help you . . . if you will see fit to take me on."

By now Lilly had finished the stolen biscuit, so Keller grabbed the last one before it too could be taken. "I'll think on it," he said. In fact, he was already seriously considering the idea, for Lilly's talk about Broadmore stock being stolen concerned him. And Lilly, despite being an obvious eccentric, struck him favorably, especially given his friendship with Till Cooke. And Keller still had the notion he had met Lilly somewhere before.

Keller was surprised to notice that Weyburn had moved from the bar and was looking in his direction. When Weyburn lifted his glass in greeting, Keller nodded back, wondering why he had been singled out.

Lilly had noticed the exchange. "Does Weyburn know you?" he asked.

"Never met him," Keller said. "I guess he just figures I'm a vote he hasn't rounded up yet."

"It's probably that he knows who you are. Most around here do. It created a lot of interest when word got out that Magart Broadmore's own brother was in Cade."

Keller fell to his meal and finished it quickly. Standing, he prepared to go.

Lilly stood too. "About that job, Mr. Keller . . ."

Keller said, "I'll talk to Till. If he gives me good word on you, you're hired. Reckon I will need a cook, and someone who knows the locals enough to keep me from hiring scoundrels . . . aw, hang it all, just come on out to the ranch tomorrow. I'm moving out there in the morning. I'll be living in the bunkhouse to start out. I reckon if you don't turn out, I can always fire you."

"A man can ask no more than a fair shake. Thank you, sir. Until tomorrow."

"Right." Keller walked toward the door. As he left, he glanced back over his shoulder toward the bar. Weyburn was looking back at him, and once again lifted his glass.

Keller pretended not to have seen. As he walked onto the street, where the Tonkawas still hooted over their dice and the music of a saloon band made a tinny sound in the night, Keller noted that Weyburn's interest had made him feel unsettled, and he wasn't sure quite why.

He headed back to the Big Dakota, spent an hour halfheartedly reading an old newspaper somebody had dropped in the hall, then blew out the light and retired. A couple of hours after he fell asleep, he heard voices in the hallway outside the door. Two men, he judged from their sound. He grimaced when he heard the door of the room beside his open, then slam. Now they were inside, talking loudly, their voices coming through the wall. At least one of them was very drunk.

Keller began to fume and was about to pound the wall for silence when he heard the door open again. One of the men left, striding loudly down the hall and stairs. The firmness of the stride told Keller this was the sober one. Sure enough, the man left in the room began to sing, his voice slurred and atonal.

Keller hammered the wall with his fist. "Shut up in there!" he yelled.

"Sorry, friend," the drunk called back. "Mighty sorry. I'm drunk, that's all. Just drunk."

After that, Keller heard no more from the man. Within a few minutes he was snoring peacefully, dreaming he was a child again and that he and Magart were playing together on the muddy bank of the pond at the old homeplace in Missouri.

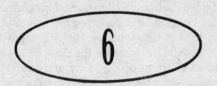

6

Keller's first thought the next morning was that he had been terribly foolish to hire a poetry-spouting stranger simply because he was interesting and insistent. Just who was Charlie Lilly, anyway? He claimed to know Till Cooke—but it was always possible he knew him only because Cooke had locked him up one time or another.

He'd just have to find out. Keller rose, washed, and after breakfasting in the restaurant that adjoined the Big Dakota, went straight to Till Cooke's office. He found his old friend coughing raggedly over a cup of coffee and a cigar—his usual "breakfast," Cooke explained.

Cooke, to Keller's pleasure, gave a good report on Lilly, confirming that he had indeed worked on the Broadmore ranch, and was considered by all a fine cook and reliable man, even if he was eccentric. Cooke then renewed his invitation for Keller to dine with him and his niece that night, and Keller again accepted, obtained directions, then headed back to the Big Dakota to check out.

He had lived at the hotel since coming to Cade, and was weary of it. Keller was no townsman by nature, despite all the years that his law enforcement duties had required him to live in or close to towns. As a rancher he would be free of that requirement; he looked forward to waking up without the bustle and clamor of streets and boardwalks right outside his window.

At the Big Dakota, Keller packed his clothing, gathered up his bundles, and departed the room, pulling the door shut behind him with his foot. Overburdened, he dropped a bundle just outside the door of the adjoining room. He was just stooping to try and retrieve it without dropping something else when the door opened.

"Give you a hand, friend?" a tired voice said.

"I'd be obliged," Keller replied. He stood, realizing at the same time that the man offering help had to be the drunk he had yelled at the night before. The man was crouching as Keller stood up—Keller noted the man's thin, sandy hair, tousled and spiked from sleep, and his rumpled clothing—and the man rose again, bundle in hand, and faced him.

It was David Weyburn. The two men looked at each other in obvious surprise.

Weyburn spoke first. "Mr. Keller, I believe?"

"That's right. How do you know me?"

"Word of your presence in Cade has made the rounds. I'm David Weyburn—I saw you last night at your meal. I'm very pleased to meet you. I was a friend, you see, of your late sister. And her husband too, of course. Please accept my condolences. Her passing was quite a tragedy."

"Yes. Thank you," Keller said.

"She thought highly of you, you know."

No, Keller didn't know, though he was glad to hear it now. At the time she died, Magart was still cut off from her family; Keller had assumed his sister harbored ill will toward him because of that.

"You look surprised, Mr. Keller, but what I say is true," Weyburn said. His voice sounded weary, and his face bore witness to a headache so bad that Keller could almost feel it himself. "I should tell you that I was aware of the division in your family. Magart . . . Mrs. Broadmore, I mean, talked about it pretty openly with her close friends. She had nothing but good, however, to say about you. She would have been happy to know you had come looking for her."

"Beg pardon, Mr. Weyburn, but how is it you know that's why I came here?"

Weyburn smiled. "Why else would you have come? Anyway, everybody in Cade tends to know everybody else's business. Or so they think. Folks here like to talk, and you've been quite a source of interest. Your little foray with Paco the Mex heated up the gossip something fierce."

Keller was amazed and offended that a man he had just met would bring up such a touchy subject. He was further offended when Weyburn took the issue a step farther.

"Let me ask you, Mr. Keller—why did you attack the Mexican?"

Keller gave Weyburn a look that should have sent him wilting back. But Weyburn continued to look him in the eye. Keller realized how very badly Weyburn wanted to know the answer.

"My business with Paco was private," Keller replied. "Why do you think it's yours?"

Weyburn shifted uncomfortably on his feet. "I heard that Paco might have been spreading false stories about me. He does that. Tells lies about people. You can't believe what he says."

"I've heard."

"He didn't say anything to you about me . . . did he?"

This conversation was becoming altogether too bizarre. Keller could have laughed in disbelief.

"He didn't say a word about anyone or anything— though frankly, Mr. Weyburn, I don't think I'd be obliged to tell you if he had. Now, if you'll be so kind as to stuff that bundle under my arm here . . ."

Weyburn did. He didn't seem offended by Keller's gruff speech; if anything, he appeared relieved. "I would offer to carry some of that downstairs for you, Mr. Keller, but I'm not fit for a public appearance right now. I'm running for sheriff, you see, and last night I drank a little too much while out stirring votes. I came up here to sleep it off instead of going home drunk."

Keller wasn't interested. He clamped the bundle between his elbow and side. "Good-bye, Mr. Weyburn."

"Good day, Mr. Keller."

Keller made it down the stairs without dropping anything else. Weyburn, a thoughtful expression on his face, turned and reentered his room, and as he walked, he limped. On his leg was a shallow bullet wound that had been healing, but which he had somehow managed to tear partly open again while he was drunk.

Keller was on his way to the Broadmore ranch before it hit him that what Weyburn had said could be construed as establishing a chilling connection between Weyburn and Magart's death. Keller had been told that Paco knew something secret about the fire at the Broadmore ranch. Weyburn, on the other hand, had said that Paco's alleged secret information supposedly involved him. Two distinct notions—unless really they weren't distinct at all. Could Paco's secret have linked Weyburn to the fire in some way?

Keller thought about that as he rode toward the Broadmore ranch. A friend of Magart's, he claimed to have been. Keller hadn't failed to notice the way Weyburn had spoken primarily of Magart, adding in Folly Broadmore as if in afterthought. He wasn't sure what it all meant, if anything. He grew tired of thinking about it.

Keller reached the ranch and was actually disappointed to find that Lilly was not awaiting him. Had the man backed out of the job he had asked for? Now that

Keller had reason to believe Lilly a sound fellow, he didn't want to lose him.

As the mounting sun warmed the morning air and drew from the land moist, organic scents that hinted of the coming spring, Keller opened up the bunkhouse shutters and doors, letting the breeze blow through and the sunshine spill in. He found an old broom and swept out the filth, sending big dust clouds into the air. He was just finishing when he saw Lilly riding in.

"Good morning to you, Mr. Keller!" Lilly brightly proclaimed as he dismounted.

"It's almost noon, in case you hadn't noticed," Keller replied.

"So it is!" Lilly replied. "If I had run any later, you surely would have thought the worst of me." He led his horse to the stable and returned, loading a pipe. " 'Tobacco, tobacco, sing sweetly for tobacco! Tobacco is like love, oh love it!' " he boomed out, then grinned. "Tobias Hume, poet. Not to be confused with David Hume, philosopher."

Keller grinned back, privately wondering how such an eccentric as Lilly had managed to hold his own among the rough-hewn personnel of a Texas ranch, for whom "poetry" meant either sentimental, sugary verse about mother back home or perhaps ribald doggerel scribbled on the wall of some sporting house privy.

Keller told Lilly that based on Till Cooke's good word about him, he wanted Lilly not only to be ranch cook, but also to help him hire other ranch personnel. In fact, Lilly would have chief authority on the matter, for Keller realized he was new here, and also knew his own inherent limitations. He was no cattleman, not yet. He was a good judge of men as men, but not necessarily of men as cowboys.

Lilly was obviously pleased by the confidence being invested him. "I will hire you the finest hands available east of the Llano Estacado," he vowed.

They worked hard the rest of the day, repairing and cleaning the bunkhouse, which was substantially run-down, and readying the cookhouse for use again. Lilly was obviously in his element in the cookhouse, and for the first time Keller was able to perceive him as a cook. Despite Lilly's poetry and faded elegance, he looked perfectly in place amid the pots, pans, and kettles, all of which had escaped theft during the period after the fire.

Keller could only hope his stock out there in the rolling cattle country had fared as well as the cookhouse dishes. He was eager to investigate just how badly the cattle thieves of the Brazos had hurt him. He didn't feel optimistic.

That evening, Keller paid the expected visit to Till Cooke and his niece. Cooke had been right: Claire O'Keefe was certainly not the skinny child Jed Keller had known. She was as tall as her gangly girlhood had promised she would be, but beyond that, all childhood indicators of her physical destiny had proven deceptive. Gone was the freckle-faced, gap-toothed, clumsy girl. Claire O'Keefe was now a shapely, poised beauty with hair the color of honey and a smile that could warm a room. Keller sat in the front room of Cooke's log ranch house, coffee cup in hand, and wondered how any man could have been fool enough to divorce a woman such as Claire.

"This place shows the feminine touch real nice," Keller said, looking around the room.

"Claire's done a lot to brighten these four walls," Cooke replied. "You should have seen it before she came."

Claire cast up her eyes at the memory. "I wasn't sure if I had found the house or stumbled into a pig-pen," she said.

"Ouch!" Cooke said, laughing. "Now, Claire, it wasn't that bad, was it?"

"I don't see how Aunt Carolina put up with a man

possessing habits like yours," Claire replied. Despite her
forthrightness, Keller could detect her affection for her
uncle.

"I wasn't like this when Carolina was still with
me," Cooke said. "She wouldn't allow it."

"Carolina was a fine woman," Keller said. "I never
figured how you managed to talk her into marrying you,
Till."

"You know, Jed, I never figured that out either," he
said, and for a moment there was a palpable dip in the
levity; Cooke's eyes became misty, and he quickly
turned his head. At that point Claire turned to Keller
and declared brightly that if he didn't have another
piece of cake she'd feel insulted.

"Make it a big one, then," he replied. And when
she was gone off to fetch it, he sat admiring the way she
had interjected herself to save her uncle embarrassment
as his emotion for his lost wife broke through. Till
Cooke had never been the kind who was comfortable
showing his feelings before others. Even at Carolina
Cooke's funeral, Cooke had staunchly refused to let
himself be seen shedding tears.

Conversation for the rest of the evening ranged all
around the various aspects of the Texas ranching business, of "Texas fever" and cattle prices, railroads and
range lands, and inevitably, rustlers. Once again Keller
was struck with the fatalistic attitude Cooke had toward
stock theft along the Brazos. "I've been unable to stop it
in all my time in office," he said. "I'm convinced there's
some things that can't be dealt with from the backside
of a badge."

Keller wasn't sure what Cooke meant by that, but
didn't inquire. He was far too distracted by Claire
O'Keefe to think deeply about much else.

When he left an hour later and rode toward his
own spread, he found he could recall only a little of
what Cooke had talked about, but every word, gesture,

and movement of Claire's was firmly ensconced in his memory.

She had asked him to come back and visit again, whenever he could. "I will," he had told her. And he had meant it.

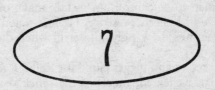

7

The next few weeks were filled with constant activity; Keller went through a paradoxical time of learning that he was anything in the world but a real Texas cattleman, while becoming more a cattleman every day. The work was harder than he had expected, but he liked it. It was healing and even pleasant at times. The only deeply aggravating part was that it kept him too busy to visit Claire O'Keefe as often as he would have liked.

His friendship with Charlie Lilly, meanwhile, had grown strong. Lilly was as good as his promise, and hired Keller a small but capable group of hands, some of whom had worked for Folly Broadmore and thus felt at home back on the familiar ranch. To a man, they treated Keller with great respect, despite his inexperience, and in time he discovered this was due to the fact that he was Magart Broadmore's brother. Magart, he found, had been revered by her husband's men. *She was a good woman,* they would say when they talked of her. *Too good a woman for Folly Broadmore.*

Two things clouded Keller's experience in rebuilding the ranch. One was the way the place kept putting him in mind of Magart; whenever he crossed the rise beyond the bunkhouse, his eyes were drawn to the two graves and the charred rubble of the Broadmore house. At last he put two of his men to work hauling the burned timbers to a nearby draw, where they burned what wood remained. And, unknown to Keller, Lilly told the men to be careful not to talk much of Magart Broadmore in Keller's presence. He had noted the way Keller's features drew tight and grim when the subject came up.

The second and bigger cloud for Keller was the discovery that, as feared, much of the ranch's stock had simply vanished. Too few of the cattle he and his men found on the hills and in the gullies for miles around the ranch bore the Broadmore brand.

"It's the thieving Wyeths," said Doyle Boston, perhaps the best of the cowboys Lilly had hired. "I'd like to stretch my rope with them Wyeths, that's for damn sure."

Keller didn't have to be told who the Wyeths were. As far away as Missouri, the Wyeths—a loosely knit gaggle of lowlifes whose name came from that of their recognized leader, Roy "Cutter" Wyeth—were cattle thieves who ranged up and down the Brazos and as far north as Dodge. Occasional forays by Texas Rangers, special posses, and soldiers out of Fort Cade had weakened the gang periodically, but had never wiped it out. Hydralike, it seemed to grow new tentacles each time one was cut off.

Not all Keller's men shared Boston's conviction about the Wyeths. Cutter Wyeth, they said, supposedly spent most of his time in Kansas now. They said that Boston tended to see the Wyeth hand in every cattle theft that happened, when in fact there were plenty of supposedly legitimate cattlemen who weren't averse to cutting into their neighbors' herds if a good opportunity came—and the death of the Broadmores had certainly been that.

Keller didn't know who to believe, and it hardly mattered. What mattered was that his herd was diminished, and his profitability would be diminished accordingly. Keller was beginning to understand why Till Cooke had been so discouraging about his plans to become a rancher.

Spring came to the Brazos country and painted the rolling terrain with a beauty that Jed Keller found awesome.

On the grounds of the Broadmore ranch—for it popularly retained that name despite Keller's ownership—daisies probed up from the greening land, moving in the breeze so their yellow and white blossoms looked like the bobbing heads of a fancily arrayed army. Texas filaree, dalea, clammyweed, and larkspur added their own touches of lavender, pink, yellow, white, and purple to the landscape. For a few brief days the pricklypear opened its big yellow-orange blossoms; these brought exclamations of delight from Charlie Lilly, who anticipated making jelly from the cactus fruit that would follow.

Once, when no one was about to see him, Keller picked a huge bouquet of wildflowers and rode all the way to the Cooke ranch to present them to Claire. It was the clearest indicator he had given of the way he was beginning to feel about her, and she pleased him by praising the flowers as if they were the rarest of beauties, even though identical ones grew all around her own residence, and bouquets like the one Keller had brought already decorated her table and mantelpiece.

Keller rode home with a grin on his face, thinking how much he loved the springtime and how benevolent the Creator had been to make womenfolk, especially womenfolk like Claire O'Keefe.

The landscape now looked lovelier than ever to Jed Keller. The best part of it, he decided, were the trees— for on a Texas landscape, trees were things that stood out to be noticed. Along the streams, pecan trees put out their leaves, and the thorny chittam shrubs grew thicker and stronger. Also welcoming spring along the waterways were elms, willows, soapberries, and an assortment of ivies that twined around and up them. On the hills and in the gullies, the white shinoak, buckeye, and elbow bushes had shaken off the winter and turned hardy again. Sumac sent out its distinctive scent, and the mesquite trees in particular were objects of delight for the transplanted Missourian.

Some days later, even the usually ugly town of Cade looked like it had put on new clothes, for gaudy banners stretched across the street and ribbon-tied garlands hung on doors and in windows. The special election had come and gone, and as had been widely expected, David Weyburn had easily taken the sheriff's post, his abundant votes bought substantially by his generosity at the local saloons. That generosity remained intact; the great victory celebration in Cade was being held at Weyburn's expense.

As evening fell on the celebration, Cade was even more crowded than usual, for the ranches and sodbuster spreads had all but emptied. Cade had plenty of festivity to offer at any time, but it usually wasn't free, so no one wanted to miss this opportunity. Jed Keller walked slowly down the decorated street, Till Cooke at his side, and watched the mounting celebration.

Till Cooke and Jed Keller were two of four men in town not in a very festive mood, though Cooke was pretending hard to be. Keller sensed that with Cooke's relinquishment of his post close at hand, the old lawman was feeling a little maudlin. Keller himself was dejected simply because Claire was not here; she was under the weather and had foregone the celebration. The other two noncelebrants were Homer and Haman Polk, both already informed by Weyburn that their employment would not continue. Their careers in law enforcement had died embryonic deaths.

"Look at him up there," Cooke said, gesturing at Weyburn, who was all smiles and handshakes on the reception platform built in front of the Big Dakota. Behind him Floyd Fells, atypically dressed up, was tugging at his stiff celluloid collar and fidgeting like a bad boy in church. "I reckon Weyburn figures Cade is all his now. And I suppose it is, in one way of looking at it. I just hope this county likes its new keeper as much as it thinks it will."

"You never have told me why it is you don't trust Weyburn," Keller said.

Cooke smiled without humor. "Instinct, Jed, instinct. And a few rumors, the really quiet kind that mean more than the loud ones."

Keller thought about Weyburn's talk of "lies" supposedly told about him by Paco the Mex, and wondered if these were the same rumors Cooke referred to. He had never told Cooke of his strange encounter with Weyburn in the Big Dakota. "What rumors?" he asked.

"That David Weyburn might not be the fine and honest rancher he puts himself up to be. There's a few who think he might have reached into his neighbors herds a few times when nobody was looking."

"You don't say?" Keller looked at Weyburn with new interest.

"No, I don't say . . . but some do. I even have to wonder, Jed, if you might not find some Broadmore stock mixed in with his herd, if you cared to look."

Keller frowned at that, and took a sip from the free beer he had picked up at one of the laden tables near Weyburn's stand. Weyburn—taking Broadmore cattle? Perhaps that, and not the Broadmore ranch fire, explained Weyburn's curiosity about him, and about the "lies" Paco supposedly had been spreading.

"Till, if Weyburn's a stock thief, then having him in as sheriff is going to make things hellacious for the ranchers. Not that it ain't hellacious enough already. I ain't heard of a cattleman within a hundred miles of Cade who hasn't lost stock this year. Cattle and horses both."

"I know of one," Cooke replied. "He's standing up on that platform with a new suit and a big 'possum grin on his face."

"Weyburn's not lost any stock?"

"Not that I've heard of."

"Maybe he's just been lucky."

"Maybe he makes his own luck."

"Till, you're a suspicious soul."

"I am indeed, when it comes to Weyburn." Cooke turned to face Keller directly. He paused for a moment before saying anything more, and when he spoke, his voice was quieter, more serious. "You know, Jed, when you have to enforce the law but stay within the law yourself, there's only so much you can do. The law's a funny thing: Maybe sometimes you have to break it just a little to put a halt to somebody else breaking it a lot worse."

There, again—another cryptic commentary from Till Cooke on lawbreaking. This time Keller didn't let it pass. "What's that kind of talk supposed to mean?" he asked.

Cooke hesitated, as if he had said too much. "Likely things will come clear soon enough, if it goes that far." He gave a fraternal punch to Keller's shoulder. "See you later. I'm going after some of that beer."

"See you later, Till."

Walking alone, Keller wondered what Cooke had been getting at. He also wondered if Cooke's suspicions about Weyburn had any meat, or if they were just the way the old lawman was expressing that inevitable tinge of jealousy toward the man who had taken his old job. Even though Cooke had stepped down voluntarily, Keller figured he had to feel slightly resentful of Weyburn, whom the public was greeting with such enthusiasm.

Keller meandered through the crowd, greeting those he knew, but keeping to himself. As of yet he didn't feel completely at home in Cade, though he did at the ranch itself. He no longer lived in the bunkhouse; he had built a small ranch house. It was still temporarily roofed with canvas, but he liked it.

"Please, please, no more . . ."

He had wandered beyond the fringe of the crowd, and heard the pleading voice from a nearby alley. Following the plea came the sounds of grunts and thuds. A man was being beaten back in that alley. Keller had no idea who, or why—but it wasn't his way to stand by while another human being was brutalized.

He darted into the alley, drawing his pistol, and came around the back of the building. He found two toughs pounding mercilessly on a third man. Keller swung back his pistol, clouted the closer of the antagonists in the side of the skull, then shoved the other to the earth with the bottom of his foot.

He saw then that the victim was Paco the Mex.

8

Paco reached up and began babbling gratefully until he saw who his rescuer was. He screeched and covered his face with crossed forearms, probably assuming that Keller had knocked the other two away in order to get his own chance at him.

Keller had no time to give reassurances, for both toughs were now up and coming at him, too mad and drunk to consider that he held a drawn pistol and they had no weapons but their fists.

Keller waited until the closer one got within striking distance, then ducked the man's wild punch. At the same time, Keller came straight up with the pistol barrel and laid open the man's chin with the sight. Groping for his split chin, the man buckled to his knees; Keller used his own knee to flatten the man's nose and lay him out on his back, his calves doubling up under his thighs.

The second man pulled up short at the last instant, seeing what had happened to his partner. Keller lifted the pistol and aimed it directly between the man's eyes; the man waved his hands, wet his pants, staggered backward, then turned and ran. The downed man stumbled to his feet and followed, dripping blood between his fingers from his tightly gripped chin.

Keller took a deep breath and holstered his pistol. Looking down at Paco, he saw a face livid with fright.

"Don't fret, Paco," he said. "You don't have anything more to fear from me. I was drunk when I attacked you, and I'd been told you knew things." He reached down to help Paco stand. "I hope you'll accept my apology."

Paco looked like he might faint, perhaps from the trauma of the attack, or from surprise at being apologized to by a man who had previously threatened his life. Almost as drunk as the men who had attacked him, Paco stood on his one real foot and one wooden peg, wobbled a bit, and then leaned back against the wall.

"Gracias, Señor Keller," he said. "You are a good man, a very good man."

"Why'd those two jump you?"

"They thought I had money, señor. They thought I had stolen money from a saloon."

"Had you?"

"Oh, no, no—I am no thief."

Keller glanced down and saw several bills sticking out of Paco's pockets, but saw no reason to say anything about them. "You seem to have come through all right, Paco. You'd best steer clear of that pair, though."

"Si, Señor Keller. I will."

Keller walked back toward the street, then turned again when Paco came after him, calling his name.

"What?" Keller asked.

"Señor . . ." Paco paused, licking his lips nervously. "Señor . . . about your sister . . . she . . ." He paused, licking his lips nervously. "Your sister . . . it is not like the people all say, about the fire—" He cut off abruptly, his eyes flickering to the left as he seemingly looked past Keller. Despite his swarthy complexion, he visibly blanched. "No, no. I can say nothing. . . . I have told you nothing, nothing!"

He turned and stumped away, grunting each time he lifted the peg leg.

"Paco!" Keller bellowed, heading after him. "Paco, come here and talk to me!"

Paco would not turn; he moved away more swiftly than ever. Keller reached him and grasped his shoulder, wheeling him around so swiftly that the Mexican almost fell.

"Tell me what you were going to say, Paco!"

"Señor, please . . . I am a dead man already! In the alley . . ."

Keller looked behind him. At the head of the alley stood Floyd Fells. Fells, who by now had yanked away his aggravating celluloid collar, was looking right at Paco with a harsh expression. His eyes flickered to Keller but did not stay on him. Fells was within easy earshot and had surely heard what Paco had been saying. Keller realized the sight of Fells must have been what made Paco blanche.

"I am dead! Dead!" Paco said despairingly. He wrenched free of Keller's grasp and stumped off in the opposite direction.

Keller watched him go and did not follow. When he turned back toward the street, Fells was gone.

David Weyburn rode home alone from the celebration, for despite his public sociability, he also required much privacy. He needed solitude in order to think clearly, to separate the public Weyburn from the private one—the real one, the one few ever came to know.

Weyburn had built his big stone house two rolling hills away from the bunkhouse, corral, and other buildings of the ranch that Floyd Fells operated on his behalf. The house was uncommonly large for its few occupants; common speculation in Cade was that Weyburn was hopeful of marrying and raising a big family someday, and had optimistically built his house to accommodate lots of youngsters. It was as good an explanation as any, and Weyburn let it stand.

He had left the celebration back in town running full tilt, as it probably would all night. With any luck, nobody would get drunk enough to spark a shooting or stabbing, especially if the Tonkawas could be kept away from the beer. Even if there was trouble, it wasn't yet Weyburn's worry, with Till Cooke still officially the sheriff for some time yet.

Though it was very dark, Weyburn's horse had learned the route back to the ranch and plodded along with no need of guidance. Weyburn slumped in the saddle and let himself relax; it had been a busy day, and he had smiled so much his jaws ached. He all but fell asleep in the saddle, but this was no accident; he had taught himself to achieve this state of near-slumber without descending deeper into full sleep, and by this means he regularly renewed his energy so efficiently that he sometimes slept only four hours at night and felt none the worse for it the next morning.

At his gate he lifted his head—and abruptly pulled his horse to a halt. A light burned downstairs, in his office, but no lamps had been lit when he left the house. Glancing up, he saw that the light was out in the upstairs bedroom of his servants, Eduardo and Maria Cruz; at this hour, they were almost certainly asleep. He dismounted, tethered his horse to the gate, drew his pistol and advanced stealthily toward the window. Probably Eduardo or Maria had entered the room for some reason and carelessly failed to extinguish the lamp, but Weyburn could take no chances.

Weyburn crouched at the base of the window. He was glad for his caution, because he heard footfalls on the floor inside. Someone was pacing back and forth in his office. Then came the clink of glass on glass, and Weyburn knew that whoever it was had gotten into his private stock of whiskey. Carefully he lifted his head and looked in. Then he swore aloud, stood, and rapped

on the window with the butt of his pistol. The man
inside was ratty-bearded, almost lipless, and possessed a
badly drooping right eye. He dropped his just-refreshed
shot glass, swung into a half crouch, whipped out his
pistol and leveled it on the face peering back at him
from the outside.

"Weyburn!" he declared, the drooping right eye
twitching a little, as it did when he was startled or nervous. "Hell, I almost shot you!"

Weyburn fired the man an angry look, then headed
around the house to the front door. Entering, he met the
man in the door of his office and jammed a finger into
his face. "Cutter Wyeth, what the hell do you think
you're doing, coming into my house with me away? You
trying to ruin both of us? What if somebody saw you?"

"Nobody saw me, Weyburn. You know I'm careful." Wyeth grinned. His way of grinning, Weyburn had
noticed long ago, only made him uglier.

"Where are Eduardo and Maria?"

"Upstairs asleep. Eduardo let me in and said I could
wait for you here."

Weyburn pushed Wyeth back inside his office and
closed the door. Moving with the swiftness of a man
much perturbed, he went to each window and drew the
heavy curtains, then lit a couple more lamps to brighten
the room. Wyeth, meanwhile, refilled his shot glass and
watched Weyburn with a vaguely haughty expression.

"Next drink you get, get it from the bottle under
the bar," Weyburn instructed tersely. "That one you're
pulling on cost me far too much to be wasted on as
rough a palate as yours."

Wyeth didn't know what a palate was, and Weyburn could tell the old thief was trying to figure out if he
had been insulted. That struck Weyburn as funny and
took the edge off his anger. He sighed and waved in
resignation. "Cutter, drink out of whichever bottle you
want," he said. "You and I will be making enough

money over the next few years to buy plenty of fine whiskey."

Cutter Wyeth smiled. "Them's musical words to my ears, Sheriff. Musical words." He lifted the glass and drained it in a swallow.

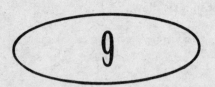

9

Weyburn went to the liquor cabinet and poured himself a shot. "I didn't expect to see you back so soon, Cutter. My wire said there was no cause to rush. The main thing was just to let you know I had won the race, and that we should be in for high cotton."

"I had to get away from Dodge anyhow," Wyeth said. "Things were getting too hot for me there." He licked the rim of his glass with a tongue that made Weyburn recall an eternally drooling beagle he had owned as a boy. "I had trouble over a woman, and shot a fellow. Didn't kill him. Just shot him, that's all. I should've killed him, though, because damned if that woman didn't turn around and take him in to nurse him back healthy again. It was all for nothing."

Weyburn had to wonder why any woman willing to associate with a maggot like Cutter Wyeth could possibly be worth shooting anyone over. The thought prudently remained private.

"Any men with you?"

"A few. They're in the old line cabins over on the Clear Fork right now. I come here to your place alone. Nobody saw me but Eduardo."

"Good. Always come alone—and only at night."

He took a small sip of his drink. "Actually, you've picked a good time to show up, Cutter. There's some cattle I want you to steal."

"Whose?"

"Mine."

"Yours?"

"That's right. I want you to steal some of my cattle. Maybe fifteen, twenty head."

"What for?"

"To avert suspicion. You think others haven't already noticed that my herd doesn't suffer like the rest? I've heard a few suspicious whispers I don't like."

"Hell, there can't be much suspicion. You got elected, didn't you?"

"There's plenty of votes for sale in Cade for the price of a few glasses of beer, and besides, I didn't have any real competition. We can't get overconfident and reckless, Cutter, or they'll be on us like a cheap suit on an undertaker. I've already heard a mention or two of the Old Boys going to work again. We sure as hell don't need that."

Wyeth walked over to an expensive stuffed chair and flopped down. Weyburn eyed the outlaw's greasy clothing and wondered how much essence of Wyeth would remain smeared on the chair when the man got up again.

"You've got you a real nice place here, Weyburn. I sure would like to have a place like this. I'd be happy just to sleep in one of them big feather beds of yours sometime."

Weyburn said nothing. When it became clear no further hospitality was forthcoming, Wyeth sighed, stretched, and stood. "I'll be going now."

"That's probably a good idea," Weyburn said.

"I'll bet I know why you want me out." Wyeth put on an odd grin.

"What do you mean?"

"I heard a woman's voice upstairs. You got you a sweet thing waiting for you up there, partner?"

Weyburn wore no smile. "You heard Maria. That's the only woman in this house."

"Didn't sound like Maria."

"It was. Now shut up and get on out of here. Be careful you're not seen riding out."

Wyeth said, "You need to talk friendlier to me, Weyburn. I don't like being talked down to. It makes me mad . . . and you don't want me mad."

"Accept my apology, then. Just get on with you—it's dangerous for you to be here."

"You fret too much, Weyburn. You always have. Good evening to you." Wyeth rolled his eyes toward the ceiling. "Yours is bound to be better than mine."

When Wyeth was gone, Weyburn went outside, fetched his horse where he had left it at the gate, and stabled it for the night. Returning to the house, he lit a lamp and walked up the dark stairs with it. He passed his servants' door; Eduardo was snoring loudly, with Maria doing her best to top his volume. He continued down the hall to his own room.

Lowering the flame of the lamp, he entered. The dim light fell on the wheelchair parked just inside the doorway. He walked to the bed.

The woman there awakened slowly, then smiled up at him.

"Hello, my dear," he said.

"David, you're here." Her hands rose toward him. "I'm glad you're here." In her voice was a quality that set it apart from other women's voices. A softness, a childishness of tone.

Weyburn didn't mind it. This was the woman he loved, the woman who was both his greatest possession and greatest risk. He set the lamp on the table by the bed and lowered himself into her embrace.

* * *

Weyburn was eating a solitary breakfast the next morning when the knocker on his door hammered three times. Both Eduardo and Maria were out, clearing the garden patch that would soon be planted with vegetables. Weyburn rose, wiped his mouth on a checkered napkin, and went to the door.

"Oh, it's you, Floyd. Come in."

"Got any coffee, David?"

"On the stove. Help yourself."

Floyd Fells moved familiarly through the house to the kitchen, and came back a few moments later with a steaming cup and a hunk of bread torn off one of Weyburn's loaves. Floyd seated himself at Weyburn's table and came straight to the point. "I saw something in town last night that may mean trouble for us."

Weyburn sighed. Fells was always smelling trouble. "Go on."

"I was meandering around in the celebration, you know, and I came to the end of an alley and saw Paco the Mex talking to that Keller fellow. Magart's brother."

Weyburn began to grow concerned. "Yes. I met him."

"Paco was about to tell him something . . . something about the fire—that much I picked up. And Paco looked scared half to death when he saw me. Turned and ran."

Weyburn had gone white. He swore. "So he *does* know! But how could he? It's impossible! We covered ourselves so well. . . ." He stood, overturning his coffee cup and ignoring it. "Do you think he told Keller?"

"No, but he came close. If he hadn't seen me when he did, he would have spilled it all."

Weyburn paced about, rubbing his chin. "So what are we going to do about it, then?"

"Only one answer I can think of."

It took a couple of seconds for Weyburn to understand Fells's implication. "No!" he declared. "No more killing. There's been enough of that already."

"Look, David, I don't like it any more than you do. But what's been done up until now has been necessary, and now it's necessary again. We can't let it fall apart now."

"I don't like it. I don't like it at all."

"You'd not like a hangman's noose or a jail cell any better."

Weyburn had nothing to say. He paced about. Fells sipped his coffee for a while, letting his employer get used to the unwelcome idea he had just been handed.

Weyburn slowly seemed to wilt. He sat down heavily. "You'll take care of it, Floyd?"

"So you agree it has to be done?"

Weyburn closed his eyes and took a deep breath. "I agree."

"That's good, because it's done already. I took care of Paco last night. I sliced his throat from ear to ear."

Weyburn looked like he might be sick.

"God, what a sorry business this is! What about the body?"

"Sunk in the Brazos."

"What if he's found?"

"He won't be. And if he is, there's nothing to link him to us. And anyway, the next sheriff won't likely find a single clue about his disappearance—will he?"

Weyburn smiled wanly. "No, he won't. That much, at least, we can be sure of." Then he sat silent awhile with his head in his hands. He looked up sharply. "Floyd, were you able to find out where Paco learned about what happened?"

"No. He fainted away on me when I grabbed him. I just made sure he didn't wake up. So I'm not sure just how much he really knew. Maybe almost nothing . . . not that we could take that chance."

"How could he have known anything at all? That's what I can't figure."

"Most likely he seen it. Think about it, David. You know how Magart always was free with the handouts. And old Paco had been around the Broadmore ranch that day—I seen him myself, walking away from the house with a loaf of Magart's bread, when we rode up. I figure that instead of going all the way back to town, he sat down out there in the grass to eat his bread. He would have been able to see it all—and we never knew he was there."

Weyburn stood up and paced around again, swearing beneath his breath and running his right hand repeatedly through his hair. "Three dead now," he said. "They'll hang us for certain, if it gets out!"

"It won't get out . . . unless your secret upstairs ends up making her presence known."

Weyburn aimed a stiff finger right at Fells. "You're starting to tread on thin ice, Floyd! You keep her out of this!"

"She's dangerous to us, David. I know you don't like to hear that, but it's true. Some things you can keep secret forever. A living and breathing woman you can't."

"She's my problem, not yours."

"You don't think so? Remember, it's my neck on the block too, David. It was me who killed the Tonkawa woman, and now Paco."

Weyburn was in no mood for further talk. Nor, for that matter, was Fells. He departed without another word passing between them.

Alone, Weyburn sighed loudly, ran his hand through his hair again, and headed to his office, where he downed a shot of whiskey, early though the hour was. He had planned to go into town today, but that idea had already been dropped. He was far too shaken to venture out in public.

He sat down and struggled to regain his composure. Finally, when his hands stopped shaking, he walked upstairs.

She was dressed now, awaiting him in her wheelchair. A tray with the scraps of her breakfast, brought up by Maria before the day's gardening began, sat on the table.

"David," she said, "is it warm outside? I'd like to go out today."

"It's too cool, my dear."

"But Maria and Eduardo are working outside! It can't be very cold. Please, let me go out! I can't stay locked up in here forever!"

"Hush, dear, hush. You need to stay inside today. Try to walk a little if you can."

She looked disappointed. Weyburn was struck, as he often was, by what an odd creature this lady was. Her body was that of a woman, but all else about her was childlike. Inwardly he cursed the man whose violence had made her this way, the man he had made pay for that violence to the fullest extent.

"Will you be here with me today?" she asked.

Weyburn smiled. "Yes. Today I stay home. Today we're together, just the two of us."

Her face became animated with happiness. "Come and hug me, David," she said. "I love you so."

He went to her and put his arms around her. "And I love you too, my dear Magart. I love you more than anything else in this world."

She squeezed him so hard it drove the breath from him. He made no protest. Magart Broadmore was his, bought at the cost of murder and deceit, and his devotion to her was one of the few things in his life that wasn't pretense or fraud.

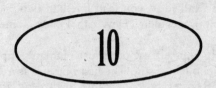

10

A Few Days Later

Jed Keller pulled the wagon to a halt in front of Till Cooke's office and threw on the brake. Dismounting, he tossed aside his tenth quirly of the day and walked up to the door. Through the pane he saw Cooke inside, pouring himself a cup of black coffee from the rusted pot on the stove. The door opened with a jangle and Cooke looked up.

"Well, hello there, Jed. How you been?"

"Fine, Till. How's yourself?"

"Tolerably well, all things considered."

"And how's Claire?"

"Talking about you every minute. That woman's affections are set for you, Keller. You'd best watch out, or she'll catch you."

Keller grinned. "I'm done caught, Till."

"I know it. I'd have to be blind to miss it."

The sheriff sat down on the corner of his battered desk and shook his head. Around the office were various crates laden with personal items that through his years in office had found their home in his office, and which now had to be moved out to make way for Weyburn.

"Looks like you've been busy here, Till."

"Yes indeed. And not just with packing up. It's been right odd. Jed, in all my time in this office I've never had anybody come in and report a missing person, and since I talked to you last, I've had two."

"That is peculiar. Hey, can I have some of that coffee?"

"Help yourself—you can use Haman's cup there, if it's clean enough to suit. The first one in was a Tonkawa they call Rooster Jack; he came in the day after Weyburn's big celebration and told me his wife has been missing for several weeks. I asked him why the devil he waited so long to report it, and he said she's took off on him before, but she's always come back. This time she hasn't. Lordy, it took me ten minutes to get him to even tell me her name!"

Keller was swabbing out Haman's rather crusty cup with his shirttail. "Why?"

"Tonkawas don't believe in saying the names of the dead. Bad medicine. They won't even give the name of a dead person to a baby—that's why they got such loco names sometimes. They run out of the usual ones, you see, and start borrowing from the Comanches and the white folks. Claire's danged scared of the Tonkawas, by the way. She can't get comfortable about folks who've occasionally been known to eat the flesh of their dead enemies."

"I'd heard something about that, I think. So this Rooster Jack believes his wife is dead, then?"

"He's beginning to think so. But I finally got out of him that her name's Winnie. If you hear anything about her, tell me . . . at least until my term is up—Lord hasten the day."

Keller took a careful sip of steaming coffee. It was as black as tar and almost as thick, but he liked it that way. "Who's the second missing party?"

"None other than your old friend Paco the Mex."

Keller's cup stopped in mid-lift. "Paco? How long's he been gone?"

"Since the night of Weyburn's victory celebration." Keller swore.

"What is it?" Cooke asked.

"I talked to Paco that night—after I helped beat off two roughnecks trying to take his money."

"Lordy! You reckon they might have done away with him later?"

"It's possible—of course, if you want to suspect everybody who has tousled with old Paco, you'd have to include me."

"No. I know you, Jed. You're no murderer. But I want to hear about them other two."

Keller told what he could, but the truth was he hadn't known either man, and hadn't paid much attention to their faces.

What really caught Cooke's attention was Keller's mention of Paco's cryptic words about the fire and Magart, and the way he ran when he saw that Floyd Fells was within earshot.

"I wonder if Paco might have really known something about Magart's death?"

Keller said, "I've tried to tell myself he didn't . . . but I don't really know. He sure acted like he had something to say—something he obviously wasn't willing to say in front of Fells. But why would he be scared of Fells in particular?"

"I don't know—but when you think about it, being scared of Fells might just be first cousin to being scared of David Weyburn."

Keller looked wryly at the sheriff. "Sounds like you're deliberately trying to pull Weyburn into this."

"Maybe I am. I don't make any bones about not trusting him, Jed, you know that. The man's trouble. It's written all over him." He paused. "Let me tell you something in confidence. I've already talked to the district attorney about Weyburn. I believe he thinks I'm crazy jealous of the man, but he owes me some favors and promised he'd check into Weyburn on the sly. He's got some good connections, and he's persistent. I've seen him learn more about a man than the man knows himself. I'll be eager to see if he finds anything on Weyburn."

Cooke walked to the stove, into which he tossed the dregs of his cup, rousing a steamy sizzle. "Weyburn's a real mystery to me. Living out there in that big house, away from everyone, everybody knowing him and liking him, but nobody really being close to him except for Fells. And did you know that every hand he has on his spread has been suspected at one time or another of being tied in with stock theft? Some even rode with the Wyeths in the past—can't prove it in every case, but I know it."

Keller finished his own coffee, mulling over the mystery. His thoughts went back to one of Cooke's past comments. "Till, who are the 'Old Boys' you talked about the other day?"

Cooke smiled coldly. "Let's put it this way: If Sheriff Weyburn turns out to be the sort I believe he is, you'll know soon enough who the Old Boys are. You might even be one of them. Now, Jed, if you'll excuse me, I've got to make a few rounds."

Keller pressed him for more explanation, but Cooke would say no more. Keller drove the wagon back to the ranch, wondering about the Old Boys and intending to ask Charlie Lilly about them. By the time he arrived, however, his thoughts had shifted to the work of the day, and Lilly was busy in the cookhouse, so the question remained unasked.

That night Keller did remember, and he called Lilly aside. Lilly's brows rose when he heard the query.

"The Old Boys? Indeed I can tell you something about the Old Boys. What I can't tell you is who they were, because nobody knows . . . or more exactly, nobody will tell."

"What do you know?"

"The Old Boys were a group of citizens, their identities well-hidden, who took matters into their own hands a couple of years ago when stock theft became a big problem. The situation, in fact, was much like it is now. The first thrust was no secret; several of the local ranchers and their hands joined with soldiers from Fort Cade and went looking for the Wyeths—the worst of the thieves—and took them on out in the hills about fifteen miles from the fort. Cutter Wyeth, unfortunately, didn't prove to be there, and the ones who were killed or taken prisoner were just small fish in the pond, so things didn't change much.

"Then, maybe a month later, the good people of Cade woke up to find a corpse hanging from the big mesquite tree at the north end of town. It was Curly Jones, a known member of Cutter Wyeth's group. There was a sign around his neck: 'Justice.' That's all it said. Then, over the next month, that tree played host to six more corpses, four of them stock thieves, the other two general lawbreakers who had been plaguing Cade. Till Cooke declared that he wouldn't put up with vigilance committees taking over the law . . . but I and plenty of others suspect he knew full well who made up that committee. In fact, some believe he led it himself. The 'Old Boys,' people began calling them. Word got out that no-accounts would not be tolerated by the Old Boys, and for about six months Cade was as trouble-free a place as you could hope to live. But it hasn't lasted. Where did you hear mention of the Old Boys, anyway?"

"From Till Cooke. He says the Old Boys might be back around soon . . . and that I might be among them."

"Do tell! And will you be?"

Keller shook his head. "Not me. I've never had use

for vigilance committees, and despite what you say, I doubt Till Cooke ever was part of one either."

"Perhaps not. He doesn't seem the type, I admit. But things about Cade are not always what they appear on the surface. A man who follows the written law by day might follow an unwritten one by night. Or maybe no law at all."

"Not me. I've killed on authority of the written law in my day. Sometimes on purpose. Once by accident . . . and I can't forget that one. I won't kill for any law again, written or unwritten."

"That's a humane ambition," Lilly said. "You obviously are a man of good conscience, Jed Keller."

Keller shook his head. "No. I'm just the opposite, and that's why I say what I do. I can't forget what it was to kill an innocent man, and I'll not risk killing another. I came to Cade to live a quiet life and live in peace, and I intend to do it. If the Old Boys come back 'round again, they'll not include Jed Keller in their number."

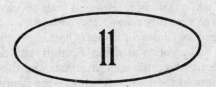

11

Three Months Later

Jed Keller was rolling a quirly when he heard the riders coming. He licked the paper into place, popped it onto his lip, and lit it as he strode toward the door. He paused long enough to remove his brand-new Winchester from the rack above the table—just in case the newcomers were not whom he anticipated.

He set the rifle aside as soon as he opened the door, for at the lead of the band was Till Cooke. Most of the fourteen men with him were cowhands from his ranch and a couple of others in the vicinity. Two, Larry Hite and Hal Allison, were ranch owners. And beside Cooke were two Tonkawas. All the men were well-armed and wore looks of grim determination.

"Hello, Jed."

"Till."

"I reckon you know who we're going after."

Keller nodded. "You have official approval?"

"Commander Wayne at Fort Cade has given his blessing. I think he'd rather see us do this than have to send out his own men."

"Has he got the authority to do that? Did you talk to the sheriff?"

Till Cooke spat contemptuously. "Believe it or not, I did, yesterday. So far he hasn't lifted a finger. Twenty-five horses stole altogether, and our fine new sheriff has let the thieves get a day's lead."

"So you're taking affairs into your own hands."

"There's no other way. You with us?"

Keller looked down, instincts battling with feelings. When he had come to the Brazos country, his desire had been to leave the pursuit of criminals and the enforcement of law in the hands of others—the hands of anyone except himself. Yet Cooke was right. The official sources of protection weren't working, and he, like almost every other rancher, was suffering for it. Since David Weyburn had taken office, theft of horses and stock had nearly doubled its already high rate—and Weyburn seemed determined to do nothing about it.

Keller looked up and nodded. "Give me ten minutes."

He strapped on a Colt and gathered ammunition and his sleeping gear while Charlie Lilly packed trail food. When he handed Keller the pouch, Keller said, "Charlie, there's enough here for two men."

"That's because I'm going too," Lilly said. He headed back to the bunkhouse on a lope, and within two minutes came out ready to ride.

They saddled horses and set off. The Tonkawas, long hair trailing behind them, rode in the lead. They were trackers beyond parallel, born of a people who lived by following the buffalo. Small in number, the Tonkawas had not been able to successfully vie with the Comanches for better range as the buffalo declined and moved, but this had only served to further sharpen their skills at tracking and survival. Keller was not surprised that the Tonkawas had joined this venture, for their tribe suffered from white thieves, just like the ranchers. Many a Tonkawa horse had been taken over the past two months.

They rode toward the west, for it was known that

the stock thieves—most certainly the Wyeths—had come this way. Cooke filled in Keller on the few details he possessed.

"We think they split up a few miles out," he said. "One of our Tonkawas yonder saw them and came to give the alert. There were may be eight of them altogether. One of the local sporting women is supposedly along with them, riding in a wagon. Her name's Nancy Scarlet, and she claims Cutter Wyeth as her man. Anyway, we think that part of the group took the stock northwest on a hard drive, and the rest, with the whore and the wagon, followed behind. I doubt they ever expected anybody would follow."

"Think we'll be able to catch them with the lead they've got?"

"We'll give it a devil of a try. I'm fed up, Jed. Good folk shouldn't be left high and dry to have their livelihood stole out from under them."

The Tonkawas found the trail easily, and this fueled the motivation of the pursuers greatly. Even Jed Keller, despite his initial trepidation, found lust for the chase rising in him. Cooke was right. Good people couldn't sit back and let themselves be rode over roughshod by thieves like the Wyeths.

They crossed the Brazos and continued, hardly resting. Night found them on the rolling plains many miles northwest of Cade. At last the weary horses and men stopped to make their camp.

Seated beside Cooke at one of the two campfires, Keller ate cold biscuits and beans and looked around at the group. "Is this the Old Boys, Till?"

Cooke shook his head. "Lord, no. But if things keep on like they are, Jed, you'll see the Old Boys."

Keller took another bite. Up until now he had firmly opposed any effort toward vigilante activity. Now he wasn't so convinced. Till Cooke's predictions of increased trouble with the advent of Weyburn in office had proven true. Might it take a stretching and bending of the law in order to set things right again? Even this posse, though bearing the informal approval of the Fort Cade commander, was legally questionable, a first move in the direction of vigilanteism.

Cooke's conversations tended to frequently drift around to the subject of Weyburn, and tonight was not an exception. "I have to admit, Weyburn has done a fair enough job in Cade itself," Cooke said. "It's safer on the streets than it has been in a long time. But beyond that—bah! I truly think the man's in league with Wyeth."

"But Weyburn's own spread has lost cattle. Horses too."

"What does that prove? If I was behind a ring of stock thieves, I'd make sure to hit myself enough times to make myself look innocent."

Keller hadn't thought of that. "So you think Weyburn has arranged thefts of his own stock?"

"It makes sense, don't it?"

"Yes. But is there any evidence of it?"

Cooke huffed and snorted. "There's my instincts."

"Instincts don't go far in a court of law."

"I ain't law anymore, Jed. Not that written law we've talked about, at least. I'm merely a rancher now, and a citizen, and I intend to see matters set right for the good folks about Cade, whatever it takes."

Cooke retired a few minutes later, and Keller rose to stretch his saddle-cramped legs and have a smoke. Charlie Lilly joined him.

"Did you hear what Cooke was saying?" Keller asked.

"Indeed I did. He's an angry man. ' "Revenge, revenge!" Timotheus cries; "See the Furies arise!" ' John Dryden."

Keller chuckled. Lilly had a poetic line for any occasion. Most of them so obscure they sailed right past, far above the heads of his less cultured listeners. Lilly

took a lot of ribbing over his quotations, which seemed
to distress him not at all.

"What do you think? You think Weyburn's as big a
fraud as Till claims?"

Oddly, the question seemed to make Lilly uncomfortable. "I don't know much about Weyburn," Lilly
said. "Before he began running for office, I never saw
him except when he came to visit Mrs. Broadmore . . .
the Broadmores, I should say." From Lilly's manner,
Keller realized the man had said something unintended.

"Wait a minute, Charlie. Are you saying Weyburn
came to call on Magart in particular?"

Lilly cleared his throat and fidgeted. "I don't wish
to imply anything you might take as a slur against your
sister, Jed."

"Charlie, say what you're thinking, straight out."

Lilly took Keller by the shoulder and moved him
farther away from the group. Outside the range of
the firelight, Keller could not see Lilly's expression well,
but there was no mistaking the serious tone of his
speech.

"Jed, David Weyburn was in love with Magart.
And it wasn't a love that went unrequited."

"Hold on, here! You mean that Magart and Weyburn were—"

"Mrs. Broadmore lived a difficult life with a difficult husband. Folly Broadmore was crude and rough.
Everyone on the ranch knew he beat her. Once he
knocked her cold. He told the doctor she had fallen on
the stairs."

"My God!"

"I've struggled for a long time over whether to say
any of this to you," Lilly said. "After all, what good
does it do you or Magart to dredge up a past that's
sealed and unchangeable?"

"So why are you telling me now?"

"Because you have a right to know the truth. And

because I want to spare you any shock if ever you hear this from some other source."

Keller remembered his conversation with Weyburn in the Big Dakota, how Weyburn had spoken easily of his friendship with Magart, while only mentioning Folly Broadmore in passing. The notion that Weyburn might have had more than a friendly relationship with Magart Broadmore was novel and unsettling to Keller—yet it fit in with what little he knew. Magart had never been what folks might call a "proper" young lady, even in the days before she had met Folly Broadmore. Her rebelliousness had caused Mark Keller to clamp down hard on his wayward daughter, which only made Magart all the more defiant. Keller had always thought she married as much to assert her independence from their father as out of any real love for Folly Broadmore, who had been a most unlovable character.

Might Magart have been an unfaithful wife to Broadmore? Knowing her ways and character, Keller couldn't honestly declare it impossible.

Later, as he lay on his bedroll, Keller found the threads of his thoughts coming together in a distressing way. There was Paco the Mex and his cryptic hints that he knew something secret about the Broadmore ranch fire, something he was afraid for Fells to hear him reveal. And then, right after that, Paco had vanished, and had remained absent since. Add to that Weyburn's own mention of "friendship" with Magart, and Lilly's suspicions that the two had carried on a secret romantic affair . . .

Keller went to sleep with a new conviction in mind: Somehow the fire at the Broadmore ranch and the deaths of Magart and her husband had something to do with Weyburn. There was a connection—a connection not yet clear. And in some way, Paco the Mex had known what that connection was. Keller recalled how Weyburn himself had quizzed him so directly about the reason for his initial tangle with Paco, as if eager to learn what Paco had said. And now Paco was gone altogether. Perhaps he had absconded out of fear of Fells or Weyburn. Or perhaps he was dead.

Despite his exhaustion from the day's hard ride, Jed Keller didn't sleep well that night.

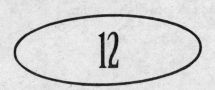

12

The morning came in cloudy, the sky gray and hanging low like a cavern ceiling. The wind drove violently across the grasslands, making the mesquite trees tremble and generating in Jed Keller the feeling that something of import was about to happen.

The two Tonkawas, riding ahead of the others, were the first to see the wagon. Crippled by a broken wheel, it sat unhitched in the midst of the rolling land, and on its seat, managing to stay aboard despite the slant caused by the wagon's sitting on one wheel and one hub, was a woman in a bright yellow dress cut low in the bustline. She held an open laced parasol above her head as though the day were sunny. The men could hear her cussing in a stream that knew no end, and the man whose name she was damning was none other than Cutter Wyeth.

"Well, look there," Till Cooke said. "Nancy Scarlet herself. It looks like old Cutter Wyeth has run off on her."

Till clicked his tongue and advanced up to the wagon. Nancy Scarlet, her face blotched and her eyes red from crying, quit cussing as Cooke approached. "Hello, Sheriff," she said.

"I ain't sheriff no more," Cooke replied. "Did they leave you stranded out here, Nancy?"

She launched into another tirade that featured several obscenities that sounded particularly vile spoken by a feminine voice. Once again Cutter Wyeth was on the receiving end of the onslaught—not that he was anywhere close by to hear it.

"Was Cutter driving this wagon?" Cooke asked.

"It was him, and him that left me sitting here on my butt!" she declared. The wind suddenly caught her parasol and threatened to turn it inside out. Trying to close it, she lost her perch on the slanting wagon seat and slid down sideways and completely out of the wagon. Nevertheless she landed on her feet.

"She's agile," one of the cowboys in the group said.

"Don't I know it!" another muttered in a wistful way that drew glances from the other men. He turned red and ducked his face.

"So that's where you been going them Friday nights," one of the others said.

"Sheriff," said Nancy, clinging to Cooke's former title, "I want you to go arrest Cutter. He was going to take me off and marry me, but when the wagon broke its wheel he just left me. He said he'd be back to fix it, and I needed to guard it for him! Can you believe that? He wants me to guard his wagon! He just wanted to be rid of me, that's all."

"Did he know he was being followed?"

"Hell, no! That was just his talk, his excuse for dumping me off! He'd been saying all along that there wouldn't be nobody following."

"Did he say anything to indicate that he has some sort of deal with David Weyburn? Something to indicate Weyburn is in league with him, you know, cooperating with him in stealing stock?"

Nancy's blank look indicated that the notion was new to her. Cooke looked disappointed; obviously he had hoped the prostitute could verify his suspicions—

suspicions that were increasingly voiced by many others, particularly cattlemen.

Keller rode forward a few paces. "Where is Wyeth now?"

"At the old cabin in Salty Basin," she said. There was no hesitation; she was a woman who felt betrayed and who would therefore betray in turn. "They keep the horses there, until they sell them to somebody up in Kansas."

"Salty Basin," Cooke said. "A thieve's hole from way on back. Hal, why don't you escort Miss Scarlet back to Cade. As for the rest of us, by grabs, let's go pay Cutter Wyeth a visit!"

The horses were still there, corraled behind the little two-room cabin. The doors and shutters of the house were open, for the day was warm even though overcast, the heat slowly thinning out the clouds. Outside, a big fire blazed beneath a black kettle and coffeepot. Nearby, a creek ran in a course cut deep into the soil.

Cooke checked his rifle one last time and glanced at the men stationed all around him, hiding behind the trees, brush, and rocks along the slope leading down to the house. Keller gauged the range and found it a little long for his liking, but to go closer would mean leaving cover behind.

"Just how are we going to do this?" Charlie Lilly asked. He was stationed on one side of Cooke; Keller was on the other.

"I wouldn't think we'd want them to fight, unless it comes to it," Keller said. "What we do, first and foremost, is get our horses back."

"I've got a little more than that in mind," Cooke mumbled.

Keller didn't understand him. "What'd you say, Till?"

"Nothing. Nothing."

"I got an idea of what to do," Keller said.

He outlined a plan, and found it matched what Cooke already had in mind. Having been trained by Cooke, Keller naturally thought along similar strategic lines.

"I'll go," Cooke said. "I can slip around and—"

"You'll stay here," Keller said. "I'll go."

"I'm in charge here," Cooke said.

"Yeah, but I'm younger—and faster." And with that Keller was up, moving at a quick lope with his head low, circling around the slope toward the corral, staying just out of sight.

By the time he reached the corral—completing his circuitous route had taken six minutes—Keller was winded but confident his plan would work. The single window on the side of the house facing the corral was closed, and the only obvious evidence of human presence at the place was smoke rising from the fire on the other side, and the muffled sound of men's voices inside.

Keller dropped to the ground when he heard a door open. There was no cover here except the grass at the edge of the corral and the conglomerate legs of the horses as they milled in the corral between Keller and the house.

Keller hoped that whoever had left the house was simply going to the cook fire to check the progress of the meal. He was disheartened to see two men stride around the side of the house, however, and head for the corral.

"I'll show the one I'm talking about, Cutter," one of the men was saying. "She's a beaut—finest I've seen, prettier even than that dun filly last fall. You remember that one?"

"Yep."

Keller's fingers wrapped around the stock of his rifle. He couldn't see enough of the men to know if they were armed; he would have to assume they were. Obviously one of them was Cutter Wyeth himself, and he would not likely give up easily. He had stolen so many horses and rustled so many cattle in his time that he would almost surely face the noose if caught.

This was not part of the plan; Keller had not anticipated anyone coming out of the house, at least, not until he had opened the corral gate and stampeded the horses. At that point those in the house would certainly rush out—and Till Cooke and the others could sweep down, overwhelm them, and take them in. If all went well, not a shot would have to be fired.

Wyeth and the man with him drew closer, closer . . . and Keller was almost to the desperate point of leaping up and demanding their surrender when they stopped, apparently having located the horse they sought. As they conversed about the form and strength of the animal—which bore the brand of Larry Hite's spread—Keller lowered his head and took a deep but silent breath. The plan might work after all. Wyeth and his companion would talk, then return to the house, and then he could proceed to free the horses as planned.

But fortune had other things in mind. Just as the two stock thieves were about to turn back toward the cabin, the sun broke through the clouds for the first time that day, pouring golden light across the entire little creek basin in which the cabin stood. And to Keller's misfortune, one of the rays glinted on the shiny hammer of his new rifle.

It was the tiniest glint of light, but it caught Wyeth's eye and aroused his suspicion. Conversation stopped, the horses began moving aside, and Keller saw Wyeth's booted feet stepping in his direction among the conglomeration of hooves.

"Wyeth!"

The yell came from up the slope, and it was Till Cooke's voice. Wyeth spun, and that, combined with the shifting of the horses, allowed Keller a clear view of him through the clumps of grass below the corral fence. Wyeth was indeed armed, but only with a pistol—

hardly a weapon to make much difference against the armed cattlemen above.

"Who's there?" Wyeth yelled.

'It's Till Cooke, Wyeth! Drop that pistol!"

Wyeth refused with an oath, and Keller chose that moment to rise. He slammed the rifle stock against his shoulder, lined up the sight on Wyeth's midsection, and advised Wyeth that obedience to Cooke's command might be prudent.

Wyeth had obviously been taken by complete surprise—as had his partner, who carried no weapon and had stuck his hands into the air at Cooke's first yell.

Wyeth swore and dropped the pistol. Keller moved in, planning to take Wyeth hostage and use him as a human shield as he edged him up the slope and away from the house. Unfortunately, some of the cattlemen on the rise were young and overeager; three of them leaped from their fighting positions and came bounding down toward Keller and the two outlaws.

"No!" Keller yelled. The echo of the word was drowned out in the roar of rifle fire from the cabin. The closest cowboy jerked and fell, blood running out of his side. A moment later the man with him also fell, crying out and grabbing his leg, his rifle rattling to the earth. The wounded men began scrambling back up the slope to safety. Wyeth, meanwhile, did a flat fall onto the ground, regained his pistol and fired sideways at Jed, all in a fluid continuum of motion. It was a graceful and effective exercise, but his aim was not good and the slug did no more than rip the hat off Keller's head.

Gunfire peppered in both directions as the cattlemen and the cabin's occupants faced off. The unarmed bandit who had come out with Wyeth ran for the safety of the creek bank, a move that seemed quite sensible to Keller as well. He loped off toward the creek as Wyeth sent another slug winging vainly after him, then turned his attention to the slope above.

Keller made it to the creek and leaped over the edge

of the cut bank, splashing into the water. He heard a curse and looked over his shoulder to see the unarmed outlaw, who had been in the process of moving belly down into the water, below bank level.

"Hold it there—stay on your belly, hands behind your head, and face down," Keller barked.

"I'll drown!" the man declared.

"Then turn your head to the side, fool! But one move after that, and you're dead."

The battle, meanwhile, was growing fiercer. Wyeth was not at the corral anymore, apparently having made it back to the house or perhaps to some other place of cover. Meanwhile, some of the cattlemen were coming down the slope, edging toward the cabin as they made use of what meager cover they could find.

"God, they'll shoot us all, and if they don't shoot us, they'll hang us!" the unarmed outlaw wailed. His mouth was half submerged in the creek water, which gave his words a blubbering quality.

Keller glanced disgustedly at his prisoner and felt torn between the need to move back into the battle and the need to guard this man, who now was beginning to sniffle pitifully.

Keller made his choice. He levered his rifle, turned to the man and said, "Get up and start running."

"You're going to shoot me, ain't you! You're going to shoot me in the back while I run!"

"Maybe I will. Or would you rather I shoot you in the head, where you lie? Get up and run!"

The man did as he was told, darting like a rabbit across the rolling prairie and up the far edge of the basin, until Keller saw him no more. No doubt the man had expected every step to be his last.

Keller took a deep breath, rose, and darted into the battle. He saw Wyeth, crouched behind a scrubby tree near the corral, still fighting with his pistol. The outlaw was so distracted that Keller realized he could probably reach him from behind before he ever realized anyone was coming.

He decided to do just that. Shifting left to put himself squarely behind Wyeth, he began loping forward with wide, careful strides. Meanwhile, Wyeth was taking aim around the trunk of the tree . . . and then he fired, just as Keller saw who his target was.

Till Cooke. Through the smoke of Wyeth's pistol Keller saw his old mentor crumple to the ground. A shiver of horror overwhelmed Keller, and he surged forward with a yell.

Wyeth, still crouched, twisted around just in time to see the butt of Keller's rifle come straight into his forehead, driving the back of his skull against the tree with the force of a sledge.

Keller didn't pause to examine the results of his work. He darted past to Cooke, ignoring the continuing gunfire on all sides.

"Till!" he yelled. "Till, are you alive?"

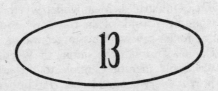

13

Cooke was pushing himself to his feet even as Keller reached him. "I'm fine, fine. He didn't even hit me; I just stumbled—look out!"

Keller, not knowing what Cooke had just seen or how to react to so imprecise a warning, instinctively ducked, putting his hands on his head. It was the correct move, for it saved him from losing his brains to a rifle wildly swung by one of the outlaws who had run out of bullets and now was panicked. Till Cooke drew his pistol and shot the outlaw in the knee, driving him down howling. Keller turned and wrenched the empty rifle from the fallen man as he lost consciousness.

Keller and Cooke, both on their feet again, headed for some nearby rocks, diving behind them as slugs spanged around them. They came up firing, Keller marveling to himself the entire while. *Why am I here? I came to Texas to escape this kind of thing—and now I'm fighting for my life.*

The battle quickly wound down, and the cattlemen emerged victorious. When Cooke and Keller converged with the others around the little cabin, they discovered their force had suffered no deaths. For that matter, neither had the surprised stock thieves. Unfortunately, the confusion had given one break to the besieged outlaws. Five of them together had made a coordinated run for some of the stolen horses and ridden away pell-mell, slugs whizzing over them. A fifth escapee was the man Keller had let run away down at the creek, and a sixth, the man Cooke had shot in the knee, who had managed to drag himself around to the far side of the house and now was nowhere to be found. The presumption was that he too had mounted a horse and gotten away.

The cattlemen were astounded and disgusted that so many had gotten away. Still, the results hadn't been a failure, for most of the stolen stock had been recovered —and best of all, one of the two remaining prisoners was Cutter Wyeth himself.

Wyeth had regained consciousness only to find himself tied up and surrounded by the grim-faced cattlemen. The man's ugly face paled beneath his scraggly whiskers, and his drooping eye narrowed to a dark slit.

Till Cooke, who as sheriff had spent long, frustrated years unable to snare the region's worst stock rustler, advanced on Cutter Wyeth and looked with dark satisfaction in his face. The scene around the cabin fell quiet and pregnant with anticipation; the cattlemen moved in close to hear what Till Cooke had to say.

He had just opened his mouth to speak when Wyeth spat on him. Cooke took the foulness in the face without even a flinch. Slowly, never letting his gaze drop from Wyeth's, he dug a cloth from his pocket and wiped off the spittle.

Wyeth grinned in a typically twisted fashion, his mouth curling like a drying leaf. "Well, Cooke, you finally trapped your rat," he said. "It's been a hell of a run I've given you, huh?"

"That you have. But every rat gets caught sooner or later."

"So what will you do with me?"

"Hang you, I reckon. Here and now."

Keller stepped forward. "What?"

"I said we were going to hang him."

"No," Keller said firmly. "We're not."

Cooke pivoted his head and looked at Keller in disbelief. "What do you mean, no? This is Cutter Wyeth himself! You saying he don't deserve the noose?"

"Of course he does. But it's not our place to do that job. You said yourself that this group isn't the Old Boys. I won't take part in lynching a man."

Cooke swore and threw his hands skyward. "So what do you think we ought to do? Take him to Weyburn and watch him walk free?"

"I don't think Weyburn could just let him go. Too many eyes on him for that. He'd be obliged to see him through to justice."

Cooke replied, "I never thought you to be so simple, Jed. These here men ain't exactly peace-loving Pennsylvania Shakers! Weyburn ain't to be trusted—especially not with a man he's almost dead certain working with in the background."

Wyeth pulled at his ropes and twitched the right side of his face. "I don't know no Weyburn," he said.

"Shut up," Cooke barked at the outlaw, still looking angrily at Keller. "Jed, there's nobody out here but cattlemen, every one of us victims of this here maggot." He waved contemptuously at Wyeth. "I say let's squash him, then keep our mouths shut."

"What about the other prisoner? You going to hang him too?"

"I don't see why not."

The other prisoner, a tall man made of beard and gristle, jerked at the ropes that bound him. "I ain't part of no stock thieving!" he bellowed. "I'm a buffalo hunter, and that's all! I come here to play cards with my cousin, and that's the God's truth!"

One of the cowboys said, "I think he's telling it true. I seen him before in Cade, down at the hide yard. And unless I counted wrong, I saw nine men down here at one time or another, and there was only eight thieves. So one had to be an extra."

This development seemed to knock Cooke off balance, so Keller pressed the issue. "See, Till? You can't hang a man you don't know is guilty. You'll have to take him back alive, no matter what you do to Wyeth, and when you do, you'll have a witness to your lynching."

"I say hang them both," Cooke growled. "He was with them, so he's guilty in my book."

"That's not the Till Cooke I worked with, saying that," Keller said. "The Till Cooke I worked with was always a man of law."

"You may not know Till Cooke so bloody well as you think!" Cooke shot back. "But I know you, Jed, and I know what's behind this high moral tone you're setting! You're still bowel-bound over that fellow you killed years ago! That's it, ain't it? That old memory has eat away at your nerve until it's gone!"

Keller clamped his teeth together, anger rising. "It's got nothing to do with anything except following the law," he retorted. "You used to believe in that yourself —in case you've forgotten."

"If our great-grandfathers had thought like you think, we'd all still be sipping English tea," Cooke said. "There's a law higher than that on the books, and sometimes it's got to be followed."

Keller forced himself to calm down. "Till, all I'm asking is that we not become murderers in the name of justice." He pointed at the self-professed buffalo hunter. It took great effort to speak calmly, but he did it. "If this man is innocent, it'd be his blood on our hands forever if we lynch him. And while I'm talking, let me be full square with you. Yes, I do think back on that poor fellow I killed—and because of what happened that day, I know what it is to kill a man wrongly. I won't be part of doing that again."

Cooke remained silent, apparently thinking. One of

the other cattlemen cleared his throat and uncomfortably contributed: "I don't much like the idea of hanging anybody without a trial." A couple of others murmured agreement.

At length Cooke sighed and nodded. He turned to Wyeth. "Looks like you've escaped the rope—for now," he said. Then, to Keller: "Jed, if we take Wyeth in to Weyburn, I guarantee you Weyburn won't do a thing but find an excuse to let him go."

"Then let's not take them to Weyburn."

"Where, then?"

"To Fort Cade. Turn them over to the commander."

The cattlemen looked among themselves. "Sounds good to me," one commented, and others followed suit, seeming relieved.

"Till?"

The former sheriff nodded. "I reckon I can go along with that. Though I ain't forgetting that you crossed me on this, Jed. I ain't forgetting."

Keller was too relieved to worry about Cooke's last statement. He glanced at Wyeth, who was still very white from realizing how closely he had brushed the hangman's noose. Keller's nose twitched, he glanced down and grinned.

"Gentlemen," he said. "Take a look—it appears the daring Mr. Cutter Wyeth has peed his pants."

Indeed, a warm, dark ring had spread down the front of the outlaw's trousers; he himself hadn't even noticed it, wrapped up as he was in the preceding debate over his fate. Now his blanched face went red and he fumed as his captors laughed at and mocked him.

"Cooke!" Wyeth said.

Till Cooke wheeled, stalked up to Wyeth and faced him at a distance no more than ten inches. "What, maggot?"

"I'll remember it was you who would have hanged

me, Cooke. Keep your eyes open . . . one of these days there'll come a settling up. You can count on it."

Cooke said nothing. Then, abruptly, he spat in Wyeth's face just as Wyeth had spat in his.

"You'll hang yet, Wyeth," he said. "And when you do, I'll be there to see you twitch your last. And believe me, I'll appreciate the show."

He stomped away, leaving Wyeth tied up and trying vainly to wipe off his face with a hunched shoulder.

"Come on, gents," Keller said to those around him. "Let's patch up the hurt ones and head to Fort Cade."

The men moved immediately in response. None of them, Keller included, thought about it, but something important had just occurred: Jed Keller had just taken on a new status. He had vied with Till Cooke's unofficial authority and won; he had given a directive and they had responded.

Without trying to, Jed Keller had just gained the status of leadership.

14

avid Weyburn shifted in his saddle and felt tension ripple through the tight muscles of his back. Putting his hands on the saddle horn, he leaned forward and wished he could find a comfortable position.

His eyes darted from side to side, noting the men with him. Unlike Till Cooke, who had operated the sheriff's office with a force of only three deputies, Weyburn had hired a force of eight, an expense he had justified to the county's governing body on the grounds that a larger force would allow him to make a greater impact on stock theft at the outlying ranches. He could send deputies on constant patrol rounds throughout the county, giving the outlying ranches greater access to the law.

In fact, Weyburn had sent men out on such rounds only twice since coming into office. He liked keeping his deputies—all of them men who had worked for him in far less legal capacities in the past—close at hand. It countered the rising sense of discomfort in office that had plagued him since he had been sworn in.

It was most disconcerting; Weyburn had expected to ease into the post as comfortably as a foot sliding into a familiar old boot. David Weyburn and the post of county sheriff had seemed a made-to-order match. As sheriff he could exercise official authority and power, keep control of forces that otherwise might be used against him, and thus work in league with Wyeth and his ring of stock thieves—all without fear of detection. As the proverbial wolf guarding the henhouse, he could feel secure and powerful. Instead he felt increasingly ill at ease.

Mostly it had to do with the district attorney, who reportedly had been asking some disconcerting questions about the new sheriff ever since he came into office. That was Till Cooke's doing, Weyburn figured; he knew how Cooke distrusted him, and guessed that he must have cashed in some due favor by getting the district attorney to check him out. Weyburn hated Cooke for it. Hated him, but didn't know how to deal with him.

Today he would have to deal with Till Cooke, if what Floyd Fells had told him was true. Fells had come riding hard to Weyburn's office, telling him that Cooke and a group of cattlemen and cowboys had gone off on their own after Cutter Wyeth and a herd of stolen horses. Now Cooke's group had been spotted returning, with Wyeth in custody.

This created quite a predicament for Weyburn. As sheriff, it would be his duty to imprison Wyeth, but as Wyeth's secret partner, he couldn't actually bring the law to bear on the man. Even now, as he, his deputies, and several of his ranch hands waited for the cattlemen and their prisoners to come into view, Weyburn wasn't sure how he was going to handle this matter.

Weyburn lifted his chin and spied out across the rolling plains. A lone rider, one of his own men, was approaching. He rode up to Weyburn. "They're heading toward Fort Cade!" he said breathlessly. "They're trying to pass us by! If we're going to intercept them, we'll have to move fast!"

Fort Cade? Weyburn hadn't expected that. Were

Till Cooke's suspicions about him so strong that he wouldn't bring his prisoners into county custody? It made chilling sense, and Weyburn cursed himself for not anticipating such a move.

He couldn't allow the military authorities to take in Wyeth. If Wyeth wound up in their hands, he would be out of his own reach; Weyburn knew he would be unable either to aid Wyeth or control him. Left to vie for himself, Wyeth might start spilling the facts about their secret alliance. . . .

No. He wouldn't let that happen. Weyburn lifted his hand. "Ride!" he ordered. And they set off, angling across the plains in a cloud of dust.

"Look yonder!" Jed Keller said, pointing. But Till Cooke needed no tip-off; he had already seen the oncoming horsemen.

"That's Weyburn in the lead," he said. "Weyburn and his bunch of deputized scoundrels, come to claim their prisoner, I'll betcha. I wonder how he knew?"

"You can't hide much in this country," Keller replied. "They've probably been spying out for us. You going to turn Wyeth over to him?"

Cooke's tone betrayed how distasteful conversation with Keller was for him at the moment. "Not by any stretch. I'll see Cutter Wyeth through that fort gate and into military custody before I let go of him."

"Think we could make a run and reach the fort before Weyburn gets here?"

"Not a chance. He's coming too fast. And what does it matter? This might be just what's needed to prove once and for all that Weyburn's what I think he is."

And so they waited. Weyburn's band grew closer. It slowed only when it became apparent that Cooke, Keller, and company were not going to attempt any scramble for Fort Cade. By the time Weyburn was within talking distance, he rode at a slow lope. He eyed the group as he approached—his gaze lingering an extra second or two on Keller—then came to a halt before Cooke. Weyburn, Keller noticed, had not looked at Wyeth at all.

For several seconds silence reigned. Keller found it fascinating and surprising to see that Weyburn, despite the badge on his vest and his band of surly armed deputies, seemed the underdog in this situation. He was amused when he detected Weyburn swallowing again and again—dry-mouthed, Keller figured, from nervousness.

"What's the nature of this band?" Weyburn asked. His voice sounded a little higher and more strained than normal.

"We're just a group of private citizens, operating under the authority of Fort Cade . . . Sheriff." Cooke put sarcastic emphasis on Weyburn's title.

"That man there appears to be Cutter Wyeth."

"You ought to know." The comment evoked a murmur of laughter from the cynical cattlemen. Weyburn's expression grew darker.

"Where are you taking these men?" Weyburn asked.

"Fort Cade. We intend to turn him over to authorities who are trustworthy and honest, and who empowered us to act."

"Fort Cade has no authority to mandate any venture like this. I'm the sheriff of this county. This is a matter under my jurisdiction."

"I don't think so. It's my opinion that you're of similar ilk to the outlaw himself, and likely in league with him. To turn him over to you would be idiocy. If you've got a squabble with the fort commander, take it up with the Army."

Weyburn was beginning to get mad now, and the effect was actually helpful to him, for it enabled him to overcome his case of nerves. "Listen to me, Mr. Cooke: I'll not have you and your—your . . . gang making like a bunch of vigilantes. You think you're the Old Boys? Well, I'll have none of that in my county. Those days are past."

"The Old Boys? That's not us, Sheriff. The Old Boys are long gone . . . though I confess that may be regrettable, given what we're forced to deal with these days. Not that I advocate vigilanteism, Sheriff Weyburn. No sir, not me."

Weyburn said, "That's a more open question than you might have us believe, Cooke. I've heard a widespread opinion that the sheriff who used to send out such loud warnings to the Old Boys to cease and desist their kind of 'justice' was in fact himself the leader of that very group."

"You can't believe all you hear. A good lawman ought to know that. But I suppose 'good lawman' doesn't necessarily apply to you, does it?"

Keller couldn't squelch his smile; Cooke was managing to insult Weyburn with almost every sentence. Weyburn wasn't missing it either, and it made him more angry. He reined in a little closer to Cooke.

"Listen to me, old man: I know you don't respect me. I know you're jealous of me because I hold your old job—jealous even though it was you who stepped down. You think you're going to ride roughshod over me, mock me before my own men, and act like a law unto yourself. Well, you can damn well forget it, Cooke. I know what you've done here. You've bypassed the elected authorities and gone out on what amounts to a vigilante raid. Perhaps you've even killed some men that I don't yet know about. Obviously, you've taken a couple of prisoners. Well, they're my prisoners now, and you can hand them over . . . or face charges as a vigilante."

That threat generated some somber glances among the cattlemen. Driven by anger and the desire to avenge themselves on the stock thieves, they were realizing only now that their actions might have legal ramifications.

Cooke's expression was a sight to see. "You dare to threaten me, rascal? You're part and parcel with scum like Wyeth."

"I'm sheriff, that's what I am. I have the force of law behind me, and you no longer do. Now, turn over the prisoners."

The self-professed buffalo hunter, his hands lashed to his saddle horn, said, "I ain't done a thing, Sheriff. They took me prisoner and almost hung me—and I swear I ain't done a thing!"

Weyburn seized the opportunity to tighten the squeeze on Cooke. To the buffalo hunter he said, "Are you willing to state that under oath, if called upon?"

"Yes sir, I am."

One of Weyburn's deputies said, "He's telling the truth. That's J. N. Tucker. He is a buffalo man, just like he says. He's no thief."

"I don't know one end of a cow from another," Tucker said.

Keller turned to Cooke. "Till, we're going to have to do what he says."

Cooke's glare upon Keller was hot enough to burn. "Do what he says? Not me! I'm taking Wyeth to Fort Cade. Hell, it was your idea, Jed! You going to back out on me now? You going to defy me again?"

"There's no choice, Till. Weyburn's the sheriff, like it or not. If he wants to make trouble for us, he can do it." Keller faced Weyburn. "Besides, this will give Weyburn a chance to prove he's the honest lawman he claims to be. If he's square, he'll see that Wyeth gets what's coming to him. If he doesn't, we'll know he's the fraud we think him to be."

Weyburn examined Keller with that same unusual interest he always gave the man. "Tell me, Mr. Keller— what has poisoned you against me?"

Through Keller's mind ran the list of events that had aroused his suspicions: the encounters with Paco the Mex, Weyburn's own insistent questioning about

Paco and the Broadmore fire, Paco's disappearance, and his knowledge that Weyburn and Magart had likely been carrying on a love affair. None of these were things that needed saying in the present context, so Keller replied, "The time may come when you and me will have to have a good talk."

Cooke spoke. "All right, Weyburn. You win. Take our prisoners. We'll be watching to see how you deal with them. If there's anything wrong in how they're handled, there'll be no lack of response. Of that I assure you."

"What's your plan, Cooke? To bring back the Old Boys? To ride in the dark and dispense your private notion of justice with a rope, but without benefit of judge and jury?"

"It's you who keeps trying to tie me to the Old Boys, Weyburn. Keep up that kind of slander, and I just may challenge you to prove your words in a court of law."

Weyburn had no more to say. He collected the buffalo hunter and Wyeth—who bore a look of relief he couldn't disguise despite all his efforts—and turned with his men toward Cade. Keller watched them ride away.

"I'm willing to bet that Cutter Wyeth will be gone from Weyburn's cell before sundown tomorrow," Keller said.

"Then why did you force my hand, Jed? What's got into you? What's turned you so against me?" Cooke's tone indicated a level of anger that startled Keller.

"Till, if we hadn't gone along, he would have put charges on us—charges that would have stuck."

"You're soft, Jed. Soft and scared as a woman. I never would have thought it of you. I thought I knew you. Reckon I was wrong. You've changed."

"It's you who's changed, Till. You used to be a man who believed in the law."

At that, Cooke swore, turned away, clicked his tongue, and rode off toward his ranch, his every movement indicating clearly that he neither wanted nor expected any company along the way.

Keller watched him go, and felt sad and angry at the same time. The sorrow came from having his old mentor take such a low view of him; the anger came from knowing that Cooke would go home and do his best to fill Claire with ill will toward him as well. He could stand having Till Cooke think ill of him. Having Claire O'Keefe do the same was quite a different thing.

Keller rode home in declining spirits. Charlie Lilly's horse plodded along beside him. "Well, it was a noble venture, even if Wyeth did wind up in Weyburn's hands. The efforts of good men bear their own rewards, thankfully. To quote Thomas Gray: 'Some bold adventurers disdain the limits of their little reign, and unknown regions dare descry—' "

"Charlie," Keller interrupted. "Here's a poem for you, very short and to the point, and I hope you take it to heart: Shut up, dear Charles, shut up."

He spurred his gelding and rode on ahead, leaving a taken-aback Lilly gaping after him.

15

Keller crossed the rise and saw Claire out by the chicken pen. It was remarkable that even so mundane an activity as feeding hens became fascinating to watch when performed by such a woman. He felt a familiar warmth rise inside him, only to have it cooled by the fear that Till Cooke's anger might have spread to his niece.

She straightened and put her hand to her brow, shielding her eyes as she saw him. Keller waved, and she waved back. *So far, so good,* he thought. *At least she isn't ignoring me or running into the house for a shotgun.*

"Hello, Jed."

"Evening, Claire. How you been?"

"Very well, though things have been . . . difficult, I guess you could say, around here the last day or two." Keller was between Claire and the setting sun, so she kept her hand at her brow and squinted in a way that he found most alluring. As a matter of fact, he couldn't think of a thing about Claire that wasn't alluring.

"Till's still mad at me?"

Claire glanced back at the house, then came a step or two closer to Keller. "He's more than mad. You defied him. To him, that's betrayal."

"How do you feel about it?"

"I'm glad you did what you did. It's always best to operate within the law, and Uncle Till himself knows that, when his temper doesn't get in the way of his sense. But we shouldn't be talking like this; if he sees us, he'll probably figure I'm betraying him too." Keller detected an edge of exasperation in the words. Apparently, life in the household of Till Cooke had taken a certain toll on Claire's patience since last he saw her.

Cooke emerged from the house, filling the door in a way that few men could. "Well, look who's here!" he said in a noticeably sarcastic tone. "Mr. Take-Charge, Turn-'em-Over-to-Weyburn Keller!"

Keller dismounted and dropped the reins. The horse, already cropping the grass, was trusty and would not wander far. "Till, I came to see if I was still welcome on your land. I think I've already got my answer."

"What? Now you're trying to make me feel bad?" Cooke said. "I never said nothing about you not being welcome. Come in." The words sounded like banter, but without the covert affection that goes with such.

Claire took Keller's arm as they advanced to the house, and Keller appreciated the support subtly indicated in the gesture as much as the affection it also spoke of.

Cooke was obviously still angry, but something intangible had changed. Over coffee the two men talked, and Keller could tell that Cooke's thoughts had traveled past the disagreement over Wyeth that had divided them. There was an underlying restlessness in Cooke's manner, and an aura of distraction about him. Cooke fidgeted like a man waiting to meet an old lover, or an heir awaiting the reading of a will that could make him rich.

Keller had not come intending to stay long, so after a few minutes of conversation, he rose to leave. He had assumed that Cooke's willingness to talk would make him feel better about things. He didn't feel better. Till

Cooke had talked with him, but not to him. The senior man's words might as well have been aimed at the corner for all the feeling that came through them.

"Take a walk with me before you go," Claire invited Keller. "This is a beautiful time of the evening for a stroll, don't you think?"

Outside, she clung to his arm and began talking about Cooke as soon as they were out of earshot of the house.

"He's been coming and going ever since he got back from chasing Wyeth and his rustlers," Claire said. "And this afternoon Ben Potts came over from the Lucky Y, and they talked for nearly an hour—shutting up real fast whenever they thought I might hear. What does it mean?"

Keller said, "I don't know for sure, but I'm willing to make a likely guess. I believe Till is reorganizing the Old Boys."

"The Old Boys?"

"Yes. Vigilantes that cleaned up the area a few years back. Nobody knew who they were, other than they reportedly included some of the finer male citizens. And I'm on pretty solid ground when I tell you that your uncle was the leader. Sheriff by day, vigilante leader by night."

"Do you really think so? I hate to consider such a thing!"

"So do I, Claire. But the fact is, Till has strongly hinted to me since I first arrived that the Old Boys were going to return to action, with me included. Or that's what he wanted."

"But he hasn't asked you?"

"Of course not, not while he's mad at me. I guess he doesn't think anymore that I have the right sort of spirit. It's not only because of our argument over Wyeth and Weyburn either. It goes back to something that happened years ago, in Missouri, when I first went to work as Till's deputy. I killed an innocent man, and it almost ended my career. In the end, that killing did end it, because it haunted me until I finally laid down my badge." Succinctly and quietly, he told her the story of the shooting in the bank. "When Till started talking about the Old Boys, I told him I didn't want to be part of it. It touched too much on that bad memory."

"But you went with him after the Wyeths. . . ."

"I know. But that wasn't intended to be a lynch mob, though it was clear at the end that Till was ready to turn it into one."

"Poor Uncle Till . . . he becomes obsessed when he gets a particular notion. It seems now that all he can think about is stock theft and David Weyburn. He despises the man so."

"I know. He believes Weyburn is in league with the Wyeths, which he very well may be. And the truth is, I'm as wary of Weyburn as Till is, and not just about stock theft." He cleared his throat. "Claire, may I tell you something in confidence?"

"Of course."

"I think David Weyburn was somehow involved with my sister's death."

"Involved? You think he killed her?"

"I didn't say that—the truth is, I don't know what I mean. It's just that since I first came to Cade, things have happened, things have been said. . . . Weyburn himself has acted peculiar around me, unless I'm just letting my imagination get out of hand. But just this week, Charlie Lilly told me something about Magart and Weyburn. They were having a love affair right before the fire that killed her and Folly Broadmore."

"A love affair!"

"That's right." He told her the story, starting with his own drunken attack on Paco the Mex and including everything thereafter. "So you see, I've got nothing that really holds together, not even enough to set up a clear suspicion. I don't even know what it is I suspect Weyburn of! But there's something there. I know there is."

"So Weyburn may be just as shady as Uncle Till thinks."

"I suspect he is. One thing you've got to say for Till, he has good instincts. He can judge a man by looking at him, and get it right nine times out of ten."

"If you feel that way, why did you let Wyeth be turned over to Weyburn?"

"There was a second man in our custody and no clear indication he was guilty of anything. Weyburn could have used that to cause us trouble if we had defied him and gone on to Fort Cade. And anyway, putting Wyeth in his hands is a sort of test. If Weyburn is honest, like he claims, he'll treat Wyeth like the criminal he is. If he lets Wyeth weasel out, then no cattleman in this county will trust him. It really puts Weyburn in a hot spot, having Wyeth in his cell."

"Is Wyeth still locked up?"

"As of this afternoon, yes. It'll be interesting to see if it stays that way. I'll bet he's chewing Weyburn's ear off, trying to talk his way out."

"I just hope Weyburn doesn't let him go. I hope he stays in jail."

"I hope so too. Mostly for Till's sake."

"What do you mean?"

"Wyeth threatened Till. It may have just been big talk, but you can't ever be sure. If he gets out, keep your eyes peeled. Watch out for Till, for he might not have the clearheadedness to watch out for himself."

"Weyburn!" Cutter Wyeth yelled through the bars as loudly as he could. The man in the next cell, badly hung over, groaned and put his hands over his ears. "Get back here, now!" Wyeth boomed out.

David Weyburn wore an angry scowl as he came out of his anterior office. "Wyeth, I'm tired of your yelling," he said. "What do you want now?"

"I want to know how long I have to put up with being locked up like common scum!"

"You're a thief, Wyeth, and thieves stay locked up a long time," Weyburn said loudly, turning his head a little to make sure Wyeth's hung-over jailed companion heard. Then he drew close to Wyeth's cell and whispered, "Watch what you're saying! You think that man can't repeat what he hears once he's on the street?"

"Then toss him out of here!"

Weyburn looked Wyeth up and down, thinking that no matter what business arrangements existed between them, he would never consider Cutter Wyeth a friend. The man was thoroughly unlikable, possessing an ugliness that went deeper than the merely physical.

Wordlessly, Weyburn went to the other cell, opened it, and told its occupant he was free to go. The hungover man stood slowly, pain scrawled across his face, and left. When Wyeth heard the office door open and close, he immediately cut into Weyburn.

"What the hell is this, Weyburn? Are you going to let me go or not?"

"I've told you already, Wyeth. If I let you go too quickly, it would only confirm suspicions we don't need."

"Till Cooke's suspicions, you mean?"

"Exactly."

"So Till Cooke still makes the decisions in the county sheriff's office? Is that it?"

"Till Cooke is a man of influence among the cattlemen. He's already burned us enough. I'm not about to give him fuel to burn us more."

"What does that mean? You're not letting me go?"

"Of course you'll go. Tonight. You'll overpower Deputy Ellsworth when he brings you your supper and break free. Deputy Ellsworth will give you no resistance. You'll steal a saddled gelding that will be hitched in front of the office. I'll mount a search, and no trace of you will be found."

"I don't like this waiting around. What if Till Cooke and his Old Boys come calling before I get out of here? They'd have me lynched to a telegraph pole, and you couldn't stop them."

"You think they'd walk right up to this office and take out a prisoner? Cooke's not that big a fool."

"Fool or not, he's a thorn in our side. He needs to be got rid of."

Weyburn stuck his finger through the bars into Wyeth's face. "You don't go getting any ideas about killing Till Cooke. You start taking that kind of risk, and it'll all come crashing down around our ears."

"I ain't worried. You're the sheriff, ain't you? What can they do to you?"

"I'll not argue with you about this, Cutter. You just mind your own affairs, lay low for a while, and for God's sake don't let anybody catch you again. If they bring you back to me, there'd be no way to let you 'escape' again and have anybody believe it was really an escape. Get out of the area awhile, and let me handle Till Cooke. There's better ways than a bullet to deal with some situations."

"Not that I've found," Wyeth muttered.

"If you can't kill a scratching cat, the next best thing is to take out its claws," Weyburn said. "Till Cooke is ripe to be ruined. One good scandal and we could bring him down. He's got that pretty niece of his living right there with him in his own house. A few stories started in the right places, among the right people, and we could scandalize his name so that nobody would so much as let him spit in their yard, much less let him lead them."

Wyeth was not a subtle thinker. What he achieved he achieved in a direct and brutal fashion. "I say let's kill him and be done with it," he said.

"I'm warning you, Cutter: Stay away from Till Cooke. You go after him, and before you can turn around, he'll be after you in turn, and he might just drag me down with him along the way."

Wyeth said nothing more. Weyburn studied him with concern, wondering if he would heed his warning. With Cutter Wyeth there was no telling. Weyburn wished he didn't have to let Wyeth go free. While Wyeth was locked up, he was under control. But keeping him here was impossible. They were partners, after all. And Wyeth could hardly do his part while in a cell. Of course, once Wyeth was out, it would be a challenge indeed to convince men such as Till Cooke that the escape was not his doing.

"Tonight, Cutter," Weyburn said. "Be patient until then."

He returned to his office. Cutter Wyeth swore and began pacing the little cell, back and forth, back and forth, like a panther in a cage.

David Weyburn sat down at his desk and took a series of deep breaths. Sweat broke out on his brow as a surge of unfocused panic passed through him. It was all he could do to keep from leaping up and running out onto the street, yelling.

After a few moments the attack of panic ended and he relaxed. Since taking office, such attacks had come to him from time to time, without warning. They frightened him, for he couldn't ascertain their origin.

Through his mind raced a boyhood memory: his grandfather, raging and fighting in a room behind a barred door in a place where they locked away people who had lost their sanity.

Weyburn thought: Could it be happening to me?

No, no. He refused to accept that. He was just wrought up, that was all. He had so many secrets to hide. Sometimes he felt like a juggler in one of those traveling snake oil shows, trying to keep everything up in the air and fearing that one slip that would bring it all crashing down.

As soon as his deputy Ellsworth arrived, Weyburn

left and headed home. He needed a drink, and the love and companionship of his beloved Magart. The mere thought of her brought him joy and comfort.

As long as he had Magart, everything would be all right.

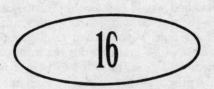

16

Maria Cruz was an ample woman; it required two towels for her to get fully dry after her baths. For years she had bathed habitually about once every week in room-temperature water, believing anything hotter and more frequent was injurious to health. But lately she had begun to bathe twice weekly, and today's bath was the third of the week.

Yet she still felt dirty, the kind of dirty that didn't go away, no matter how many times she washed. She brushed away the water in her eyes. Most of it had not come from the tin washtub she stood in.

Continuing to wipe away tears, she dressed herself in her nightgown, a long cotton frock given to her by her husband. She wouldn't let herself cry aloud for fear Eduardo would hear her. At the moment he was upstairs, taking his shift at keeping the Lady company. The Lady. That was how Maria thought of her now. She knew that David Weyburn preferred that she be called Mrs. Weyburn, but Maria hadn't been able to do that. No matter what Weyburn said, the Lady wasn't his wife just because she shared his house and bed. She wasn't anybody's wife at all, now that her husband had died in that fire. If she was Mrs. anyone, it was Mrs. Broadmore.

Of course, Maria dared not call her by that name in this house. To do so would invite the fury of David Weyburn. He had despised Folly Broadmore in life, even as he had loved Broadmore's woman. And so, for Maria, she was and would remain simply, the Lady.

When she was dressed, Maria sat down at the little dressing table that Weyburn had given her two years ago as a show of his gratitude for the loyal service she and Eduardo had given him. It had been a wonderful gift, highly prized by her. Yet now even the dressing table could not delight her as it once had. It was tainted by its very association with David Weyburn. David Weyburn the fraud, the thief . . . the murderer.

The latter fact was the part that Maria couldn't bear. She had known for years that her employer was not honest, not the good man he pretended to be. And she hadn't much cared. She herself had been no angel throughout her earlier life; she could hardly condemn her employer for being dishonest when she had been far worse herself. But murder . . . that was a different matter. She could overlook a multitude of David Weyburn's sins, but try as she might, she couldn't bear the knowledge that he had killed Folly Broadmore, then burned his house down around him to destroy the body and cover the evidence of how Broadmore had really died. Eduardo had told her that it wasn't as bad as it sounded. Folly Broadmore had beaten Magart so severely that her brain had been damaged; that was why she was now so childlike. So he had deserved to die, according to Eduardo.

If only Eduardo hadn't told me about it all, Maria thought. *If only he had kept it to himself . . . then I wouldn't have to bear the weight of it on my soul. I wouldn't feel so dirty all the time.*

When she was honest with herself, Maria could not really blame Eduardo for having told her. After all, she had pushed him to it. Knowing something significant and secret had happened between Weyburn and the

Broadmores, she had harangued Eduardo into telling her. Now she regretted it, for what he had revealed was a crushing burden on her soul.

The worst part was the poor Tonkawa woman Floyd Fells had killed. She was the truly innocent victim in this scandal. Fells had dressed the woman's corpse in some of Magart Keller's clothing, and put her alongside the body of Folly Broadmore before the house was set ablaze. And so everyone had believed that Magart Broadmore had died along with her husband. No one dreamed she was still alive and living in the house of David Weyburn, where Weyburn intended she should stay for perpetuity.

It was so foolish, and so impossible! Maria knew that such a house of cards could not stand. Only Weyburn's fierce love for Magart Broadmore kept him under the delusion that she could be hidden from the world forever. Only a handful of people knew about the woman in Weyburn's upper room: Weyburn himself; his ranch manager and associate, Floyd Fells; Eduardo and Maria. And Paco, the poor old fellow who used to come around begging at the ranches. Maria had told him the entire story, simply to unload the weight of it. What harm could have come from telling him? He was harmless and simple, and probably hadn't even understood it.

But since then, Paco hadn't come around, and Maria wondered why.

She knelt beside her bed and took up her rosary. It seemed an alien thing in her hands. Closing her eyes, she tried to pray and could not. How could one as guilty as she send up any kind of prayer and expect to be heard? The very idea was sacrilege.

She was a woman living in secret sin, the sin of helping hide a murder. Every day that she and Eduardo helped perpetuate Weyburn's secret, keeping their silence, her guilt only grew. Surely she would pay the divine penalty for this sin, and Eduardo too. She felt she should confess it, not only to a priest, but also to the law . . . but now the law was Weyburn. And even if she told someone else—the commander at Fort Cade, or the former sheriff, Till Cooke—what would become of her? Would she and Eduardo not both be liable for the parts they had already played in this matter?

She put away the rosary and crawled into bed. There she huddled silently, still weeping, until Eduardo came to join her. He undressed without words and crawled in beside her.

He knew his wife was upset as soon as his hand touched her tight and tense shoulders.

"What is wrong with you, Maria? Are you crying again?"

"No, Eduardo, I . . . yes. Yes, I am crying. I cry every night. I cry as we will both cry in eternal Hell for the sin we are committing."

Eduardo sat up and made her roll to face him. "Hear me, wife: You must not think like this. Don't even think of confession. If the truth came out, we would be punished for what we have done."

"Yes . . . I know that. But I can't carry this weight forever. It crushes me"—she thumped her large and sagging bosom—"here . . . I can feel the weight of it, like a stone."

"We are only being faithful servants. Señor Weyburn has been good to us through many years, Maria."

"But Señor Weyburn is a murderer."

"He killed a man who would have beaten an innocent woman into her grave . . . and he did not mean to kill him. It was the anger of love that made him do it. Perhaps, in God's eyes, that isn't murder."

"Yes, it is murder, and even if it wasn't, what of the Indian woman? The poor Tonkawa?"

"She was only an Indian, Maria."

"If we were killed, there are those who would say of us, 'They were only Mexicans.' Only an Indian? She was a woman made by God's hands, and he will surely smite us down for helping hide her death."

"Keep your voice low, Maria! What if he should hear you? He might fear you will talk, and then—"

"It's too late. I've already told someone."

"Mother of God!"

"It's true—I told the story to Paco."

"Paco—the old thief and beggar?"

"Yes. I couldn't bear to not talk of it, Eduardo. It was a fire inside me. I chose him because he was simple and couldn't understand."

Eduardo took a deep breath. "Maria, Paco is gone. He has been gone for a long time. In town they say he claimed to know a secret about the Broadmore fire. No one believed him . . . but now he is gone, and no one knows where."

"Oh, Eduardo . . ."

"Paco understood what you told him, Maria. It was you who was the fool, the simple one. Not Paco."

"If he is gone, then he is dead, Eduardo! He must be! Señor Weyburn and Señor Fells, they have killed him! Oh, God forgive me!"

"Hush, woman! If they have killed him, then at least we are safe. You were a fool to talk to Paco about what I told you. Because of you, we might have been discovered."

"My husband, is that all you can think of, what would happen to us? Have you no pity for those who have died? Have you no fear of the sin that has been done?"

"I cannot bear the thought of being imprisoned, Maria. And hanging—that would be even worse."

"And what about the sufferings of Hell? Have you no fear of that?"

"Go to sleep, Maria. We will talk no more of this."

They turned their backs on each other. Maria cried for a long time, keeping her sobs silent. As for Eduardo, he simply stared into the darkness.

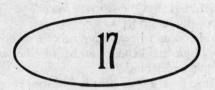

17

"Three head a month?" Weyburn asked, scratching his chin and leaning back in his chair. He was in his office, and across the desk from him sat Floyd Fells, holding a document that bore the imprints of the U.S. Army and Fort Cade. "I see no problem in meeting that demand."

"Neither do I." Fells dropped his voice. "And seldom, I think, will it be necessary to even touch our own herd. We can easily cut three beeves a month out of neighboring herds, dispose of the hides to hide the brands, and deliver the meat to Fort Cade without lifting any eyebrows."

"Yes, but be careful," Weyburn replied. "There's Till Cooke and his ilk already breathing down my neck. They'll be looking for anything they can find against me. Now that I've let Wyeth make his escape, there will be trouble enough for us."

"It would be convenient if our former sheriff met with an accident, don't you think?" Fells ventured.

Weyburn jerked forward, pounding the bottom of his fist on the desktop. "No! You're talking like Wyeth now. There's already been enough killing, and it doesn't sit easily with me. There are lines I don't like to cross."

"Yes," Fells said coldly. "I know."

"Don't worry about Cooke. I have a plan to discredit him in the public eye. Now, let me see that contract."

Fells handed the paper to Weyburn, who studied it for a minute, then signed. He had just handed it back to Fells when the front door burst open and Jed Keller stomped in. Ignoring Fells, he went straight to the side of Weyburn's desk, leaned over on his palms and looked the sheriff in the face.

"I hear that Cutter Wyeth escaped this jail last night."

"Yes. He overpowered one of my deputies and forced his way out. Believe me, I regret it deeply."

"I'm sure you do, Sheriff Weyburn," Keller said mockingly. "Overpowered your deputy, you say? There's no reason for that ever to happen. I know a little about the jail business, you know. A properly trained deputy never puts himself in a position to be overpowered by a prisoner."

Weyburn's eyes flicked to Fells. "Floyd, perhaps you should go now."

Fells stood, looking at Keller like the man had just tangled with a skunk and neglected to clean himself. "Later, David." He waved the contract. "I'll go deliver this paper."

"Weyburn, you and I both know that Cutter Wyeth didn't escape from this jail. You let him walk out."

"That's a serious charge to bring against a legally elected peace officer. Do you have any evidence to support it?"

Keller hesitated. "No," he said. "But sometimes a man knows what he can't prove."

"That carries no weight in a court of law . . . if it's your plan to go that route."

"I have no plan. But there are others who might not be so lenient. And they don't require the kind of proof a court demands."

"You're talking about the so-called Old Boys, I take it? You're treading thin ice, Keller. I might take that comment as a threat."

"I'm not one of the Old Boys, Weyburn. I don't control them, if they even exist. This is no threat, but a warning. You're going to have to prove yourself honest, or you'll start an avalanche that will crush you. I went to the wall for you when I argued to let you take custody of Wyeth. You could have vindicated yourself. You didn't. You let him go free."

"I told you—he escaped."

"Then why are you here? Why aren't you out looking for him?"

"I have a sizable force of deputies doing that as we speak."

"Deputies? The deputies you hired are no more than a gang of trash who've spent more time occupying jail cells than tending them. You're a fool, Weyburn, and you're tying your own noose, one twist at a time."

Weyburn stood and walked to the stove, where he poured himself a cup of coffee. Returning to his desk, he sat down and began drinking, looking Keller up and down. "You know, Jed Keller, there's something about you that I like, and God only knows I can't say what it is. No, no, that's not true. It's because Magart Broadmore was your sister. I look in your face, and I see her. She was a fine woman, and for the sake of your kinship to her, I want to see good things come to you. But you make it hard for me to be so charitable when you act like this. Just let it go, Keller. Leave me to my business, and mind your own."

"Cade is my home now, Weyburn. I have a life here, and an investment. All I want is a peaceful existence and an honest trade in the cattle business. You and your ilk are threatening both." He paused; it was on the tip of his tongue to present to Weyburn his troubling questions about Magart's death and the way that Weyburn seemed somehow connected to it. He didn't get the

chance to ask, however, for right then the door opened
again and Till Cooke entered, his face as grim as a thun-
derhead about to burst.

"Weyburn!" Cooke shouted. "Weyburn, you did it,
didn't you! You let Wyeth go free!" Cooke wheeled
toward Keller. "And you're as much at fault as he is. If
you'd let us take Wyeth on to Fort Cade, this wouldn't
have happened!"

"Calm down, Cooke," Weyburn said. He was trying to sound composed, but Keller detected a tremble in
his voice. Weyburn, he realized, was truly afraid of Till
Cooke. He could hardly blame him.

"Calm down? I'll tell you when I'll calm down, you
maggot! I'll calm down when you're out of office and in
a cell, where you belong. Or perhaps when you're
swinging from a mesquite tree somewhere outside town!
And don't think that can't happen!"

"Till!" Keller cut in. "You watch your mouth, or
you'll say something that you'll later regret."

Cooke shot back, "Are you working for Weyburn
now, Jed? Lord knows you seem to take his side of
things enough!"

Weyburn was getting mad. "Mr. Cooke, you've just
threatened the life of the duly elected sheriff of this
county. I could jail you for that."

"You try it, you foul little swine! I'll knock your
head down your throat and pull it out your bung!"

"Mr. Cooke, I'm putting you under arrest!"

"Come and get me, then, if you think you're man
enough!"

Weyburn moved as if to come around from behind
the desk, but then he faltered. The fear on his face
couldn't be hidden. Keller saw Weyburn's eye drift
down toward his desk drawer and saw his hand twitch
restlessly. He knew then that there was a pistol in the
drawer, and that Weyburn was thinking of getting it
out. And he also knew what would happen if he did: Till

Cooke would draw his own Colt and kill Weyburn where he stood. Keller had to intervene.

"Sheriff, I apologize for my friend here," Keller said, deliberately grasping Cooke's gun arm. Cooke tried to shake him off, but Keller hung on. "Don't arrest him, please. I'll get him out of here and talk sense into him. Just let it be. It would be best for all of us."

Weyburn glared at Cooke, his lip trembling. Then he nodded curtly.

"Come on, Till," Keller said.

"Let go of me, Jed."

"Till, I'll not see you hang or spend the rest of your days locked away for murder. Think of Claire, if nothing else. Come on. Let's get out of here before things get worse."

Till Cooke, still staring at Weyburn, jerked his arm free. But he did not draw his pistol. "All right," he said. "I'll leave. But hear me, Weyburn! The cattlemen are getting sore weary of you. They know what you are. If Cutter Wyeth is found by any of them, you won't have a chance to lock him up again. All you'll be able to do with him is deliver him to the coroner."

"That's a threat of murder, Mr. Cooke. I won't forget you made it."

"I hope you won't. And while you're remembering that, remember this too: A noose can choke the life out of a crooked sheriff as easy as out of an outlaw like Wyeth. You think on that, Weyburn. Think on it when you lie down at night. And from now on, you might want to make sure your pistol is always on your hip, instead of in your desk. You might be called on to use it."

Cooke wheeled and went out the door. Keller followed. At the door he glanced back to see Weyburn, white-faced, sink back down into his chair. He looked like a man who had just heard a judge sentence him to death . . . and that, Keller realized with a chill, was not far from what had just happened.

Cooke was mounting his horse at a hitch post two buildings down when Keller caught up with him. "Till, you just made a bad mistake," he said. "If anything happens now that remotely looks like vigilante revenge, Weyburn's going to come straight to your door."

"Let him come," Cooke said. "I'd welcome the opportunity to settle with him, man to man."

"Don't be a fool, Till."

Cooke looked down at Keller from the saddle. "I'd rather be a fool than a traitor and a coward, Jed." And then he rode off, spurring his horse to a gallop, which drew much attention from those on the street.

It was clear that Cooke had intended his last words to sting Keller, and he had succeeded. Keller watched Cooke ride away, and wished he had never come to Cade at all.

When Eduardo Cruz went to his bedroom in David Weyburn's big stone house that night, he found Maria crying again.

His voice was cold. "Why are you crying now?"

Maria dabbed her eyes. "I am crying because now it is worse than before," she said.

"How? What has happened?"

"I was with the Lady all day today," Maria said. "I should have seen it earlier . . . but it was only today that I realized it."

"What?"

Maria put her arms around her husband and began weeping again. Through her crying she said, "There is another one now that will surely suffer when all this ends. An innocent one."

"Who do you speak of?"

Maria looked into her husband's eyes. "The Lady is pregnant, Eduardo. She has been pregnant for a long time now, and I've been blind to it. She is carrying his child, Señor Weyburn's child, and she is too much a child herself to even know it. And what will become of it when it is born? How will an innocent child fail to suffer, born into this house of sin?"

She began to sob loudly, and nothing Eduardo could do would comfort her.

18

For three days there was a tense lull, and then the time of vengeance began and the word went out up and down the Brazos: The Old Boys are back.

The first to fall victim was a man named Vincent Calvin, a stock thief who had been driven from Cade during the earlier days of the Old Boys, but who had returned at the first of the year and stolen horses both from ranchers and a small settlement of Tonkawas. His body was found hanging from a mesquite tree a mile north of Cade, and around his neck was a hand-lettered sign that said, *Justice.*

The incident generated great excitement up and down the Brazos. Keller walked the streets of Cade and heard nothing but talk about the hanging. "The Old Boys are stringing up the criminals again," people would say. "There'll be plenty more no-accounts who taste their justice before it's done."

Sure that Till Cooke was leading the Old Boys, and fearing he would be immediately arrested for it, Keller rode to his house. He hadn't seen Cooke since the encounter in Weyburn's office, and didn't know if he would even be allowed on Cooke's property.

Claire was there alone. "Weyburn sent deputies to

115

talk to Uncle Till," she told Keller. "But they didn't arrest him, because he was able to prove he had been in a saloon in Cade at the time the hanging happened."

"He really was in that saloon?"

"Absolutely. There were several witnesses."

Keller was surprised, and mystified. "Then who led the Old Boys, I wonder?"

"I don't know, but it wasn't Uncle Till—thank God."

"Amen to that, Claire. Where is he now?"

"Out somewhere on the ranch. He'll be back soon."

Keller said, "Maybe I shouldn't be here when he returns."

Claire nodded sadly. "Maybe you shouldn't."

That same day in Cade, Sheriff David Weyburn issued a public proclamation: Vigilante activity would not be tolerated, and any members of the so-called Old Boys would be prosecuted to the fullest extent of the law.

The people of Cade were divided on the issue of the proclamation. Some, aware of the cattlemen's mounting suspicions of their sheriff, and believing that Cutter Wyeth's escape from Weyburn's custody had been no accident, declared that Weyburn was simply scared of the Old Boys, fearing their noose would find his own neck. Others, mostly those who had not been in Cade back in the days when the Old Boys first rode, agreed with the proclamation and said vigilantes were worse than those they persecuted.

Two nights later the Old Boys struck again. This time they hanged two men in an old stable right on the edge of Cade. Both were suspected horse thieves, and one was said to have ridden with the Wyeths. Keller was in Cade when these two bodies were brought in, and he recognized one as the man who had hidden behind the creek bank during the gun battle.

The next day, Weyburn issued another proclamation, even more sternly worded than before, and included a thousand dollar reward on behalf of the county for information leading to the arrest and conviction of any of the Old Boys. The sheriff's detractors laughed loudly at this new declaration, and whispered among themselves that some of the county solons who had approved the reward were most likely Old Boys themselves.

Once again a visit was paid to Till Cooke, and once again he had a clear alibi. He had attended a "singing" at the local church, in clear view of three-score congregation members, at the time of the lynchings. This word brought amusement in Cade, for everyone knew that Till Cooke hadn't attended church in years up until that particular night.

Keller continued to be mystified. If Till Cooke was behind the revival of the Old Boys, he was certainly handling himself carefully, and taking no direct part in the lynchings. Perhaps he wasn't involved at all; perhaps others had actually taken up the gauntlet in his place.

Keller hoped that was true, and quietly investigated to see if he could determine who was leading the mysterious nocturnal lynch mob. He asked Charlie Lilly to make similar investigations, knowing that Lilly was more knowledgeable than he of the subtle workings of life around Cade. Keller was unable to find even a hint of who made up this new incarnation of the Old Boys, and Lilly reported no better luck.

After the double lynching, everything was quiet for two weeks. Talk about the Old Boys subsided, and life began to seem more normal again. There were a few noticeable differences; the streets of Cade were quieter than ever before, and horse theft declined, even though it did not vanish. Suspected stock thieves who had openly showed themselves in the saloons and dance halls of the town were now conspicuously hard to find.

Weyburn continued to search for the vigilantes, and even persuaded the commander at Fort Cade to send out a party of soldiers to patrol the county nightly in search of any lynch mobs. After a week the searches were discontinued, and the general wisdom had it that the military leadership of Fort Cade actually supported the Old Boys' efforts, and had agreed to Weyburn's request primarily as a token favor based on his contract to deliver three beeves a day to the fort to feed the soldiers.

That contract itself was a point of discussion among the cattlemen who were already suspicious of Weyburn. Since the beef deliveries had begun, the cattlemen had quietly watched their own herds, and Weyburn's, and it was noted by some that Weyburn's stock didn't seem to decrease at the rate his delivery schedule would indicate. Yet cattle from other herds continually declined. Might the sheriff, through Floyd Fells, be raiding his neighbors' holdings to fulfill his contract at no expense to himself?

Till Cooke was at the lead of those cattlemen who spread that suspicion. Keller kept close watch on his old friend, who was growing quite reckless in his willingness to publicly slander Weyburn. Cooke's escape from official linkage with the Old Boys had made him rather cavalier and mocking, and on three occasions he shouted at Weyburn himself on the streets of Cade, taunting his inability to halt the vigilante activity. He also voiced his own suspicions about how Weyburn was fulfilling his contract with the Army. Before long the animosity between the former and current sheriff became a source of great entertainment all over the county.

And then the animosity took on a darker aspect, one that hit Till Cooke like a hammer. Rumors began circulating that Cooke's relationship with his niece was not innocent. Whispers of scandal rode on the undercurrents. Till Cooke was so stung and surprised that he took ill to his bed.

Keller was just as angry, and confronted Weyburn. The sheriff denied any part in the rumors, but Keller didn't believe him.

It was the beginning of a great change of attitude for Jed Keller. So far, he had managed to remain a relatively stable force in the tense atmosphere around Cade. But now Claire, the woman he had come to love, was being slandered. He could no longer stand by.

But what could he do? How could he fight something as intangible as a rumor? He knew Weyburn was behind it all, yet there was not a thing he could do to prove it or combat its effects.

Keller began to feel like a man standing on the edge of a windy precipice, barely able to hang on.

Time passed, and the Old Boys rode several times again. Each time there was no forewarning, no sightings of mysterious riders in the night, and—seemingly—no one who had any idea who comprised the vigilante group. Each night after they had ridden, only one piece of evidence would remain: a fresh corpse or two swinging from mesquite branches, telegraph poles, or barn rafters, and on each a sign bearing the word that was the Old Boys' signature: *Justice*.

And each time, Till Cooke had an alibi. Keller was completely stumped, and wished he could ask Cooke about it. That, however, was out of the question. As weeks rolled into months, Till Cooke remained angry at Jed Keller for what had passed between them.

His estrangement from Cooke was a sad thing for Jed Keller. It also made it difficult to carry on his growing romance with Claire O'Keefe. At first he tried to avoid calling on her when he knew Cooke was home, until finally that became too inconvenient, and he began going to see her whenever he felt like it. She would always meet him in the yard, and whenever Cooke was home, Keller would know it by the slamming of the shutters.

19

Calvin McBrearty, district attorney, was a strapping fellow, broad of face and body, with an overflow of unkempt white hair and a pale mustache that was well-groomed, pampered, and much admired by its owner. McBrearty was a clearheaded man who lived under only one significant delusion: that his flourishing facial ornament was greatly admired by the local female population. Everyone knew his conviction and laughed up his sleeve about it, and many a woman deliberately stared at McBrearty's mustache when he passed her on the boardwalk, just to keep his delusion alive for its entertainment value.

Another well-known fact about McBrearty related to his love of courtroom battle, the bloodier the better. He prided himself on his ability to maintain a poker face in the midst of debate, never revealing by any flick of the brow or twitch of the lip, whether he perceived himself to be losing or winning. But unbeknownst to him, the mustache provided a public barometer of his thoughts. When the case was going his way he would stroke that mustache lovingly. When the defense was showing up better than his prosecution, however, he would tug on the left side of the mustache. "He's the first man I ever met whose mind could be read in his nose hair," Till Cooke had once commented to his friends.

Keller, still haunted by suspicions that his sister's death had something to do with David Weyburn, and remembering that Cooke had asked the district attorney to investigate Weyburn's past, called on McBrearty one bright Wednesday afternoon. He wondered if McBrearty would even be willing to talk to him, since he had come to ask for information he wasn't legally entitled to. Keller was pleased when the prosecutor welcomed him openly, saying he had heard of him and knew him to be a good man. When McBrearty heard Keller's question, however, his hand drifted to the mustache; Keller noted he tugged instead of stroked, and took that as a bad portent.

"The truth is, Mr. Keller, that it violates the policy of this office for me to comment to a member of the public about the nature or results of any investigation," McBrearty said. "As a matter of fact, I'm not actually at liberty even to state an investigation is taking place." A long pause, and then he stroked rather than pulled. "In this case, however, I'm inclined to talk to you not as district attorney to citizen, but as man to man. I know that Till Cooke has certainly told you that he asked me to investigate Weyburn, so I see no cause to hide that from you. Come on—let me buy you a beer, and I'll tell you what I can about our good sheriff. Of course, if you ever reveal I spoke to you about this, I'll deny it and find some pretext or another to make your life a legal hell for a good spell. Will you buy those terms?"

"I'll buy them. I want to know what you know about David Weyburn."

They crossed the street to the nearest saloon, and McBrearty signaled for two beers. They sat at a back table, where they could talk without being heard. McBrearty drank half of his beer before he began speaking.

"Sheriff David Weyburn has a background that is as checkered as this tablecloth," McBrearty said through his napkin, with which he lightly dabbed beer foam off his well-waxed facial treasure. "He's faced a variety of charges in a variety of places. Only one ever stuck to him, and that was a charge of stealing two cattle from a neighbor when he was twenty years old. Through the kindness of the victim, he was let off with payment for the cattle, plus a modest fine.

"It's the charges that never were proven that concern me. David Weyburn, who has also gone by the name of Daniel Weyburn, David Way, and William Burns, has been accused of everything from rustling to embezzlement. The man was born in Georgia, lost his father, a shopkeeper, when he was twelve, and his mother when he was fifteen. After her death, he left Georgia, headed first into Illinois, where he supposedly was run out of one town for stealing bread from a bakery shelf not once, but three times. His movements after that I can't trace, but it seems he wound up in eastern Colorado, working on a ranch, and from there came to Texas. While in Colorado he was accused of rustling for his employer, but his superior apparently got him out of trouble by agreeing to pay a heavy fine on his behalf in lieu of prosecution. Why he did this is hard to understand until you learn that Weyburn was later accused of blackmailing his employer. Suffice it to say he came away from Colorado a relatively well-off young man.

"He came to Texas after that and operated a ranch near the Arkansas border, where he apparently did quite well until he abruptly sold out and moved in our direction. My counterpart in Weyburn's former county tells me Weyburn was more or less driven out. The accusation was horse theft, and he came nigh getting himself lynched."

"I would think that would give him a decent respect for vigilantes," Keller said.

"I'm sure it has," McBrearty replied. "Though

from what I hear these days, Weyburn may well not have been scared enough to change his ways."

"There's one thing I can't figure," Keller said. "That big stone house of his, two hired servants, fine ranch land—you're saying he got money enough for all that through blackmail and stock theft?"

"No. Most of his money came from his wife. He inherited it when she died."

"Weyburn was married?"

"Yes. Most people here know he was married once, and that his wife died. In fact, he was married twice. He married his first wife five years ago; she died the year after. Through an earlier inheritance out of New York, she was quite a wealthy woman, several years older than Weyburn."

"How did she die?"

"In childbirth. She was too old for it, I guess. The child died as well. Weyburn apparently took his wife's death badly. He married soon after that, out of grief and loneliness, I suppose. That marriage didn't last a year."

"Divorce?"

"No. Weyburn attempted to obtain one, but his wife wouldn't grant it."

"So he's still married?"

"Legally, yes. But he lives alone, except for two servants, who have been with him since his first marriage. Two Mexicans, a married couple named Cruz."

Keller said, "Mr. McBrearty, let me ask you something. Have you heard any whispers that there might have been something, say, unusual about the fire that killed my sister and her husband?"

"No . . . well, wait a moment. I did hear that Paco the Mex had made a comment or two to that effect —but nobody ever believed Paco. He was a known liar. Full of fantasies."

"And now he's gone."

"Mr. Keller, do you know something about Weyburn that you should tell me?"

Keller fixed his eyes on his beer and pursed his lips. Then he shook his head. "Nothing substantial . . . nothing but feelings, really. But maybe I'll know more soon."

"If you do, you tell me." McBrearty shifted the subject. "Mr. Keller, as a man of the cattle business, do you know anything about the current vigilante activity?"

Keller grinned. "If you're asking me if I'm one of the Old Boys, I can truthfully tell you I'm not."

"Good. And I hope you'll stay out of such affairs. They aren't legal, you know." He glanced from side to side before continuing. "Though I admit, the Old Boys are certainly efficient, and they target just the right people. They achieve the same ends I seek, but without the legal mumbo-jumbo I'm bound to follow. Now, my friend, I must say good day. I seem to stay endlessly busy of late."

Keller stayed at the table alone for several minutes after the district attorney left, not sure why he had stopped short of revealing that Paco had been afraid of Floyd Fells and had vanished the very day Fells had seen him and the Mexican talking in the alley. Perhaps he would tell McBrearty about it . . . but not today. It wasn't yet time for that; he needed to know more.

When he left the saloon, Weyburn was standing on the other side of the street, looking in his direction. Both men stared at each other, and Weyburn turned away.

I'll bet he saw McBrearty leaving too, Keller thought. *I wonder if he figured out we were talking? If he did, I'll bet he's sweating.*

The thought made him smile. He waved at Weyburn and strode off whistling as the sheriff glowered and turned away.

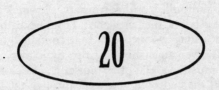

20

The hour was eleven at night, the wind was up, and Till Cooke had just sat up in bed, roused by something he had heard in his sleep, but which had vanished like a dream upon awakening.

"Claire?" he called, sitting up in bed. "Have you come home, Claire?"

Claire was supposed to be away visiting Charlotte Allison, wife of neighboring rancher Hal Allison, and had planned to stay the night. The Allisons were among those who knew better than to believe the vile rumors being spread about Cooke and his niece—rumors Cooke was convinced originated with David Weyburn. Charlotte Allison's invitation for Claire to visit had been issued out of kindness, to give Claire a chance to get away from home for a time and enjoy some diversion. Being home around her brooding uncle seemed hard on Claire these days.

"Claire?" Cooke called again, swinging his feet off the side of the bed. White legs sticking out from beneath the tail of his nightshirt, Cooke stood and left his tiny bedroom. It was dark outside, but enough light remained to illuminate the little house.

Then he heard a noise and realized that this was

what had penetrated his sleep. It was the nicker of a horse, and not one of his own, if he judged the sound rightly.

He rubbed his stubbled chin, slipped back into his bedroom and pulled on his trousers. He stuck his bare feet into his boots, then crouched. From beneath the bed he pulled a long wooden box that contained a maple-stocked twelve-gauge shotgun, already loaded.

The horse made another noise; it was closer now. Cooke left the bedroom and went through the house to the window. He peered around the corner of it.

A rider was outside, though at first he looked not so much like a man as a sack of grain heaped onto a saddled horse. Cooke heard a groan. "By heaven, that man's hurt!" Cooke muttered.

He couldn't see the man's face, for his head was down and crowned by a broad-brimmed hat. Cooke shifted the shotgun to his left hand, opened the door and went out.

"I'm Till Cooke, mister—you shot or something?"

A groan, filled with pain.

"What's wrong with you?"

"Help me . . ." Cooke couldn't recognize the whispering, raspy voice.

"Hold on, I'm coming. We'll get you down from there and see just what—"

The man straightened suddenly, and moonlight bathed his face. "Howdy, Till Cooke," Cutter Wyeth said, grinning. "How are you this fine evening?" Then he shot him through the center of the chest.

"That's for trying to get me hung," Wyeth said, swinging his smoking pistol upright. "I told you I wouldn't forget it."

"Wyeth . . ." Cooke had dropped his shotgun when he fell. Now he groped for it, his hand straining toward it. Wyeth lowered his pistol again and shot Cooke through the arm. The groping hand went limp.

"You're a stubborn old squat, Cooke, that much I'll

say for you. Now tell me, old man, where's that pretty niece of yours? Inside?"

"I'll kill you, Wyeth, kill you . . ."

"No," Wyeth calmly said. "It's me who's doing the killing tonight—remember?" He shot a third time, striking Cooke in the forehead and killing him instantly.

Wyeth dismounted, keeping his pistol out in case Cooke's niece showed up in the door with a gun. He toed Cooke's body. Satisfied Cooke was dead, Wyeth stepped over him and entered the house. He came out again a minute later, disappointed to have found no female inside. Too bad. Had she been home, he could have made his revenge against Till Cooke all the more complete, and all the more personally gratifying.

Cutter Wyeth holstered his pistol and mounted. Looking down one last time at Cooke's body, he grinned. "Hope that when they find you, the buzzards have left enough to bury, old man." He headed for his horse, then paused a moment. Stooping, he picked up Cooke's shotgun. A fine weapon, costly and well-kept, and for him a meaningful souvenir.

Hefting up the shotgun, he mounted and rode off into the darkness.

Jed Keller longed to comfort Claire O'Keefe, but didn't know how. What comfort could he give another when he had none himself? Till Cooke . . . dead, murdered. It was inconceivable. When he had first heard it, Keller became sick to his stomach.

Now he stood beside Claire on a windy hillside, listening numbly as a final psalm was read before Till Cooke's body was given back to the earth. Keller was an inwardly severed man at the moment. One part of him was a grieving human being, emotional and consumed by the realization that an old friend was forever gone. The other part, the lawman portion that would not die no matter how much Keller tried to kill it, was cold and rational and busily engaged in an evaluation of Cooke's murder. Who had shot him, and why?

Might it have been Weyburn or one of his deputies? Weyburn certainly bore enough hatred of Cooke to make him do it. Perhaps when Weyburn had seen him talking to the district attorney, it had somehow set him off. Yet Keller doubted Weyburn was behind this. For one thing, it didn't seem quite his style, and for another, he had already found his own means of dealing with Cooke: He had destroyed his reputation with rumors. Keller had no question that Weyburn had started the tales about Cooke and Claire. He doubted Weyburn would have felt the need to murder Cooke's physical person as well as his reputation.

As a former sheriff, Cooke was bound to have made enemies. His killer might have been the holder of some old grudge from years past. Or perhaps the grudge had a more recent origin.

If so, Keller had a good idea who the killer was, for he clearly remembered Cutter Wyeth's threat. It racked him with guilt. *It was me who urged that Wyeth be turned over to Weyburn. I knew the odds were good that Weyburn would let him go, but I encouraged it anyway. I was a fool . . . and now Till is murdered.*

After the burying, Keller helped Claire into her buggy, then climbed into the driver's seat. "I don't think you should go back home just yet," he said. "The memory is too fresh."

"No," she said. "Take me back. I'm not running from what happened. I'll not do that."

Cooke's ranch house seemed terribly empty and forlorn when they arrived. Keller tried to steer Claire away from the bloodied spot where her uncle had died, but she would not be led. She walked to the rust-colored stain on the earth and looked sadly down at it.

"Murdered," she said. "That's the part I can't accept. To die naturally is one thing. But to be killed because of someone's hatred . . ." She said no more, ending her thought with a shudder.

"He was a brave man, Claire. I was at his side for many a day, and I know what his mettle was. I'd like to know how whoever it was got the jump on him. He wasn't one to be fooled easy. And why was he out here unarmed? That has me confused. It wasn't like Till to be careless."

Claire frowned thoughtfully. "Wait a minute," she said. She entered the house. Keller, puzzled by what she was up to, rolled a quirly and was just lighting up when she emerged.

"Uncle Till kept his shotgun under his bed," she said. "It's gone."

"Gone!" Keller let smoke drift out through his nostrils. "So he didn't come out here unarmed. He was tricked, or overpowered, and his killer took the shotgun. Is anything else missing?"

"Not that I can tell."

Keller swore. The thought of Cooke's killer making off with that particular gun made him seethe. That was a special gun, one he himself had given Cooke many years ago, at the time he left his service.

"I'm going to find Till's killer, Claire," Keller said. "I'm going to find him, and make sure he pays for what he did."

"Jed, don't get into the middle of this," Claire pleaded. "You can't bring him back—and I'm afraid I'll just lose you too. I couldn't bear it. Leave this to the law to deal with. You yourself have said so many times that you just want to be through with this sort of thing."

"I can't leave this to the law, Claire. Not while the law is David Weyburn."

"Jed, do you think Weyburn might be behind the killing?"

"Maybe . . . perhaps just indirectly, but he could be behind it."

"Indirectly?"

"Yes. I think it may be because of Weyburn that Till's killer was free and able to do this."

It required only a moment for Claire to comprehend the implication. "Cutter Wyeth?"

"Yes. It's just a suspicion, but a strong one. He did threaten Till, after all. And if he did kill him, then that's all the more reason I have to hunt him down. It was me who talked Till into letting Weyburn take custody of Wyeth. And Weyburn, whatever talk about 'escape' he might make, let Wyeth go free. So it's partly my fault Till is dead, Claire. I owe it to him to find his killer. Do you understand?"

"Yes," she said. "I do." Then she came to him, put her arms around him and held him as if she feared never being able to hold him again.

Back home that night, Keller sat up alone, smoking and thinking. He was recalling Till Cooke's words about written law and unwritten law, and his own stubborn rejection of that way of thinking.

Keller had been sure he was right in his own thinking at the beginning. Now nothing seemed sure at all. Perhaps Cooke had known far better than he the depth of wickedness being dealt with when one took on the likes of Cutter Wyeth and David Weyburn. Perhaps the unwritten law that Cooke had believed in was the law of right and wrong, and of good men being free to take a stand against bad ones.

Keller fell asleep at last, still in his chair. He woke himself up crying. Crying—and he hadn't cried in years.

He cried because Till Cooke had died still estranged from him, just as Magart had. It seemed absurd and tragic. And it was too late to do anything about it.

He stood, stretching and yawning. Walking to his window, he looked out over the dawn-lighted land.

It may be too late for me to patch my differences with Till, he thought, but there are still some things it's not too late to do. And now, for the first time, I'm ready to do them. I never would have thought I would come to it, but I'm ready.

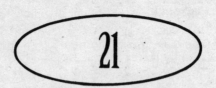

21

For the next forty-eight hours Jed Keller was a man in torment. He ached to find Cooke's killer, but as one man, there was little he could do. Twice he caught himself thinking that since he needed some guidance on how to begin his investigation, he ought to go talk to Till Cooke. Till would know what to do . . . and then Keller remembered the truth, and his pain and distraction grew all the worse.

On the second day after Cooke's burial, clouds began to roll across the sky and the temperature fell several degrees. "Looks like bad weather may be rolling in," Doyle Boston said, studying the sky. "Cattle are restless; look at them. Don't know what to do with themselves."

"I'm restless too," Keller commented. "But I know what I need to do with myself. If the Old Boys were to ride up right now and ask me to join them, I'd be with them in a second."

Darkness fell, and the anticipated storm still had not come, though the threat of it lingered.

Keller was outside, beneath the overhang he had built onto his house, watching the wind rise and whip dust across the yard. He was smoking, though the wind burned up each quirly within a minute of lighting it. Keller's spirits were no brighter, but for some reason he had a sense of ominous anticipation, as if the wind was carrying a hint of something new.

Keller closed his eyes, trying to relax. When he opened them, Charlie Lilly and Doyle Boston were standing before him, dressed to ride.

"Jed, get ready to go," Lilly said.

Keller, puzzled and surprised, opened his mouth to ask why, and where. Before the words were out, Lilly shook his head. "It'll be clear soon enough," he said.

Keller stood and nodded. He understood now, without being told. He retreated inside, then came out again. His Colt was in his gun belt, strapped around his waist, and he carried his Winchester.

He noticed that Doyle Boston had a stout coil of rope over his shoulder. Keller's eyes flicked over to meet Lilly's, and he exchanged his unspoken question for a silent confirmation.

It was a time for decision. What he had said before was mere talk. This was the real thing.

He stood silently and thought about Till's coffin being lowered into the open grave. "I'll saddle up," he said.

"Things look different now than before, eh, Jed?"

"Yes," Keller said. "They do."

They rode through the night as clouds roiled above and distant thunder shook the Brazos country. The smell of the coming storm was strong, and matched the rising fire in Keller's spirit. No more holding out or holding back. No more bowing the head at the altar of old memories. No more conundrums over written and unwritten law, or over surface loyalties and deeper ones. He was where he should be.

They came to the old picket house where the late cattleman Sayler Todd once lived. The light of a small campfire flared in the middle of the old stable yard. Keller, Lilly, and Boston rode up close and stopped.

"Who goes there?"

"Justice by hemp," Lilly replied.

"Come in, then," the voice called back.

Keller could tell by the lack of reaction to his appearance that he was expected tonight. He looked around at nearly a score of faces that were reddened by the firelight. Most of these men he knew. The majority were ranch owners or foremen, and a couple were particularly trusted cowhands. But in addition there was a shopkeeper, a butcher, and even a saloon operator, these three being Cade townsmen.

Keller scanned the group, mentally clicking off the names of those he recognized: Will Cornmiller, Arden Spann, Larry Hite, Hank Kelvin, Irwin Dunbar, Joe Decatur, Levon Hatley, Sheller Calahan, Gunter House, Ben Potts, Manfred Burroughs, Gordy Snow, Bonner Elrod, and others, all of them men of high reputation and known stoutness of heart. Even Hal Allison was here.

"Gentlemen," Keller said, nodding a general greeting.

Nods and mumbles in return, then Lilly went to the side of the fire. "There's no turning back for us now," he said. "The death of Till Cooke shows us there's yet a lot of cleaning up to be done along the Brazos."

"It was Wyeth who done it," Kelvin said.

"We don't know that, Hank," Lilly replied. He paused. "But I believe it too. It was Wyeth. Had to be."

"He's been seen back in the county within the past week," said Arden Spann.

"Maybe we'll find him tonight," Lilly said. "Or maybe not. One thing I know—no, two: We'll find somebody worth the finding tonight, and sooner or later we'll catch up with Wyeth himself. And this time there'll be no men with badges or soldiers in uniforms to get in the way of justice. That right?"

A rumble of assent broke from the group. Then Lilly looked at Keller.

"That right, Jed?"

"That's right," he said.

They found three of them together, camped in a big Sibley tent left over from the previous decade's war. They resisted only a little, for canvas walls gave no protection from bullets, and three against a score was no odds at all.

"Calahan?" Lilly said when the three were lined up, their pale faces tight with fright and illuminated by the light of a pine-tar torch that one of the Old Boys had lighted.

Sheller Calahan, who owned a medium-sized spread bordering the south bank of the Brazos, nudged his horse forward a step. "Them's the three," he said.

Arden Spann, Calahan's ranch boss, came around the other side of the tent, leading a pair of horses. "These are ours," he said. "They got a passel of them inside a rope fence. Gunter, Manfred, Gordy, I seen horses belonging to you in there too. And there's others."

"I don't want to hang!" one of the thieves pleaded.

"Too late to be begging—you could have avoided all this by not stealing our horses to begin with," Calahan said. There was not a trace of sympathy in his voice. He, like the others, had been victimized too long by men such as these, who stole without conscience and gave thought to mercy only when it was they who wanted to receive it.

"At least give us the chance for a trial," one of the others asked. He was more composed than the first, though obviously scared. "Hanging us without a trial ain't fair."

" 'None but the brave deserves the fair,' " Charlie Lilly quoted. "That's John Dryden."

The thieves seemed confused by the quote; one of them loudly denied that any of them were named Dryden. The Old Boys, familiar with Lilly's poetic quotes and citations, laughed, but it was a harsh and serious laughter.

Calahan had a more direct answer for the horse thief's plea for a trial. "There's several hundred of your kind already indicted in this state, and most will never go to trial as it is. Not one stock thief in ten gets caught —unless it's by men who won't stand around waiting for the official law to work. You want a trial? All right, we'll give you one." Calahan looked to his partners. "These men stand charged as thieving scum on the face of Texas. Guilty or not guilty?"

"Guilty!" the cry came back.

Calahan smiled a very fearsome smile. "There you are, men. Fairly tried and fairly convicted."

"Doyle, yonder limb looks stout enough to suffice," Charlie Lilly said to Boston, pointing at a nearby tree.

"Wait," Jed Keller said. Every face turned to him; Lilly gazed at him intently. Was Keller again about to waffle?

Keller dismounted, took the torch from the man holding it, and walked up to the thieves. He looked into the face of the first, who had been maintaining only the most tenuous hold on his emotions. The man began to sob; he sank to his knees, face in hands. Keller moved on to the second man, the one who had pleaded for trial. This man didn't break down, but managed to look Keller in the eye, though falteringly.

"Friend, you've got nothing to gain by refusing to answer my question, for you'll be no more dead after telling me the truth than you'll be after lying. Do you ride with Cutter Wyeth?"

"I have . . . I don't no more."

"You're independent?"

"Yes sir."

"Do you know if it was Cutter Wyeth who killed the former sheriff, Till Cooke?"

"No sir, I don't know who killed him. It sure wasn't me."

Keller moved to the third man, who had said nothing at all. He was thin and had a nose like a hawkbill knife. "What about you? You know who killed Till Cooke?"

"I do."

The forthright and unhesitant answer surprised the entire group. "Who was it, then?"

"Is it worth my freedom for you to know?"

Keller glanced at Lilly, then at the others. In the darkness they were phantom men on phantom mounts. Keller held up the torch to illuminate Lilly's face, for this was Lilly's decision to make, not his.

"They have to hang," Lilly said.

Keller turned back to the man. "You heard that—I can't offer you freedom. But telling the truth is a good thing for a man to do, especially one swing away from his judgment day."

The man swallowed and pulled his lips tight. "It was Wyeth who killed the lawman," he said. "He come back in the county two weeks ago, looking for Nancy Scarlet. I reckon he pined for her. But he also come back to kill Till Cooke. Told me that himself." The man nodded. "Well, I told it. Makes this old dirty soul feel that much cleaner."

Keller turned away and climbed back onto his horse. His heart was hammering, and he sweated like he had just finished a fast run up a steep hill. He knew what would happen now, and that once it had happened, he would undeniably be the very thing he had sworn never to be. A vigilante. An Old Boy. He couldn't back out now. So be it.

Doyle Boston threw his rope over the limb and tied a noose. A couple of others in the group joined him with ropes of their own. The three horse thieves watched the process wordlessly; the first had gotten control of himself and now only whimpered a little. Keller was glad the man had stopped his crying. It was a sorry thing to die like a coward; he couldn't wish that kind of shame even on a horse thief.

Keller didn't want to watch the actual hangings, but he made himself do it. Having come this far, he wouldn't falter at the last minute. When the horses ran out from under the men and the ropes pulled tight, the Old Boys watched in silence until it was clear that death had come.

"Well, that's three more gone," Charlie Lilly said. He glanced from the swinging bodies up into the branches of the hanging tree. " 'Casting the body's vest aside, My soul into the boughs does glide.' Andrew Marvell, 'The Garden.' " He snorted. "Of course, in the case of these three, I suppose the souls are more likely working their way down through the roots than up through the boughs."

Several others chuckled, but Keller couldn't join in. What had just happened was, he believed, the working out of justice, however rough, but to him it was also a somber event. He had made a major transformation to-night, for the sake of Till Cooke's memory, and he hoped it was the right one.

Spann left signs, each bearing the word "Justice," on all three bodies—signs made in advance, with loops already attached so they could be slipped over the vic-tims' heads like medals on chains. This, Keller realized, was a purposeful and efficient group of men.

They rode back home, and Keller fell into his bed, fully clothed, and slept without dreams.

22

Keller went to Lilly's cookhouse the next morning after breakfast. Lilly was cleaning his pots, whistling, and cutting up various beef organs to add to a stew that was already in the works on the stove. A battered book of English poetry was propped open against a flour sack on a shelf, so that Lilly could read as he worked.

Keller helped himself to a cupful of coffee. "Charlie, I never would have guessed you to be the one," he said. "Wouldn't have guessed it in a century."

"Which is precisely why Till Cooke asked me to do it on his behalf," Lilly replied. "Obviously he couldn't do it himself, not with Weyburn's eyes on him—and the eyes of about everybody else too. He might have asked you instead of me . . . had circumstances been different."

"I would've turned him down."

"I know. I guess he knew it too."

"Why did you agree, Charlie? Night-riding doesn't seem to fit my impression of you."

"I believe in justice. And in this county, with Weyburn in office, there's no justice except the kind that's dealt out directly. Nor is there a hand to deal directly but our own."

139

"I want to get Cutter Wyeth, Charlie. I want to see him brought to justice for murdering Till Cooke."

"So do I."

"So when do we ride again, and look for him?"

"Tomorrow night. And if we don't find him then, another night hence. And so on and so on, until this county is clean again."

Keller took a swallow of the strong coffee. "This county won't be fully clean until David Weyburn is gone. Till Cooke was right about him. He smells like trouble from a mile away, and trouble he'll be as long as he's got power."

Life was different for Jed Keller after he began riding with the Old Boys. For the next two months, hardly a week passed that didn't see Keller, Lilly, Boston, and at least a few of the other Old Boys speeding through the darkness, often with hooves silenced by muffling pads and always with ropes at ready, to leave behind them one, two, sometimes three corpses hanging with signs about their necks. So common did the sight of the bodies become that the people in and around Cade lost their sense of shock upon seeing them hanging limp and white in the morning sunlight. They would cut them down, haul them into town, and turn them over to Sheriff David Weyburn.

Weyburn, everyone noticed, was growing increasingly distressed by his inability to stop the vigilante activity. Some wondered why he even wanted to stop it; by all common sense, it was making his work easier. Unless, folks would whisper, doing the job of a proper sheriff wasn't David Weyburn's true work at all, but only a cover.

Questions abounded. Where did the man's money come from, anyway? And how was he fulfilling that contract with Fort Cade without depleting his own stock? And why was it, for that matter, that half the scoundrels who swung at the end of Old Boy ropes had either worked for Weyburn's spread at one time or another, or were tied in with others who had? And another thing: Wasn't it odd that Till Cooke was murdered just when he was grinding Weyburn's nerves the hardest? What kind of man was the good sheriff anyway? Was he a murderer?

For David Weyburn, the days of Old Boy vengeance were also the days of personal decline. Bit by bit the public favor he bought with free drinks, big smiles, and friendly jokes began to fade. The same public to whom he had fed rumors of scandal involving Till Cooke and Claire O'Keefe quickly forgot those stories in the shadows of the far more intriguing speculations about Weyburn himself. Suspicions against him rose as respect for him declined—and then word got out somehow that District Attorney McBrearty was building a file on the sheriff, and talk grew all the hotter.

Weyburn became increasingly consumed by his difficulties, and it showed in his face. People speculated that he was ill, and in fact he had begun missing many days of work. He let deputies do his job for him while he remained closed up in his big stone house, mulling over his problems, thinking of resignation, then giving up that idea when he realized that sacrificing his office would make him lose almost all control of the stock theft network he operated from behind that sheriff's desk.

Locked away in his own private castle, Weyburn found little peace. As Magart's pregnancy advanced, she grew weak and ill, her joints swelling and her color draining away. Weyburn was reminded of the dearly beloved wife he had lost to childbirth some years before, and began to fear fate was about to hand him the same tragedy again. He spent much time beside Magart's bed, staring at her swollen belly, drinking, and saying things that frightened and repelled Maria Cruz. When Maria would repeat them to Eduardo in their room at night, he was just as horrified.

"He hates the child in her," Maria whispered to her husband. "He says he wishes it had never been conceived, and he hopes it dies before it kills his 'wife.' "

Eduardo would not comment when Maria repeated things like that. She could see the cowardice in him, and feared that in the end he would stand by and let even greater evils be done, rather than endanger himself. She began to despise him for it.

Weyburn didn't devote all his bedside rantings to Magart and her unborn child. He talked much about Till Cooke, cursing the former sheriff for dying in a manner that cast suspicion back on him. And he talked to Magart about her brother Jed—though Magart, in her brain-damaged state, had no more memory of him —and said he believed that Keller had taken up with the Old Boys in his fury over the death of Till Cooke. Even so—and this seemed odd to Maria Cruz—Weyburn didn't talk about Keller in the same tone as he talked of the late Cooke. He clearly held a certain odd respect for Keller, a deference to him that Maria could not understand.

Maria tucked away Jed Keller's name in her mind. When the time came for revealing hidden things, perhaps he could be the one she would turn to. After all, the Lady was his sister, and the child in her his blood kin.

When the autumn came, Cade's newspapers carried news of the wedding of Jed Keller and Claire O'Keefe. It was a sizable affair, and well-attended. Weyburn, to no one's surprise, was not invited to the wedding, but he made his presence known outside the church, watching the men who came out and noting down their names. Keller himself noticed the odd activity and wondered what Weyburn was up to. He would realize later that Weyburn operated under the assumption that he was a leader of the Old Boys, and that the men attending his wedding were likely to be Old Boys themselves.

And indeed many were. But Keller didn't worry

about it. In fact, he didn't fret nearly as much about Weyburn as he had before. He knew the man's prestige and power were declining—and that the nocturnal activities of the Old Boys seemed to lead ever closer to Weyburn's own door.

Cold nights descended on the Brazos country, and still the Old Boys rode, though the frequency of their excursions lessened as the number of thieves and rustlers plaguing the ranches was reduced.

Jed Keller was on the whole a happy man. Marriage to Claire brought him great joy and satisfaction, and for the first time in years he ceased to be haunted by dreams of that tragic shooting in the Missouri bank. Claire was a healing balm, soothing the most roughened and raw areas of his life.

But one thing undercut Keller's satisfaction: Cutter Wyeth remained at large. Everyone knew he was frequently in the county, for he was often seen, and he sometimes even sent out public taunts. The Old Boys, he declared, would never put a hand on him, and any who tried would draw back a bloody stump.

The Old Boys concentrated their efforts toward finding the outlaw. All they found was frustration. Wyeth had an uncanny ability to disappear like smoke, only to reappear somewhere else and issue another taunt and steal another horse. Keller began to despair of ever bringing Wyeth to justice.

One night Charlie Lilly came galloping up to the ranch house with exciting news for Keller. He had received information that Wyeth was holed up in a house at the remote area of Brock Spring, on the very western border of the county. Furthermore, he reportedly had some two dozen head of stolen cattle penned nearby, and was planning to steal more from Keller's herd—for Wyeth was said to believe that Keller now headed the Old Boys in Till Cooke's place, and was deliberately targeting his herd in retaliation.

"Where'd you hear this?" Keller asked Lilly.

"From Nancy Scarlet herself," Lilly answered. "She came here specifically to inform on Wyeth. She's mad at him again, and wants to be rid of him . . . with her own safety guaranteed, of course."

"I think we can accommodate her on both those scores," Keller said. "I think it would be advisable for us to pay a nighttime call on Brock Spring."

And so began the planning for what Keller and Lilly hoped would be the largest and most productive Old Boy excursion yet. This time, Keller was determined, Cutter Wyeth would not get away.

Then came an unexpected development. The day after Charlie Lilly brought his news, none other than David Weyburn himself rode onto the ranch, along with three deputies. When Keller came in answer, Weyburn dismounted, walked up to him, and informed him he was under arrest.

"Why am I being arrested?" Keller demanded.

Weyburn, his face so pallid and drawn that he looked like a different man than the Weyburn whom Keller had first met, looked him in the eye. "Night-riding and lynching, Mr. Keller. I'm taking you in for your part in the crimes of the so-called Old Boys."

"Do you have evidence to back your charges?" Keller said.

"That's a matter for later discussion," Weyburn replied. "You'll have an opportunity to defend yourself—which is more mercy than you have granted those who swing at the end of your ropes."

They unceremoniously hauled him off. He didn't even have time to say good-bye to Claire, nor to talk with Charlie Lilly, who watched the entire event with great concern.

Doyle Boston sidled up to Lilly as Keller was being taken down the road. "Do we ride, or does this stop us?"

Lilly seemed unsure. "Jed has wanted his personal

chance at Wyeth for a long time now. I despise taking it from him. But we may not find a better opportunity to get him. I think we ought to gather as many of the boys as we can and see what the feeling is."

Doyle Boston spat tobacco amber. "Fair enough—but I already know how I feel about it. I say let's ride, and let Cutter Wyeth stretch some hemp before sunrise. And if the others don't want to come, we can do it ourselves, just you and me. Cutter Wyeth ain't too much for two good men to handle, in my way of looking at it."

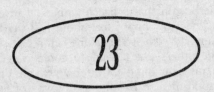

23

The events that followed the arrest of Jed Keller did so swiftly. Like dust devils that gust up separately, then join to form a large whirlwind, they combined to form an end that Keller himself could have never foreseen.

Keller paced in his cell, the lone prisoner in the jail. Claire had been here earlier, holding his hands through the bars and vehemently expressing her anger over his arrest. Keller had urged her to go home before darkness fell, and finally she had.

He went to the cell window. Somewhere out there, in that darkness to the west, the Old Boys were riding even now on a raid aimed at bringing down Cutter Wyeth once and for all. Keller wished himself among them. It was a shame to be stuck here while such an important event was taking place.

Restless, he shifted over to the cell door. "Deputy! Hey, out there! I'm thirsty! Can't a man get anything to drink in this lousy jail?"

The door leading to the front office opened and a man came through. Keller had expected one of the deputies. He had not expected David Weyburn.

"I'll be—so the devil himself oversees Hell tonight, eh?"

Weyburn smiled tightly. "This is far from Hell, and tonight I'm more your deliverer than your devil."

"I want a drink of water."

Weyburn reached up as if to tip a nonexistent hat. "At your service, Mr. Keller."

Keller was surprised when Weyburn actually did fetch him a cup of water. He couldn't imagine why the man would be kind to him.

"What was that talk about your being my deliverer, Weyburn?"

"Time will answer that question, Mr. Keller."

"Tell me: Why do you believe I lead the Old Boys?"

"Everything will come clear enough soon. As early as in the morning, I expect. Just be patient." The sheriff drew closer. "There's no cause for division between us, Mr. Keller. We have something in common, you and me."

"I've got nothing in common with you."

"Indeed you do . . . if only I were free to tell you about it."

Keller found Weyburn's cryptic manner irritating. He had heard enough obscurity; the time for free talking had come. "The truth is, Weyburn, I think I do know what you mean. You're talking about my sister."

Weyburn's reaction was more extreme than Keller would have anticipated. His eyes widened and he backed away. "What do you mean by that?" he said in a sharp whisper, even though there were no others present to hear.

"I know about the love affair between you and Magart. The one you carried on right under Folly Broadmore's nose just before Magart's death."

"Before Magart's death . . ." Keller wondered why Weyburn sounded almost relieved as he said those words.

"That's right. And since I'm speaking so freely, let me say something else that's been on my mind for a long time now. When I first came to Cade and found Magart was dead, I heard a rumor that Paco the Mex—remember him?—was hinting around that there was something out of the ordinary about the fire that killed the Broadmores. You know already that I tried to beat information out of Paco once when I was drunk. I didn't learn anything that time, but later on I had occasion to help out Paco, and he was ready to tell me. Only one thing stopped him, and that was the sight of Floyd Fells close by, within earshot. It nearly scared Paco to death. 'Weyburn's man,' he called Fells. That was the last day Paco was seen. You know what I think, Weyburn? I think Paco is dead, and that Floyd Fells killed him so he wouldn't have another chance to tell what he knew. And whatever it was that he did know, I think it comes around somehow right back to your doorstep."

Weyburn wore the darkest of expressions. "You're insane, Keller. You seem to be making some sort of major accusation against me."

"You catch on fast, Sheriff."

"Then what is it you're accusing me of? Spit it out!"

Now Keller could find little way to express himself. "The truth is, I don't know what I'm accusing you of," he said. "I've had a bad feeling about you ever since I first met you that day in the hallway at the Big Dakota. And it's not only because of your dealings with scum like Wyeth. It's because of Magart, and Paco, and whatever it was he would have told me if he had been given the chance."

"What could an old Mexican drunk have known that would be worth the telling?"

"You tell me, Sheriff. You sure enough seemed worried about what he might have told me the first time you and me ever talked."

Weyburn evidently was growing tired of this conversation. "I've got only one thing more to say to you, Keller, and that's that I've done you a favor you don't yet know about, though you will soon enough. And yes, you're right—I did love your sister. That's the thing we've got in common, and it's for her sake that I've helped you today. Because she spoke so highly of you. Because she loved you."

"I'm glad to know she did. That's information I can truly thank you for. But tell me, Weyburn: How is it that dragging me away from my own ranch and locking me up in this jail equals out to 'helping' me? This is help I can do without. You think Magart would have wanted her brother treated this way?"

Weyburn smiled mysteriously. "Be patient, Jed Keller. Soon you'll understand." He turned on his heel and headed out of the cell block. At the door he stopped and looked back. "You think you're so clever, Keller. You think you know so much. But you know nothing, nothing at all. There are things I could tell you that would knock you onto your backside. If only you'd have the sense to mind your own affairs."

For Keller, the moment was one of those when sudden insight rises with the clarity of a winter dawn. The jumble of vague suspicions he had been carrying around for months suddenly patterned themselves into a picture, or at least a potential picture. "Weyburn, did you kill Folly Broadmore? Because he had beaten Magart?"

The sheriff held his silence, staring at Keller for several seconds with a peculiar expression. When he entered the front office, he slammed the cell-block door behind him very hard.

It would have pleased Calvin McBrearty's healthy sense of irony if he could have known of the conversation that was taking place between Keller and Weyburn even as he was roused from sleep by a series of violent knocks on his door. The big district attorney sat up, rubbed his face and grumbled, "Hold your horses, whoever you are! I'm coming as fast as I can!"

He rose and put on his trousers, then stumbled through his dark house to answer the knocking, which continued despite his yells for patience. Just as he was reaching for the latch, he remembered something and paused long enough to slip off the mail-order, black-net mustache-shaping device he always wore to bed to make sure his most precious personal ornament didn't lose its beautiful form. He thrust the embarrassing item into his pocket as he opened the door.

"What the devil is it?" he blared as the door swung open. "Do you know what hour it is?"

The face on the other side was that of former Till Cooke deputy Haman Polk, who lately had been unhappily vegetating as a clerk in a local tack and feed store. Polk looked very upset.

"Mr. McBrearty, I'm awful sorry to bother you right now, but you need to come quick."

"What is it, Haman?"

"We've found something, Homer and me. A body. A dead body."

"A body? Where?"

"In Cade Creek, where it pools up deep behind the stone dam. We were out there camping and fishing and such. The corpse had rocks and things tied to it to keep it sunk, but the water had rotted away the ropes enough to let him come up . . . what's left of him. I'm sure it's a murdered man. Homer's still out there guarding him while I fetch you."

"Why did you come to me and not the sheriff?"

"Pshaw! It was Sheriff Weyburn who fired me and Homer, Mr. McBrearty. I won't go to him for nothing. Besides, I just plain-old don't trust him."

"You have keen insight, my friend. I don't trust him either." McBrearty stretched and yawned. "Well, so much for sleeping tonight. Come in and have a seat—we'll be off as soon as I get dressed."

Polk sat and fidgeted in his chair while he waited. McBrearty bumped around in his room, dressing too slowly to suit Polk. The district attorney called out through the half-open door, "Could you tell who the dead man was?"

"Not from the face," Polk said. "You know what water does to a body. But we think we know who it was anyway. He had only one leg, you see."

McBrearty all but lunged out of his room. "Paco the Mex?"

"Yes sir, I think it was. And from what little remains of him, I believe his throat was cut."

Keller sat up abruptly, making his cell bunk squeak. He had just experienced a second burst of insight. Weyburn's cryptic talk of "helping" him had suddenly taken on a grim kind of sense.

"No, no! Not that!" Keller leaped up and went to his cell window, looking out across the dark alley and toward the west. "God, please don't let it happen, not that. Not that."

He stared out into the dark, ridiculously trying to see what was impossible to see, for Brock Spring was many miles away. "Charlie," he whispered. "Charlie, what have you ridden into? God help us, what fools we've been!"

It was one of the darkest moments Jed Keller would know in his life.

Meanwhile, a couple of miles away, David Weyburn was also awake. Downstairs in his home office, he was dressed in a robe and was still very rumpled from sleep. Like Calvin McBrearty, he had been roused by a knock at his door.

His caller was Floyd Fells, and from Fells's expression, Weyburn knew his partner was not a happy man. Fells pushed his way in without waiting for an invitation.

"David, is it true?"

"Is what true?"

"You know what I mean! Is it true you arrested Jed Keller to keep him from going on the Old Boys raid?"

"I arrested him, yes."

"Damn! Do you know what you've done? You've brought the whole thing down around our heads!"

"What? You're talking loco, Floyd."

"No, David, no. It's you who's loco. Once Keller understands that he was arrested to protect him from that ambush, it's going to be obvious that you had knowledge of the ambush beforehand. In other words, you've as much as verified to the Old Boys that you and Wyeth work together, David. The Old Boys will be hanging you and me next!"

Weyburn glowered, spluttered, then said: "You worry too much, Fells. Nothing is going to happen." He didn't sound as confident as he intended, and in fact Fells saw that his words had shaken Weyburn. It astounded him to realize that such an obvious and dangerous flaw in planning had been both made and overlooked by the sheriff. Fells knew right then that Weyburn had already crossed a line. He had broken under the strains of the past weeks.

"It's over, David. There's no hope now."

"I did what I had to do! What else could I have done?"

"What else? You could have left well enough alone! You could have let Jed Keller ride into Brock Spring with the others. You could have let him die, and there would have been one less worry for us!"

"I couldn't let that happen—not to Keller."

"Why? Where does this great love for Jed Keller come from?" Fells waved his hand violently in a gesture of disgust. "Hell, I know where it comes from. It's because of *her*. That's it, ain't it!"

"He's her brother, Floyd! That means something, you know! I can't let the brother of my wife die like some dog out there under Wyeth's guns!"

"She ain't your wife, David, no matter how much

you call her that. She's nobody's wife now, just a widow. A widow who was beat into such a pulp by her late husband that she ain't hardly even a real woman anymore! But she is woman enough to bear a child, ain't she? And that child will be the death of us for sure, for there'll be no keeping that a secret, no matter what notions you have. God, I was a fool to have ever gone to work with you! I was a fool to have ever thought we could get away with all this! At one time I thought this might have worked—but now you've ruined it . . . all because of that mindless she-dog you've thrown away your good sense over!"

Weyburn drew back his fist and swung. Fells reached out and stopped the blow with a deft catch of Weyburn's forearm. The two men faced off silently, both drawing great heaving breaths. Fells said, "Don't you try to hit me again, David. Don't even think of it."

"If you ever talk to me like that, Floyd, I'll kill you. You don't talk about Magart that way and expect me to overlook it."

Fells slowly smiled, and the smile evolved into a cold laugh. "You know, David, we just handled it all wrong, didn't we! We made it too complicated. After you killed Folly Broadmore, we should have just taken Magart out, burned the house down around Broadmore's corpse, and had you marry Magart right out in the open sometime after. It would have been so simple, if you'd only have allowed it."

"It wouldn't have worked," Weyburn replied. "I'm still legally married to somebody else, and trying to marry Magart would have revealed that sooner or later. And even without that, there would have been no way. If I had married her, it would have generated talk. People would have figured out what had been going on between Magart and me; they might have even investigated Folly Broadmore's death a lot more closely and found the truth. And I sure as hell could have never been elected sheriff in the midst of all that suspicion. We did it the only way we could have."

Fells said, "That's clear thinking, David. I wish you could have been that clearheaded when you thought up the notion of saving Jed Keller from that ambush, for then you'd never have done such a fool thing. But it's too late now, ain't it! Before we know it, the Old Boys will be on us."

"Now it's you who've lost your clearheadedness. After tonight there won't be any Old Boys, remember? Except for Keller, they'll all be dead."

"If we're lucky."

"We will be. Trust me."

"I've already trusted you," Fells said. "And that's what's liable to get me hung."

He strode to the door and out into the night, leaving Weyburn staring after him through the doorway.

24

J ed Keller was released after breakfast the next morning. No explanations, no appearance by the sheriff. Just a deputy who turned a key and told him he was free to go, that his arrest had been an unfortunate mistake.

If not for the insight that had come in the middle of the night, Keller would have been surprised. There was no surprise now. This newest piece fit the puzzle perfectly, and only gave more credence to the terrible suspicion already in mind.

Keller had been hauled to jail on the back of a wagon, and therefore had no mount upon which to ride home. He headed for the South Brothers Livery to borrow or rent a horse, but he never made it that far. Along the way he was hailed by Calvin McBrearty. Veering across the street to meet McBrearty on the boardwalk, Keller was surprised when the district attorney yanked him into the closest alleyway, as if to avoid their being seen together.

"McBrearty, I'm glad to see you. Let me tell you what happened to me."

"No time, Keller. Listen to me: Paco the Mex has been found."

"Alive?"

"Anything but. He was murdered, and his body was sunk in the pool behind the Cade Creek stone dam."

"Murdered! Then I'll bet the farm it was Floyd Fells who did it."

"I agree; the problem is, we have no clear proof."

"I'll be glad to testify as to Paco's fear of Fells."

"Thank you, but you are not the most credible witness where Paco is concerned, given the row you had with him."

"So what can be done?"

"What I want to do for now is nothing, at least nothing public. I don't want it known that Paco has been found, not until I can gather more concrete evidence. The Polk brothers found him; they can be trusted to keep quiet. The county coroner—who quite conveniently is married to my sister—has put the body on ice above his apothecary. He'll be conducting a quiet autopsy today or tomorrow. Thank our lucky stars that Paco had no immediate kin here who would require notification; otherwise we couldn't do this."

"What are you going to be looking for in the meantime?"

"Anything I can find, my friend. Any evidence at all that would more firmly establish Fells as Paco's murderer. But I won't be able to wait long. You can only sit on a murder so long, you know."

Keller said, "I'll help you any way I can. Now let me ask you something that isn't as unrelated as it might sound. Have you heard anything this morning about gun battle around, say, Brock Spring last night?"

McBrearty looked puzzled. "No. Should I have?"

"I hope not. Let's just say I have reason to suspect such a thing."

"You've both confused and intrigued me, Jed."

"I'm a mite confused myself. I was just turned out

of Weyburn's jail, hardly minutes before you yelled for me."

"You were jailed? For what?"

"For allegedly leading the Old Boys. That was the charge. As of this morning it must have been dropped, because they turned me out and said it had all been a mistake."

"But why—what—"

"Let me confuse you even more. According to Weyburn himself, I was arrested for my own protection."

"Protection from what?"

"From death at the hands of Cutter Wyeth—or that is my suspicion. I have reason to believe that the Old Boys rode last night. I have reason to believe they were lured to Brock Spring on hopes of finding Cutter Wyeth there. I believe it was all bait for an ambush."

"Jed, are you in fact leading the Old Boys?"

"If I wasn't, I'd be truthful and deny it. If I was, I'd be untruthful and still deny it. Suffice it to say that Weyburn believes I'm an Old Boy, and it was because of that he locked me up. So I wouldn't get killed."

"Why, in the name of heaven, would he want to protect you if he believes you are an Old Boy?"

"For the sake of my late sister, that's why. He was in love with her. He carried on an affair with her right under Folly Broadmore's nose. I even suspect he may have murdered Folly because he beat my sister so badly. Maybe he had beaten her badly enough to kill her, and so Weyburn killed him and set the fire to cover what he had done. Maybe Paco knew about that some way or another. I don't know—it's all guesswork. But whatever the case, Weyburn sure didn't want me roaming free last night."

"So the question is: Was there an ambush at Brock Spring last night?" McBrearty said. "If there was, then David Weyburn has made a fatal mistake. He's proven that he knew in advance that such a thing was planned, and that links him firmly with Cutter Wyeth."

"That's one piece of evidence I hope we don't find," Keller said. "Because if there was an ambush last night, you can bet the aim was to kill as many Old Boys as possible. And I hope to God that didn't happen. There's a lot of good—" And he cut off. He had been ready to say there were a lot of good men among the Old Boys, but at the last second had remembered that vigilantism was not legal, and this *was* the district attorney he was talking to.

McBrearty, keen-minded as he was, easily figured out what Keller had been about to say. He grinned. "Don't worry, my friend. At the moment I have more important fish to fry than trying to ascertain who makes up the Old Boys. In fact, I suspect that I'm so distracted right now by other matters that I might not recognize evidence of any individual's Old Boy participation if it were to stare me right in the face. Do you understand me?"

Keller grinned now. "I do. Now come on, McBrearty. Let's head out to my spread and see if we can pick up any information about what might have happened at Brock Spring last night."

"We can take my buggy, if you'd like."

"Very good. Very good."

Taking back alleys to avoid public notice, they went around to McBrearty's private stable to fetch the rig. Within a few minutes they were rolling out of Cade toward Keller's ranch.

Within a mile of the ranch, they were met by Claire, who was riding at a fast clip back toward town. Keller was surprised not only by the meeting itself, but also by Claire's unkempt condition. She rode astride a man's saddle, wearing a pair of his trousers and an old shirt, her hair tucked up under a man's hat. Keller could think of only one reason Claire would go out publicly in that state: that she was in too great a hurry to do otherwise.

"Oh, no," he said to McBrearty as Claire drew near. "It must have happened. Just like I feared."

Claire, of course, was just as surprised to see Keller as he was to see her. She rode up and halted as Mc-Brearty pulled the buggy to a stop.

"Jed, how did you get out?"

"I was turned loose, flat-out. Claire, this is Calvin McBrearty, district attorney."

"District attorney . . ."

"Don't worry. It's all right, and you can speak freely. Claire, was there trouble at Brock Spring last night?"

"Yes . . . but how did you know? That was what I was coming to town to tell you."

"Never mind. Was it an ambush?"

"Yes. Jed . . . Doyle Boston is dead."

Keller lowered his head. "I had hoped they got away clear."

"They didn't. And Charlie Lilly is hardly alive himself."

"What about others?"

"There were no others. When you were arrested, Charlie and Doyle were determined that . . . Jed, is it really all right to talk about this in front of the district attorney?"

"Ma'am, I seem to have gone deaf as a post," Mc-Brearty said.

"Go on, Claire. He's with us on this."

"Charlie and Doyle wanted to go on after Wyeth just like they had planned. But when the others found out you had been arrested, they got wary and backed out. Charlie and Doyle went on alone."

"Alone? What a fool thing—"

"That's what I told them. They wouldn't listen. They went on and rode right into an ambush. Doyle fell dead at the first volley. Charlie managed to ride away—but he was shot up, bad. I don't think he would have gotten out alive at all except that Wyeth and his men were looking for a bigger group, and that distracted them from finishing Charlie off as quickly. He's back at the ranch right now, Jed, and I've already sent to town for the doctor. I don't know that he'll live."

"This clearly establishes that Weyburn and Wyeth are in league with one another," McBrearty said. "Not that I've been listening in."

"Jed, when I think how close you came to riding into that ambush . . ."

"You can thank David Weyburn for my safety," Keller said. "I was arrested to spare me from being with the Old Boys last night. He knew the ambush was coming, and he spared me, because he had loved Magart and I was her brother. Now let's get on to the ranch. I want to see Charlie Lilly."

The doctor arrived only minutes after they got back to the ranch. Keller was denied the opportunity to talk much to his injured friend. Not that Lilly was in shape to talk anyway; he had been shot three times, and was now hardly conscious and showed signs of losing his rationality.

It deeply depressed Keller to see the condition his friend was in. He sat brooding. McBrearty came to him, tugging his mustache and looking concerned.

"Change of plans. I'd best get Fells into custody soon, given what's happened," he said. "Fells is smart enough to figure out that Weyburn has tipped his hand by arresting you. He'll take out for parts unknown as soon as he sees things beginning to unravel."

"Who will you send to arrest him, with the sheriff being who he is?"

"If necessary, I'll get help from Fort Cade. I'm hoping, however, that some assistance will arrive today from the Texas Rangers. I wired for one or two men to come, if possible, to help me investigate Weyburn. They wired back that at least one would arrive today. If so, we'll go after Fells."

"What about Weyburn? Now that we can show he and Wyeth were in coordination on that ambush, you've got the nail you needed to hang him on."

"Yes . . . but only at the price of revealing your participation—not to mention that of Charlie Lilly and Doyle Boston—in the Old Boys. There may be legal repercussions coming from that that I'll be unable to control."

"In other words, I'll have to confess to being a vigilante, and take the potential consequences, if we're to bring down Weyburn."

"Exactly."

Keller drew in a long, deep breath. "All right. If that's what it takes, so be it."

"Not so fast, my friend. Give me time on this, and maybe there'll be evidence found that isn't so costly. For example, Mr. Fells himself might be persuaded to turn evidence against Weyburn in return for some sort of leniency. It's worth a try, at least—so don't go making any confessions just yet. Good day, my friends. And take good care of Mr. Lilly."

Keller and Claire sat up most of the night with Lilly, waiting for him to die. Fever rose in him and he went out of his head; throughout the night he spouted twisted and garbled poetry, yelled at sights no one else could see, and groped the air above him with his right arm, the left one being injured and immobile. When morning came he was still alive. Keller stayed with him all day, dozing in his chair, and when night came, Lilly was yet living.

Keller began to hope that Lilly would pull through. That became the only important thing to him. David Weyburn, Cutter Wyeth, the murder of Paco the Mex . . . none of it seemed to matter now. All Jed Keller cared about was seeing Charlie Lilly come through alive.

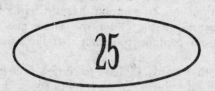

25

Floyd Fells tilted up the bottle and took another swallow of rye. It was four in the morning, and since his confrontation with Weyburn the previous night, he had been up drinking and worrying, hidden away in his little hut near the bunkhouse.

He knew it was time to leave, yet he was afraid to make the break. The idea of abandoning Weyburn filled him with fear. It would represent the final break between the two men, and while it might save him from being dragged down with Weyburn, it also would end any protection the sheriff had to offer. If he fled, Weyburn would certainly use him as a scapegoat, should one become necessary.

It was a matter of weighing risks, and Fells couldn't make up his mind. He drank again, then put the bottle aside. He was close to being drunk already, and if he fled, he needed to have his wits about him.

The longer he thought about it, the more appealing flight became. Especially now that he knew the outcome of the ambush at Brock Spring. Rather than destroy the Old Boys, as had been the hope, the ambush had succeeded in killing one, maybe two men—the only two who had snapped at the bait of Cutter Wyeth. The ambush had been a failure—and no doubt the reason was that Jed Keller's arrest had spooked the majority of the Old Boys off the chase. Thanks to Weyburn, the Old Boys were still around, and now had every reason to focus their attention on Weyburn . . . and on he himself, by extension.

The risk of remaining in Cade was simply too great. Fells made up his mind right then. He would go. Let Weyburn deal with the outcome of his own foolishness alone. Even if what Weyburn had already done didn't bring him down, the birth of Magart Broadmore's child would. And that was due to occur at any time.

"Yes, sir," Fells said to himself. "Time to get while the getting's good."

His spirits brightened now that his mind was made up. He knew he had made the right choice. *I was a fool to stay this long. I'll ride to Arkansas, Kansas, Missouri, even Mexico—anywhere but Texas. I can change my name, line myself up a job, and be safe. They'll never find me once I'm out of Texas.*

He took two horses, one belonging to him and the other to Weyburn. Fells owned few personal possessions, and what he couldn't pack with him on horseback he simply left. None of those things mattered now. What mattered was freedom.

He rode through the predawn darkness over toward the main road. When he reached it, the sun was sending the first splinters of light across the horizon. When Weyburn's big house came into view, Fells paused only a moment.

"Good-bye, David Weyburn," he said aloud. "When you hang, you'll hang without Floyd Fells beside you."

He spurred his horse and headed down the road, wanting to put as much distance as possible behind him before full daylight.

*   *   *

Fells was unaware of the three men who watched him traveling over the rolling terrain. One of the three was Calvin McBrearty, who studied Fells through a pair of binoculars borrowed from one of the two men beside him. Both of McBrearty's companions wore the badge of the Texas Rangers. The men had arrived late the prior day, and the first order of business today was the arrest of Floyd Fells for the murder of the Mexican named Paco.

"That's Fells, all right," McBrearty said, handing back the binoculars. "If we'd have waited another hour, we'd have lost our chance at him."

"Reckon he was tipped off about the Mexican's corpse being found?" one of the Rangers asked.

"I doubt it," replied McBrearty. "I'd say the reason that bird is flying its coop is simple common sense. He knows that Weyburn made a bad mistake when he arrested Jed Keller."

"We'll find out soon enough, I reckon." The Rangers began riding forward.

"Gentlemen—when you take him in, don't tell him about the murder suspicion right away. If need be, let him believe his arrest relates to stock theft. I'm interested in hearing what he'll have to say on his own steam."

"Whatever suits you," one of them said. They put spurs to flanks and headed out after Floyd Fells. McBrearty watched them a little while, then rode back toward Cade to await their return.

Fells felt the beginning of panic when he realized there was someone behind him on the road. Two men, he believed, though he had caught only a distant and fleeting view and could not be sure. Why were they following him—or were they merely other travelers who happened to be on the same road?

He couldn't bet on the latter. He would have to

assume he was being followed until given proof to the contrary.

The land made a steady upturn for the next quarter mile. Fells pushed his mount harder until he topped the rise, then descended just as quickly. Ahead and to the right was a thick grove of oaks growing along a stream. He left the trail, entered the trees, dismounted and tethered the horses. Drawing his rifle from its saddle boot, he crept to the edge of the tree line and took shelter behind a stump.

From here he had a good view of the road, while remaining out of sight himself. Leveling his rifle, he watched the spot where the two riders would appear.

Within a few moments a rider came across—only one. Fells was confused. What had happened to the second man? He began looking furtively around, thinking some sort of trick was afoot. The lone rider continued on, his horse moving at a steady but unhurried pace. The rider whistled to himself and didn't appear to be looking for anyone or anything in particular. By all appearances, he was merely a traveler on his way to wherever he was going. He rode on over the next low hill and was gone.

Fells frowned. Might he have been mistaken about there being two riders? Surely he had been. He stood and leaned against a tree trunk, giving himself comforting mental counsel. Of course there had been only one rider, and he wasn't in pursuit of anyone.

Fells returned to his horse and booted the rifle. He felt much better now. Downright secure, in fact. He had made it out. He would be long gone before Weyburn or anybody else even noticed.

He waited to give the rider ahead a longer lead, then headed out onto the road again. He traveled more slowly than before. The ups and downs of the road increased, so that Fells had less and less range of view both in front and behind. He paid no attention to this; he was relaxed now, halfway dozing in the saddle.

Something jerked him out of his daze. He stopped, confused and concerned, realizing that he had been completely asleep for a few moments. He straightened and looked all around him.

And behind him. His heart surged. Another rider was there. Traveling alone, just like the first. Fells watched him coming over the rise. Fells turned and began riding forward more quickly, wary of this newcomer. *Calm down,* he told himself. *This is just another traveler, like the first one. Mind your own business, and he'll mind his.*

Then he came across the next rise. In the middle of the road ahead sat the first rider, his horse crossways in the road and his rifle out and resting butt down against his thigh. Fells stopped, gaping. The man pulled back his coat, and the sun caught the glint of a badge.

Fells pivoted his horse to run, and saw the rider behind him coming up. His rifle was out as well, and he too wore a badge. Fells looked around, and crazily pictured himself bolting across the countryside, all pursuers left behind as he rode to freedom. Then reality set in. He couldn't run. He knew those badges. These were Texas Rangers, men trained in pursuit, men who would hound him until his horse fell from under him, then hound him some more until he had run himself into the ground.

They advanced from both sides. "Floyd Fells?"

"Yes. I'm Fells."

"Mr. Fells, my name is Bill Childress, and yonder is Landal McTavish. We're officers of the Texas Rangers, and we're authorized by the district attorney of this county to bring you in for questioning."

Fells bowed his head, and to his own surprise began to cry. "I'm sorry," he said, swiping at his tears. "It's just that I thought I had made it out safe. I really thought I had. I reckon this is about the cattle and such. At least you aren't the Old Boys, huh?"

"No, we're not. We'll take those weapons, Mr.

Fells," McTavish said. "You won't be needing them at the moment."

Fells cried all the way back to Cade, shaming himself, yet unable to stop. "I'm sorry," he said again and again. "I'm mighty embarrassed."

As for the Rangers, they had nothing to say at all.

26

Only with great effort did David Weyburn force himself out of bed with the sun. It took an even more excruciating push to get through his breakfast and onto his horse for the ride into town.

Weyburn was a frightened man. Despite his deliberate bravado in assuring Fells that his worries were groundless, Weyburn knew now that he had made a major mistake. He felt like a fool. How could he have failed to understand what he was doing?

He felt weary, confused, and had a sense of mounting desperation so intense that it caused a buzzing in his ears. He feared that his days as sheriff were numbered, and that probably it had been a mistake to take this job in the first place. He had believed that as sheriff he could control with impunity the entire network of stock thieves on the Brazos. It hadn't worked that way, thanks to the Old Boys, and thanks to his own obsessed devotion to Magart.

Weyburn looked around as he rode, and longed to ride out of this county and not look back. But he couldn't. There was Magart to think of, and the child she was about to give birth to. Maria Cruz believed the baby would be born this very week, possibly in the next

day or so. Weyburn had left word with his servants to
come fetch him as soon as the first signs of labor came
on.

Lord, but I'm tired this morning, Weyburn
thought. He hadn't slept much the night before. Too
much on his mind. And when he had slept, he dreamed
about the Tonkawa woman Floyd Fells had killed, and
about Paco the Mex. He felt guilty for their deaths, even
though it hadn't been his hand that killed them. They
had both died because of him, and that didn't sit easily
on his mind. Perhaps Floyd Fells had no conscience, but
David Weyburn did. More of a conscience than he had
realized.

Weyburn had broken out in a sweat by the time he
reached his office, and as he dismounted he felt dizzy.
Might he be getting sick? He was actually happy to consider that possibility, for an oncoming illness would explain the nightmares, the sense of coming doom, the
buzzing in his ears.

He stabled his horse in the shed behind the jail and
went inside. The night deputy at the desk was snoring,
and looked embarrassed when he woke up and saw
Weyburn looking at him. He stood.

"Morning, Sheriff."

"Morning."

The deputy frowned. "Are you feeling all right,
Sheriff Weyburn? You look a little green this morning."

"I think maybe I'm coming down with something.
But I'll be fine. Go on home, and we'll see you back
tonight."

Weyburn felt relieved when the deputy was gone.
An examination of the cell block revealed that the jail
had no prisoners. Even better. Weyburn poured himself
a cup of coffee, spiked it with whiskey from a pocket
flask, added a dollop of molasses from the shelf above
the stove and a chunk of hard candy from a sack in his
desk. Looking for further signs of illness, he had con-

vinced himself his throat felt raw. This concoction should help.

When he had finished drinking, he rose, went to the window, and surveyed the busy main street of Cade. He turned his face in the direction of his own house and wondered how Magart was faring. Her labor could be starting even now. He remembered the death of his first wife in childbirth, and wished he could call in a doctor to help Magart through her own delivery. That was out of the question, of course. Magart was supposedly dead and buried. What help she received in labor would have to come from Maria Cruz.

Weyburn went back to his desk, rubbing the back of his neck and letting his thoughts proceed a step further. He had managed to hide Magart well enough, but what would he do with the baby? Fells was right; there would be no hiding an infant.

It's not going to work. There's no way it can work. I'll have to get rid of the baby. Maybe Eduardo can haul it off and drop it at the door of some church or orphanage.

The idea made him feel even more conscience-stricken. That was Magart's child he was thinking about —Magart's, and his own. Perhaps the thing to do would be to leave, as soon as the baby was old enough . . .

. . . if the Old Boys allow me that much time. After what happened at Brock Spring, they'll be out for my blood. God above, what's going to happen here? Magart, how are we going to get ourselves out of this?

David Weyburn pulled the flask from his pocket, turned it up, and took a long, shaky swallow.

"I must go get him at once!" Eduardo Cruz held his wife by the shoulders and virtually spat the words into her face. "He has given us clear instruction, and if we disobey, he will hold us to account!"

"And you fear him, don't you, my husband? You are more afraid of the wrath of David Weyburn than of the wrath of the God who will smite both him and us if we continue to do wrong!"

"And what would you have us do, woman? Deliver her child and steal it away?"

"Yes, that is exactly what I would have us do. This child is an innocent one, Eduardo. Nothing good can come to it, being born into this household! It would be sent away . . . maybe killed. When the child comes, the days of Señor Weyburn's secrets will be short. The baby would be discovered in time, and the truth would come out, all of it. There is danger for this child here . . . we cannot let harm come to a baby, my husband! We cannot!"

Eduardo cursed and pushed her away. Pacing back and forth, he sought escape from the predicament and could not find it. He went to the bedside of Magart Broadmore and looked down into her ashen face. His fear increased, for even he, who knew nothing of childbirth, could see that Magart's labor was not proceeding correctly. What if she should die in childbirth, like David Weyburn's first wife had? Weyburn would blame him for that—especially if they failed to notify him promptly, as they had been directed.

"Maria, there is no other way—I must go to Señor Weyburn. There is nothing else to do."

"Yes, there is," Maria said. "We can bring the child into the world and take it away to safety, out of his reach. We can for once in our lives do what is right!"

"Take it away? How would we care for a newborn child, wife? There is no milk in your old breasts!" He paused, then tried a shift of tack. "And Señor Weyburn would certainly pursue us, and when he found us, he would be angry, and then the child truly would be in danger. For the sake of the child, we must go to Señor Weyburn now."

"For the sake of the child, you say? Bah!" Maria spat at her husband's face. "It is only because of your cowardice, Eduardo. The man I have married is a cow-

ard! Very well, then! Go to Señor Weyburn, if you must!
But may the blood of this child be on your hands!"

Eduardo's face was red with fury. He pivoted and
stalked out of the room. Maria listened as he stomped
down the stairs and out the door. At the window she
watched him cross to the stable and saddle a horse. A
few minutes later he was galloping off toward Cade.

Now it was her turn to be fearful. Maria closed her
eyes and prayed fervently. *God, bring the child quickly,
before Weyburn returns. Give me time to take it away
to a safe place . . . but where?*

She lifted her head. Yes! Now she knew where she
could take the child—if only it would be born quickly
enough. Repeating the prayer in her mind, she went to
Magart's bedside.

Magart opened her eyes, and from her throat
boiled up a yell of pain. This was a fast and painful
labor, and Magart's suffering brought tears to Maria's
eyes. She put her hand on Magart's brow.

"Be strong, Lady," she said. "You must push the
child from your body. Be strong. I am with you."

It was a mustache-stroking moment for Calvin Mc-
Brearty, for he was satisfied. Before him sat Floyd Fells,
a very scared man. *But not nearly so scared,* McBrearty
thought privately, *as he will be when I show him the
iced-down body at the coroner's. That will probably be
enough to make him start crying again.*

"Mr. Fells, may I ask you where you were going
this morning?" McBrearty asked, pulling a cigar from
his pocket.

"Riding. That's all. Just riding away."

"For good?"

"Reckon so."

"You were leaving Mr. Weyburn's employment,
then?"

"Yeah, yeah I was."

"Why?"

Fells shrugged. "Just wanted to. Tired of working there, you know."

"Tell me, Mr. Fells: How have you been fulfilling Mr. Weyburn's contract with Fort Cade? What is it . . . three beeves a day?"

"That's easy enough. I cut out three good beeves from the herd, slaughter and skin the hides off them, and haul them to the fort."

"What do you do with the hides?"

Fells paled a little. "Just get rid of them, you know."

"Where?"

His Adam's apple bobbed toward his chin and down again. "Throw them in the water."

"Mr. Fells, I think you know what I'm trying to get at. What water?"

"There's a pool by the slaughter pen. A stream we diverted and dammed. I throw them in there."

"I see. Thank you, Mr. Fells. Let me tell you something. I believe that when we go fish some of those hides out of that water, we'll find lots of brands on them other than Weyburn's. In fact, I suspect we won't find any Weyburn cattle at all. What do you think, Mr. Fells?"

No answer.

"The water may yield up some interesting evidence for us. It has a way of doing that, you know. As a matter of fact, let's walk down a couple of buildings here and let me show you something else the water has revealed for us. I think you might find it of personal interest."

Fells looked for all the world like a man walking to the gallows as they trudged behind the building row to the local apothecary. The druggist had some medical training and doubled as county coroner, and whenever he had to keep a body in storage, he iced it down in a sealed room on the second floor of the building, a big empty room like a warehouse.

The coroner was a tall and rather coarse man, and

the more dramatic McBrearty was somewhat disappointed by the slow and mundane way his brother-in-law opened the ice chest and lifted the top block to reveal Paco the Mex's much-decayed face. The disappointment was short-lived. What the coroner's performance had lacked in dramatic flair, Fells more than made up for by his reaction. He looked as if Hell itself had opened before him.

"That's Paco the Mex in there," McBrearty said. "I'm willing to bet you can tell us how he managed to get his throat so terribly sliced."

Fells darted out of the little room so quickly that not even the Rangers—who were distracted by the hideous corpse—could stop him. "No!" Fells screamed. "I didn't kill him! I didn't do it!"

He lunged for the stairs and made the top of them before the stunned lawmen could even get out of the ice room. McBrearty came out just in time to see Fells slip and tumble down the stairs. He made a horrible racket that ended with a thump like an unripe melon dropped on the bottom of an overturned barrel.

McBrearty pounded over to the stairs. Fells lay at the bottom, blood pulsing out of his nose and his eyes staring upward. In the process of falling, he had managed to strike his head very hard against the corner of one of the stairs. The pulsing of the blood stopped as McBrearty came to the bottom of the stairs.

"I'm confounded!" he said. "He's dead!"

Texas Ranger Bill Childress said, "Well, in all my days I ain't never seen one go out like that! No sir."

The coroner reached the bottom of the stairs last of all. He examined Fells's corpse briefly and said, "Well, if you carry him out through the apothecary, please try not to drip any blood on the floor."

When they hauled the body of Floyd Fells out of the apothecary and laid it out on a board, it drew a crowd very quickly. Down the street, David Weyburn had just stepped out of his office. Noting the tumult, he strode up the boardwalk.

The people murmured as he drew near, for they knew Fells worked for Weyburn. The crowd parted and let Weyburn through. He stared wordlessly at the body, then turned away. At that moment he looked almost as corpselike as Fells himself.

Eduardo Cruz galloped around the corner on the opposite end of the street. His goal was the sheriff's office, but he also was attracted by the crowd. He was about to descend from his horse and go over to see what was getting so much attention, when a momentary shift of the crowd allowed him to see the corpse.

A great fear gripped Eduardo. Fells . . . dead? He looked up and saw Weyburn striding away, his back toward him, his stride stiff, and the crowd looking from Fells to Weyburn and back again, and all Eduardo could think was: *Señor Weyburn has killed him. Señor Weyburn has become loco and killed Floyd Fells!*

The notion made little sense, but Eduardo was already agitated beyond clear thought. And Weyburn indeed had been acting lately like a man about to go over the edge of sanity.

Panic set in, and Eduardo wheeled his horse, riding away as fast as he could, out of Cade and onto the plains beyond, his mission of announcing Magart's labor forgotten.

27

McBrearty walked into the sheriff's office without knocking. A trace of Floyd Fells's blood had remained unnoticed on his fingers, and it wiped off on the knob as he turned it. McBrearty shuddered. He was a tough man, but blood always bothered him.

Weyburn was sitting at his desk. He looked like his spirit had been beaten out of him. His pallor was so deathly that McBrearty had to struggle not to gape at the man.

"Weyburn, you aren't looking so good these days," McBrearty said.

"It's not been an easy time for me. Vigilantes, rumors and accusations in the streets . . . and now it appears my foreman is dead."

"Yes. It was accidental." McBrearty told the story, starting with Fells's arrest. When he mentioned the part about the body of Paco the Mex, Weyburn gave a little spasm, like he had been kicked.

"So Paco the Mex was murdered?" Weyburn asked.

"Yes . . . but you knew that already."

Weyburn held his silence. No denials, no confirmations. Just that sad, blank stare. McBrearty had seen

176

that expression before, on the faces of murder defendants when the evidence was strong against them and conviction inevitable. It was the expression of men looking over the nearing horizon and seeing death grinning and waiting for them to arrive.

"Mr. McBrearty, is it true you've been investigating me?"

"Yes, sir. I started it at the request of Till Cooke while he was still in office. What began out of his interest has continued out of my own. Mr. Weyburn, I believe that you have been, and are continuing, an involvement in stock theft. I believe that you, mostly through Mr. Fells, have worked in cooperation with Cutter Wyeth. I believe you had advance knowledge of the planned massacre of the vigilantes at Brock Spring. Is my line of thinking generally correct?"

Weyburn said, "You know I can't answer a question like that, Mr. McBrearty."

Interesting, McBrearty thought, *that he doesn't simply deny it. What has happened to this man?* He recalled what he had learned of the madness of Weyburn's grandfather, and wondered if Weyburn was moving toward a similar breakdown.

"There's more, Mr. Weyburn, though it is much less precise. You may be aware that Mr. Jed Keller has some vague suspicions that you know something about the death of his sister, something that Paco the Mex was killed to cover up. We believe it was Mr. Fells who killed him, though obviously that matter won't come to trial, given what has just happened. Might there be any substance to these suspicions?"

Weyburn gave no indication he had even been listening.

"Mr. Weyburn," McBrearty said gently, "I think you should consider turning in your badge. Difficult times are ahead for you, and for the sake of the operation of this county office, I think your resignation would be a helpful and appropriate gesture. You needn't admit guilt to any crime by so doing. It would merely be, as I said, a gesture showing your concern that this office's reputation not be sullied."

Weyburn reached under his vest, unpinned his badge, and laid it on his desk. "I was tired of it anyway," he said. "It seems I'm tired all the time now, Mr. McBrearty."

"Yes." McBrearty reached over and took the badge. "Perhaps a letter to the county court would be in order."

"Yes. I'll do that. I will." Weyburn's weary eyes lifted to McBrearty's face. "Am I under arrest?"

"No. I do anticipate the likelihood of an indictment soon, with later ones probable. I see no reason not to tell you. You are an intelligent enough man; you would have figured it out for yourself soon enough."

"Yes."

"I advise you, sir, don't try to flee the area. You know you would soon be found, and even if not, what kind of life would it be, looking over your shoulder the rest of your days?"

Weyburn nodded. He stood, still wearing that same sad and listless expression. Oddly, he thrust out his hand to McBrearty. Surprised, the district attorney shook it. It was like grasping a wet roll of newspaper.

"You are a credit to your position, Mr. McBrearty," Weyburn said. "Our county is well-served by its prosecutor."

Weyburn put on his hat and coat and walked out, leaving McBrearty thinking that in all his career in law, this conversation was the strangest he had ever held with any man, be he criminal, victim, judge, or juror.

David Weyburn spent the rest of the day riding alone on the plains around Cade. No longer did he feel that his world was about to crash around him. The crash had already come. Floyd Fells was dead, the district attorney apparently had a strong case building

against him, and there was no way out now by denials
and alibis.

Odd though it was, **David Weyburn** was relieved.
He had tried to shoulder too big a burden, and now it
had fallen back on him. He couldn't hope to lift it off
now, even though it certainly would crush him. There
was no more need for struggle, and the end of struggle
was welcome.

As the day waned, Weyburn turned his mount
toward his ranch. The sight of his big house brought a
smile. Inside was Magart, the one being in the world he
loved more than himself. Once they came after him,
even Magart would be lost to him, and he knew it. Tonight he wouldn't let it matter. He would be with her, a
man and his beloved, for whatever time they were given.

He wondered when the baby would come. It
brought him pause, and he recalled the thought he had
played with that morning, that the child would have to
be sent away to preserve his precious secrets. Well, it
didn't matter now. Soon enough there would be no
secrets. The truth was going to come out, and not a
thing he could do would stop it now.

He halted. Why was the house so dark? Why did it
seem so empty?

"*Magart . . .*"

He dismounted at the gate and ran toward the
door. It was ajar; he pushed it open and went inside.
Not a light burned inside.

Weyburn drew his pistol and edged farther in.
"Hello?"

No response. "Maria? Eduardo? Where are you?"

Silence. Then a scuffling, a movement upstairs—in
Magart's room.

"Magart? Magart, are you all right?"

He ran up the stairs, taking four at a bound. Turning down the hall, he stopped, overcome by the darkness of the enclosed space. Just as he was digging in his
pocket for a match, a light flared in Magart's bedroom.

Weyburn heard the clink of a lamp chimney being set in place, and the light smoothed and regulated.

Weyburn drew in a breath, edged forward, and leaped into the doorway, pistol leveled before him.

Eduardo Cruz looked back at him. He was holding the lamp, standing by Magart's bed. Weyburn lowered the pistol. "Eduardo?" Then he looked at Magart.

That she was dead was obvious at first glance. Unbreathing, gray of pallor, her head turned to the side, she lay between sheets bloodied by birthing, and her belly, formerly large with child, was flat under the top sheet.

"Magart, oh God, Magart!" Weyburn dropped the pistol and went to the bedside, falling to his knees. "Magart, have I lost you too? Have I lost you too?"

"I am sorry, Señor Weyburn," Eduardo said. He was shaking, making the flame of the lamp quiver, the distorted shadows of broken men it cast onto the wall in shuddering motion. "I came to town today to tell you of her labor, but I saw the body of Mr. Fells and grew afraid. I hid on the plains all day, but when it was dark I came back to see what had happened. I didn't know she had died, Mr. Weyburn. I didn't know. I'm so sorry, so very sorry."

"Where is Maria?"

"I don't know, Mr. Weyburn. She is gone."

"The baby . . ."

"There is no baby here, sir. Maria must have taken it."

Weyburn stood. "Taken it? Where?"

"I don't know, sir. I truly don't."

Weyburn looked at his pistol where it lay on the floor. Eduardo saw it too, and gave a little gasp of realization. He moved as if to go toward it, then his cowardice asserted itself and he cringed back. Weyburn walked over and picked up the pistol. He lifted it and aimed it at Eduardo.

"Señor Weyburn, please . . ." Eduardo knelt, setting the lamp before him on the floor and putting clenched fists on each side of his head. His eyes looked up pleadingly at Weyburn.

"You should have found me, Eduardo. You should have told me what was happening."

"I was afraid, sir. I am sorry—please don't kill me!"

Weyburn held the pistol up a quarter minute more, then lowered it. His manner softened. "Go away, Eduardo. Take a horse and ride away from here. One more death will solve nothing. It's over. It's all over."

Eduardo, trembling and cringing like a kicked dog, edged for the door, then went out it on a run.

Weyburn stood, stoop-shouldered, pistol in hand, in the center of the room. On the bed lay the shell of what had once been Magart Keller Broadmore, now cold and silent, and outside there was no sound but the receding hoofbeats of Eduardo Cruz's horse.

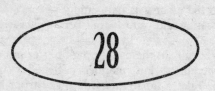

28

Magart Broadmore's baby boy wasn't born for almost three hours after Eduardo left to find David Weyburn. Maria could not guess what kept Eduardo and Weyburn from returning during that time—but whatever it was, it was a blessing. It allowed her time to get the child into the world and safely away from Weyburn's house.

She had cried when she realized Magart Broadmore had not survived the birthing. To see the life depart from one body even as it pushed a new life into the world seemed infinitely sorrowful, especially considering the sad condition in which Magart had lived during her last months. It made Maria despise David Weyburn. If not for the necessity to preserve his vile secrets, Magart Broadmore could have had the assistance of a doctor as she gave birth. She might have lived.

After the child was born, Maria was in a quandary. The baby was screaming for its mother's breast, but its mother could give it no sustenance now or ever. Maria cleaned the squalling newborn as best she could and wrapped it in a blanket, struggling against panic. "Don't cry, little one, I will take you to safety," she said. "I will find a breast to give you milk. I promise you. All will be well."

As she took the baby outside and over to the stable, she was grateful that Weyburn had built his house out of view of the working headquarters of the ranch. It gave her privacy to hitch a horse to a wagon without being observed or heard, for at the moment there were no living humans here except for herself and the crying baby. With nervous fingers she had finished the hitching —an unfamiliar job for her—and then climbed aboard, the enwrapped baby in her arms. She gave one last, tense look around to reassure herself that Eduardo and Weyburn were not coming into view, then drove off toward the ranch of Jed and Claire Keller.

Claire hadn't felt so sad since the day her uncle Till had died. She was alone in the ranch house. Jed was gone, along with a couple of the hands, taking Charlie Lilly into town to be put under the full-time supervision of the doctor. Despite his tenacious clinging to life, Lilly had taken a turn for the worse in the night, and it was evident, to Claire at least, that he was not going to survive.

Wiping her moist eyes on her cuff, she went to the window and looked across the ranch land. It was barren this time of year—as barren as she felt inside. It would be a sad thing to lose Charlie Lilly, a man ever bright and full of poetry. And all because the good men of the area had found themselves without any help in the official legal structure of the county. Even while reluctantly acknowledging the need for the Old Boys and their rough justice, Claire despised the fact they had existed— and especially that they had involved her husband so deeply. She had also come to despise David Weyburn, whose corruption and ineffectiveness as a law enforcement official were the ultimate reasons the Old Boys had been revived. If not for Weyburn, Till Cooke would probably still be alive, and Jed Keller wouldn't have violated his own pledge never to become a vigilante.

Claire's thoughts were interrupted by the sight of

an approaching wagon. At first she thought it was Keller and the hands returning from delivering Lilly to Cade and the doctor. Quickly she saw that it wasn't; this was a strange wagon, being driven by a woman—and clumsily driven at that. As it drew closer, Claire saw that the woman had a bundle in her arms, carefully held . . . like a baby.

It *was* a baby. Surprised, Claire threw her coat over her shoulders and left the house. The woman, who appeared to be Mexican, saw her, steered the wagon directly toward her, and came to a stop. The baby was squalling, but it was a weak and meager squall, like that of a newborn. Claire looked more closely, and was amazed to see that the baby appeared to be mere hours old at the most.

"My heavens, is that your child?" she asked, rushing forward with arms out. "Have you driven yourself here after giving birth?"

"No, señora, no . . . it is not my child. But please, we must find food for him."

"Yes, you are right. Come in, Miss, Missus . . ."

"I am Maria Cruz. Señora Keller, how will we feed him?"

After a few moments of thought, Claire said, "There's a camp of Indians west of the ranch, and one of the women has given birth. I'll send a man to tell her she can make good money as a wet nurse at the Keller place."

"Gracias, thank you so much," Maria said. "I can see you are a good woman, señora. And I have much to tell you and your husband."

"My husband is away at the moment."

"But I must see him. I have news for him, about his sister."

"About Magart Broadmore?"

"Si, señora. The child, you see, it is hers."

"But this is a newborn, and Magart Broadmore has been dead for almost a year."

"I will explain it all, señora, as soon as the child is fed."

The process of sending for and awaiting the Indian woman took a little more than an hour. During that time Claire was immensely curious, and also wondering if this Mexican lady was a madwoman. Might she have stolen this child from someone nearby? The baby's increasingly hoarse and weak crying made it impossible for Claire to question Maria Cruz very closely. Only when the somber-faced young Tonkawa arrived and put the hungry infant to her milk-swollen breast did the opportunity for explanation come.

"Tell me, now, Mrs. Cruz, how it is possible for a woman long dead to have given birth to a newborn baby."

"I see you do not believe me, señora. I don't blame you. What I have to tell will be difficult for you to believe. But you must believe it—and forgive me for my part in this terrible thing."

Then Maria Cruz began to talk, telling the story from the beginning, and when she was done, Claire Keller was a woman astonished. Maria's tale was as astounding as she had indicated it would be, but the more Claire thought about it, the more it fit the facts of the past year's experiences.

Jed Keller did not return home until late in the night, and from the expression on his face, Claire knew that Charlie Lilly had not lived. She met Keller outside, while the hands who had accompanied him saw to putting away the wagon.

"He went out easy, at least," Keller said. "At the end, for a couple of minutes, he was as lucid as he could be. That happens sometimes with folks who are dying. He gave me the name of his brother in Missouri and told me how to get hold of him. I've already had a wire sent. Charlie will be buried in the city cemetery." Keller paused, having heard something he couldn't identify. "What was that? It sounded like a baby."

"It is a baby."

"What? Here?"

"Yes. Come inside, Jed. There's a Mexican woman here, named Maria Cruz."

"Maria Cruz? Isn't that one of David Weyburn's house servants?"

"Yes. Jed, she has brought a baby here. A newborn. And she has a story to tell that you may find hard to bear. It has to do with your sister, and David Weyburn, and this new baby . . . but come in. I'll let her tell it."

Maria Cruz had calmed significantly since the morning, and spoke in a steady, even voice. Jed Keller sat holding the sleeping newborn as he listened in astonishment, trying to fathom what he already had been told: that the baby had been born that very morning to none other than his sister; that Magart had died only hours before, not months ago, as he had believed.

"What I tell you is what I know from my own experience, along with what has been told to me by my own husband. I will not pretend that I have no guilt; I ask only that you forgive me as best you can.

"I and my husband have worked for Señor Weyburn for several years. We knew well the kind of man he was, and had learned to turn our backs on it, God forgive us. We were with him when he came to the Brazos country and built his big house. We knew of his thieving and rustling, and that he dealt with bad men like Cutter Wyeth—but we said nothing, and did nothing. He was our employer, and we were faithful to him. Too faithful, I now know.

"Señor Weyburn fell in love with Magart Broadmore almost as soon as he first saw her. She was not a free woman, but a married one. And Señor Weyburn was not free either, though only those closest to him—my husband and I, and in time, Floyd Fells—knew he still had a wife who had refused to divorce him. But Señor Weyburn is not a man who can resist what he wants, and soon he and Magart Broadmore were involved in a love affair. At the beginning, Folly Broadmore knew nothing of what was going on, but in time he grew suspicious. He was a harsh man, Folly Broadmore, and cruel to his wife. As he grew more sure she was being untrue to him, his cruelty became worse. He began beating her—and that was what finally led to his end.

"Though no one now living knows exactly what happened, somehow Folly Broadmore found out it was David Weyburn who was seeing his wife. He grew terribly angry, and beat his poor wife until her head was almost crushed. It changed her, robbed her of her mind. She became simple, like a child, hardly knowing who she was, and remembering very little of her own life.

"When Señor Weyburn saw her in this way, he became furious. Floyd Fells was his foreman and partner by then, and they were together when Señor Weyburn went to make Folly Broadmore pay for what he had done. I don't know exactly how he killed him, but I think he stabbed him to death, right in Folly Broadmore's own house, and right before Magart's eyes. But she didn't understand what she saw—that was how much of her mind Folly Broadmore had beaten out of her.

"When Señor Weyburn realized what he had done, he knew he had to hide the murder. He decided to burn the house down, to make it seem Folly Broadmore had died in the fire. But there was still Magart Broadmore to deal with. Señor Weyburn couldn't marry her for fear that his own marriage would be discovered, and for fear that people would realize he had been carrying on a love affair with a married woman. Señor Weyburn had plans to run for sheriff as soon as Till Cooke stepped down, and he couldn't afford scandal.

"And so they decided there was nothing to be done but to make it appear she had died with her husband. That way Señor Weyburn could take her secretly into his own home, and live with her as a man lives with his wife. And so Floyd Fells murdered a Tonkawa woman, and they dressed her body in some of Magart's clothing, and burned the house down with her corpse lying near that of Broadmore. The trick worked; everyone believed that both Folly and Magart Broadmore had died in the fire.

"My husband and I had to be told some of what had happened, because it fell to us to take care of Magart Broadmore—though Señor Weyburn wished us to call her 'Mrs. Weyburn.' My husband was told more than I was . . . they trusted him more, because they could tell he was more like them than I was. They were right. My husband is an evil coward, and he doesn't know I have come here tonight. I hope never to see him again.

"I knew there were things I hadn't been told, and I begged my husband to tell me. At last he did, and then I wished I hadn't been told at all. The evil of what had been done, and the evil Eduardo and I were doing in helping hide it, was too much for me. I had to tell someone, and at last I did. It was only Paco, a simple old beggar who would go from ranch to ranch looking for food or something to steal."

"So that's how Paco knew!" Keller cut in.

"Yes, Señor Keller. And then it only grew worse. I realized that Magart had become with child—Señor Weyburn's child. I began to fear what would become of the child once it was born, because I knew it would mean the end of all secrets unless it was sent away or done away with. I decided then that when the time of birth came, I would somehow get the child to safety. And so I have brought it here to you, Señor and Señora Keller. And I throw myself onto your mercy, because I don't know what will become of me, now that I've betrayed Señor Weyburn."

Keller stood, holding the baby out before him and looking into its little face. He remained silent for a long time. Then he turned to Maria. "You have nothing to fear from me, Mrs. Cruz. You have done the right thing in coming here. This baby is now safe, and so are you. But I have to leave. I'm going to Weyburn's house."

Claire stood. "Jed, you're not thinking of—"

"Don't worry, Claire. I doubt David Weyburn is anywhere within miles of here now. I'm going to claim the body of my sister, if he hasn't done away with it already."

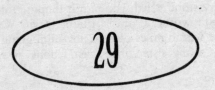

29

The funeral and burial service for Magart Keller Broadmore drew one of the largest crowds in the county's history. The story of David Weyburn's deception, and the tragedy of Magart's death and the other aspects of the remarkable story, made all the rounds, and even drew the attention of the newspapers from the big cities.

One portion in particular seemed to be told the most frequently and with the most dramatic flair: that being the way Jed Keller had found the body of his sister. After hearing Maria Cruz's revelations, he had ridden to the Weyburn house and found it deserted and dark—dark, that is, except in the upper bedroom, where a score of candles and lamps burned around the bed upon which Magart's still body lay. Weyburn had closed her eyes and laid her straight, and in her hands had placed a bouquet of dried flowers taken from a vase downstairs. With the flowers was a note, written in his own hand: *Forgive me.*

Weyburn was nowhere to be found, though he was sought extensively throughout and all around the county. He, like his servant Eduardo Cruz, had vanished, no doubt having fled far away.

"He was afraid of the Old Boys," some speculated at Magart's graveside. Others said his fear was more probably caused by Calvin McBrearty, who was reportedly about to bring damning information about Weyburn before the next grand jury. One of the charges, according to the general wisdom, would be an accessory to murder charge involving the death of Winnie, the murdered Tonkawa woman, and possibly another related to the slaying of Paco the Mex.

Many, both private citizens and press, sought to question Jed Keller about the unique events he had found himself in the middle of. He answered no queries. Keller had no desire to discuss the matter, and it was evident that his grief was deep both for his sister and for his friend Charlie Lilly. The background of Lilly's death was a matter of speculation among the people. Information about the fight at the remote Brock Spring had been kept out of public circulation by McBrearty and the few others who knew of it, so no one was really sure Lilly's fatal wounding had come during an Old Boy excursion. Still, rumors flew.

Jed Keller called on Calvin McBrearty two days after Magart's burial in the city cemetery—Keller had forbid that she be buried on the ranch grounds beside Folly Broadmore—to ask him his views on the likelihood of David Weyburn ever being brought to justice.

"Eventually he'll turn up, somewhere," McBrearty said. "Frankly, I'm surprised he even fled—I didn't think he would do it. Otherwise I'd have never—" He cut off.

"Go on."

McBrearty sighed and tugged the left side of his mustache. "I may have made an error of judgment. I told Weyburn that I was planning to bring evidence against him before the grand jury."

"For land's sake, McBrearty! Why the devil—"

"Don't jump down my throat, Keller. At the time, I knew nothing about Magart, or the Tonkawa woman's death. And it was certain that Weyburn had already heard that charges would probably come against him. The man had a big home and a sizable ranch investment. The idea of him running away from all that seemed inconceivable. And quite honestly, I still don't believe he would have left if Magart had not died. I think he would have stayed at her side. Whatever his flaws—and they were legion—Weyburn apparently was devoted to Magart. He committed murder because of her, for God's sake."

"Weyburn is an odd mix," Keller conceded. "On the one hand he killed the husband who had beaten her nearly to death—then on the other, he locked her away and denied her the care she needed in childbirth. He took a personal risk to save my own neck by locking me up the night of the Brock Spring fight, but at the same time he allowed two of my best friends in the world to ride to their deaths under Cutter Wyeth's guns. He proved himself devoted to Magart, just like you said, but he also let Floyd Fells murder an innocent Indian woman just to cover his own guilt. And it was Weyburn who let Cutter Wyeth go free, and because of that, Till Cooke was murdered." Keller paused thoughtfully. "I guess when you weigh him in the balance, there's not enough good to offset the bad. And what good he had was generally tainted with his own selfishness."

"Jed, I vow to you: If Weyburn can be found and brought into court, I'll do my best to see him dealt with to the fullest extent possible."

Keller smiled coldly. "If it's me who finds him, you won't have to worry about prosecution, McBrearty. All you'll have to do is send out for a good pine box and a grave digger."

"It might be counted a foolish thing to voice such a threat right in front of the county prosecutor," McBrearty said.

"It might—but it's far from the first foolish thing I've done," Keller said.

"I'm serious about this, Keller. I've overlooked a lot with you. But you listen to me: I'm sworn to uphold the law, and there's only so many things I can turn my back on. Don't get some fool notion of going after Weyburn yourself, or Wyeth either, for that matter."

Keller stared right into McBrearty's eyes. "I used to talk about leaving the law in the hands of the official lawmen myself, you may recall. A man named Till Cooke gave me a new perspective on that. He taught me that sometimes a man has to deal with wrongdoing in a direct way. Charlie Lilly believed that too."

"And Till Cooke and Charlie Lilly are both dead. Don't become a loose cannon on the deck, Keller. That'll do no good for you, me, this county, or the memory of your sister. Take that as a warning."

"Warning heard. Now if you'll excuse me, I've got to go down and meet the stage. Charlie Lilly's brother's coming in today to see to his things, few though they were."

"Give him my condolences."

"I will."

"Jed Keller, you heed what I've said—hear?"

"Good-bye, McBrearty. See you around."

He left the district attorney's office and strode down the street toward the stage office, hands in the pockets of his mackinaw. McBrearty stood at his window, watching him go, and tugged at his mustache so hard that it hurt.

That night, Claire noticed that Jed Keller was quiet and somber. He had been like that since Magart's death, but tonight he was unusually so. In their bed, she put her arms around him and asked him what was on his mind.

"I talked to Charlie Lilly's brother today," he said. "He came in to claim Charlie's things and to pay his respects at the grave."

"I knew he was due in soon."

"He told me something . . . I don't quite know how to feel about it."

"What was it?"

"Ed Lilly—that's his name—he's a lot like Charlie was. Clever and keen, you know. We talked, and I told him I intended to see Wyeth and Weyburn pay for what they've done, and pay by my own hand if at all possible. What he told me sort of shook me up, I admit."

Now Claire was intrigued. She pushed up on one elbow and looked into Keller's face. "What did he say?"

"He told me not to try and avenge Charlie. He said he understood what I was feeling, because he'd been through it himself. Seems he and Charlie had a younger brother once, a simple fellow. He got killed in an accidental shooting."

"That's sad."

"It's more than that, Claire. That shooting happened in a Missouri bank where this young fellow worked, and the man who shot him was a greenhorn deputy."

"Jed . . . he was talking about you!"

"He was, though he didn't know it. He said that for a long time after his brother died, he was determined to kill that deputy in payback for the death. It was Charlie who talked him out of it. Said it wasn't worth it, and that it was just an accident, after all. Charlie told him that the poor fellow who shot their brother likely would suffer more punishment in his own mind than any avenger could inflict. He was right. God have mercy, he was right." Keller choked up as he talked. "Claire, Charlie Lilly went to his grave never knowing he was working for the very man who shot his brother all those years back. I never talked to him in any specific way about what had happened to me back in Missouri. I'm glad now that I didn't." Keller wiped at his face. "You know, the first time I saw Charlie, I knew there was something familiar in his face. It was the family resemblance to that fellow I shot. That's what it was. The family resemblance."

Claire held her husband for a while. "Jed, do you think that maybe what Charlie said to his brother might apply to this situation too?"

"You mean about Weyburn's mind inflicting more punishment than what I could give in vengeance? Maybe so, Claire. He must have loved Magart a lot, in his own selfish way. He's got to feel responsible for her death. Remember the note he left on her body? 'Forgive me,' it said."

"Maybe you should just let it go, Jed. Let Weyburn pay for what he did in his own way."

"Maybe . . . but what about Wyeth? There's no conscience in that man at all."

"Leave it be, Jed. Leave it be. Maybe he'll be required to pay too."

"But how?"

"I don't know. But just leave it be. I lost my uncle Till after he decided that it was up to him to settle all the scores and right all the wrongs. I see more and more of him in you. I don't want to lose you like I lost him. Just let it be, Jed. Please."

He leaned over and kissed her. "I think maybe I will, Claire. I think maybe I will."

30

Weeks rolled past, and the year of 1876 came to a
close. Often Jed Keller thought about David Weyburn, out there roaming free somewhere while the
woman who had borne his child lay in her grave; and
about Cutter Wyeth, living his worthless life with the
blood of Till Cooke on his hands. The thoughts would
bring him fury, and he would consider going to search
for them. But he never did. He didn't know where to
look, for one thing. And he wasn't even sure anymore
that it was his place to look, for another. The thing that
Charlie Lilly's brother had told him had greatly tem-
pered his thirst for vengeance.

Meanwhile, Magart's little baby boy thrived and
grew. It was the image of Magart herself, and Keller was
glad of that, because it made it easier to forget that
David Weyburn was the father. The Kellers grew to love
the baby, and named him Charles Doyle Keller, in memory of Charlie Lilly and Doyle Boston.

Maria Cruz remained in town, and occasionally
came to visit the baby. The Kellers held no hard feelings
toward her for her part in helping Weyburn cover his
many sins; if not for Maria's honesty and courage at the
end, the truth might have never come out. Maria struck

a deal with Calvin McBrearty to serve as chief prosecution witness against Weyburn, should he ever come to trial, in exchange for her own immunity. Meanwhile, she found employment as a cook and maid at the Big Dakota, began attending almost every mass at the local Catholic church, and seemed to be a happier woman than she had been in a long time. As for Eduardo Cruz, he never appeared again. Maria grieved over him some, but as time passed, that pain lessened significantly.

The Old Boys rode no more after the Brock Spring incident. Their work, however, had already been substantially done. Stock theft had declined significantly, and after the disappearance of David Weyburn, it fell off even more. His hands deserted the ranch—several of them plundering the big stone house on their way out—and the court seized his property. McBrearty took every step possible to prepare for a thorough prosecution, but as time went by, anticipation of David Weyburn ever being seen again around Cade finally waned.

Keller was never called upon to face charges stemming from his vigilante activities, and for that he owed the sheer grace of McBrearty. Like almost everyone else around Cade, McBrearty knew Keller had certainly been part of the Old Boys, but he was quick to point out that he had no legal proof of it. Keller had never admitted outright to it, and all the incident of his jailing by Weyburn proved was that Weyburn *believed* Keller to be an Old Boy, not that he in fact *was* an Old Boy.

When the spring of 1877 swept in, matters changed for Keller. A newly hired cowhand fresh in from Kansas offhandedly commented that the infamous Cutter Wyeth had been taken into custody in Dodge City a few days before, right at the time he was leaving. Interestingly, Wyeth was wounded at the time he was arrested.

Keller asked if a lawman had wounded Wyeth. No, the cowboy replied. It was another fellow who had been riled by Wyeth. He had gotten away without being caught.

Keller was stirred by this new reminder of Wyeth. He lay awake most of the night, thinking back on his younger days with Cooke, and about the tragic way Cooke had died. He thought about Doyle Boston and Charlie Lilly too, riding into Wyeth's ambush at Brock Spring.

The next morning Keller informed Claire that he was going to Dodge City. He had to see if Wyeth was actually in custody, and do what he could to make sure he faced justice for the killings he had committed.

Claire was sad to see her husband's obsession renewed. At the same time, she knew there was no point in trying to sway him. She kissed him and told him she would pack him some good clothes to wear while he was in town.

The next morning he set off.

Jed Keller had never laid eyes on Dodge City until the morning he rode into it. Not much to see, really, especially given its wild reputation. It was pretty much just another frontier plains town. Keller had expected nothing else; he knew the tendency of Americans to develop overblown images of places with reputations . . . sort of the reverse of the way he had developed such a positive image of Cade before he first saw it.

Keller found himself a room at the Dodge House and headed out into the streets. Already the town was preparing itself for the arrival of the herds from the south. The saloons and faro houses and dance parlors were being cleaned and painted, and signs going up here and there announced higher prices on liquor, beer, and cigars. Keller only half observed it all; the only thing he was concerned about was finding Cutter Wyeth and having a talk with the county sheriff to assure that he was aware of Wyeth's crimes in Texas.

An hour later Keller was walking the streets again, with such an expression of anger on his face that two women actually crossed the street rather than pass him on the same boardwalk. He had just talked to the county sheriff, a man named Charles Bassett, and heard news that distressed him.

Cutter Wyeth, with his seemingly unending luck, had escaped. Bassett was embarrassed and angry over how it had happened, for Wyeth, he felt, had played him for a fool.

"He had a wound when we took him in," Bassett had said. "A gunshot, just a shallow furrow on his leg. Oh, but he moaned about it something fierce, declaring it was mortifying on him. He begged to be put in the care of a doctor, and finally I had my fill of his mouthing and sent him off to be patched. Well, he clouted my deputy and got away clean. It's a shameful thing he was able to do it so easy, and I'm embarrassed to be telling you."

Keller found the news depressing. There truly was no justice when men such as Till Cooke and Charlie Lilly died, while scum such as Wyeth couldn't even be held in custody. There was no changing what had happened, though. Keller had to be satisfied simply to tell Bassett about Wyeth's killings in Texas and ask that word be wired immediately to District Attorney General Calvin McBrearty's Cade office if Wyeth should be recaptured.

"Who was it that shot Wyeth, by the way?" Keller had asked Bassett. An odd and intriguing possibility had just crossed his mind.

"A redskin," Bassett answered. "Wyeth was giving him some sort of devilment, and he had his fill of it, I reckon. Why you ask?"

"Just wondering, that's all. Thank you, Sheriff Bassett."

Well, that was it. He had traveled this far merely to be disappointed. Keller decided to remain only one night and begin his ride home the next morning. There was plenty to do back in Texas—cattle to round up and brand, and a trail drive to engage later.

At the moment, the most important business was filling his stomach, however. Keller headed back for the Dodge House down on a corner of Front Street. He entered the restaurant, seated himself, ordered a steak and coffee, and settled back to read a copy of a local newspaper somebody had left on the chair beside him.

He read for about ten minutes, then lowered the paper. At the same moment, another man across the room from him went through an identical motion, lowering his own newspaper. Keller was situated so as to look him squarely in the face. He gasped and stood.

It was David Weyburn.

A wild jumble of feelings rolled through Keller. Before him, and just now seeing him in turn, was the one man he had come to believe he would never see again. Weyburn stared back at Keller with wide eyes and a pallid face.

Keller strode forward and came to a stop just beside Weyburn's chair.

"Keller . . . I didn't expect to see you here."

"And I didn't expect to see you, Weyburn." He inspected the despised man closely. "You look like pure hell. You been sick?" Indeed Weyburn did look bad. Downright terrible, as if he had just checked out of a deadhouse, as most folks still sardonically termed hospitals.

Weyburn didn't seem interested in answering. "I suppose you're thinking you might kill me."

"Well, Weyburn, I'm impressed. You've become quite a mind reader. You ought to turn it into an act and book yourself into one of the local show halls."

"I don't blame you for hating me, Keller," Weyburn said. "God knows I've learned to hate myself. I didn't want her to die, you know. I truly did love her."

"You locked her away like she was no more than a dog in season. You left her to go through her travail alone, when a doctor might have saved her."

"The servants were supposed to come for me when she began to have the baby," Weyburn said. "It wasn't my fault they didn't do what I told them."

"You don't fault yourself? Then why do you hate yourself over it, like you say you do?"

Weyburn lowered his head. "Because I do fault myself, truth be told. I failed her. I should have . . . but it's too late now."

"Indeed it is. And it is your fault, Weyburn. Just like it's your fault that Till Cooke was murdered."

"That was Cutter Wyeth's doing—I had nothing to do with that!"

"Other than turning Wyeth loose so he was free to do it, you should say! And I fault you the same for what happened at Brock Spring."

"You owe me your life for that one, Keller, and you know it! If I hadn't locked you up, you would have ridden right into the same ambush."

"Maybe so—but don't expect me to thank you for any favors. You let two good men, one of them in particular a fine friend of mine, ride to their deaths, all so they'd quit hanging the scum of your county and let you run your stock thieving ring without interference! And even if you did save my neck, it was to appease your rotten conscience for the way you locked away my sister like she was a sack of old potatoes."

Weyburn stood, drawing the attention of the others in the restaurant. "I was always good to Magart. I loved her! She was my wife!"

"Your wife? No, Weyburn. She was never your wife. More your prisoner, a captive kept for your pleasure."

Weyburn swung at Keller. Keller ducked and came up with his own punch, striking Weyburn in the jaw and knocking him back onto his seat.

A man in an apron came out of the kitchen, shotgun in hand. "Here, now—that's enough of that in here!

This is no south-of-the-tracks dive here! You men take it outside!"

Keller dug into his pocket, pulled out a few bills, and tossed them at the man. Then he grabbed Weyburn's collar and all but dragged him out of the saloon and down to the nearby railroad tracks. "Weyburn, if you want to take another swing at me, do it. Give me an excuse to beat you to death!"

But Weyburn seemed deflated and weak now. He slumped where he stood and let his hands hang limply at his sides. "I won't fight you, Keller. If you want to kill me, kill me. Save me the trouble of doing it myself."

Those words surprised Keller and took a little of the fight out of him. "What—you're trying to tell me you're some conscience-tortured soul or something?"

"That's exactly what I am. You think you know what it is to hate someone, Keller? Do you? I know about hate. I hate exactly the same man you do. I hate David Weyburn."

"You're making no sense."

"This life we live makes no sense, Keller. I've been low, then high, then low again, and wherever I am, I'm still the same foul piece of . . . but forget the talk. It makes no difference. You want to kill me, then kill me. Go ahead. I won't stop you."

Keller was flabbergasted; Weyburn really seemed to mean it. "I think you really are sick, Weyburn. You look like death itself."

"The look will fit soon enough. I wanted the chance to kill Cutter Wyeth first, but what does that matter, when it comes down to it? I'd still feel just as dirty."

"Wait a minute . . . you're saying you came to Dodge to kill Cutter Wyeth?"

"Yes. He's here, you know. Locked up in the county jail yonder at the courthouse."

"Not anymore. He got free. This time he had to work for it a little . . . he didn't have a partner as sheriff, you know, somebody who would just turn him loose and call it escape."

"Wyeth is gone?"

"That's right."

"So I've come here for nothing."

"Maybe not. Maybe fate brought you here, Weyburn. So I'd catch you. I'm taking you back to Cade with me. I want to see you stand trial on those indictments McBrearty has waiting for you."

Weyburn wasn't listening. "I'll bet I know where he is!" he said. His tone indicated the words were self-directed.

"You mean Wyeth?"

"Yes . . . let me go, Keller. Let me go find him. Let me kill him."

"Why the devil would you want to kill Cutter Wyeth? You expect me to really believe that?"

"Appeasement, Keller. Payback. Justice—the same kind of justice you and your Old Boys had in mind when you looped those signs around the necks of your victims. Don't you see, Keller? I have to set things right. Make everything square. Wyeth and me, we're two of a kind. We're both guilty . . . we've both got to pay."

Keller had a dawning awareness of a surprising but likely notion: David Weyburn was no longer fully sane. Something had been grinded down in the man until it finally gave way. The thought was so startling that Keller was left speechless a moment.

Weyburn looked at him with a fearfully inquisitive expression. Then he began to back away. A few steps back, he turned and headed down the street.

"Weyburn!"

Weyburn turned. Keller had drawn a pistol from beneath his jacket and leveled it. Weyburn licked his lips. "I can find Wyeth," he said. "I know some of his haunts—I can find him, and kill him."

Keller began to squeeze the trigger. At the same time his arm began to shake. He looked around. This was broad daylight, at the end of a public street. He couldn't gun down Weyburn here. He lowered the pistol. Who was he trying to fool? He couldn't have gunned down Weyburn if it were midnight and this was a back alley in China.

"All right, Weyburn. You find him, and I'm going to be right at your side."

31

Weyburn frowned. "You want to track down Wyeth
. . . with me?"

"That's right. I'm not fool enough to let you
out of my sight. If you're going after Wyeth, I'm going
with you. If you're serious about wanting to see him
punished, then I'll give you the chance to prove it."

Weyburn eyed the ground and looked discomfited.
He nodded. "All right. All right. If that's the way you
want it."

"Where are you staying?"

Weyburn said, "Right there," and thumbed back at
the Dodge House.

"Do tell! So am I. It's no wonder we ran across
each other, then. Go on—we're getting our gear and
heading out. Where do you think Wyeth is?"

"There's an old cluster of dugouts out east of here,
on the road that leads to a little town called Eldridge.
Wyeth has holed up there before."

"Then we'll pay us a little visit out that way."

They went to Keller's room first. There was little to
gather; Keller had packed only what would ride in his
saddlebags or rolled inside his bedroll. They went next
to Weyburn's room, and there Keller made his mistake.

Perhaps it was overconfidence or simply bad judgment, but he went to the window of the room and looked out onto Front Street while Weyburn gathered his own goods. Something warned Keller at the last moment, and he turned, but it was already too late. Weyburn had a pistol in his hand, already uplifted and swinging down. Keller tried to dodge and failed. The heavy barrel struck him across the brow and knocked him to the floor, his vision spinning, twisting, sparkling away into darkness.

When he came to, the shadows in the room were different. Not greatly so, but different. Time had passed. He dug out his watch as he pushed to his feet. An hour. A full hour had gone by.

He squinted against the pain in his brow and touched his head. At least he was alive. Weyburn could have killed him—and he wondered why he hadn't. Keller swore at himself. He had been quite a dunce to let this happen. Now he was disarmed and Weyburn was gone—probably off to join up with his old partner Wyeth and have a good laugh at how he had pushed over such a pile of fool truck on Jed Keller. All Weyburn's talk, all his professed grief and dirty conscience—it had all been a fraud. He should have known. It was likely that the real reason Weyburn had come to Dodge City was to try and get Wyeth out of jail. All that talk of guilt and punishment and setting things right . . . he had been almost ready to really believe it!

Keller looked for his saddlebags and bedroll; they were gone. Weyburn had taken not only his weapons, but everything else he had carried. Keller veered toward the door, still dizzy. He almost overran a man in the hall and a woman on the stairs before he made it out onto the street. He headed for the livery and took his horse from its stall. His saddle was locked up in a room to the side, and Keller rattled the door futilely, trying to open it. "Liveryman!" he yelled. "Where are you?"

The aging livery keeper emerged from an outhouse

out back of the stable. Still pulling galluses over his shoulders, he said, "Hold on, hold on—give a man a chance to answer, durn you!"

"I need my saddle. The name's Keller. Hurry!"

"All right, all right . . ."

The man moved too slow to suit Keller. He fidgeted and muttered under his breath as the fellow dragged out the saddle and heaved it onto Keller's waiting horse— not noticing that Keller was taking advantage of the moment to reach into the momentarily unlocked storage room and slip a pistol out of a gun belt that hung on a peg in the wall, stored there for safe keeping by some livery customer who intended to abide by Dodge's ordinances against carrying guns in town. Hooking a loaded pistol was a stroke of luck Keller had not anticipated. He stuck it under his belt, in the back.

As he tightened the cinch, the old liveryman looked up and eyed the reddish mark on Keller's forehead. "Looks like somebody walloped you right good, friend."

"They did," Keller said. He swung up onto the saddle. "Then they cleaned out my pockets and took everything I had."

"Wait a minute . . . you got no money?"

"Not at the moment. Don't you worry—I'll send it on from Texas." He urged the horse out of the stable before the old liveryman could stop him, and rode off down the street with the man yelling after him.

What he was doing was probably foolish, and he knew it. Surely Weyburn had lied about the place he expected to find Wyeth. Nevertheless, Keller was heading in that direction, just in case. There was certainly nothing else to do; Weyburn could have ridden out in any direction. He would follow the only lead he had, even if the odds of it being a good one were virtually nil.

Or maybe not. Maybe at the time Weyburn had talked about the dugouts on the Eldridge road, he had been telling the truth. Maybe he hadn't known at that point that he would have an opportunity to escape, and so had not bothered to lie. They were remote odds, but worth putting to the test. If the gamble paid off, he would be led to both Weyburn and Wyeth.

And given that he had only a pistol and six rounds of ammunition, he would probably have to make that opportunity work to his advantage—if he could at all.

An hour outside of Dodge, Keller began to pick up sign of a lone horseman riding ahead of him. It might be Weyburn—or it might be any other man in Kansas, for that matter. When the road divided and the tracks veered toward Eldridge, Keller was encouraged.

He became lost in the mid-afternoon, and by dusk felt he was no closer to finding the right way again. He had followed the horseman's track off the main road, gambling that the rider was in fact Weyburn, and then he had lost the trail altogether. Now, in gathering gloom, he gave up any hope of finding where Weyburn had gone.

He rode back in the direction of the main road. Tonight would be spent beneath the stars, blanketless, his head on his saddle. He didn't look forward to it. And he was terribly hungry.

He was about to stop when he saw the light. A distant flicker, as if a shutter had been opened and closed. Yet strain his eyes as he might, he saw no sign of a habitation out there. Perhaps it was too dark to make out the form of the house . . . or perhaps there was little form to make out. Perhaps this house was part of the earth itself.

"A dugout!" Keller said aloud. Immediately hunger and weariness were forgotten. He had found them—he was sure of it.

The light flickered again, and he rode toward it. When he was close enough to see that it was in fact a dugout, he dismounted and tethered his horse to a bush. It was almost totally dark now. He drew the pistol he had stolen—it was a Remington, unfamiliar and uncomfortable in his hand—and advanced. He heard a faint wickering and noted two horses in a pen behind the dugout. One was unfamiliar. The other was a black he had seen Weyburn riding many times.

He went to the window and looked in around the edge of the shutter. There, seated at a table with one hand holding a fan of cards and the other curled around a glass of whiskey, sat Cutter Wyeth. Across the table from him was David Weyburn, also drinking and playing cards. Wyeth was talking, telling some profane story or another. Weyburn was silent, and very somber, yet he didn't seem to be listening.

Keller examined Wyeth. He wore no gun belt, but his pistol lay on the table before him, within easy reach. Weyburn also was armed; his pistol was in his gun belt. Keller looked around the room as best his limited field of vision would allow. Against the wall and close to Weyburn he saw a familiar shotgun. Till Cooke's shotgun, the one Wyeth had stolen the night he murdered the old lawman.

The sight of the shotgun sent a fire through Keller. He gritted his teeth, hard. His fingers squeezed the grip of his pistol, harder. He stepped back three paces, advanced, and hammered the shutters into splinters with his foot.

It all happened in a blur of speed. Wyeth cursed in surprise and reached for his pistol. Keller raised his own pistol and aimed it through the window, yelling for the men inside to give up and not touch their weapons. The call made no difference. Keller was aware of Wyeth scooping up his pistol, and of Weyburn reaching for his own even as he stood, shoving his chair toward the wall behind him.

With a yell of fury Keller cocked his pistol and squeezed the trigger. Cutter Wyeth was in his sights. The hammer clicked; no explosion, no smoke and fire, no roar. The pistol was faulty. Keller backstepped, started to turn. Wyeth cursed again and fired. Keller felt something like fire rip through his torso, felt himself fall. At the same time he saw David Weyburn lifting his pistol, aiming it, firing it. Cutter Wyeth's head jerked as if struck by a club, sent forth a red spray, and then the outlaw pitched sideways and fell to the floor.

As Keller's world began to spin and darken, he knew that Cutter Wyeth was dead, and that David Weyburn had killed him. Maybe he had been sitting at that table waiting for the first good opportunity to do it, or maybe his violent act had been just another case of David Weyburn impulsively protecting the brother of the woman he had loved. Keller had no chance to decide that question. A numbing darkness crushed in against him, seeped into the inside of his skull, and he knew no more.

The next hours—days? weeks? Keller could not tell —passed in a disjointed series of nightmarish images, odd sounds, peculiar pains, and hellish music that came from inside his brain. And then, one day, he was well enough to know that he was still living, and in Dodge City, and in a bed. There were faces of strangers, strangers who told him he was fortunate to be alive.

He asked how he got where he was, and they told him a sandy-haired man had brought him in, then vanished. Keller knew it must have been David Weyburn.

He had them wire Claire and tell her he had been hurt, but was now getting better and would be home soon. And then he wrote her a detailed letter, telling her that Cutter Wyeth was dead, that David Weyburn had killed him, and how it all had occurred. He added that they would almost certainly never lay eyes on Weyburn again.

Claire wrote him back. Her letter said only that she loved him, and was eager for his return, and was sending a couple of ranch hands to Dodge with a wagon to bring him home as soon as he was fit to travel.

He rested and healed and counted the days.

*   *   *

It happened only two days after he was home again. Keller awoke in the night, hearing the dogs barking furiously. He rose and put on trousers, a shirt, and his boots, and went to the door. When he opened it, he found a shotgun leaned carefully against the door frame. It was Till Cooke's old shotgun, the one Cutter Wyeth had taken. Whoever had put it there had shined the maple stock to perfection and oiled and rubbed the double barrel.

The dogs were barking over across the rise, where the Broadmore house had stood, and where Folly Broadmore lay buried beside a Tonkawa woman named Winnie. Keller picked up the shotgun and walked in that direction. What he found was unexpected, but oddly, it didn't surprise him. How could anything David Weyburn did surprise him, given all that had already happened?

Weyburn's body swung from a mesquite tree, his feet no more than three inches above the ground. Lacking a rope, he had torn the sleeves from his shirt, tied them together to make a cord, and done the job with that.

The placard that hung against Weyburn's chest was lettered in his own hand, and all it said was: Justice.

LOOK FOR

DEAD MAN'S GOLD—

CAMERON JUDD'S NEWEST EXCITING INSTALLMENT IN THE UNDERHILL SAGA—

NOW AVAILABLE FROM ST. MARTIN'S PAPERBACKS!

AN EXCERPT FOLLOWS...

Ten horsemen rode in the mountains, horses struggling in the snow, breath and bodies steaming.

"It's no use, Jordan!" one of the riders called to the man in front, a weathered, lean fellow with a pitted, dark countenance and black eyes. "We got to turn back!"

"Not without Dehaven!" the pitted man replied firmly. He urged his weary horse on, through the next fresh drift of snow.

"We're going to get ourselves trapped in these damned mountains!"

"We're not giving up, Remine! Not until we find Dehaven!"

In a clearing on the other side of the drift, the riders stopped, letting their horses rest. The ten horses drew close together, seeking one another's heat.

"Ross is right," said a dark-haired young man who was in many ways the image of the pitted leader, but without the pox scars. This was Searl Mahaffery, younger brother of Jordan. "He's got away from us, Jordan. We may as well admit it and go back."

"Back to where, Searl? And to what? Dehaven has took it all! The gold . . . everything we've worked for! We planned it all perfectly. Performed it all perfectly. Got away perfectly. I'll not have it ruined by one man. He took everything we earned."

"Everything we *stole*, you mean," muttered one of the other riders.

"What was that, Perry?" said Jordan Mahaffery, the pitted man. "You got something to say, you say it out to be heard!"

"All I said was, we didn't earn that gold, we stole it. And Dehaven stole it from us. Sure, it makes us mad. Sure, it leaves us back where we begun. But the man, and that gold, ain't worth dying for. There's a lot of gold in California. We can steal more of it. I say forget about Dehaven. Give the man his due for outwitting us, and let's get out of these mountains before we freeze to death."

Jordan Mahaffery replied, "It's the principle of the thing. I want my gold back."

An even-featured man who appeared to possess a mix of racial bloodlines cleared his throat and spoke in a smooth, almost soothing voice. "Jordan, listen to me. You've got to consider our situation. We've come out here without being ready for this kind of weather, particularly in these mountains. The horses are worn out, and there's no trail to follow. Perry is right. Dehaven has gotten away from us."

"Besides," threw in Emmett Fish, another of the band, "Dehaven has probably froze to death by now. No reason for us to do the same." Fish had a strong Georgia drawl and teeth the color of rust.

Jordan Mahaffery appeared to be thinking very hard. At last he spoke. "You got to ask yourself: why would Dehaven have run to such a place as this, especially in the winter? Why not take that gold and go to San Francisco or some other town, where he could spend it?"

"Because he'd know that we'd search every town until we found him," replied Searl Mahaffery.

Jordan Mahaffery nodded. "That's right. So he was coming up here to huddle with the gold through the winter. Figuring that the snow and such would keep us from following. Figuring that before the springtime come, we'd forget about him and move on. Then he could take that gold at his leisure and go off and enjoy it.''

"I can't believe Dehaven would try to winter over in such a place as this," said Conner Broadgrass, the dark-complexioned man with the smooth and diplomatic way of speaking. He was one of the few who could counter Jordan Mahaffery and get away with it. "There's no place here for a man to live, no settlements or diggings, no shelter. And Dehaven is no mountain man. He'd never survive."

"There *are* some diggings nearby," Mahaffery said. "There's Dutch Camp."

"Never heard of it," Emmett Fish said, spitting into the snow.

"I have, though I admit I'd forgotten about it," Broadgrass said. He'd been in California since well before the start of the Gold Rush, and had robbed, gambled, and womanized his way through almost every mining camp that had sprung into being since color turned up in Sutter's millrace. "But even if there's still shelter to be had at Dutch Camp, Jordan, the camp is abandoned. There'd be no food, no company. Dehaven would never go to such a place."

"I've heard Dutch Camp ain't empty," Mahaffery replied. "There's a new group who come in and started prospecting there again. Word is just beginning to get out. More rumors than anything else . . . but the talk is, there was a group of folks who bought enough food and supplies to last a full season for twenty or so folks, and hauled it up into these mountains."

"I don't believe it," said Bert Mongold, the burliest of the ten. The son of a St. Louis swindler who himself was the offspring of a Natchez Trace bandit, Mongold had been criminal since he'd been able to walk. "Why would anybody prospect played-out diggings?"

"Because maybe the diggings didn't prove to be played out after all," Mahaffery replied. "And maybe they figure to winter over to guard their find, and to get the fastest start on the mining season come warmer weather. And maybe Dehaven heard about it, and figured that kind of place was the safest for him to be. If I heard rumors about Dutch Camp, then he could have, too. Hell, the man talked to every stranger he met, anyway, so he'd be likely to hear the latest rumors. I despise the man for what he's done to us, but even I'll admit he's got a winning way about him with people.'' Mahaffery paused. ''Maybe that's why I was fool enough to trust him.''

Broadgrass spoke again. ''Even if Dehaven is at Dutch Camp, Jordan, we still face a problem if we go after him. Look at the sky. This snow isn't going to stop. If we stay in the mountains much longer, we're likely to be snowed in. Maybe until spring. And what if Dehaven isn't there? What if we go to Dutch Camp and find the people there have abandoned it like the first group did? We could be trapped in these mountains without food or supplies.''

''We'll take the risk. I ain't giving up that gold,'' Mahaffery said firmly. ''Dehaven *is* at Dutch Camp. I can feel it. And we're going after him.'' Mahaffery looked from face to face. ''Anybody wants out of this, let him leave. But whoever doesn't stick around gives up his cut of that gold once we get it back.''

''*If* we get it back,'' muttered Emmett Fish.

''We will get it back,'' Mahaffery said. ''But we've wasted enough time jaw-flapping. This snow is piling up by the minute. We're going to Dutch Camp, gents, and we're going to peel the very hide off Dehaven when we catch him.''

The other nine cast glances at one another. There was fear in the eyes of all but Broadgrass, whose immobile countenance always hid whatever he might be feeling. But no one countered Jordan Mahaffery. It wasn't wise to do such a thing.

''Let's go, big brother,'' Searl Mahaffery said. ''Lead the way to Dutch Camp. You reckon they got any pretty little ladies there?''

"At a mining camp? Ain't likely," Mahaffery replied. "Probably just a bunch of greasy miners with beards to their bellies."

"And Dehaven with them."

"That's right. And Dehaven with them. Now let's go."

The snow fell harder, but the riders pressed on.

Arianna Winkle shivered under her heavy coat and trudged through the piling snow, thinking how much better things were back home in Texas.

Just now she didn't remember the miseries she had suffered in the height of Texas summers, when she'd fantasized about dwelling in snowy, cold mountains just like those now surrounding her. Now that she was living out that midsummer's fantasy, she found little to like about it.

"Enoch!" she yelled, her breath gusting white. "Enoch! Here, boy!"

She waited and looked around. There was no sign of Enoch, no barking or scrambling in the snow.

A dreadful thought came: might somebody have done something to Enoch because of his habit of barking at night? She instantly suspected Herbert Colfax, whom she despised. Or Crain Brown, who put on such a nice front to cover the unpleasant, harsh person he really was. Arianna was good at sensing the personalities and characters of people, despite what veneer they put over their true selves. Either Colfax or Brown were the kinds who might have shot or poisoned Enoch on the sneak.

"Here, boy! Enoch!"

Still the dog did not appear. She looked all around in the vast whiteness. What if Enoch was hurt, and buried in the snow, unable to help himself?

"Enoch!"

She continued on toward the pass. Because of the lay of the land, the snow was drifted more heavily toward the wide, notchlike opening. She never much liked going beyond the pass into the mountains; it made her feel cut off from the protection of the little society of Texas Gulch. But for Enoch's sake she went on, whistling and calling the dog's name.

Unexpectedly, she heard her own name called, from behind her. "Arianna!"

Arianna winced. That was Daniel Chase's voice, an unwelcome one. She didn't really dislike Daniel—she felt very sorry for him as an orphan, in fact—but right now she didn't really want him bothering her. Besides, she could tell that he liked her, which made her uncomfortable. He was a year younger than she, after all. And he was not the kind of boy who could appeal to her, even if he were older.

She went on, pretending not to hear, hoping she could clear the pass before he caught up with her.

"Arianna!"

He was too close now for her to pretend she hadn't heard him. Oh, well. Maybe he could help her find Enoch. She turned and saw Daniel lumbering up through the snow, stepping high and wide and kicking up white dust all around. He had his usual big grin on his face.

He reached her, out of breath, red-nosed from the cold. "Where you going, Arianna?" he panted.

"Through the pass," she said.

"He's gone again?"

"Yes. I'm worried about him. There's snow now. He could get trapped out in it."

"I saw him yesterday. When I was coming in to tell about the dead man. He was heading up toward the pass, right up through this very place, matter of fact. He goes out of the pass a lot. I've seen him chase varmints and such a long way beyond it. He'll be back."

"Not if he can't make it through the snow."

"He can do it. You know how a dog his size travels through snow, don't you? He jumps!" Daniel performed a little demonstrative hop, advancing himself another couple of feet. "Then he does it again." Another jump, and suddenly he was uncomfortably close to her, grinning more broadly. She backed away a little.

"Want me to help you look for him?" he asked.

"Well . . . yes."

"Come on, then."

They walked together through the ever-deeper snow. "Hey, Arianna, I got you something," Daniel said. He stuck out his hand.

She looked at the ring that lay on his palm.

"Where'd you get it?"

Daniel remembered Sam Underhill's advice about not telling her it was a dead man's ring. "Sam Underhill told me I could have it. I put it on and it got stuck on my finger, but a few minutes ago, I was able to get it off. I don't want it no more. So you can have it. It won't stick on your finger, your hands being smaller and all."

Given the romantic symbolism associated with the acceptance of rings, Arianna wasn't sure she should take it. But she did like baubles, and didn't own a ring just now.

"Thank you," she said, reaching out and taking the ring off his palm. She slipped it on her biggest finger and found it too large, her hands being very slender. So she tried it on her thumb, and it fit perfectly.

"Wearing a ring on your thumb!" Daniel declared, and laughed. "I never seen nobody do that before!"

She shrugged and continued walking, battling the snow, hoping he understood that there was no significance in her acceptance of his ring. "Enoch!" she called. "Here, boy!"

Daniel fell in beside her. The snow grew more obstructive as they entered the pass, but both of them managed to keep going.

An hour later, well out into the craggy Sierra wilderness, a somber Daniel turned to Arianna and said, "We have to go back."

"But we haven't found Enoch."

"But the snow, Arianna. Look how deep it's getting. If we don't get back, we may not be able to."

Arianna looked around, and knew Daniel was talking sense. They'd wandered far, calling for Enoch and getting no response. The snow was deep enough now that it was hard to hold out much hope for the dog, if in fact he'd been caught out here. It broke her heart to think about it.

A noise made Arianna pause.

"Daniel, did you hear that?"

"I didn't hear nothing."

"I did. It might have been Enoch."

Daniel listened hard, but shook his head.

"It came from over that way," Arianna insisted. "I'm going to go look. Then we can start back."

"Arianna, I don't think we're going to find Enoch."

Arianna was paying no attention, already pushing through the snow in the direction from which she'd heard the noise that had drawn her ear. "Enoch!" she called. "Enoch! Can you hear me?"

Daniel started after her. "Arianna, come back."

She kept going, calling for her dog.

"Arianna!"

She clambered over a fallen tree that was piled and slick with snow. She slipped, coming down hard on the log. The snow, however, softened the impact and she got up quickly.

"Are you hurt?" Daniel reached her and put out a hand toward her.

"Leave me alone!" she declared, irritable. "Go away! If you're worried about getting home, then go home now. I'll come later, with Enoch."

"Arianna, you got to go back. It's too cold. There's too much snow."

"I'll not! Not without Enoch!"

"Enoch may be waiting for you at home right now. I think we should—" He cut off suddenly, turning his head slightly.

"Do you hear him, too?" she asked.

"I hear something. But I don't think it's . . ." His voice trailed off.

"What is it?"

"Be quiet!" he said in a sharp whisper.

"Daniel . . ."

"Look!" he said, bending slightly at the knees and pointing down a slope to their west.

Arianna saw them. Men on horses, making their way along through the snow, and having a hard time of it. They were traveling along the foot of the ridge.

Daniel and Arianna slowly knelt, letting the deep snow hide them.

"Who are they, Daniel?" Arianna whispered.

"Don't know. Odd, men traveling like that in this snow. Who in the world . . ."

"Daniel, let's go home."

Daniel nodded. When the riders had passed below, boy and girl stood and began walking as fast as they could, which was not fast at all, toward the pass. It seemed terribly far away, and Arianna felt foolish for having come this far, even for Enoch.

"Those men scare me," she said to Daniel between harsh gasps for air.

"Nothing to be afraid of," Daniel said, trying to sound manly. Arianna could tell, though, that he was scared of them, too. There was something out-of-place and disturbing about such a group, in these mountains, during a season such as this. Only some desperate reason could make men willing to plunge into this wilderness at this time of year.

Arianna and Daniel were halfway back to the pass when another sound brought them to a stop. They glanced at one another, then veered to the left, scrambling over some fallen timber that was deeply encrusted with fresh snow, forming a distorted natural sculpture. Both Arianna and Daniel fell more than once as they clambered over the timber, but in the end they made it, and were rewarded by the sight of Enoch, the straying dog, yapping at them from a recess among the logs. The dog had apparently climbed on the timber, probably chasing some woodland creature, and had slipped into the deep recess, from which he had not been able to get out again. Though the crevice had imprisoned Enoch, it had also protected him from the snow and wind.

"I'll get him," Daniel said. He flopped onto his belly, reached down, and extricated the twenty-pound mongrel.

"Here you go," Daniel said blandly, handing Enoch to Arianna, knowing he was very much the hero of the moment, but trying to be nonchalant about it. Arianna hugged the dog and planted a big kiss on the side of his snout. Daniel was instantly and obviously jealous of the dog.

He made a face. "You know, I've thought a time or two that I might like to get a kiss from you sometime. But now that I know you kiss dogs, I ain't so sure."

She was too happy at the moment to worry about insult. "Thank you, Daniel," she said sincerely. "He'd have died in there if you hadn't found him."

"It was nothing. Now we'd better keep moving. Look

yonder—it's so white you can't make out the far peaks. That means the snow's coming in even heavier.''

"Do you think those riders are near?"

"I think they've moved on. Come on."

They continued, Arianna insisting on carrying her dog, even though it slowed her.

"Let him down, Arianna," Daniel said. "He'll follow us."

"No. He'll run away again."

"You're making us have to drag along, way too slow."

"Just keep going. I'll keep up."

They rounded the side of a hill, taking heed to their footing. Daniel was cheered to catch sight of the familiar pass into Texas Gulch, but the vision was quickly erased by a new sweep of falling snow, driven hard on the wind. For a frightening moment Daniel realized just how easy it would be to become hopelessly lost in such weather. He recalled campfire stories about mountain people who had frozen to death mere yards from their own homes, as lost as if they'd been a hundred miles out in the wilderness. He tried to lock in mind the exact spot where he'd seen the pass, so he wouldn't lose course.

The wind shifted again, and he saw the riders. They were riding single file, laboriously, on a diagonal path up the face of the final slope leading to the pass. Daniel stopped at once, and Arianna, having also seen them, stopped just behind him.

"Daniel, they'll get to the pass before we do," she said.

The wind swirled, and the falling snow thinned out for a few moments.

Enoch snarled in Arianna's arms, barked, and leaped free of her grasp.

"Enoch!" she said, sharply, but hardly louder than a whisper.

Her caution was pointless now. Enoch bounded through the snow, down the slope, barking loudly at the riders. The two youngsters saw the riders turn their heads, see the dog

. . . and then one pointed. Up the slope. At them.

Daniel and Arianna glanced nervously at one another, both knowing it would be futile to run.

"It's probably all right," Daniel said, watching as three of the riders turned their horses off-course and began riding up the ridge toward them. Enoch was barking and bounding, making a defiant show, but keeping well away from the advancing horses and men. "They're probably just travelers wanting shelter. Nobody to worry about."

"Yes," Arianna said. "Just men lost in the snow. They'll probably help us get in safe to Texas Gulch."

They stood there together, waiting for the advancing men to reach them.

"I'm worried, Sam," Leora Winkle said. "Arianna disappeared earlier, looking for her dog, and she hasn't come back."

Sam looked into Leora's face, pretty despite the lines of concern that tracked along it just now like thin trail marks traced on a map. "Do you think she'd have gone beyond the pass in this weather?" he asked.

"I don't know . . . I didn't think she would. That's why I let her go. Maybe I didn't think at all. I was . . . distracted today."

Distracted. Sam knew what that meant. She'd been grieving again for her lost husband. Sam felt sorry for Leora, but at the same time wished she'd find a way to put that loss behind her and take notice that there were other good and available men in the world, the most prime example he could think of being the one standing before her now.

"Might she be visiting at someone's cabin? Have you asked around for her?"

"I've been almost everywhere, every place she'd go," Leora said. "She's nowhere. And Daniel is missing, too. Mr. Colfax said he saw Daniel earlier, looking for her. I suppose they're together somewhere."

"I doubt they're far away, Leora. I'll go look for her. There's still a lot of daylight left."

"There's a place she likes to go, farther back in the valley. Where those white rocks are that the sun shines on in the evening."

"That's where we'll find her, I'll bet. Or more likely, I'll meet them already coming back. I'll find her for you. I promise."

"Thank you, Sam."

"My pleasure."

Leora left the cabin and hurried back through the snow toward the lodge house. Sam watched her go, and frowned. He'd just promised to find Arianna, a foolish pledge. His father had taught him never to make a vow he couldn't be sure of keeping. There was always the terrible chance that Arianna and Daniel had wandered too far, and had gotten lost or cut off from getting back. If so, they might not be found until the spring thaw, and maybe not even then. But Sam decided not to dwell on that possibility. He'd assume for now that he'd find both youngsters quickly.

Sam filled his water bottle from the drinking bucket, and dropped some sun-dried meat into a pocket. He considered loading himself up with his rifle and other gear, but it was hard enough to move through thick snow even without burdens. He'd forgo the weaponry in favor of unencumbrance.

If Ben Dillow was handy, he'd ask him to come too. But Ben was off somewhere else, and Sam wasn't inclined to go looking for him. He'd just make a quick hike out into the valley, round up the children, get them home, and enjoy Leora's praise.

He paused once before he set out, wondering if he was taking this all a little too lightly. Maybe he should organize a full search, take gear and weapons . . . but no. Leora was a worrier, always exaggerating things. It was possible that the youngsters were right here in the camp, just hidden away. Maybe Daniel had finally persuaded Arianna to give him a kiss, and they were off holding hands somewhere.

Probably the boy had given her that ring by now.

Tightening his hat onto his head, Sam left his cabin, paused to strap snowshoes onto his feet, and trudged out into the white.

CAMERON JUDD
THE NEW VOICE OF THE OLD WEST

"Judd is a keen observer of the human heart as well as a fine action writer."
—*Publishers Weekly*

THE GLORY RIVER
Raised by a French-born Indian trader among the Cherokees and Creeks, Bushrod Underhill left the dark mountains of the American Southeast for the promise of the open frontier. But across the mighty Mississippi, a storm of violence awaited young Bushrod—and it would put his survival skills to the ultimate test...
0-312-96499-4___$5.99 U.S.___$7.99 Can.

SNOW SKY
Tudor Cochran has come to Snow Sky to find some answers about the suspicious young mining town. And what he finds is a gathering of enemies, strangers and conspirators who have all come together around one man's violent past—and deadly future.
0-312-96647-4___$5.99 U.S.___$7.99 Can.

CORRIGAN
He was young and green when he rode out from his family's Wyoming ranch, a boy sent to bring his wayward brother home to a dying father. Now, Tucker Corrigan was entering a range war. A beleaguered family, a powerful landowner, and Tucker's brother, Jack—a man seven years on the run—were all at the center of a deadly storm.
0-312-96615-6___$4.99 U.S.___$6.50 Can.